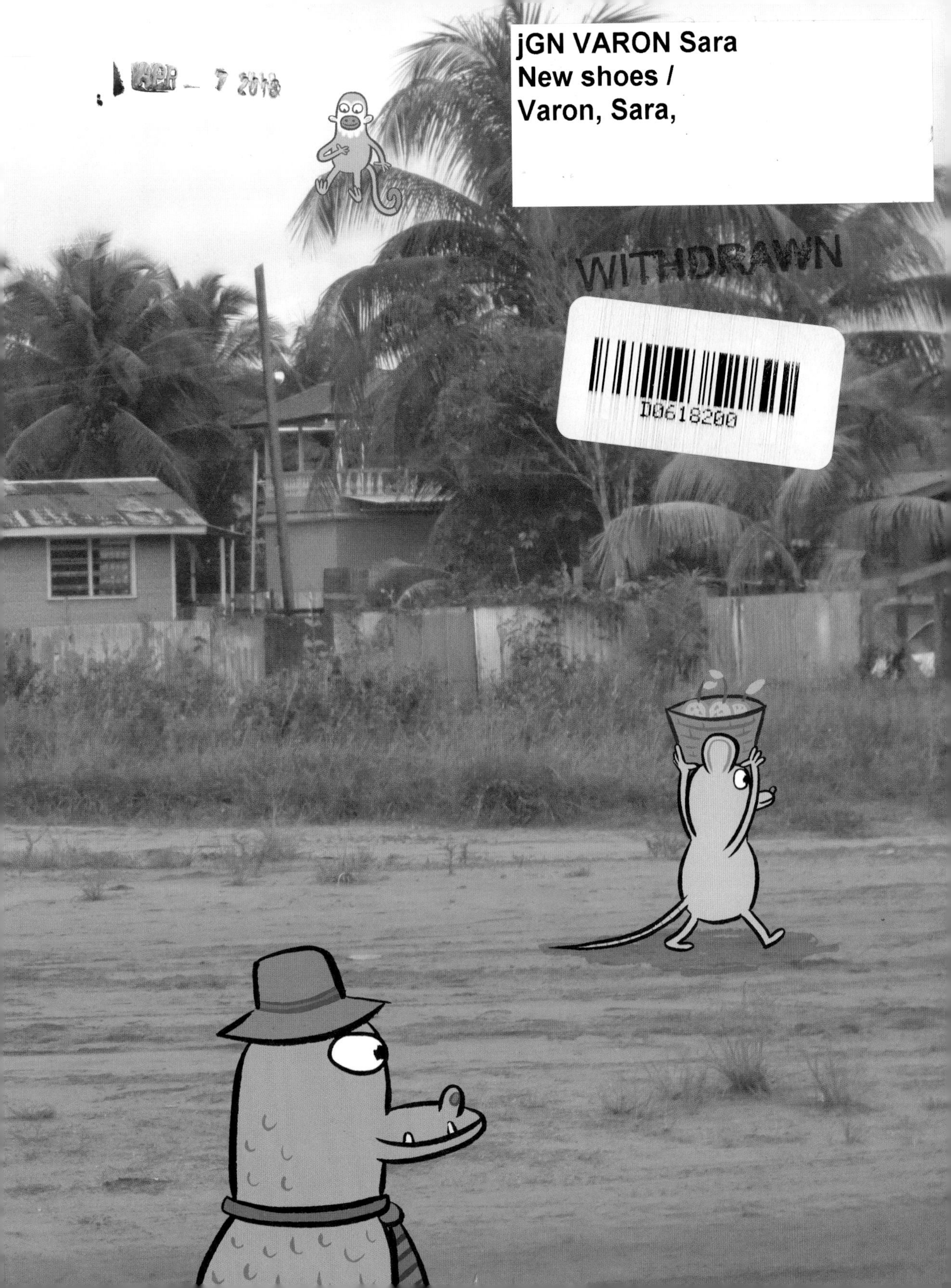

NEW SHOES

SARA VARON

:01

First Second
NEW YORK

For Miles and Eily:
Wishing you many great adventures

And in memory of Nina Frenkel,
Friend Extraordinaire

First Second

Copyright © 2018 by Sara Varon
Illustrations in Francis's guidebook copyright © 2016 by George Boorujy

Published by First Second
First Second is an imprint of Roaring Brook Press, a division of
Holtzbrinck Publishing Holdings Limited Partnership
175 Fifth Avenue, New York, NY 10010

Library of Congress Control Number: 2017941164

ISBN: 978-1-59643-920-7

Our books may be purchased in bulk for promotional, educational, or business use.
Please contact your local bookseller or the Macmillan Corporate and Premium Sales Department
at (800) 221-7945 ext. 5442 or by
e-mail at MacmillanSpecialMarkets@macmillan.com.

First edition, 2018
Book design by Danielle Ceccolini and Sara Varon
Printed in China by 1010 Printing International Limited, North Point, Hong Kong

Penciled on Canson Bristol paper with a Kohinoor Rapidomatic 0.9 mm mechanical pencil and 2B lead.
Inked with a Windsor & Newton Series 7 size 2 brush and Dr. Martin's Black Star Hi-Carb ink.
Colored digitally in Photoshop.

1 3 5 7 9 10 8 6 4 2

chapter one

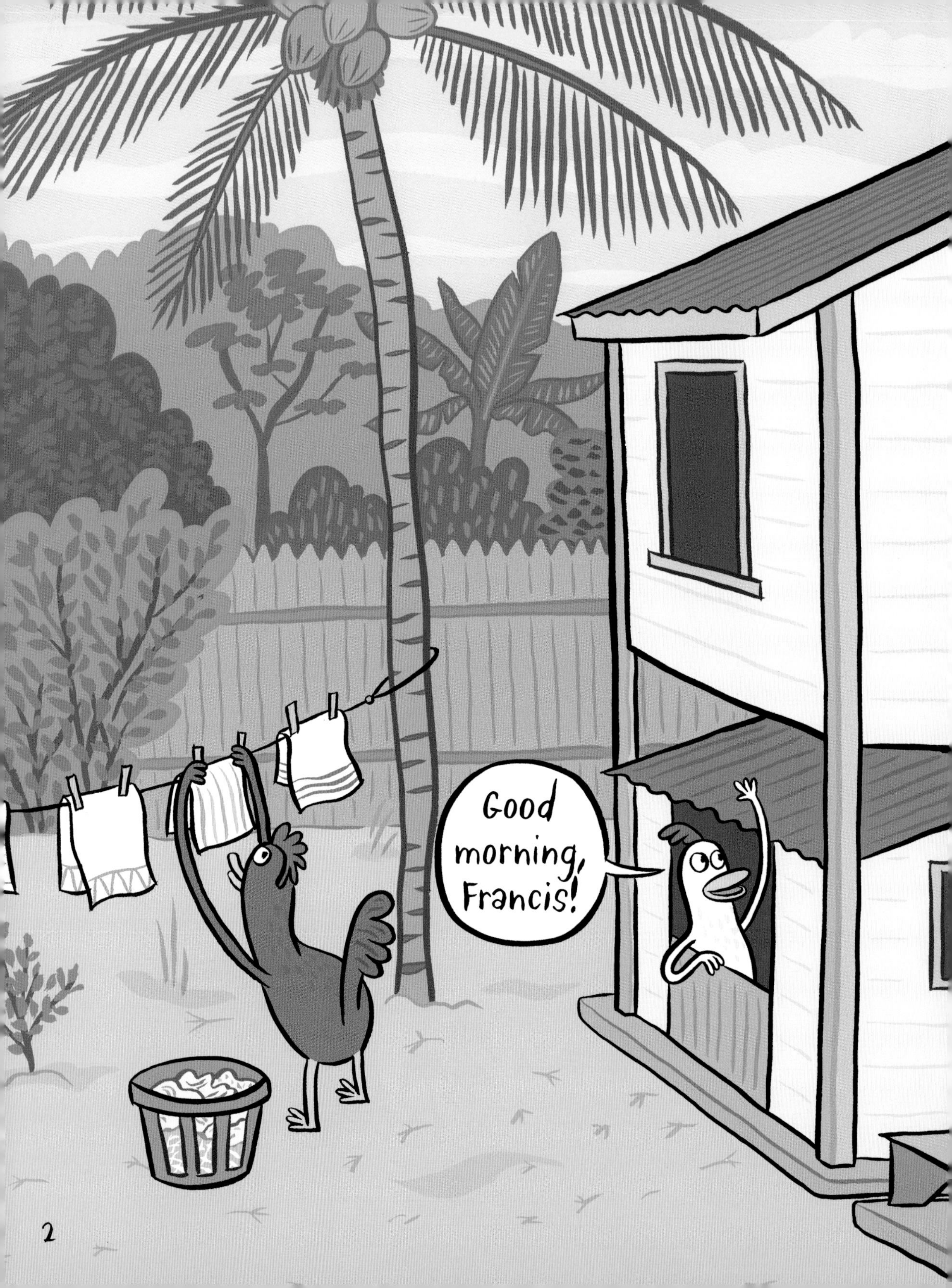
Good morning, Francis!

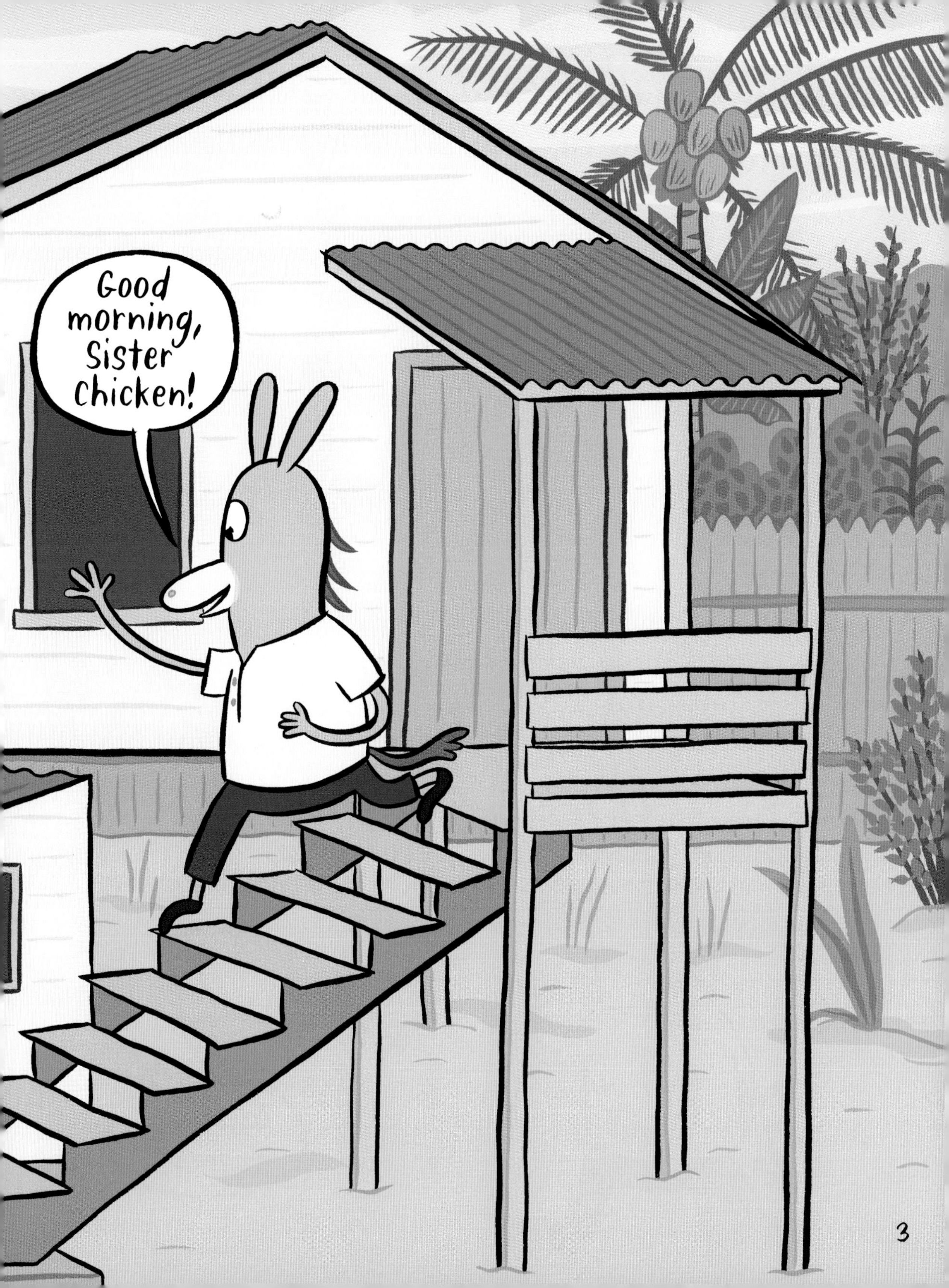
Good morning, Sister Chicken!

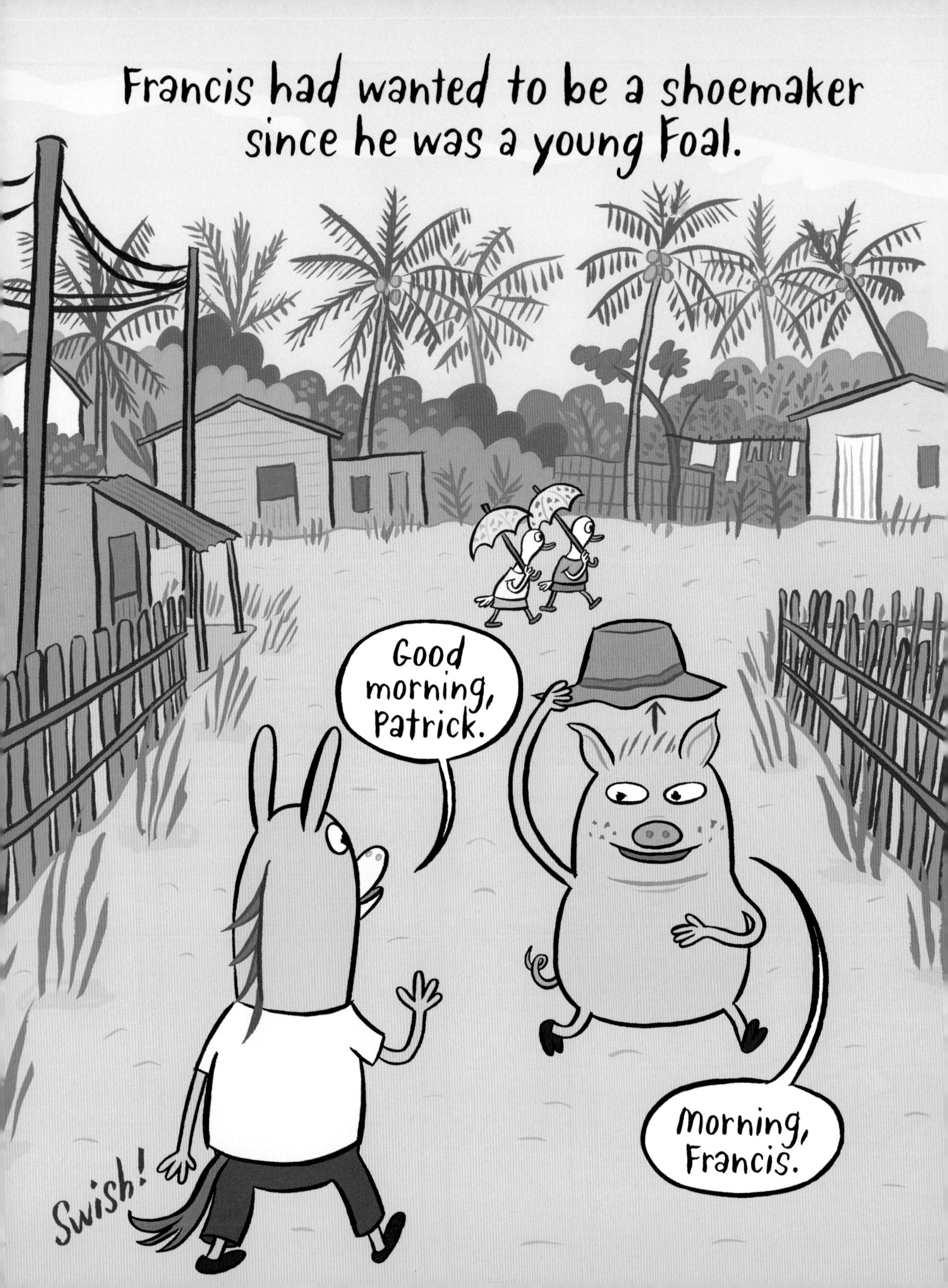
Francis had wanted to be a shoemaker since he was a young foal.
Good morning, Patrick.
Morning, Francis.
Swish!

As a grown donkey, it was his aspiration to make the best shoes he possibly could.

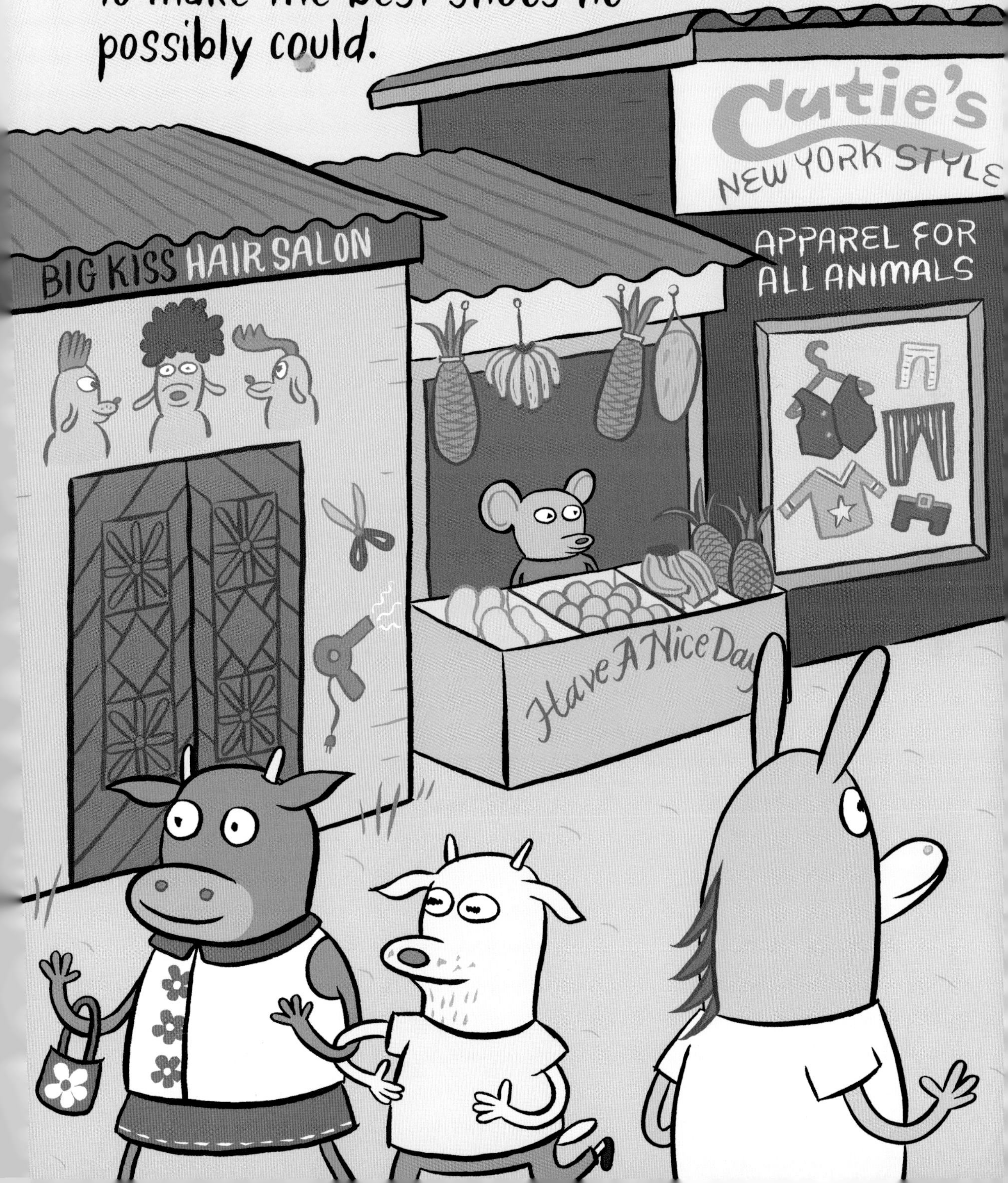
Cutie's
NEW YORK STYLE
BIG KISS HAIR SALON
APPAREL FOR ALL ANIMALS
Have A Nice Day

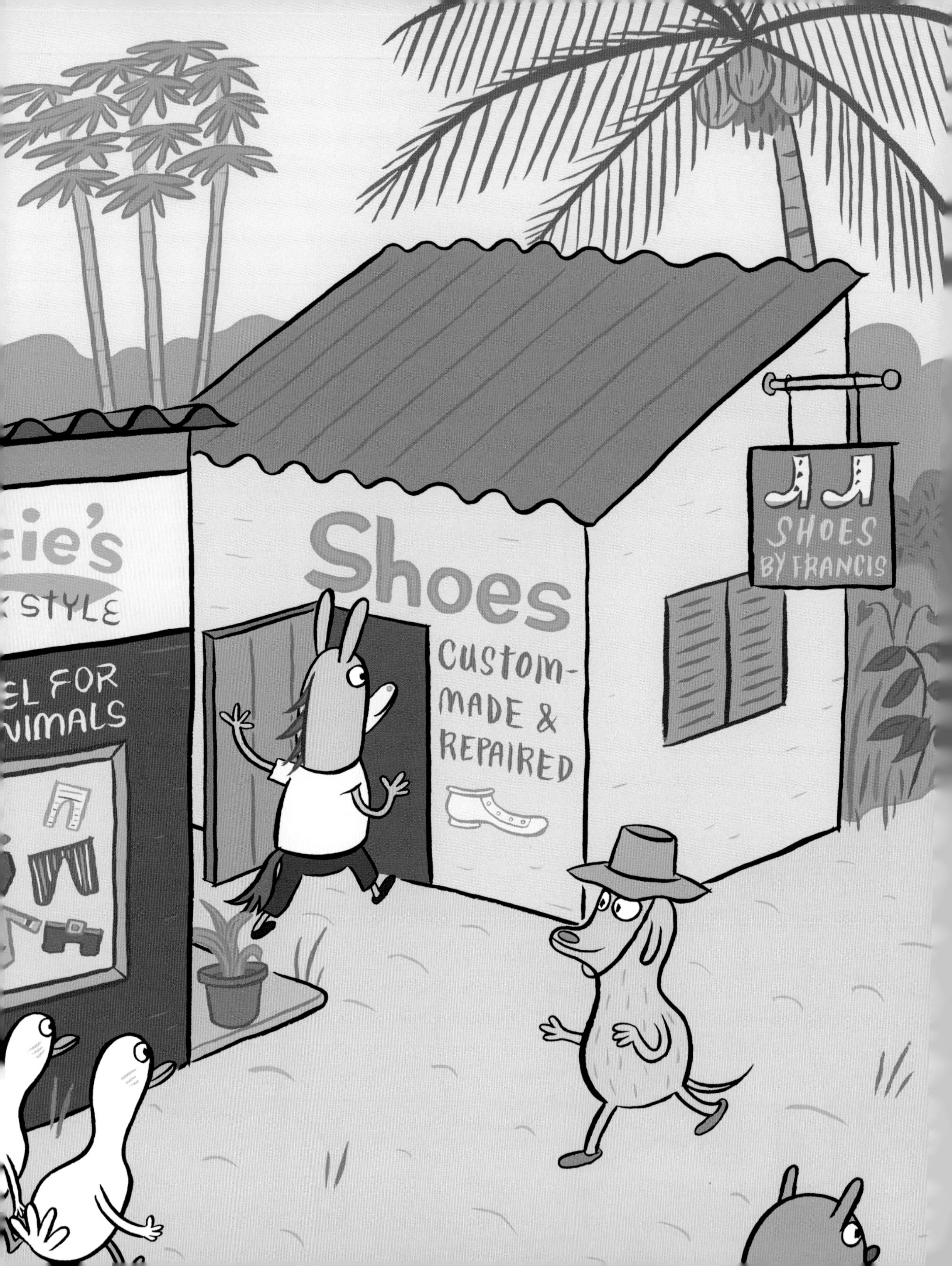

cie's
STYLE
EL FOR
NIMALS
Shoes
Custom-
MADE &
REPAIRED
SHOES
BY FRANCIS

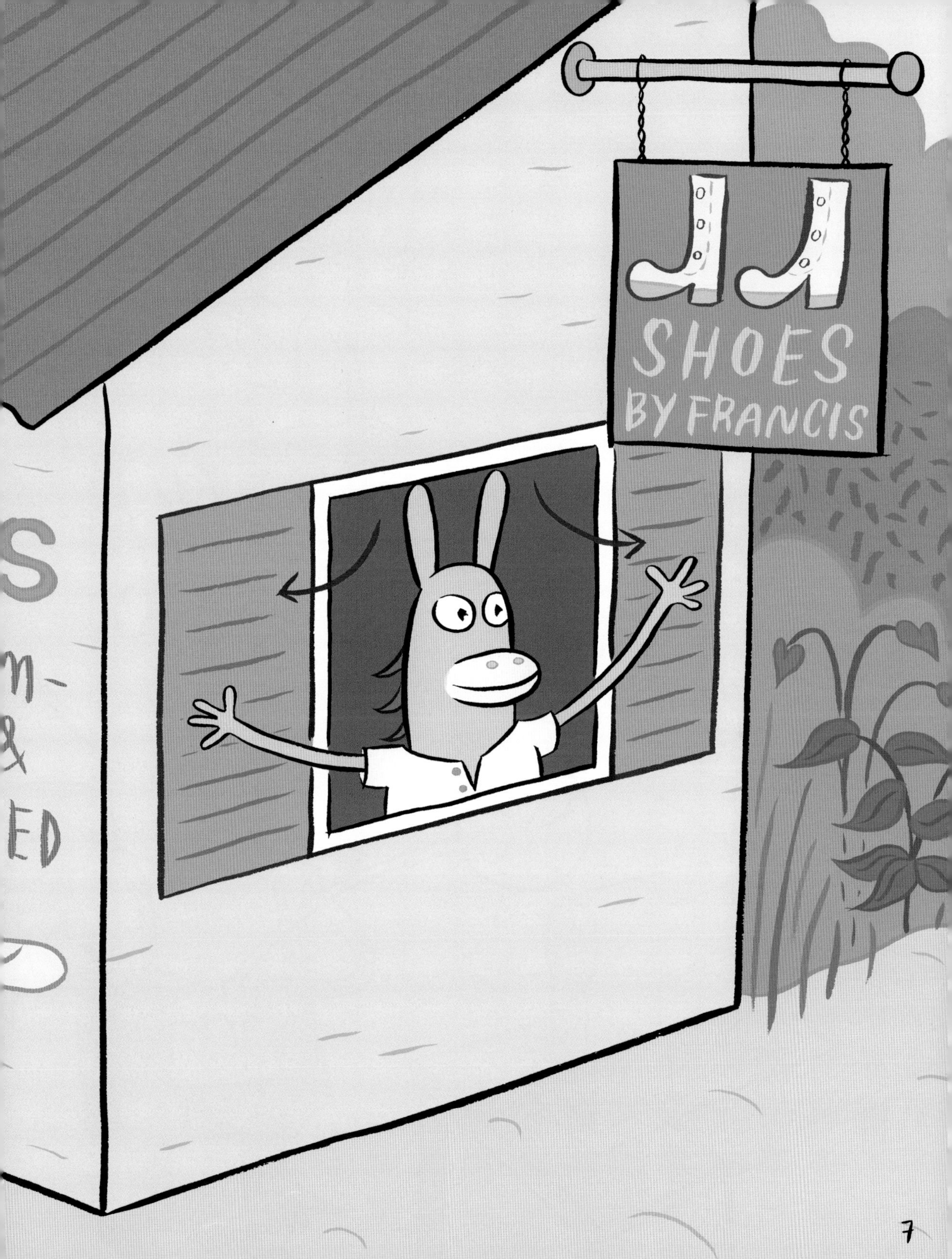
SHOES
BY FRANCIS

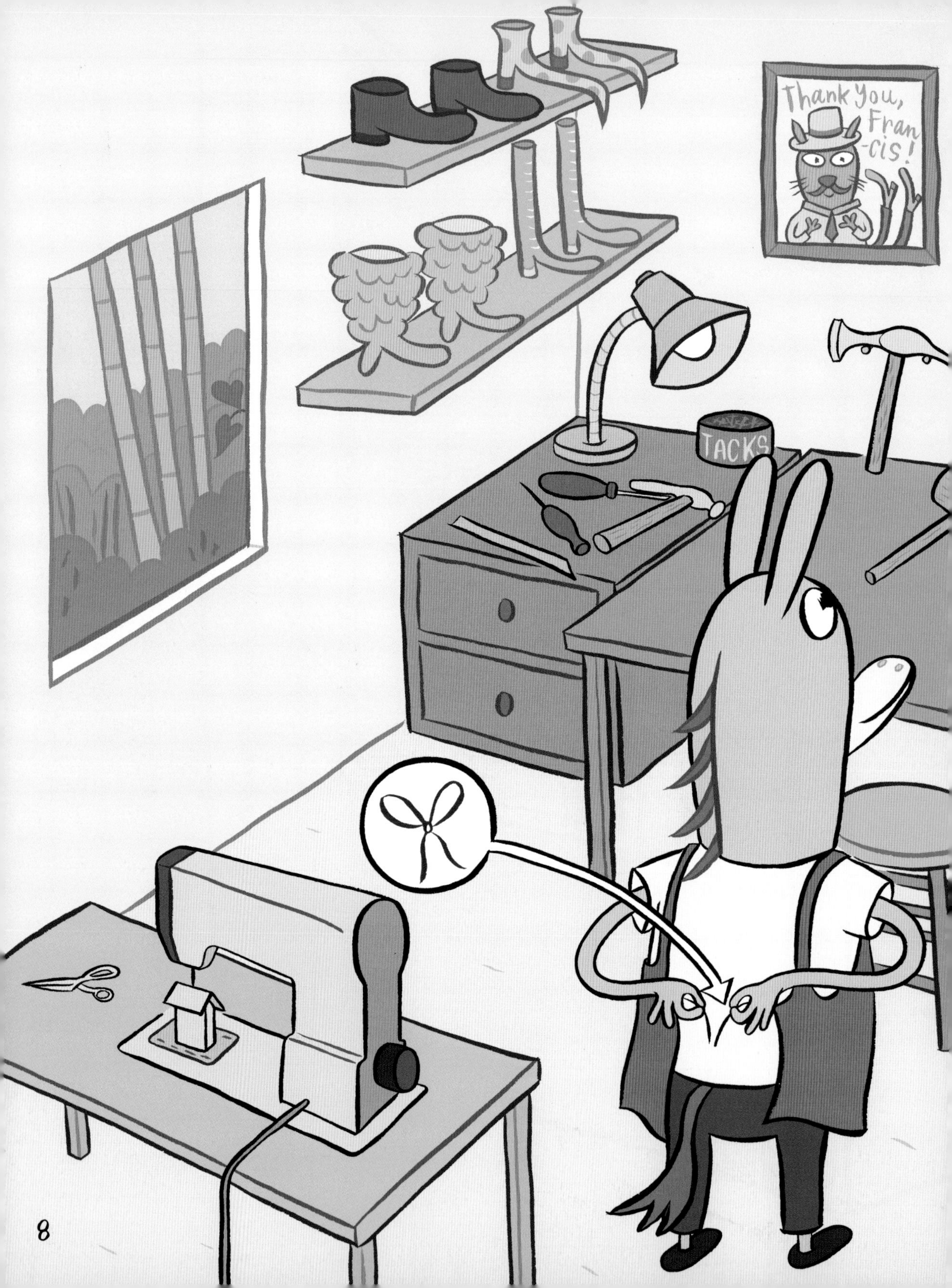
Thank You, Fran-cis!
TACKS

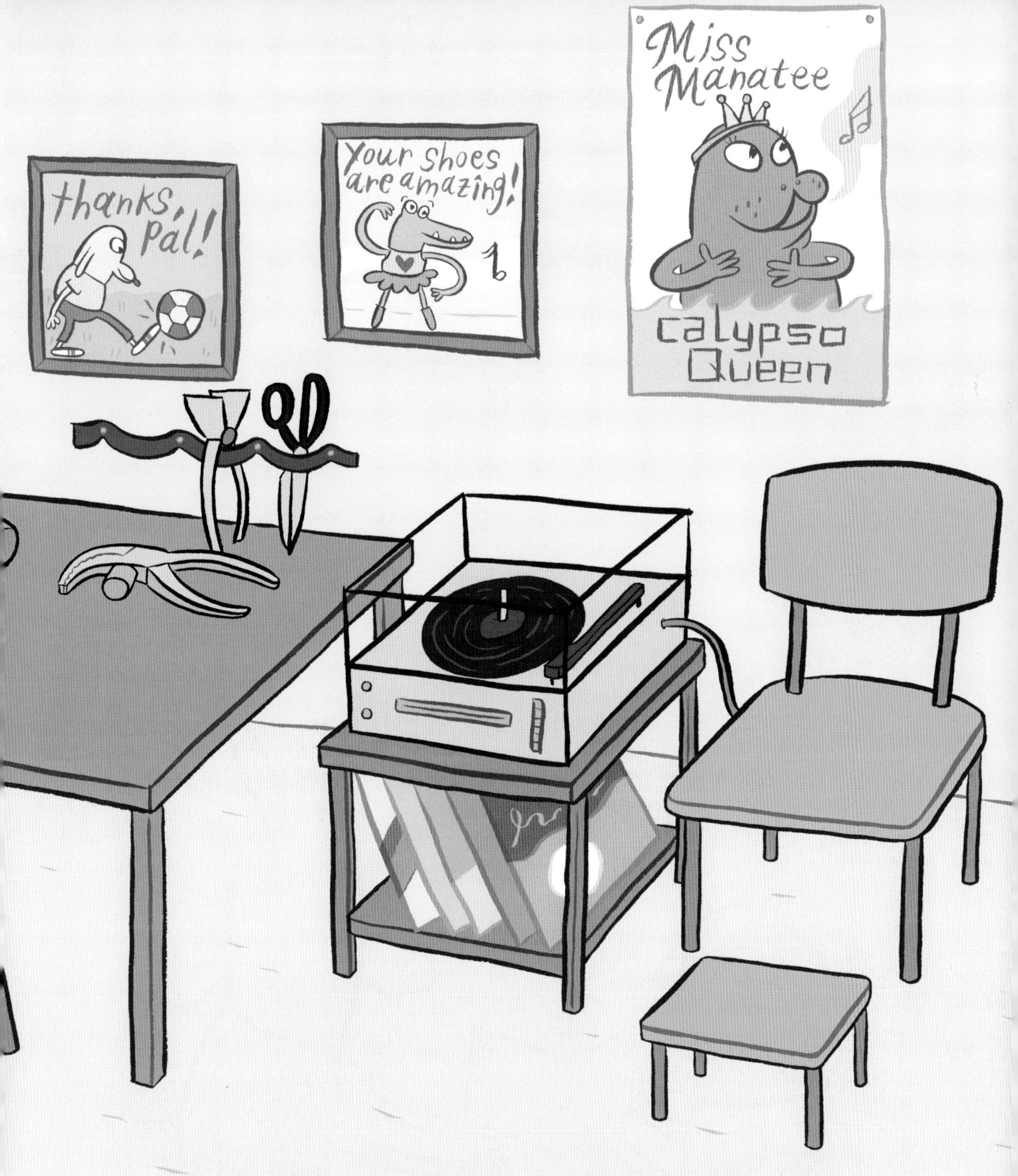
thanks, pal!
Your shoes are amazing!
Miss Manatee
calypso Queen

Animals came from far and wide
to purchase shoes made by Francis.

He used only the finest coconut wood for the soles.

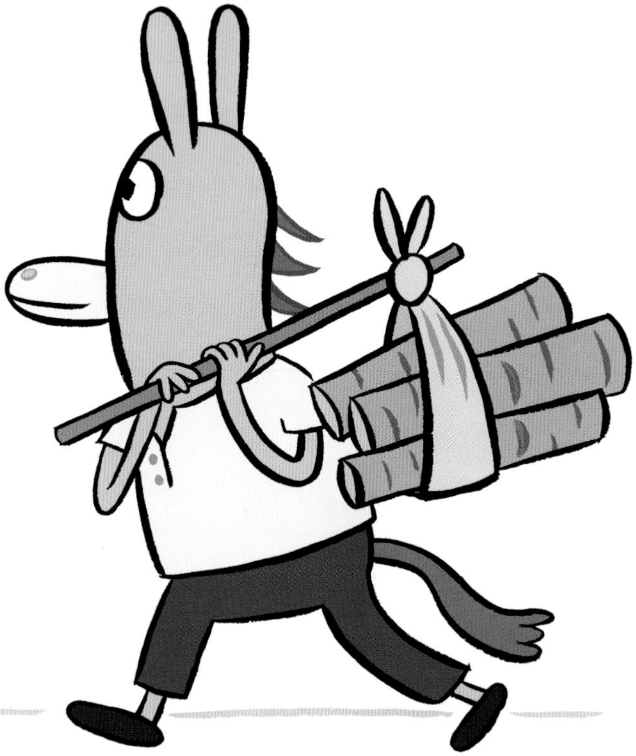

He padded the insoles with wool so they'd be extra comfortable. This came from the goats down the road.

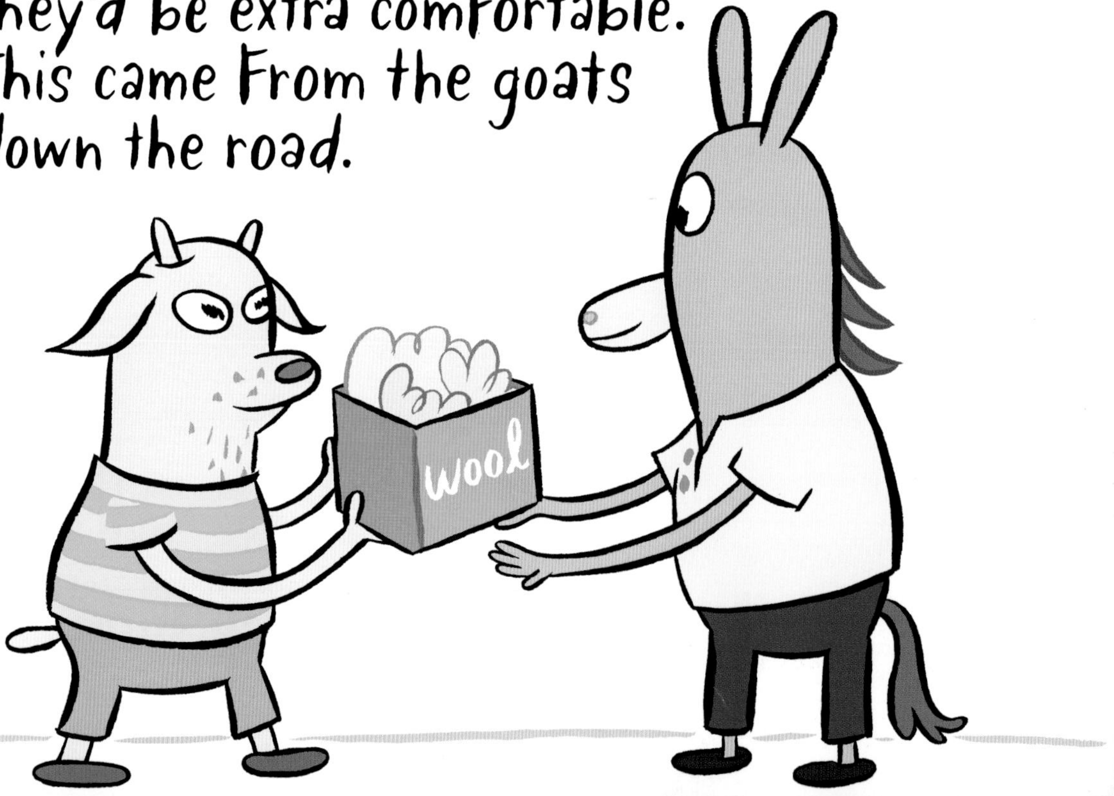
wool

the uppers were made from special fibers called wild tiger grass, which he purchased from his friend and neighbor Nigel, a squirrel monkey.

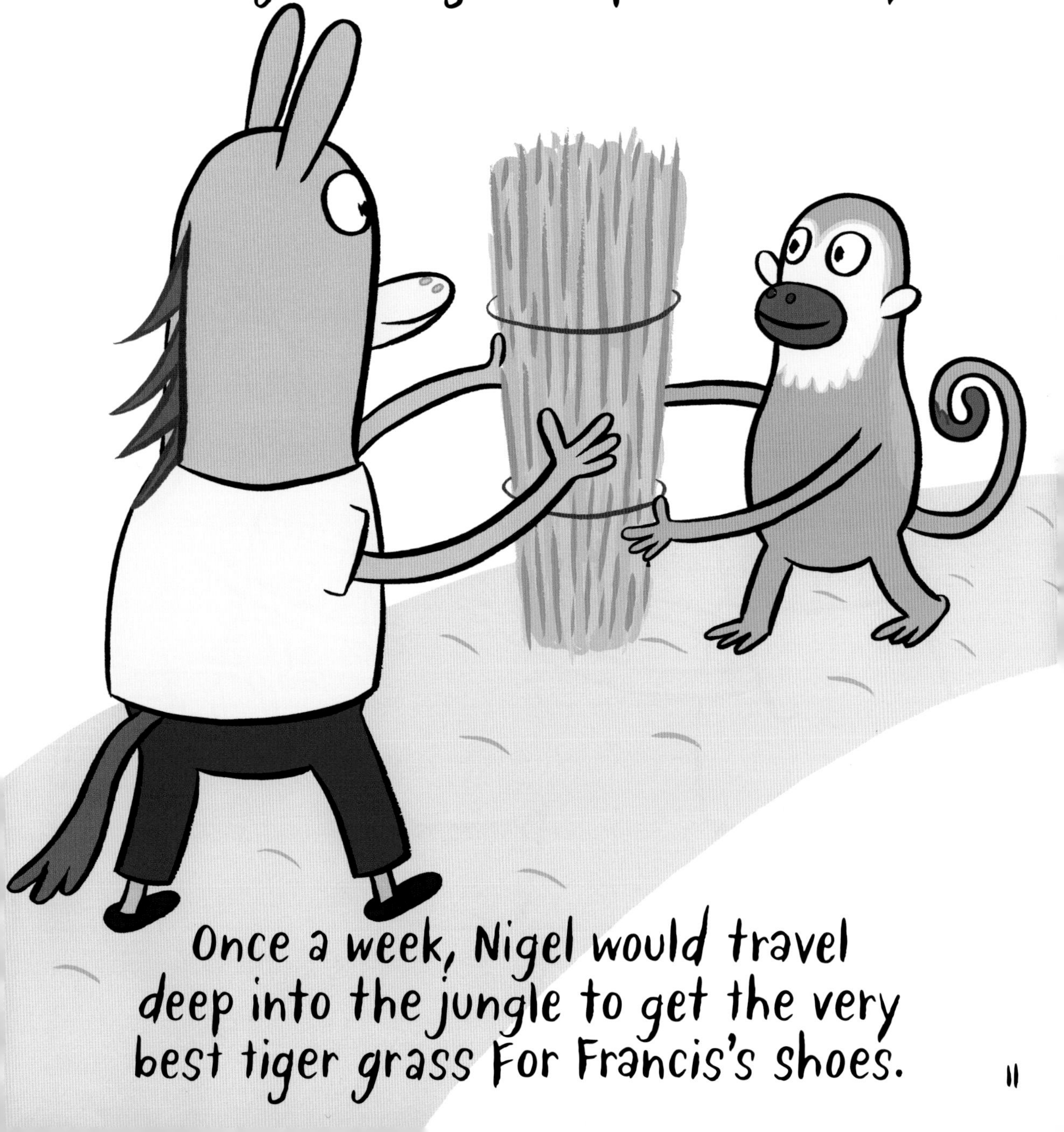

Once a week, Nigel would travel deep into the jungle to get the very best tiger grass for Francis's shoes.

The downstairs chickens wove the tiger grass into a very sturdy fabric that was so durable, Francis advertised, that you could trek through jungles in his shoes.

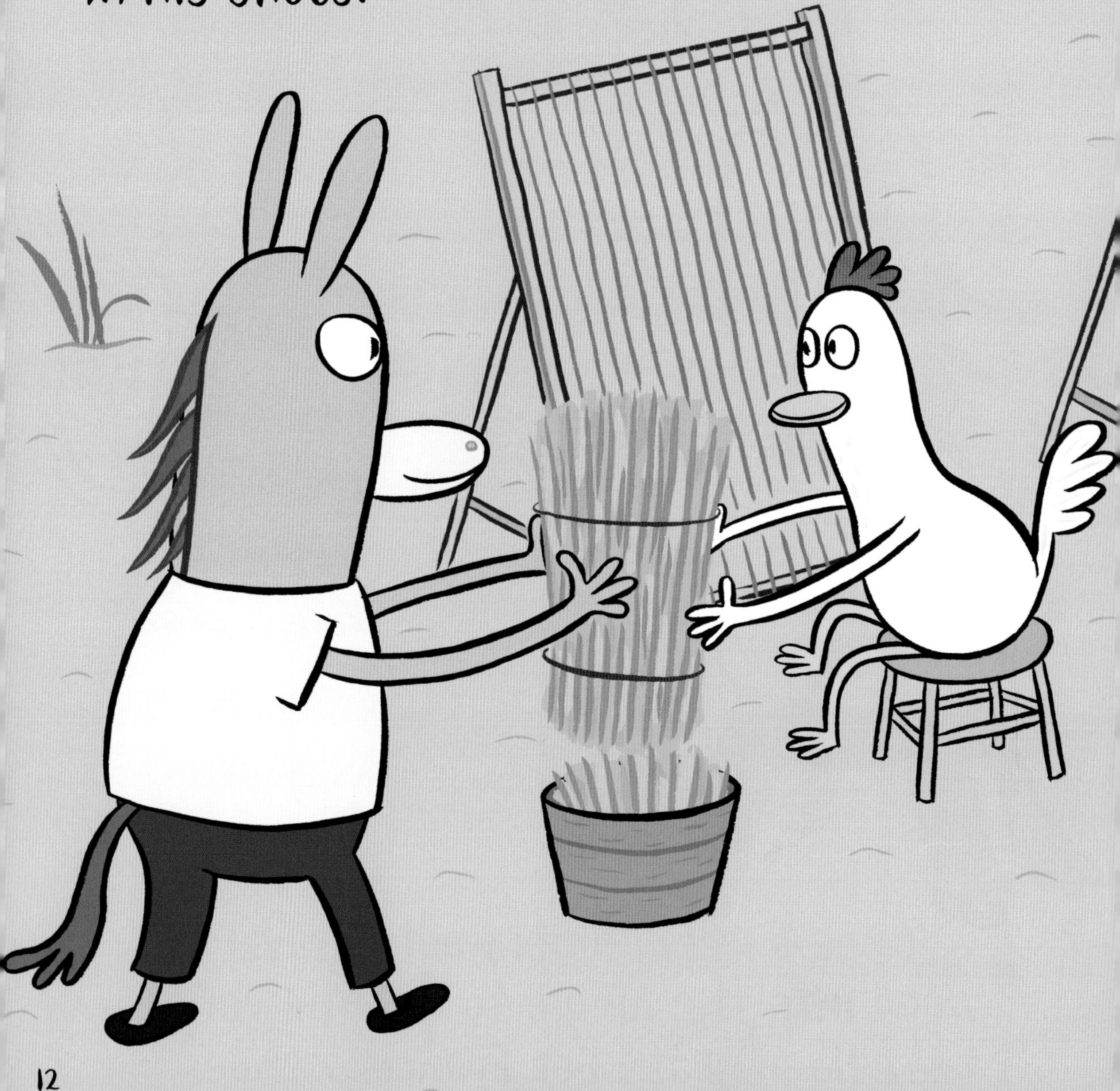

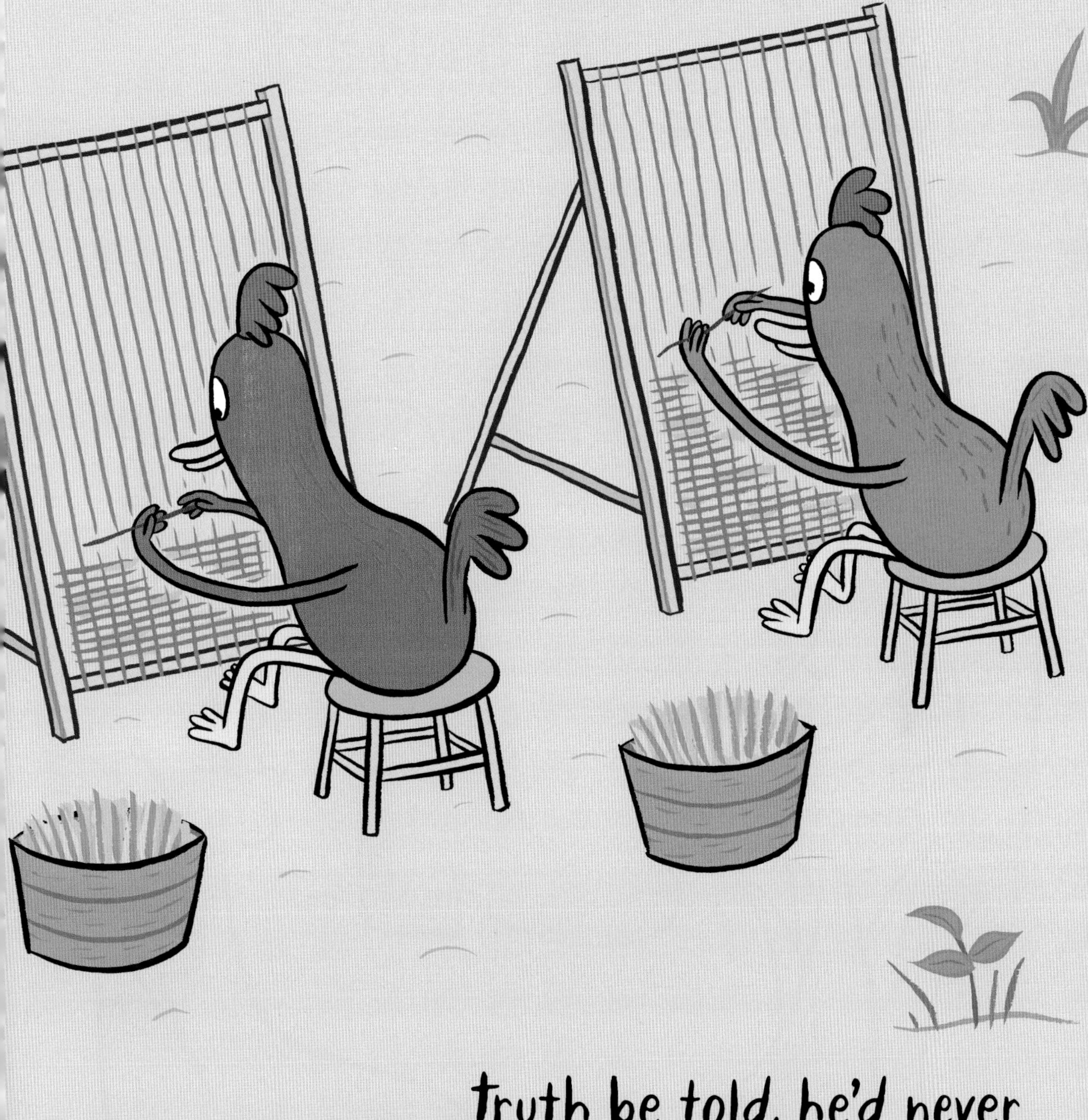

truth be told, he'd never
been to the jungle, or even outside
the village, but he was certain it was true.

He was especially good with embellishment. He loved to embroider leaves along the ankles, flowers on the heels, or fruits on the toes.

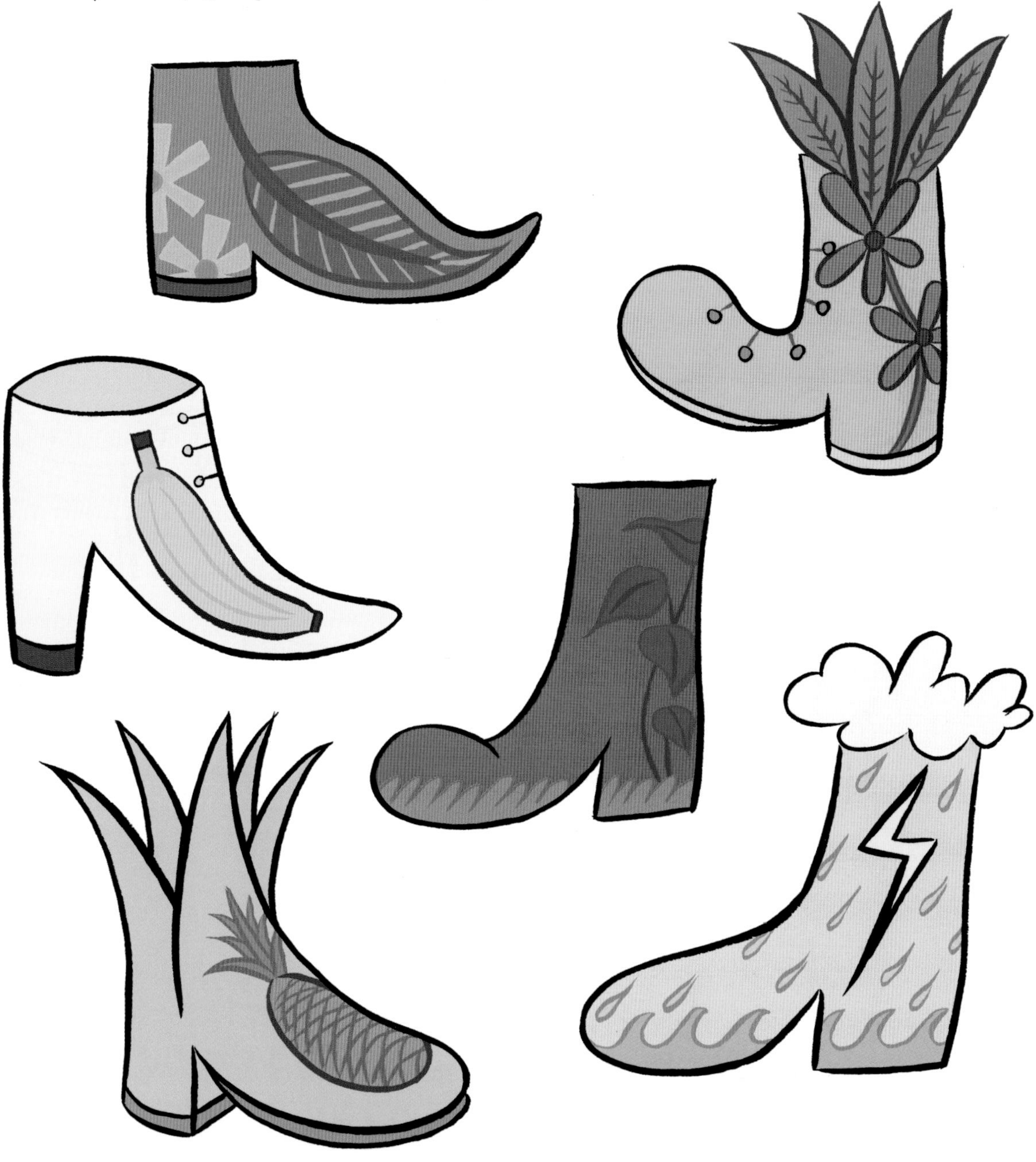

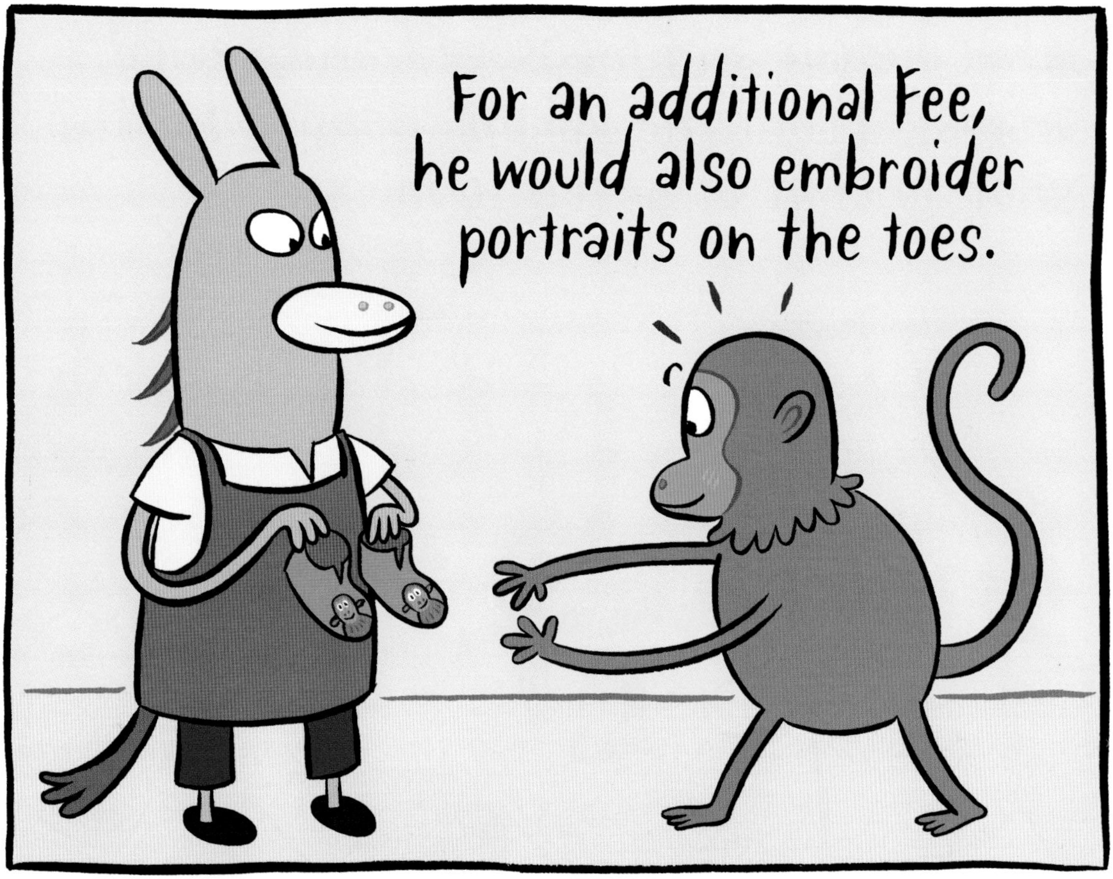
For an additional fee, he would also embroider portraits on the toes.

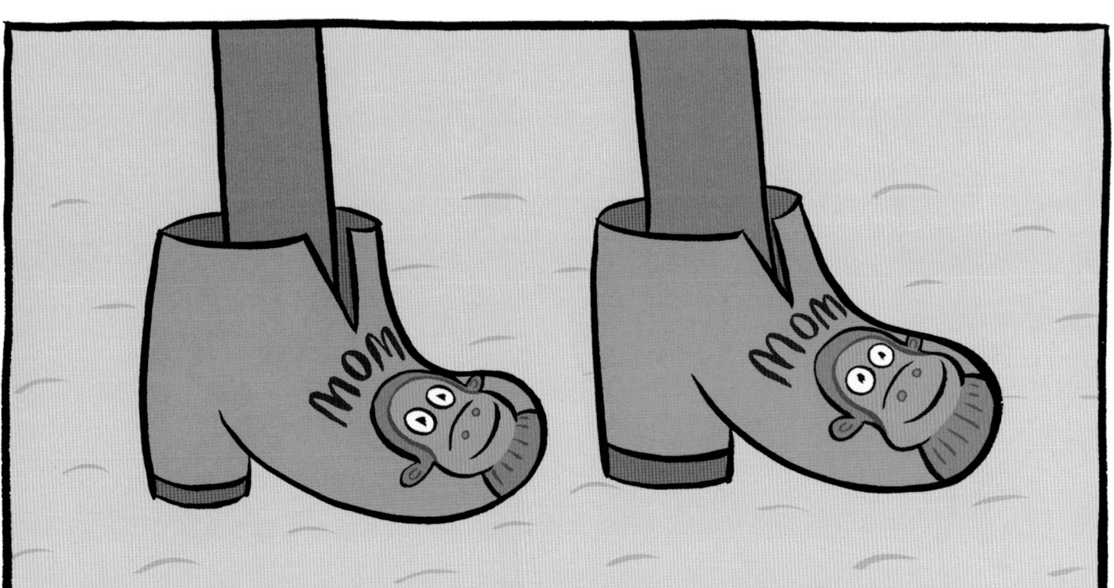
MOM
MOM

While he cut and measured and sewed, animals from the village stopped by the shop to chat or listen to music.

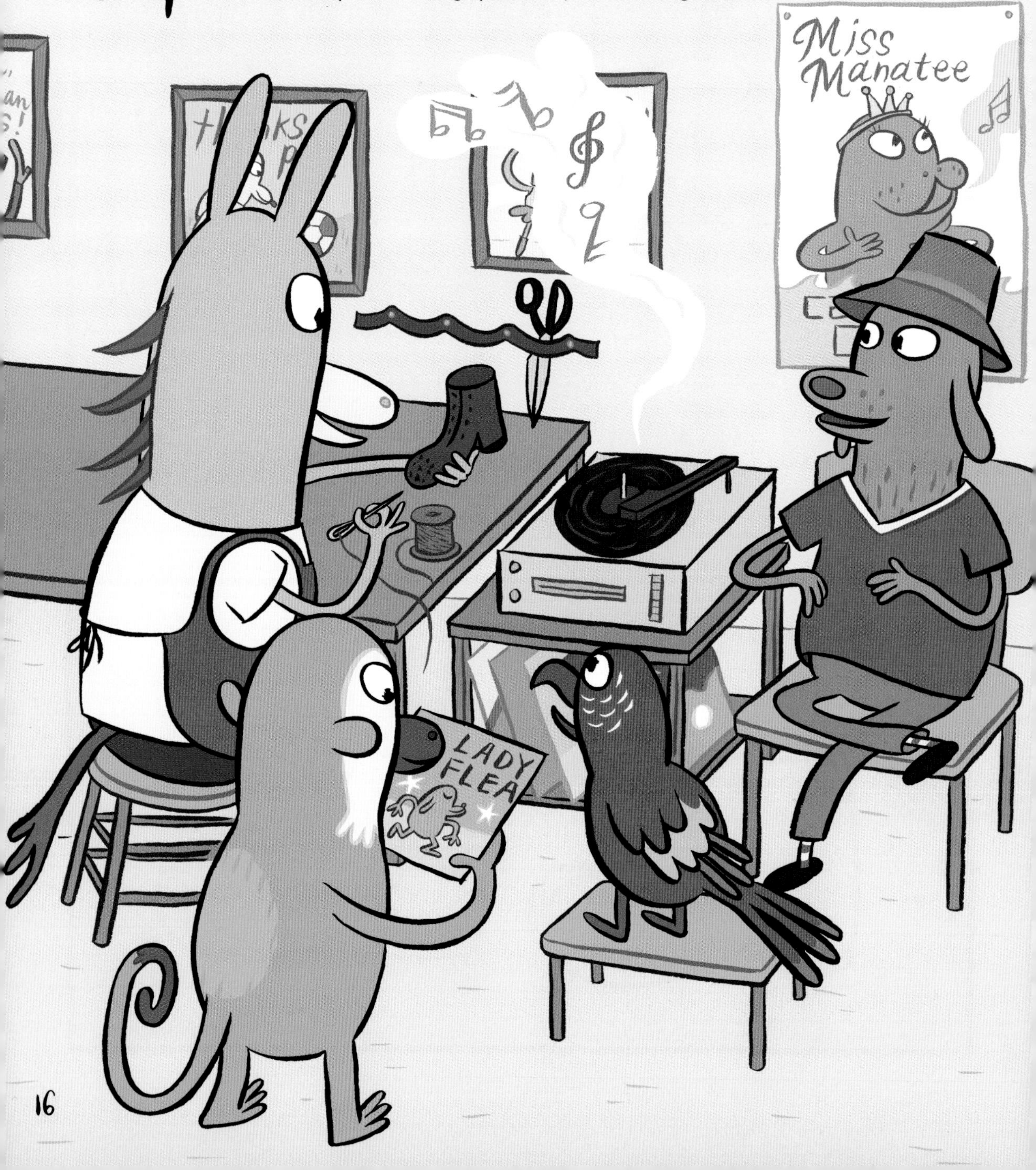
Miss Manatee
LADY FLEA

Francis had a renowned record collection. His Favorite music was calypso.

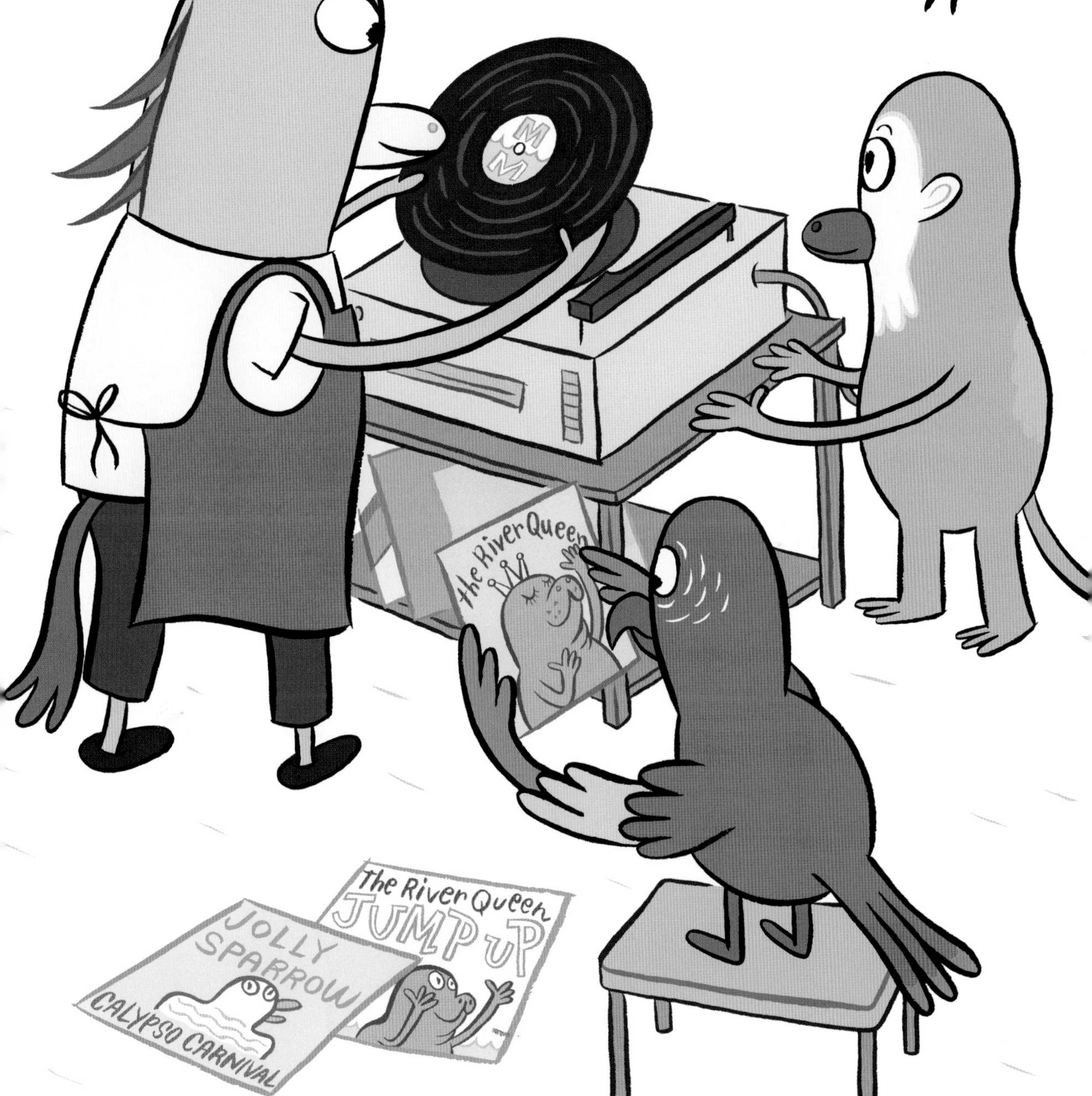

The River Queen
The River Queen
JUMP UP
JOLLY SPARROW
CALYPSO CARNIVAL

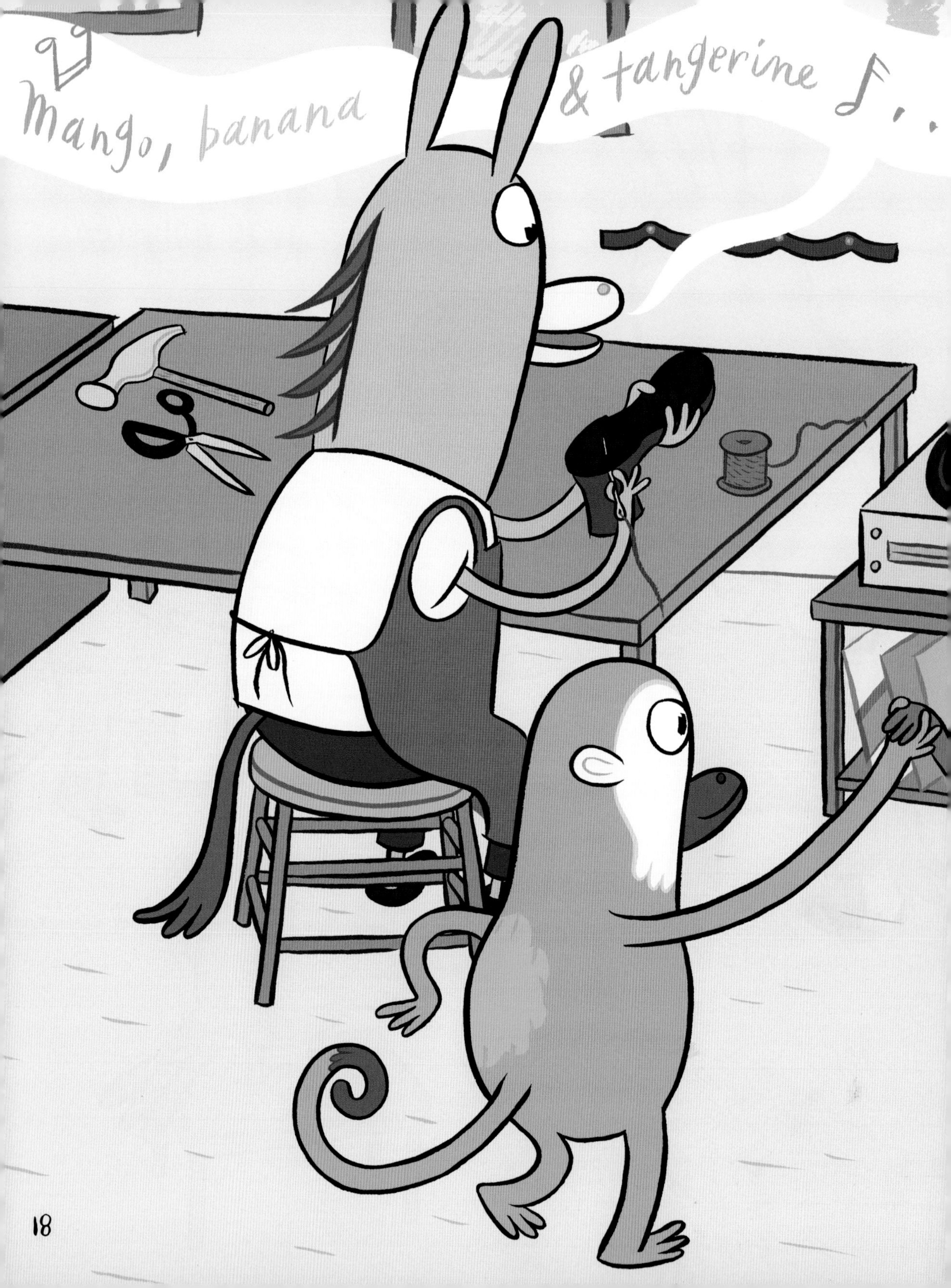
Mango, banana & tangerine ♪...

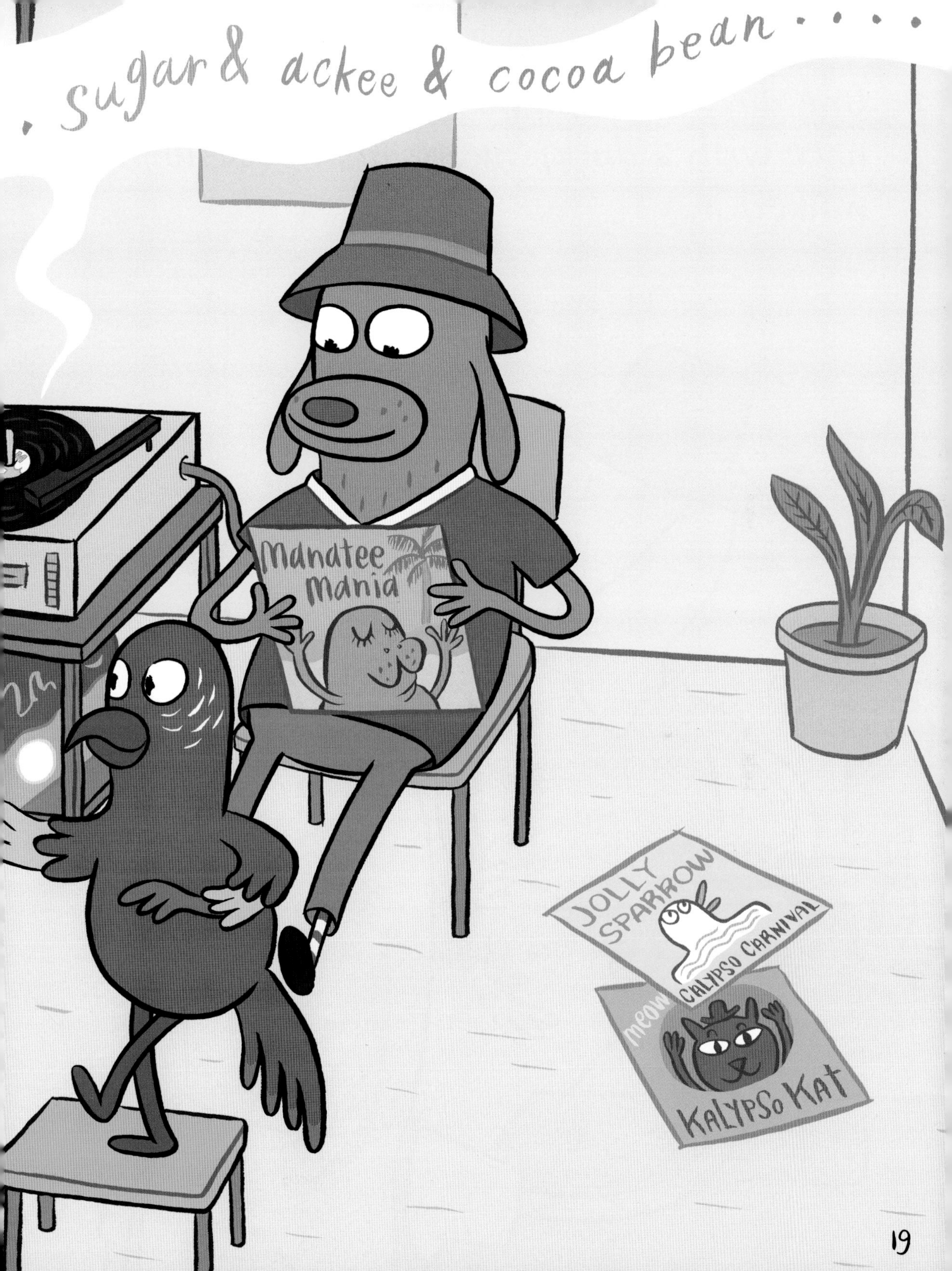
. sugar & ackee & cocoa bean . . . .
Manatee mania
JOLLY SPARROW
CALYPSO CARNIVAL
meow
KALYPSO KAT

One day, while he was having tamarind juice with a duck, an unfamiliar customer walked in.

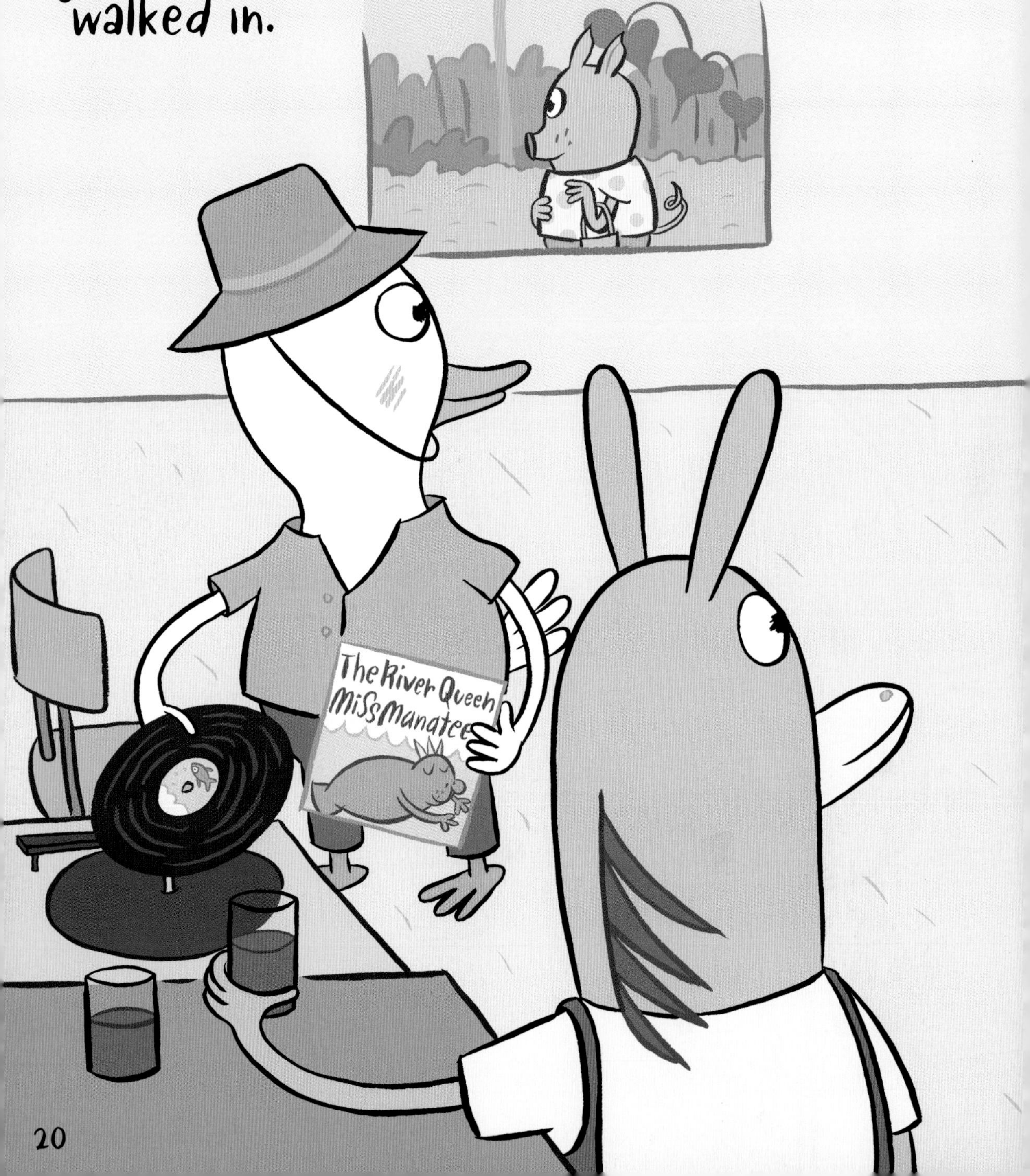
The River Queen
Miss Manatee

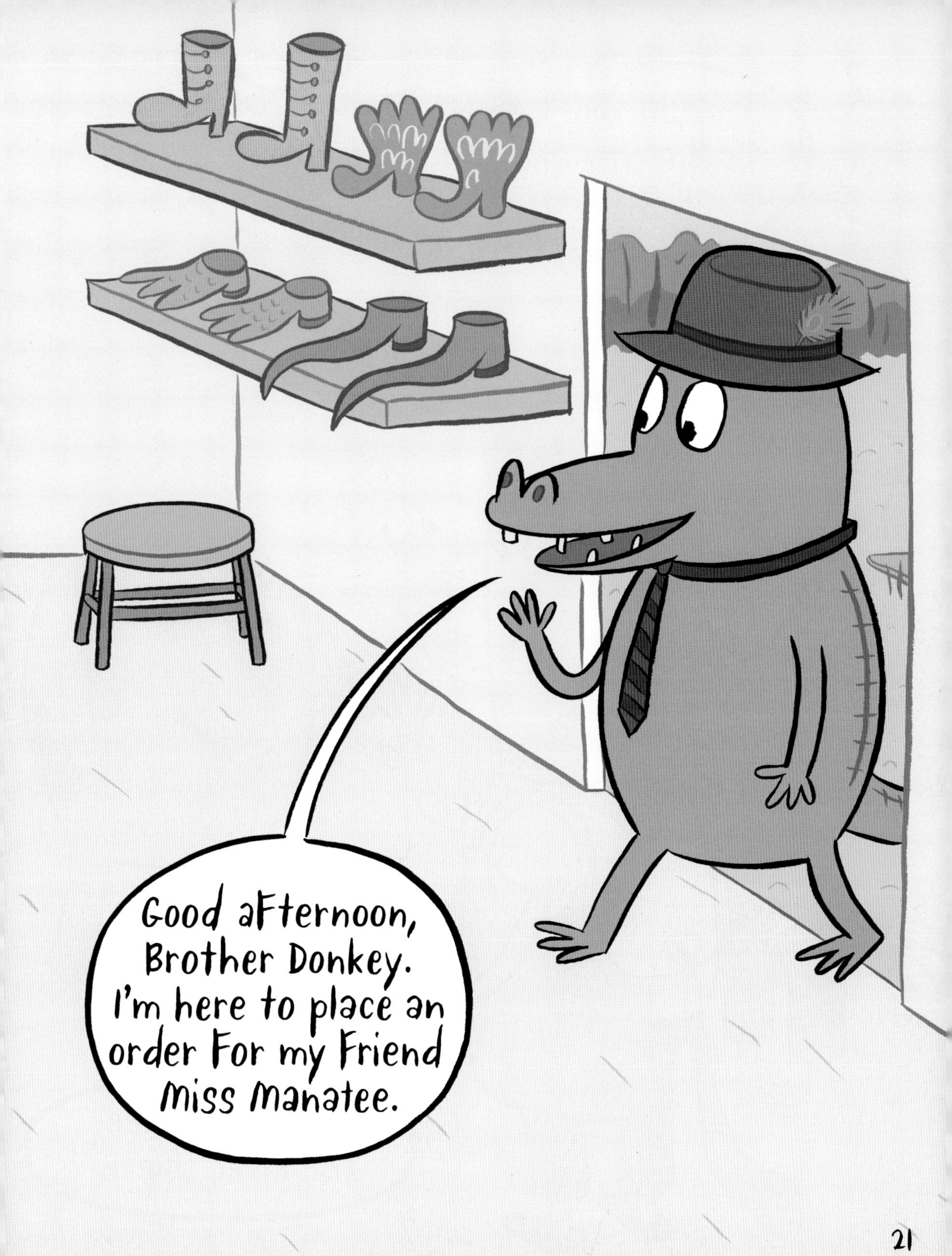
Good afternoon, Brother Donkey. I'm here to place an order for my friend Miss Manatee.

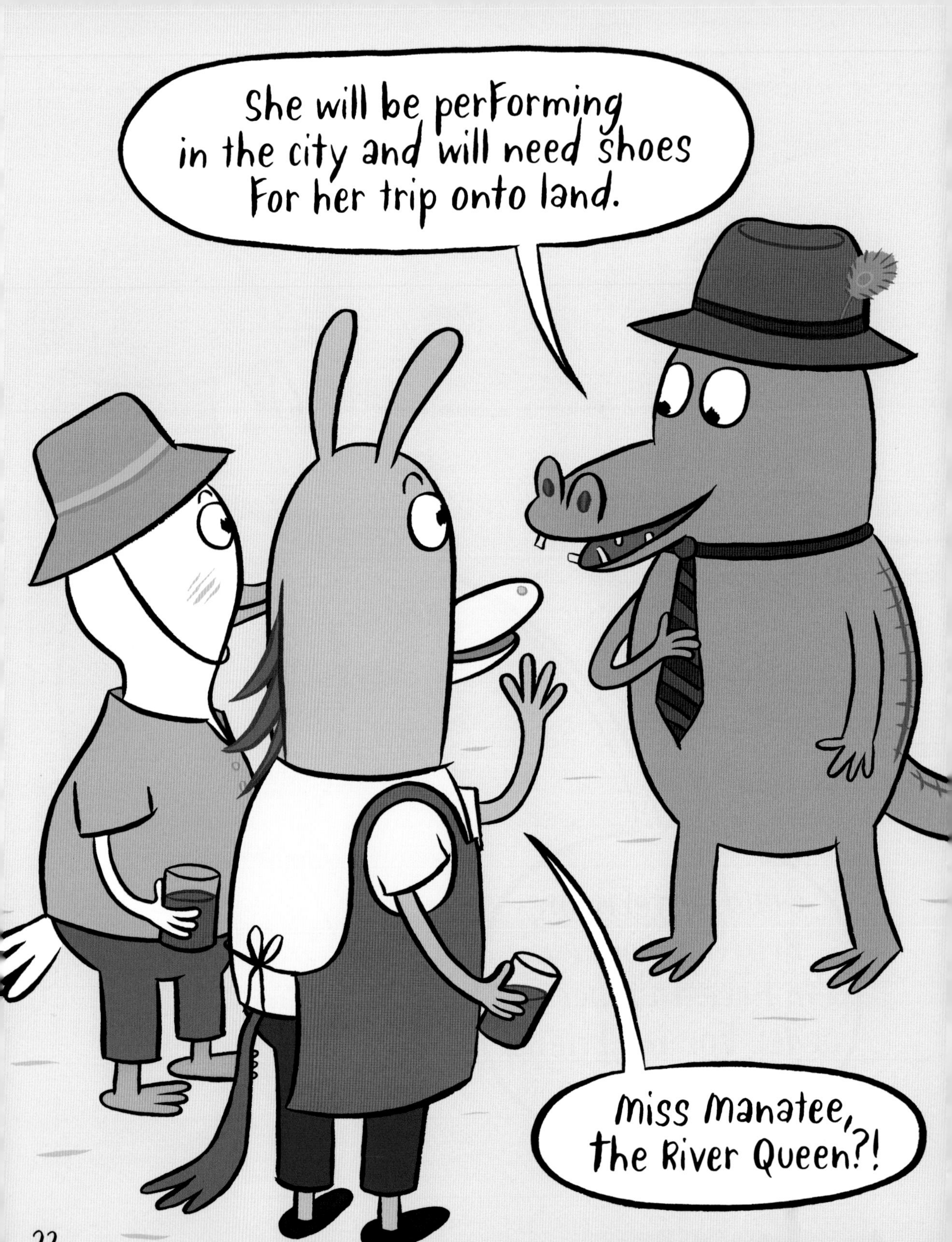
She will be performing in the city and will need shoes for her trip onto land.
Miss Manatee, the River Queen?!

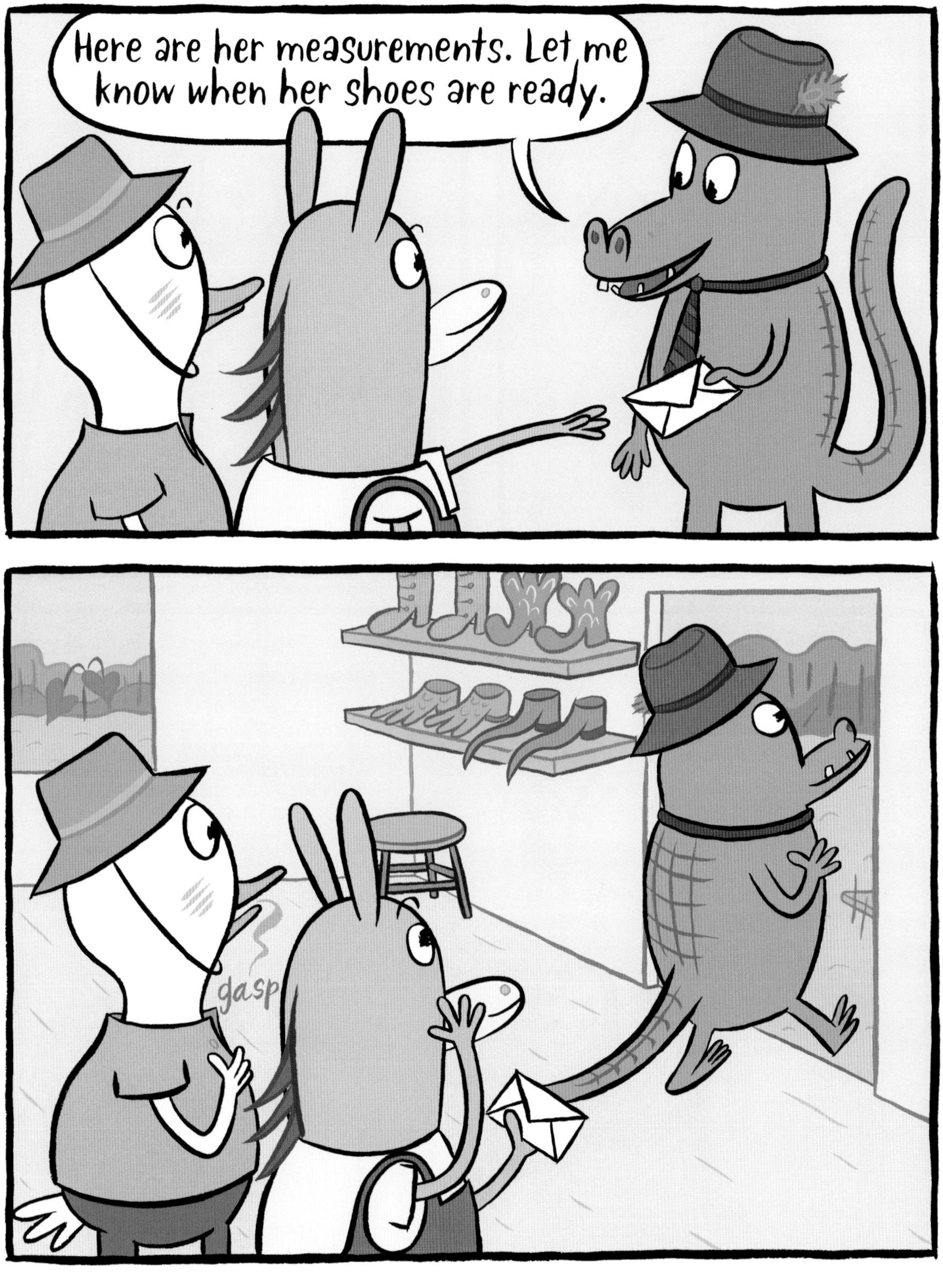
Here are her measurements. Let me know when her shoes are ready.
gasp

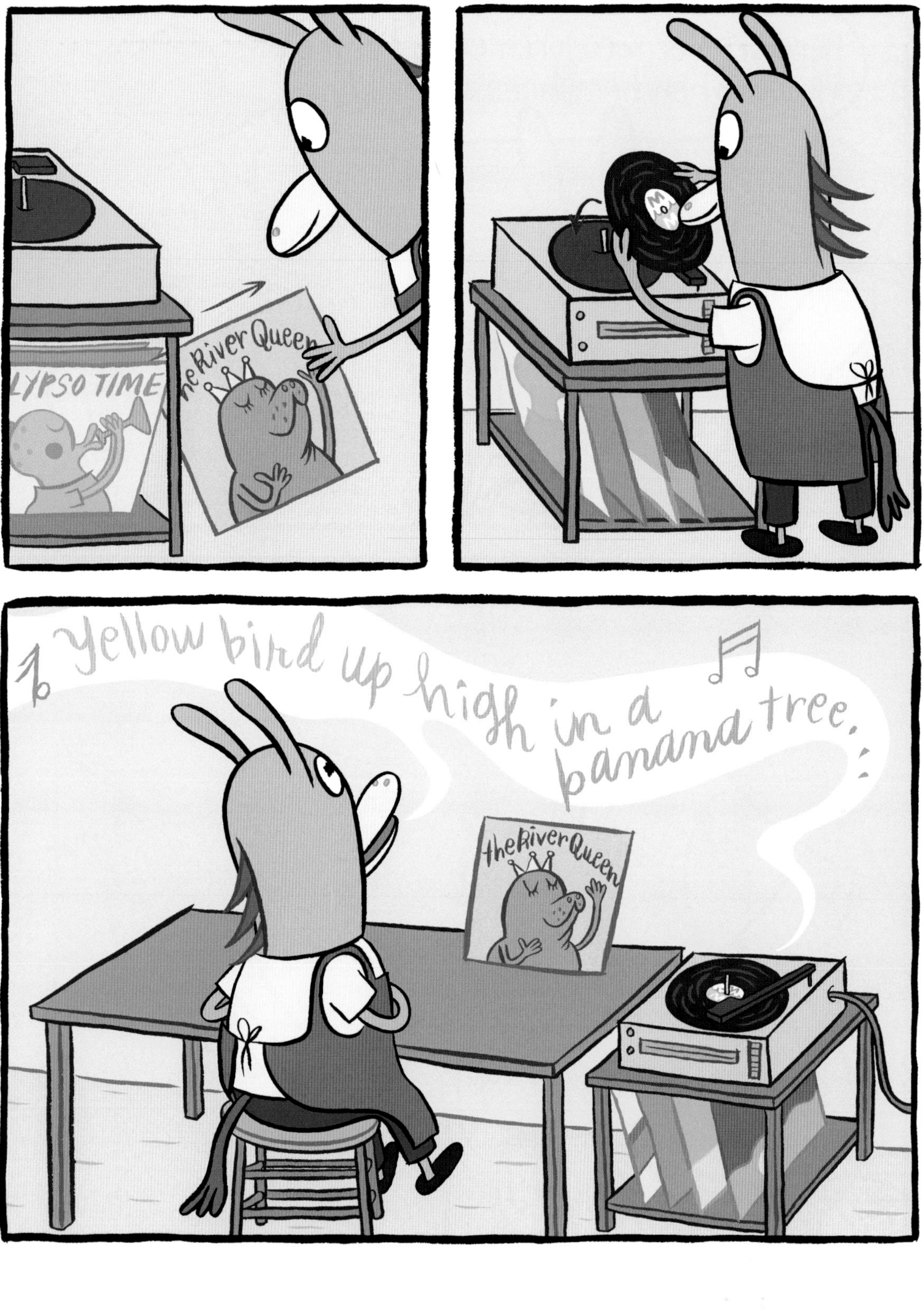
LYPSO TIME
the River Queen
the River Queen
the River Queen
Yellow bird up high in a banana tree...

All afternoon, Francis imagined how to make shoes for his favorite singer.

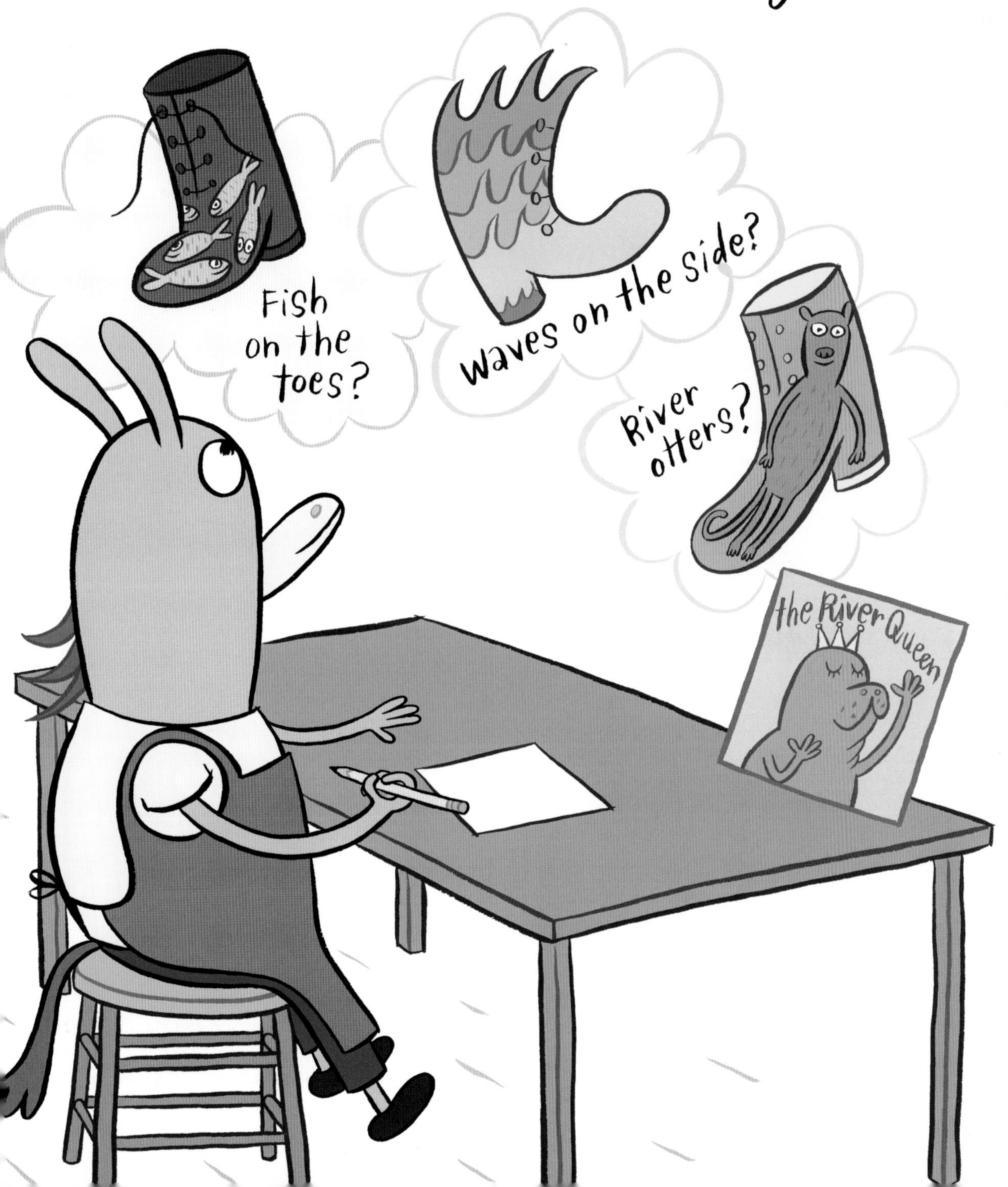
Fish on the toes?
Waves on the side?
River otters?
the River Queen

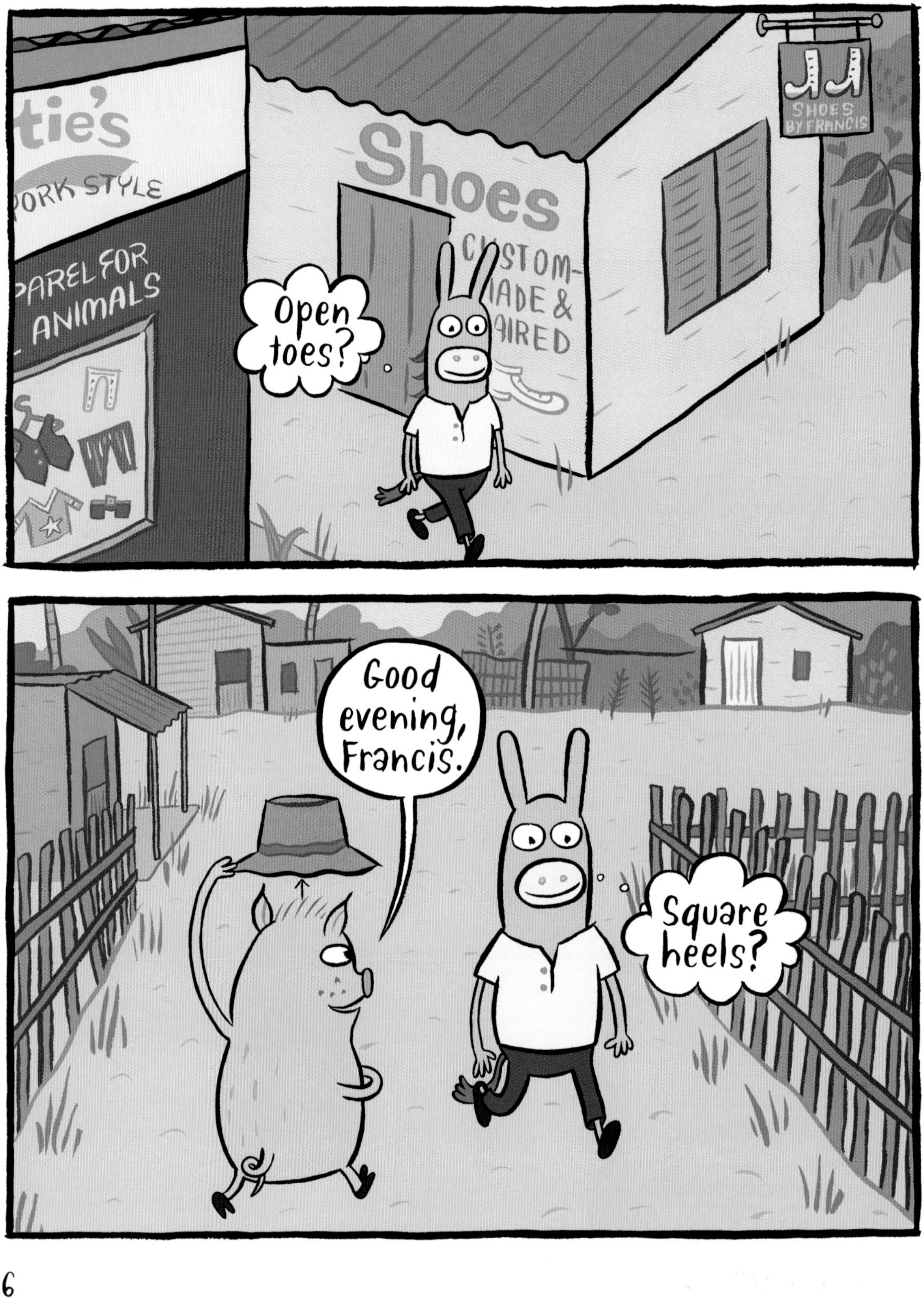
tie's
PORK STYLE
PAREL FOR
ANIMALS
Shoes
CUSTOM-
MADE &
AIRED
SHOES
BY FRANCIS
Open toes?
Good evening, Francis.
Square heels?

But the best part was imagining the moment when he could present them to her.

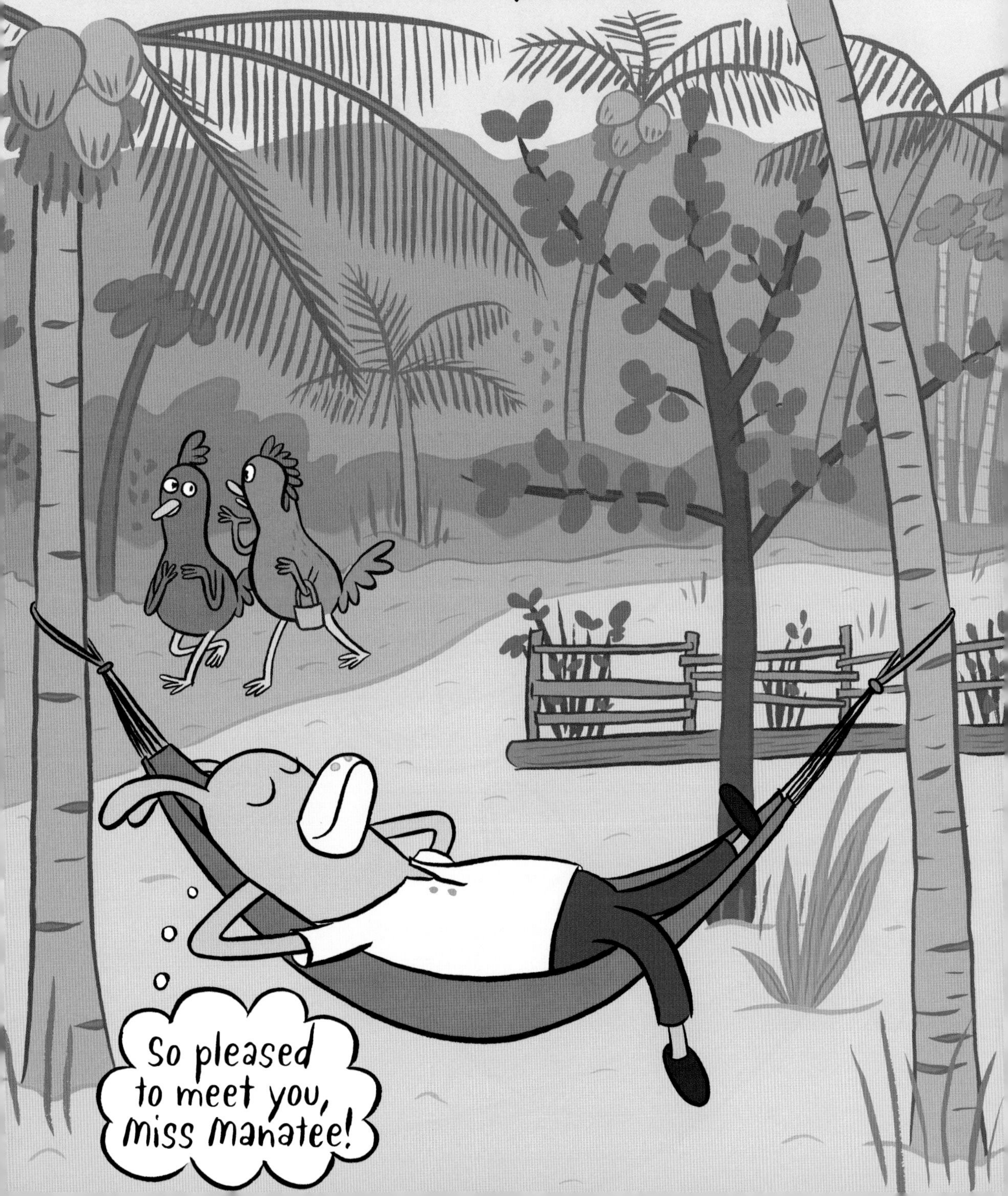

That night, Francis could hardly sleep.
He couldn't wait until morning to visit Nigel and pick up the wild tiger grass that would become Miss Manatee's shoes.
He could tell Nigel all about it over a game of dominoes.
Nigel would be thrilled.

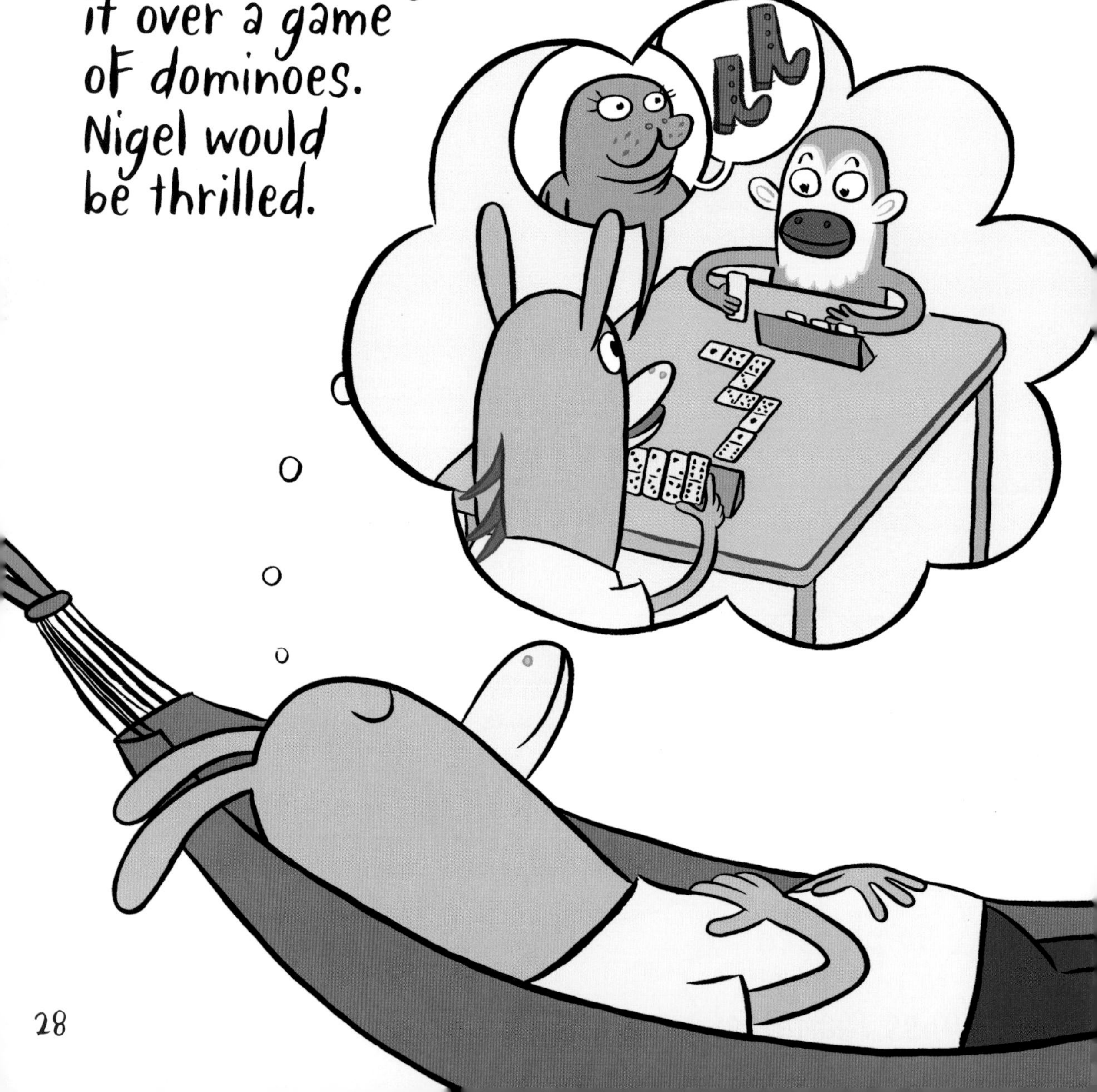

chapter two

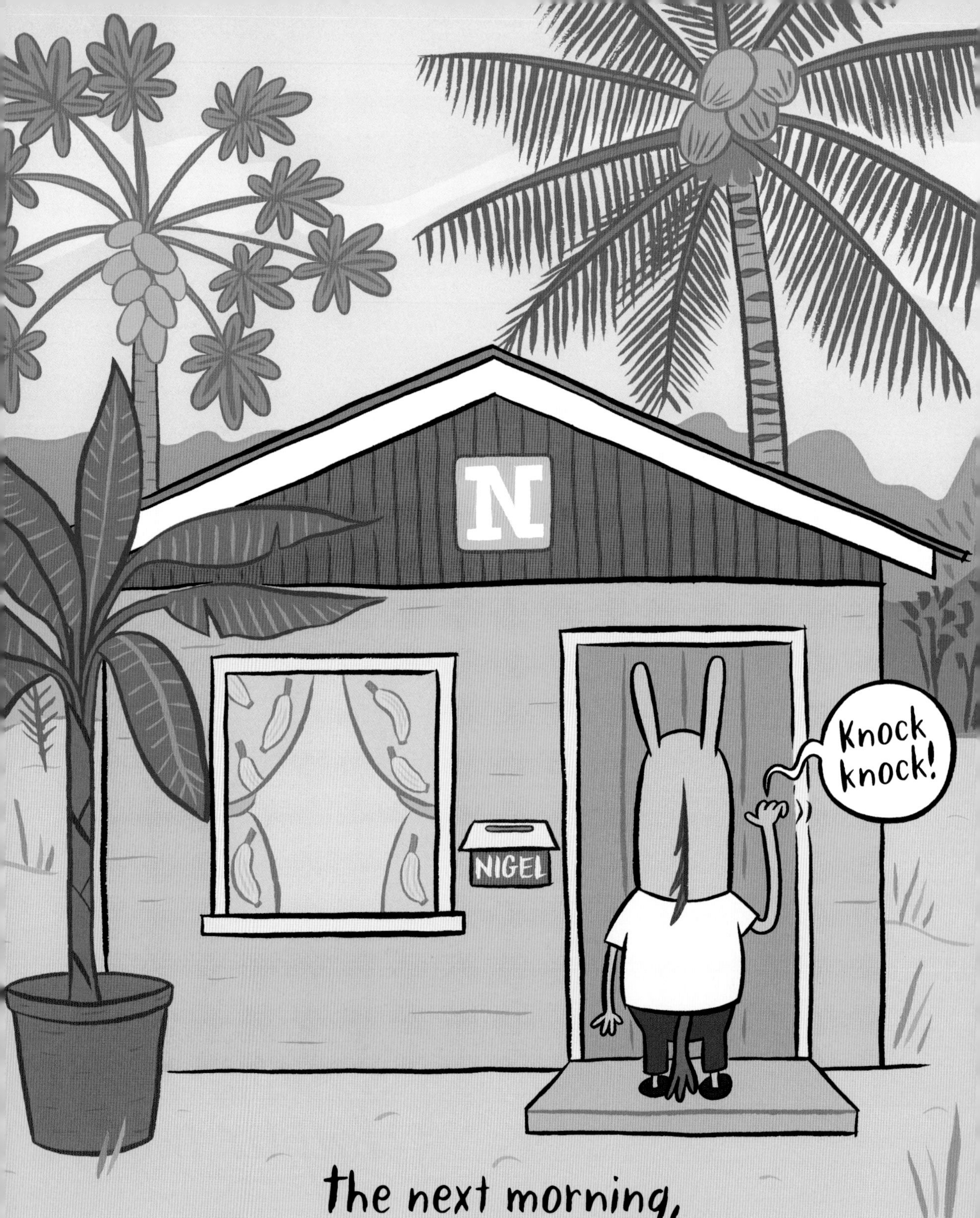
N
NIGEL
Knock knock!

The next morning,
Nigel was nowhere to be found.

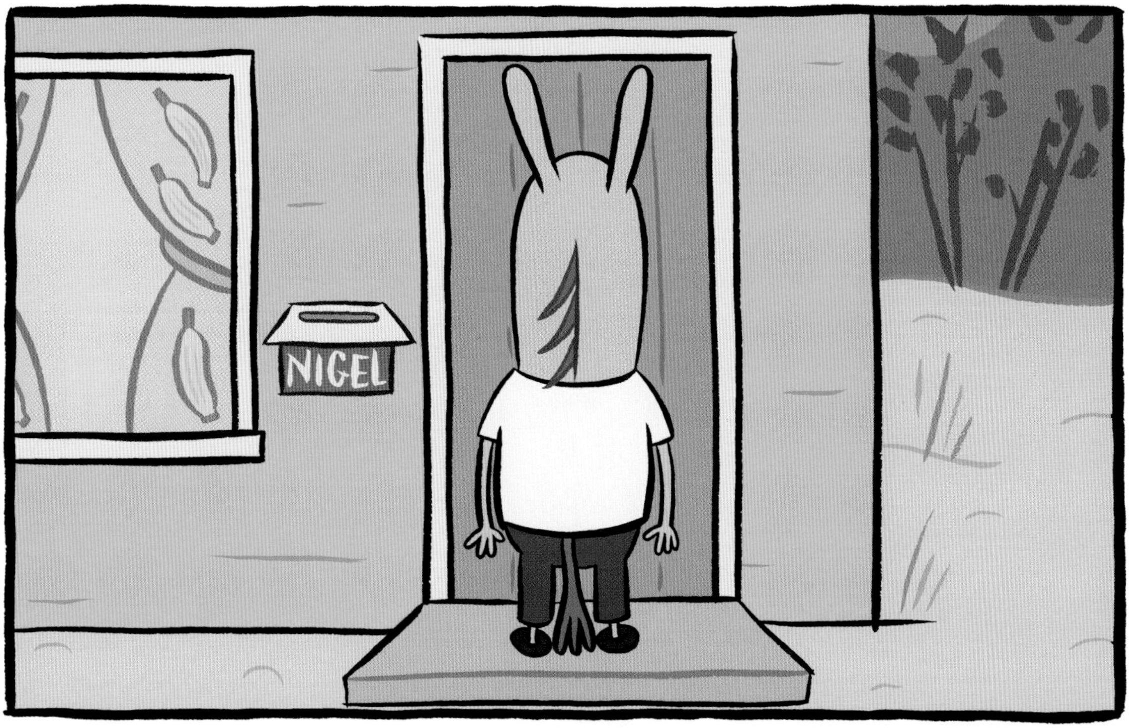
NIGEL

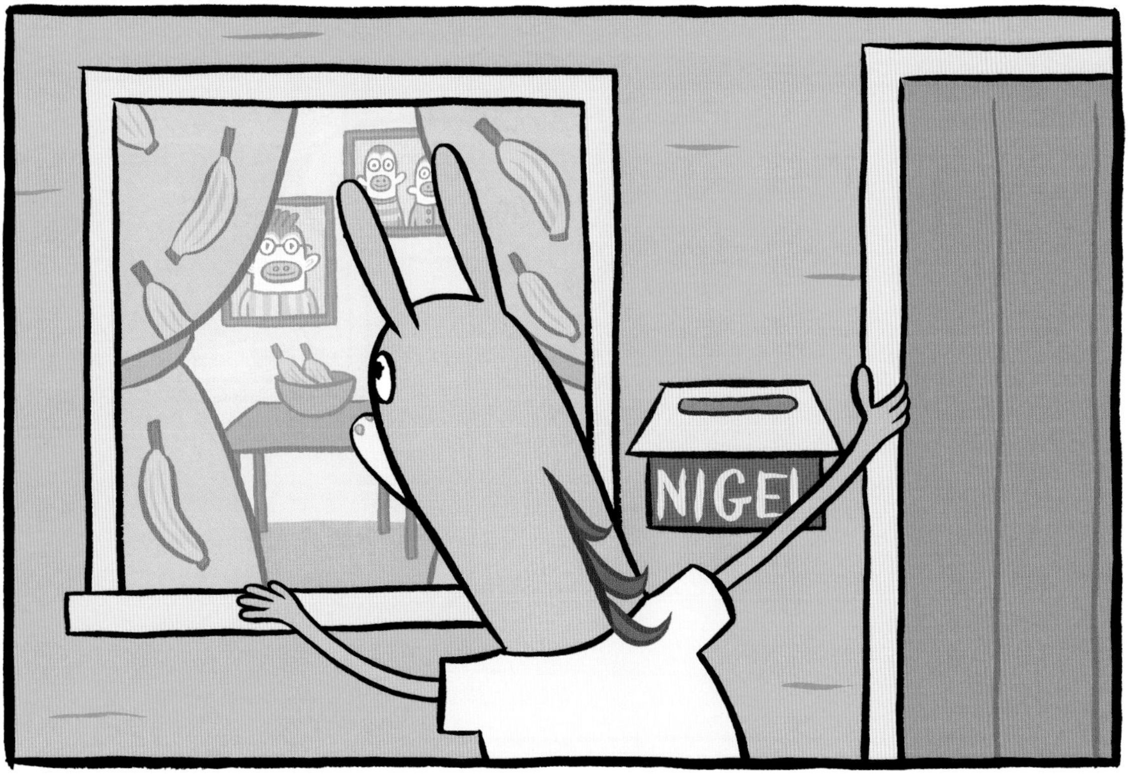
NIGEL

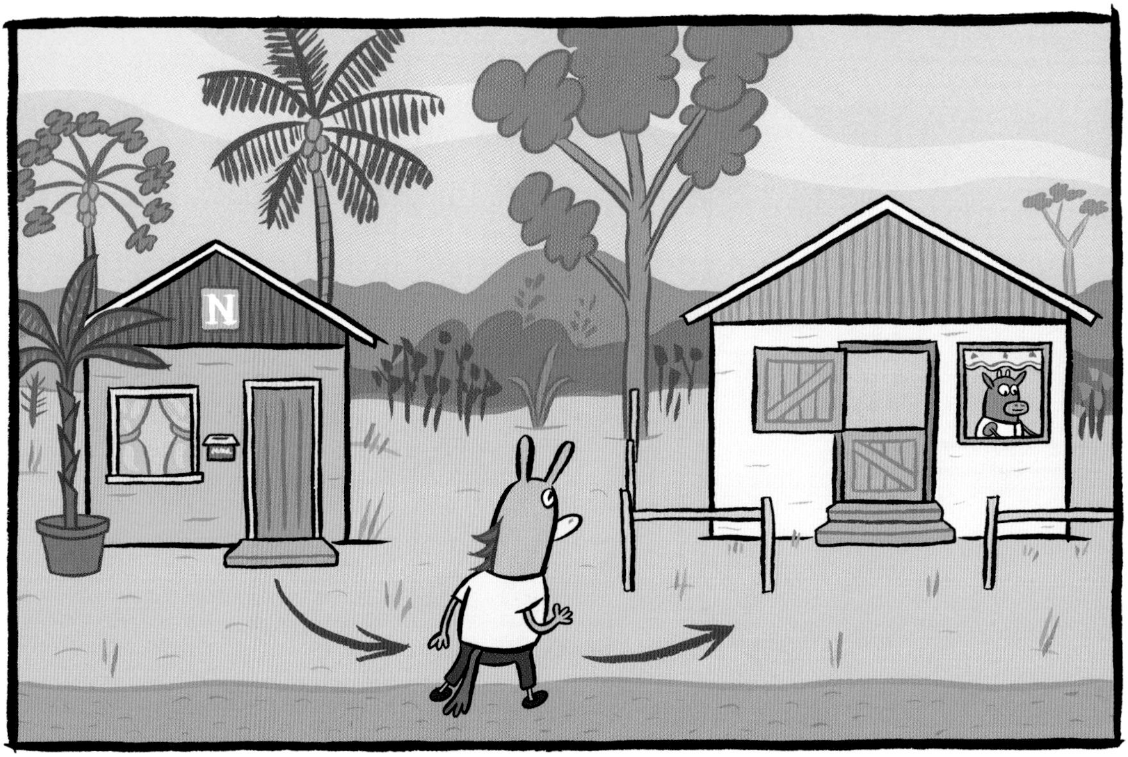
N

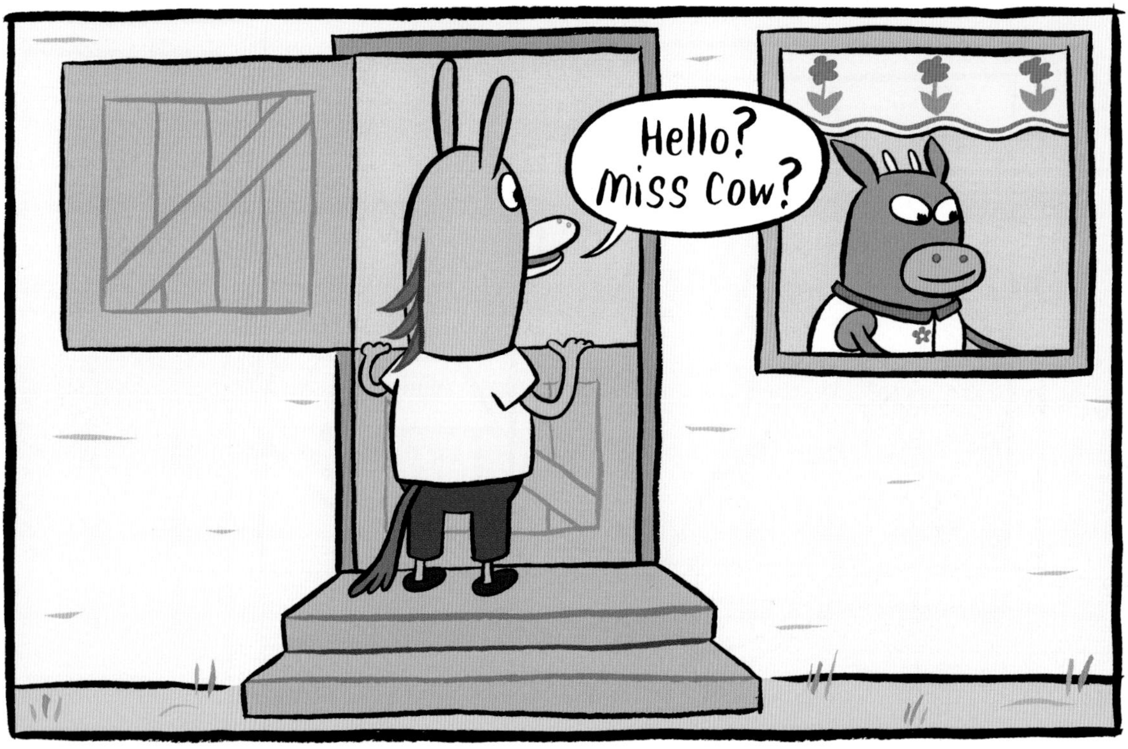
Hello? Miss Cow?

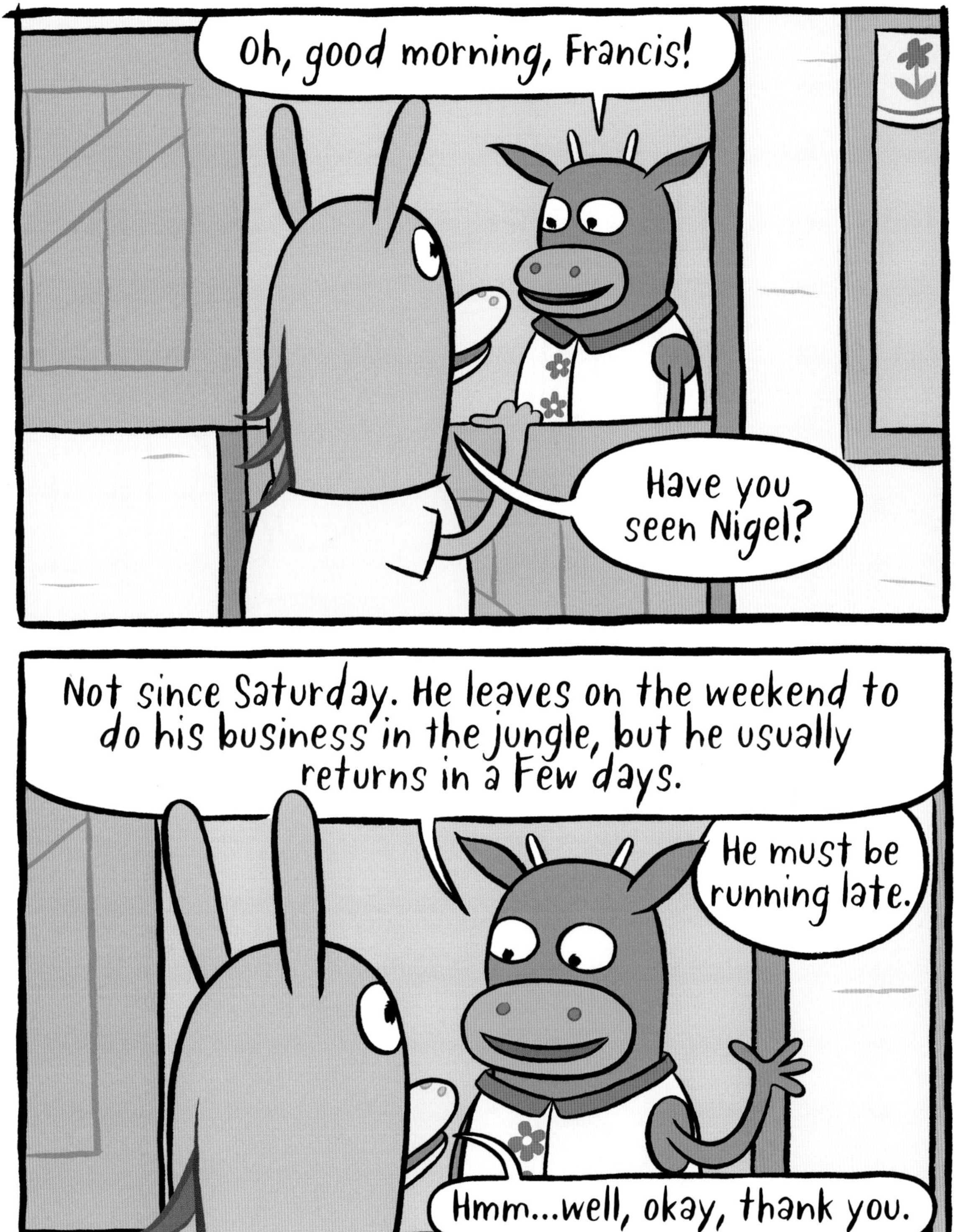
Oh, good morning, Francis!
Have you seen Nigel?
Not since Saturday. He leaves on the weekend to do his business in the jungle, but he usually returns in a Few days.
He must be running late.
Hmm...well, okay, thank you.

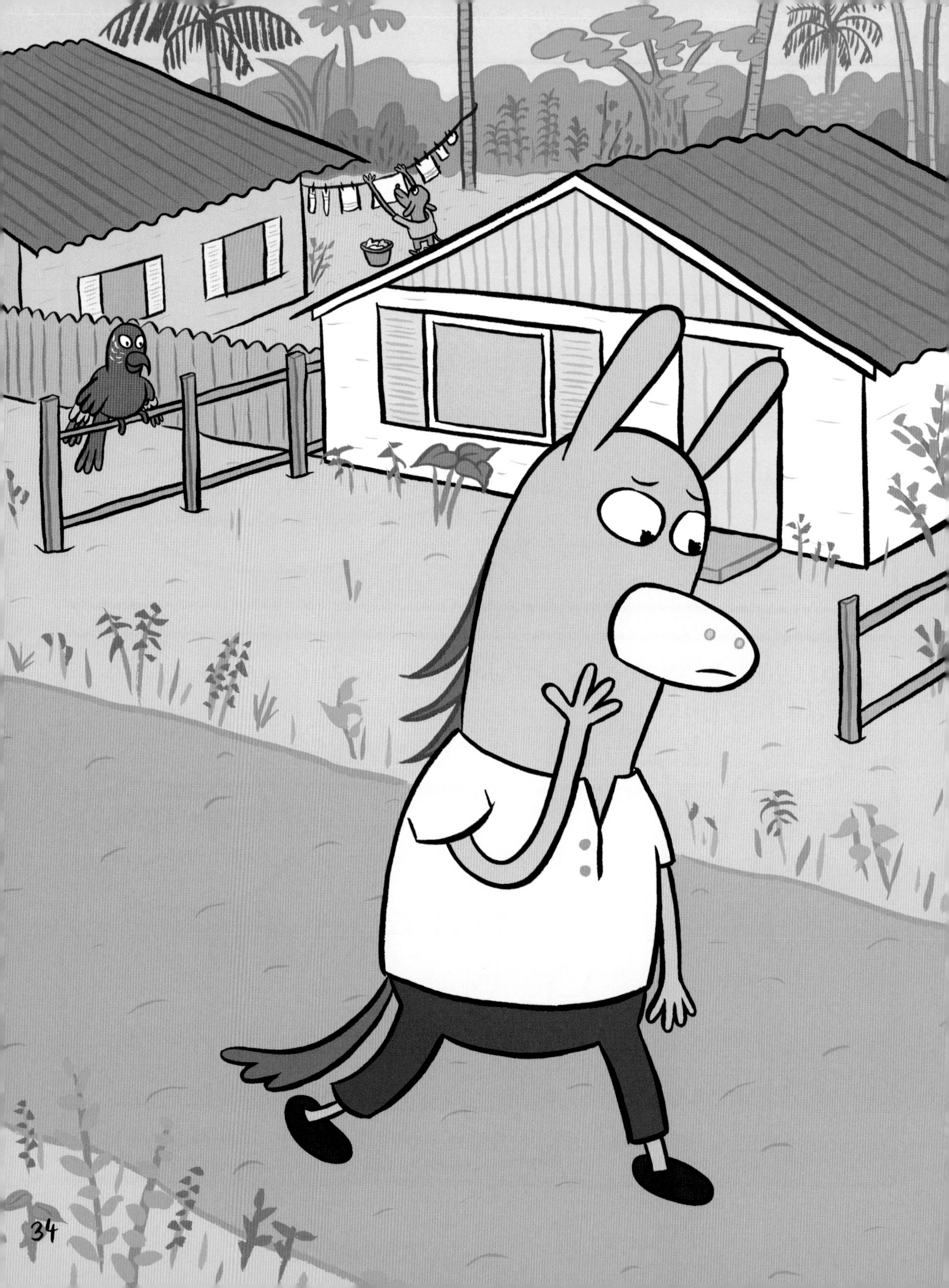

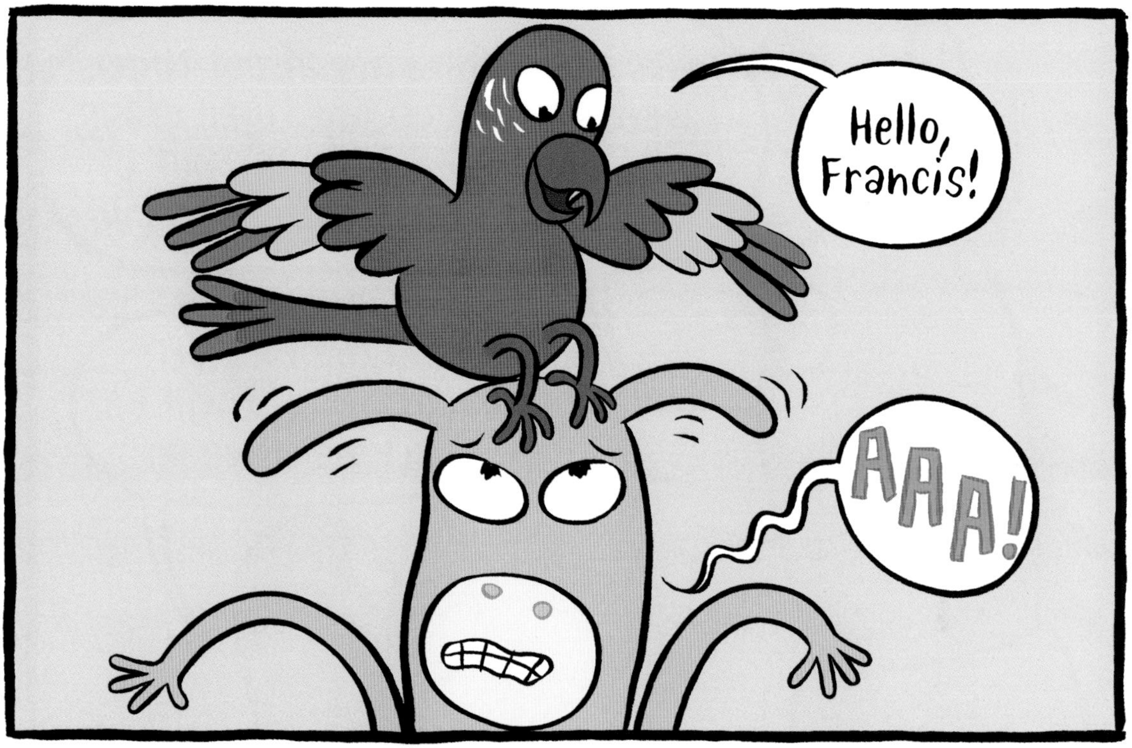
Hello, Francis!
AAA!

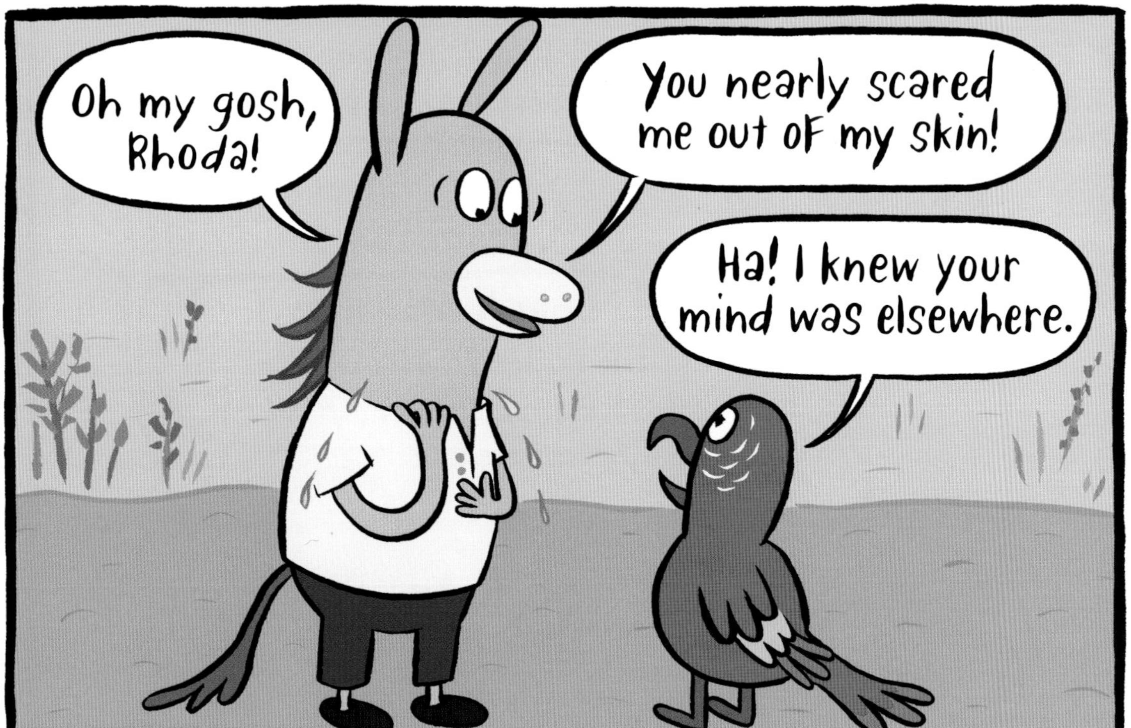
Oh my gosh, Rhoda!
You nearly scared me out of my skin!
Ha! I knew your mind was elsewhere.

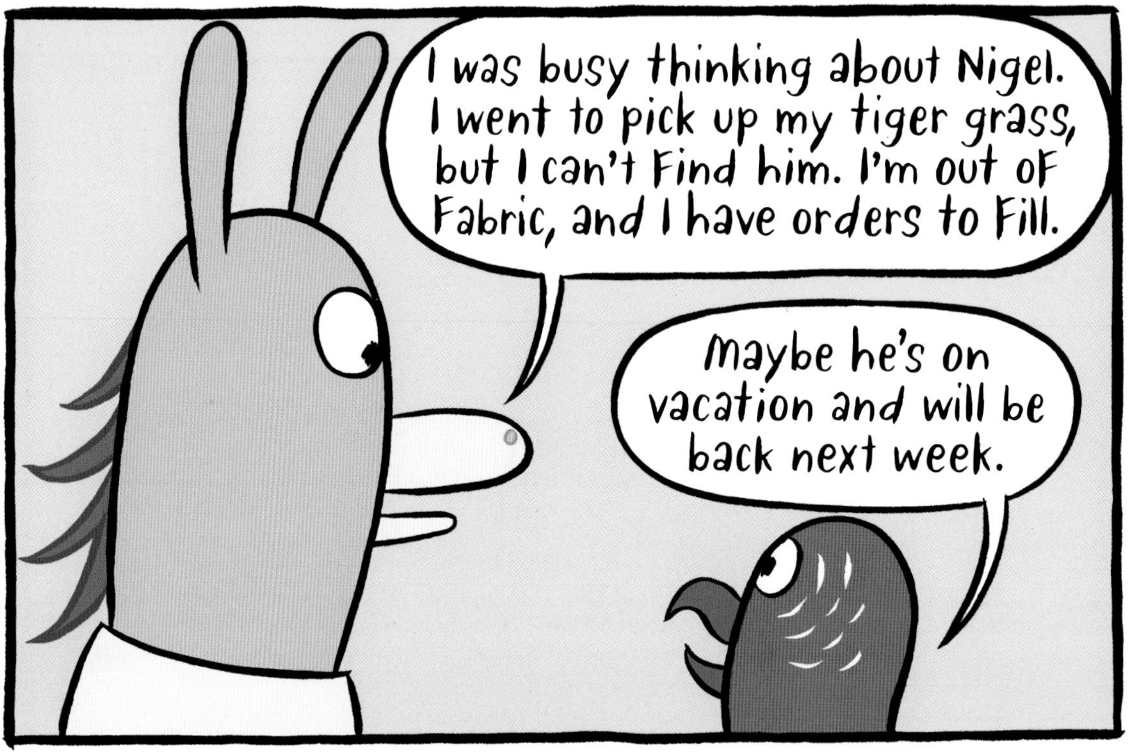
I was busy thinking about Nigel. I went to pick up my tiger grass, but I can't find him. I'm out of fabric, and I have orders to fill.
Maybe he's on vacation and will be back next week.

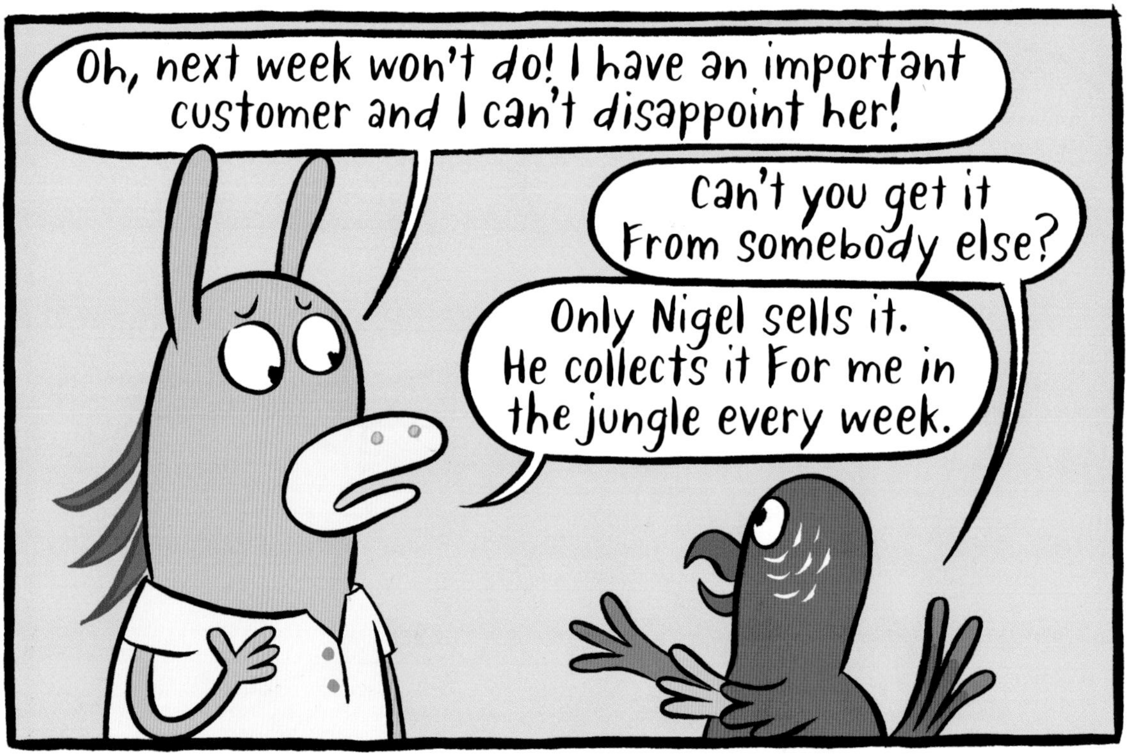
Oh, next week won't do! I have an important customer and I can't disappoint her!
Can't you get it from somebody else?
Only Nigel sells it. He collects it for me in the jungle every week.

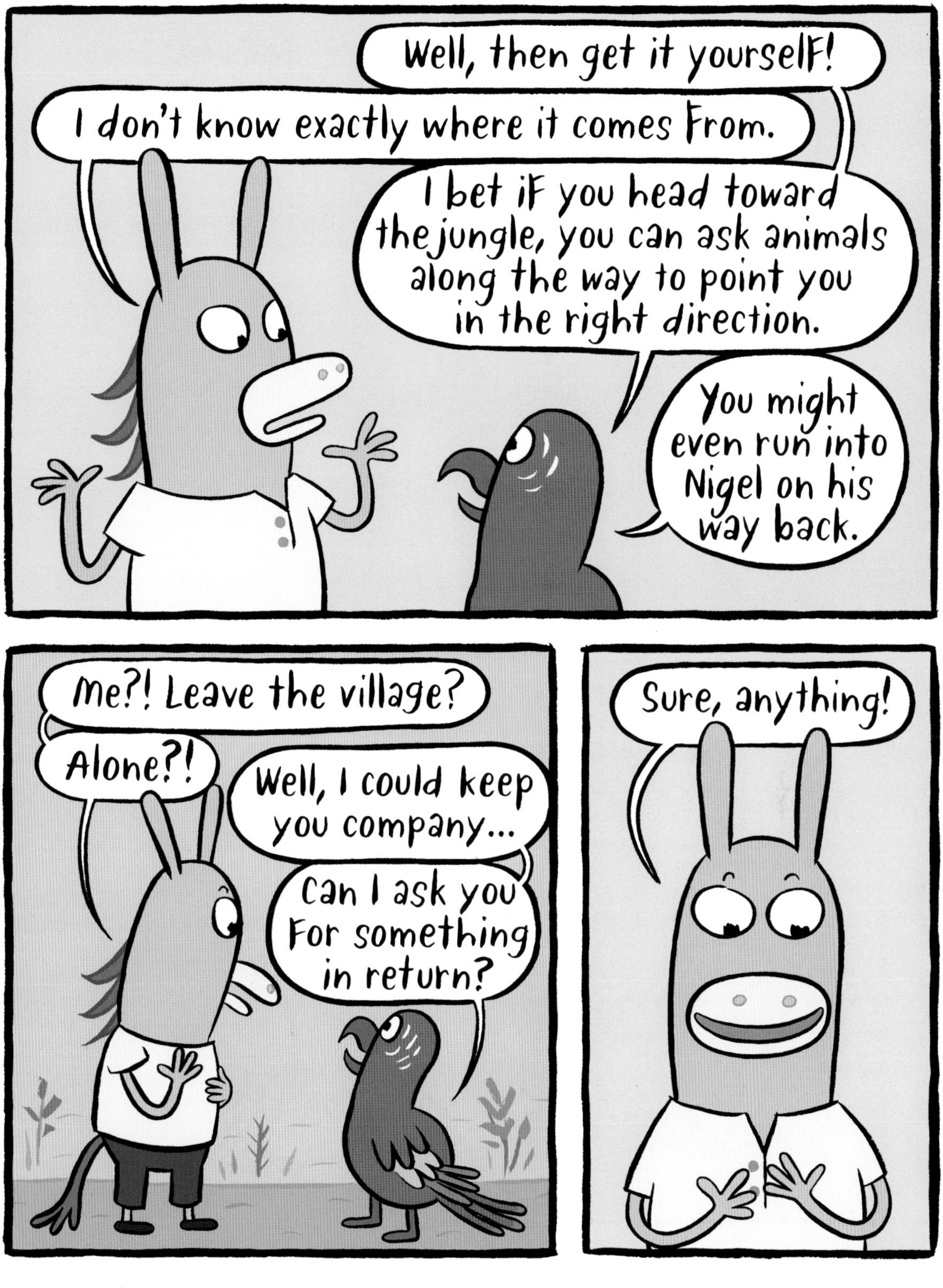
I don't know exactly where it comes From.
Well, then get it yourselF!
I bet iF you head toward the jungle, you can ask animals along the way to point you in the right direction.
You might even run into Nigel on his way back.
Me?! Leave the village?
Alone?!
Well, I could keep you company...
Can I ask you For something in return?
Sure, anything!

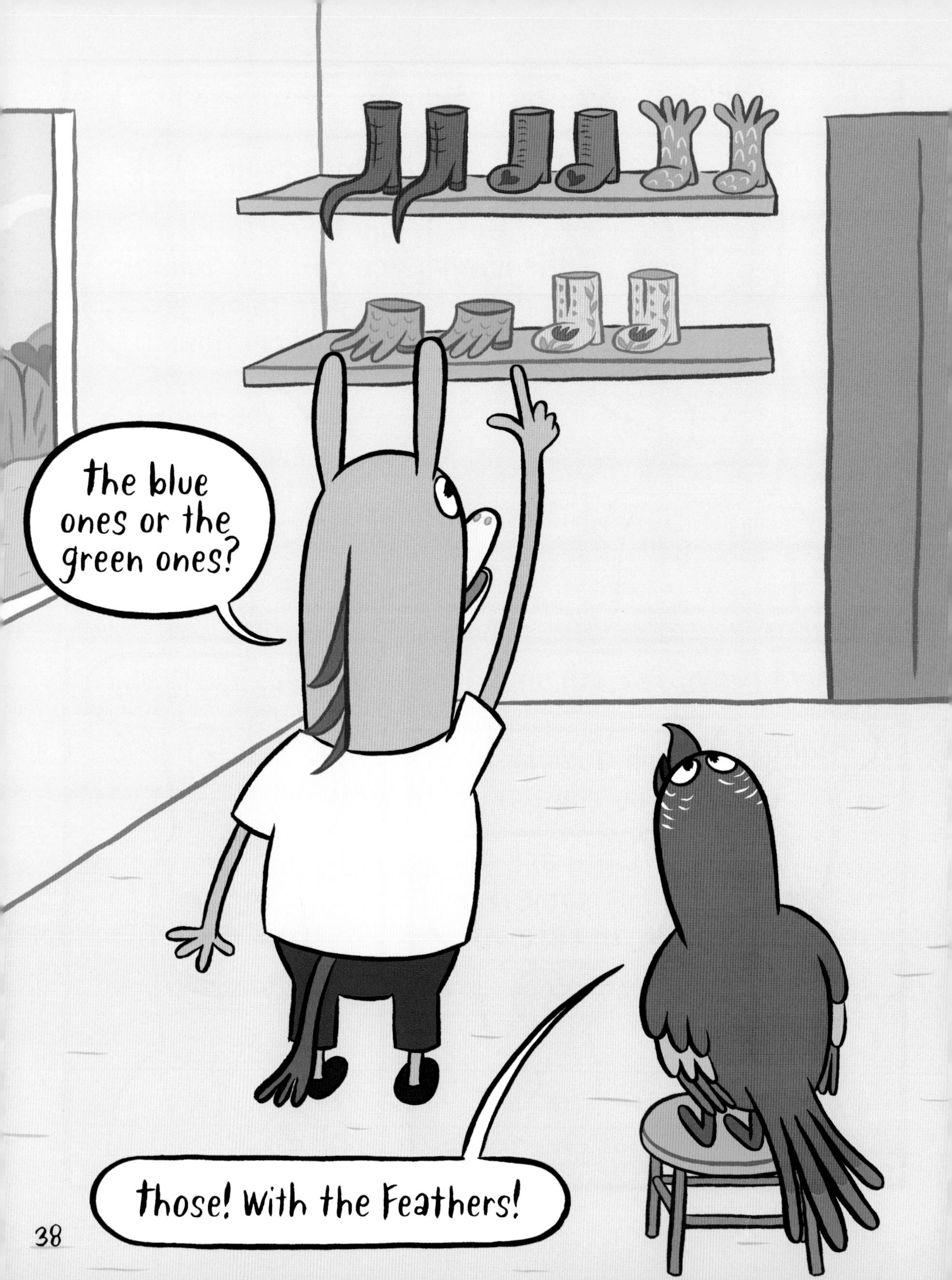
the blue ones or the green ones?
those! With the Feathers!

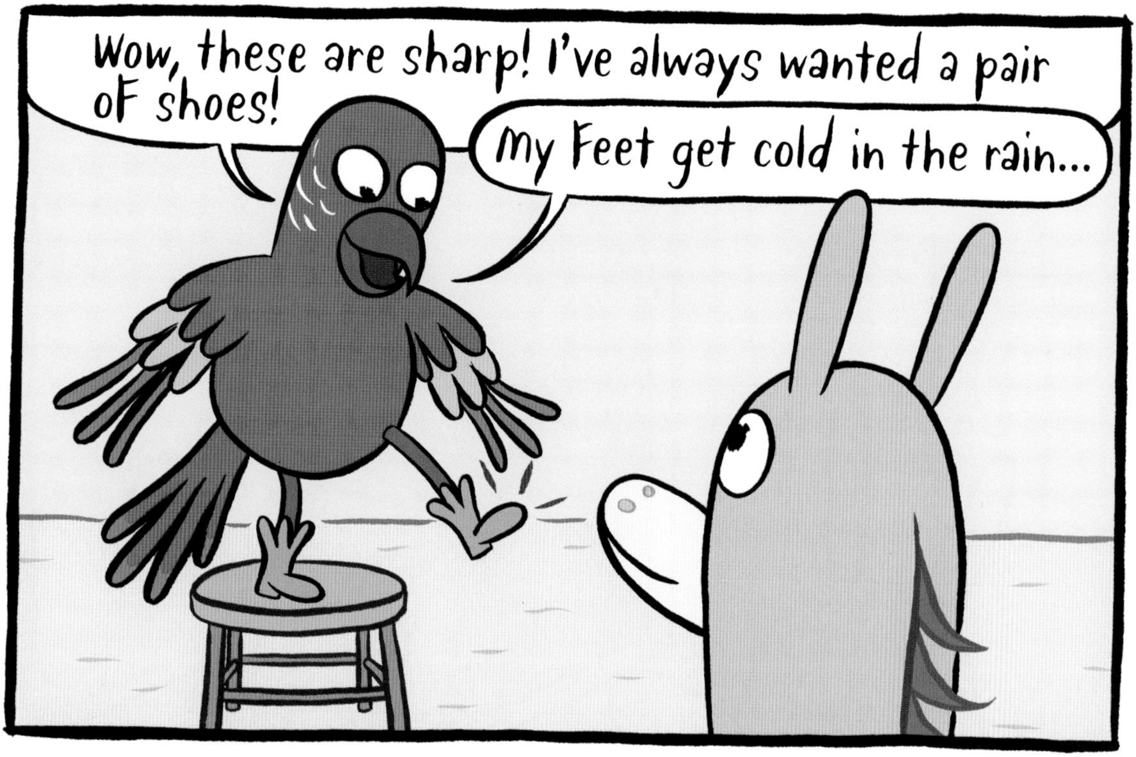
Wow, these are sharp! I've always wanted a pair of shoes!
My feet get cold in the rain...

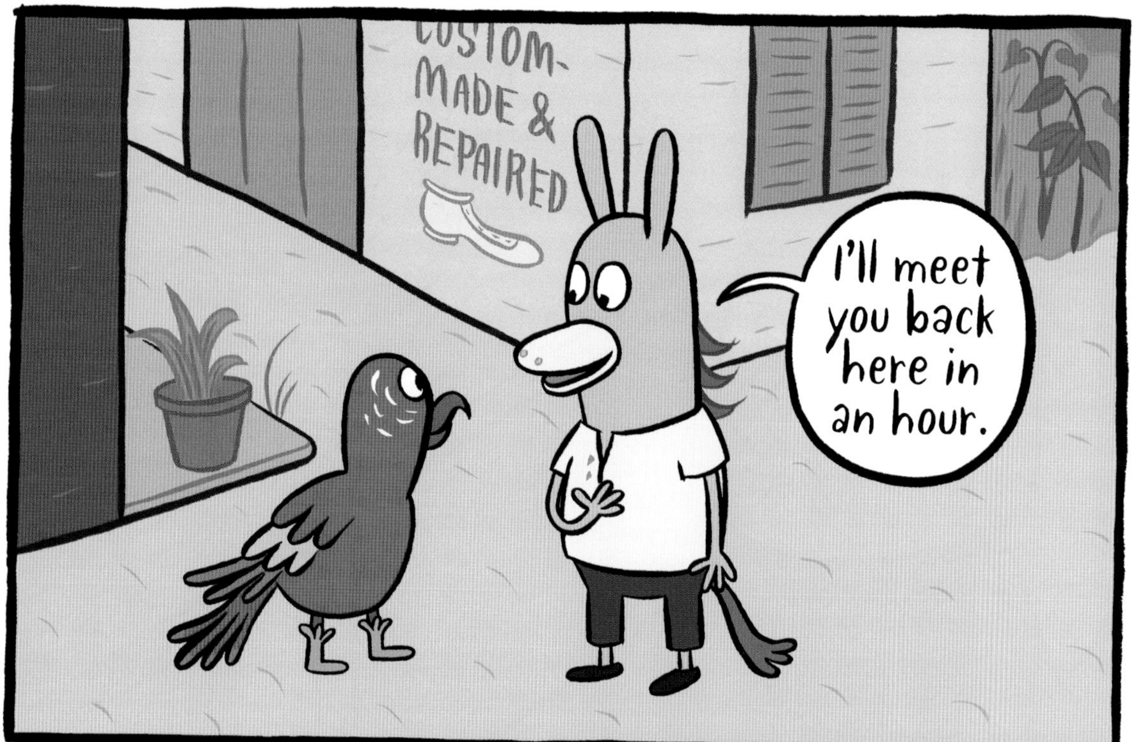
CUSTOM-MADE & REPAIRED
I'll meet you back here in an hour.

Francis wasn't quite sure what he'd need for his journey.

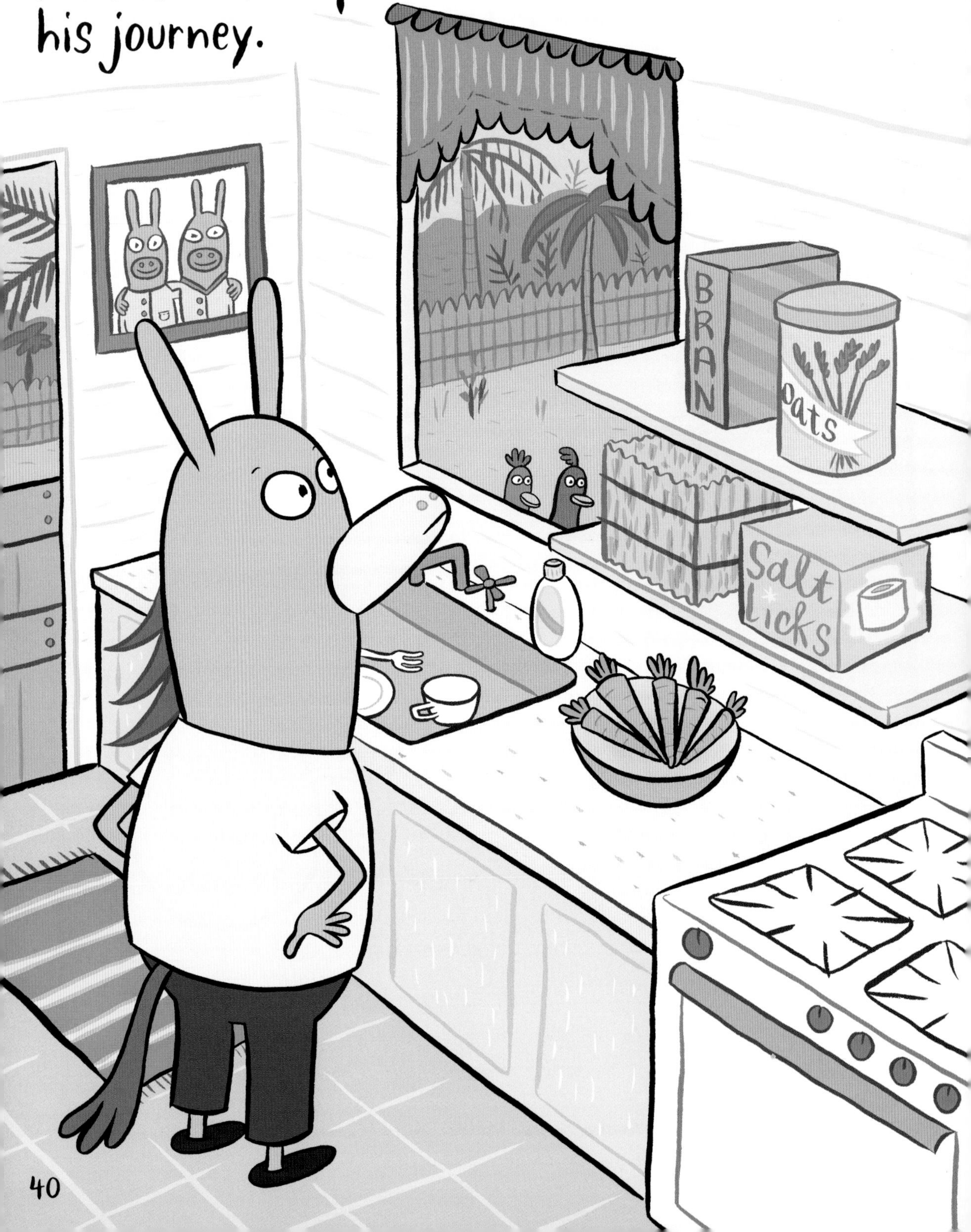
BRAN
oats
Salt Licks

He decided to pack a loaf of bread,

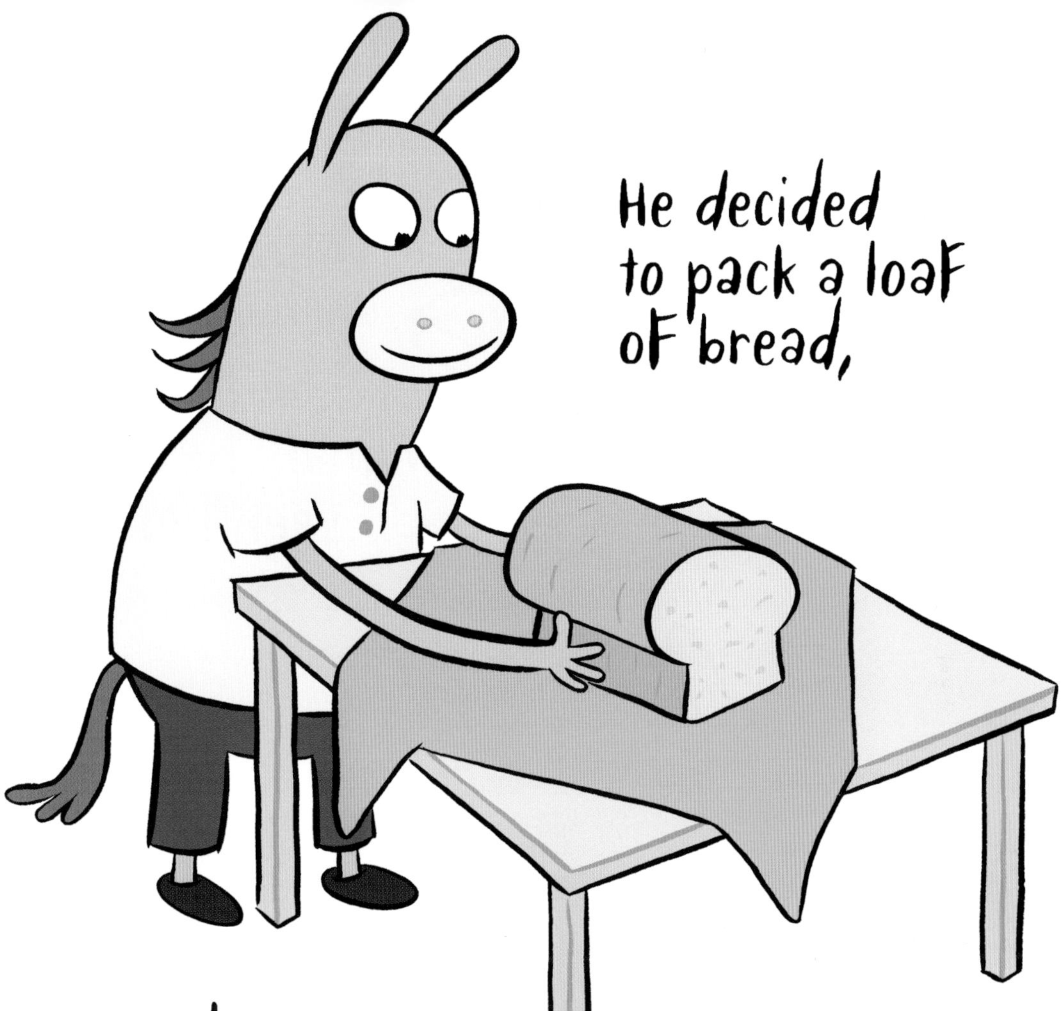

some hay for snacks,

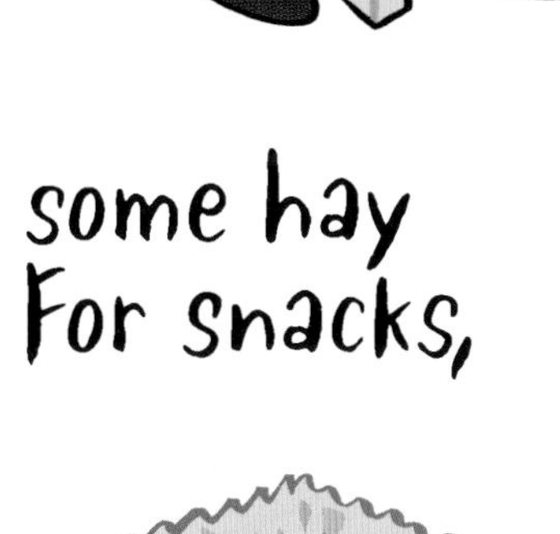

and a hammock for sleeping.

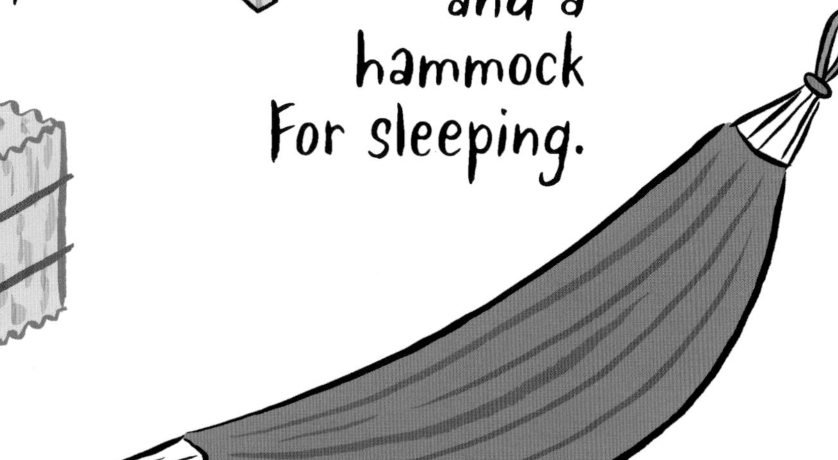

He also brought some guidebooks about animals. He didn't want to seem provincial if he ran into animals he'd not seen before.

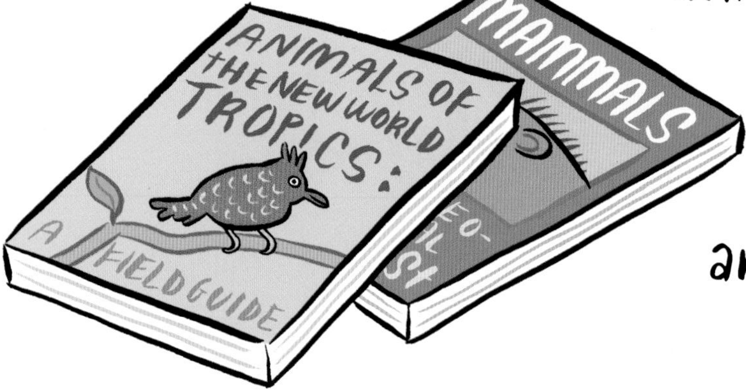
ANIMALS OF THE NEW WORLD TROPICS:
A FIELD GUIDE
MAMMALS

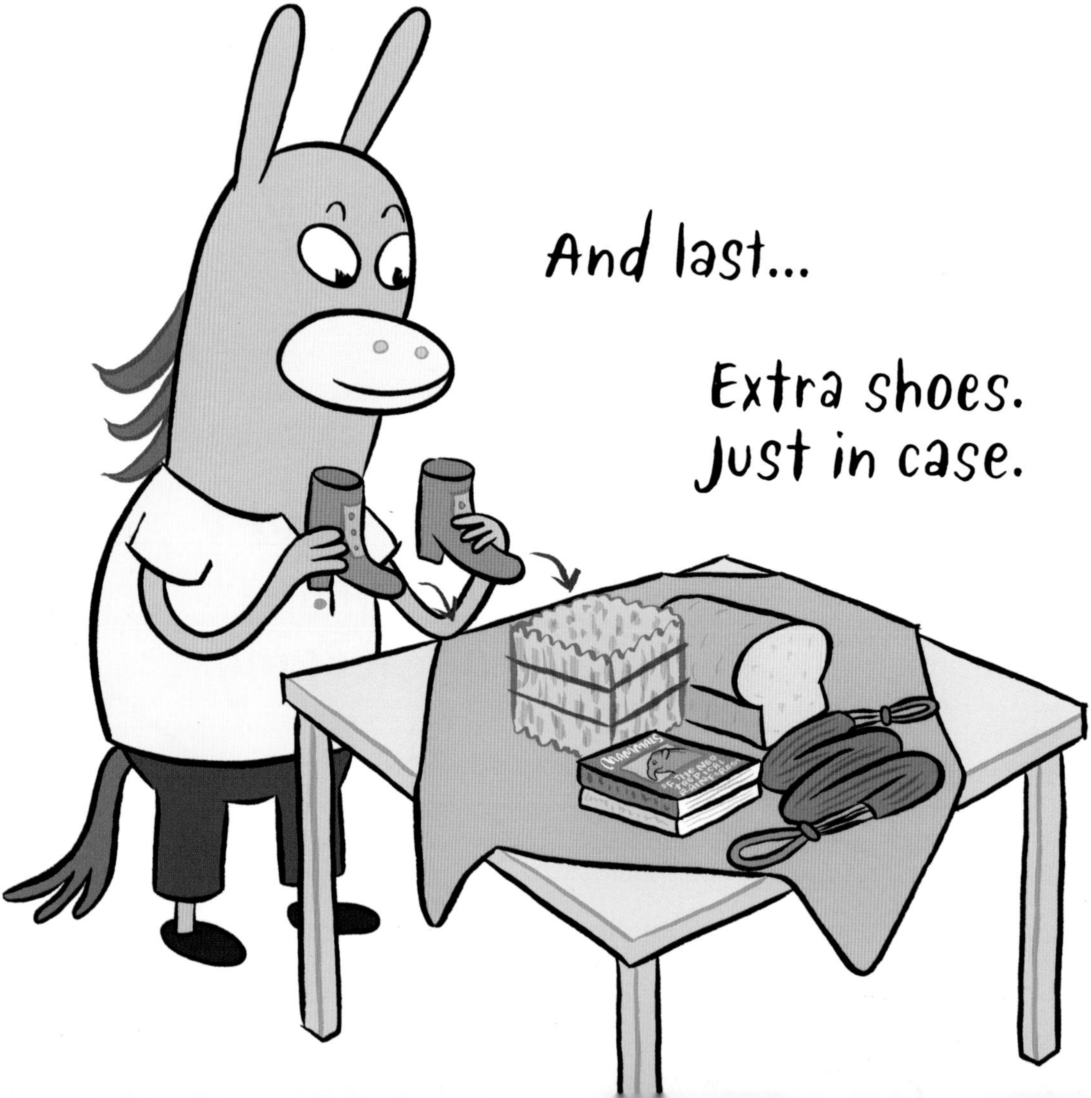

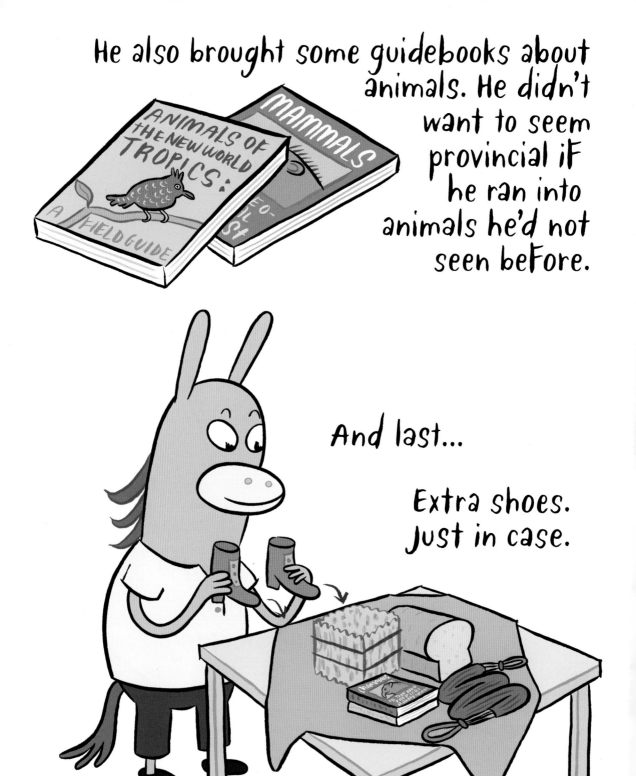

And last...

Extra shoes. Just in case.

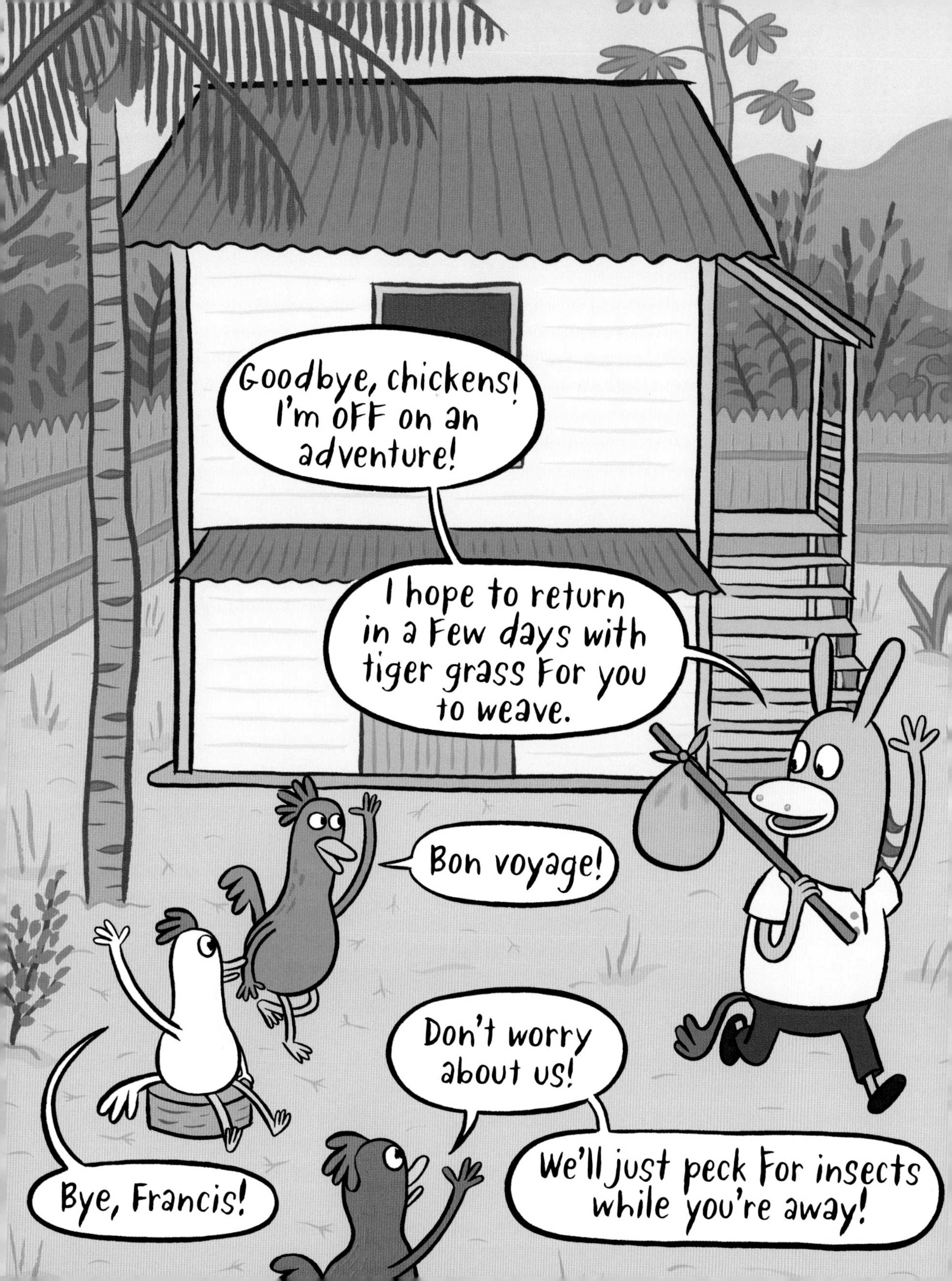
Goodbye, chickens! I'm OFF on an adventure!
I hope to return in a few days with tiger grass for you to weave.
Bon voyage!
Don't worry about us!
We'll just peck for insects while you're away!
Bye, Francis!

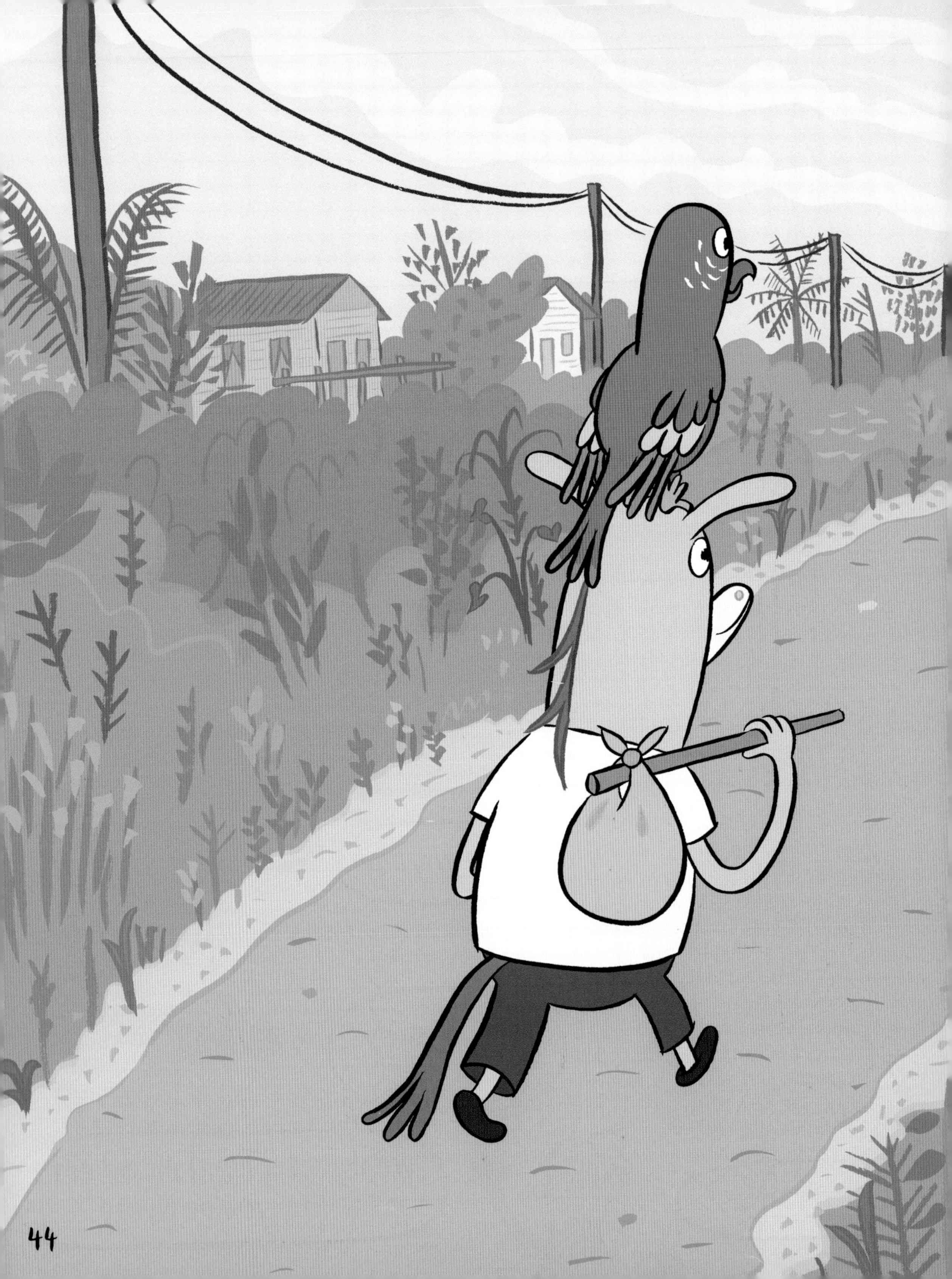

chapter three

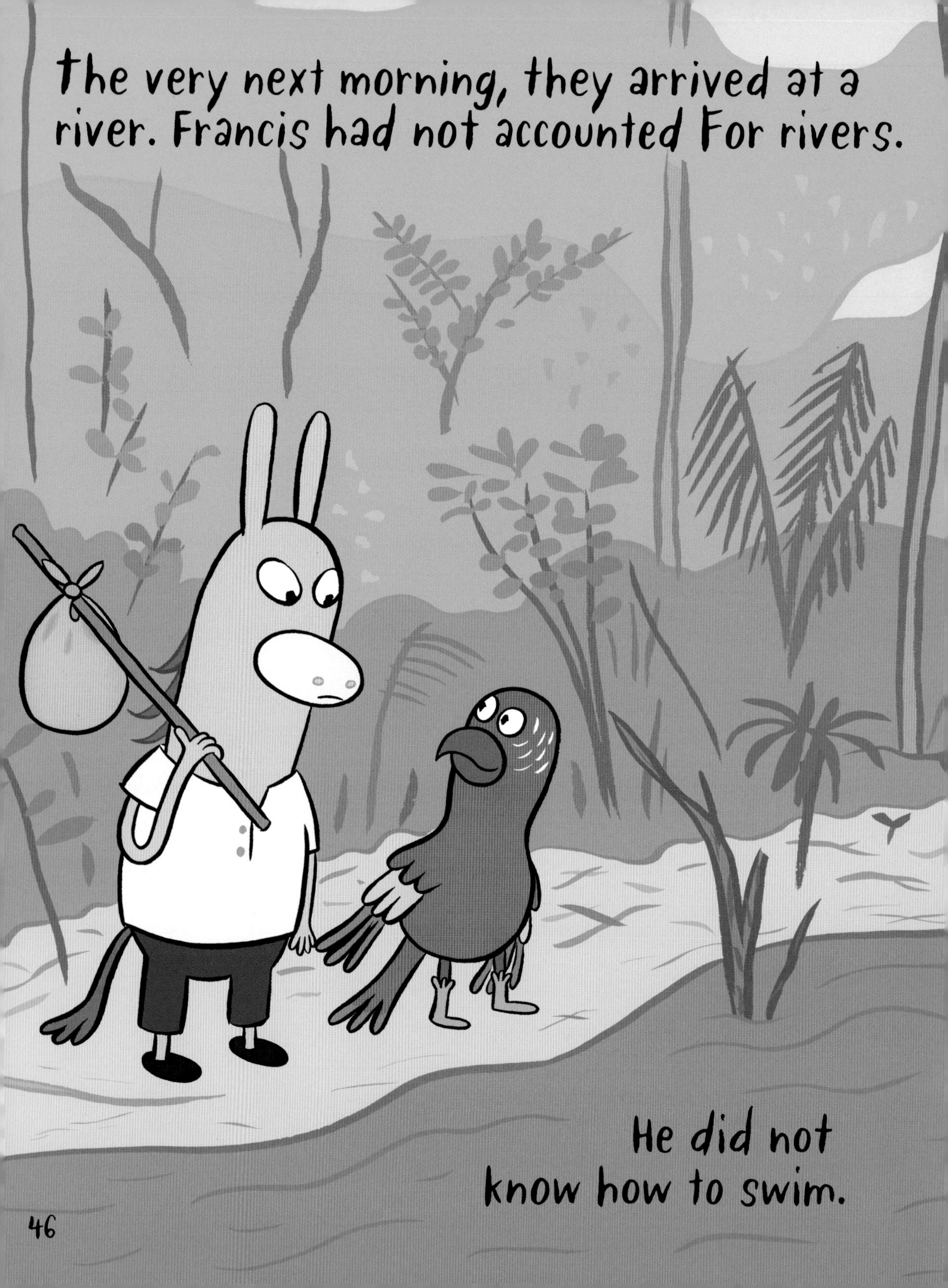
The very next morning, they arrived at a river. Francis had not accounted for rivers.
He did not know how to swim.

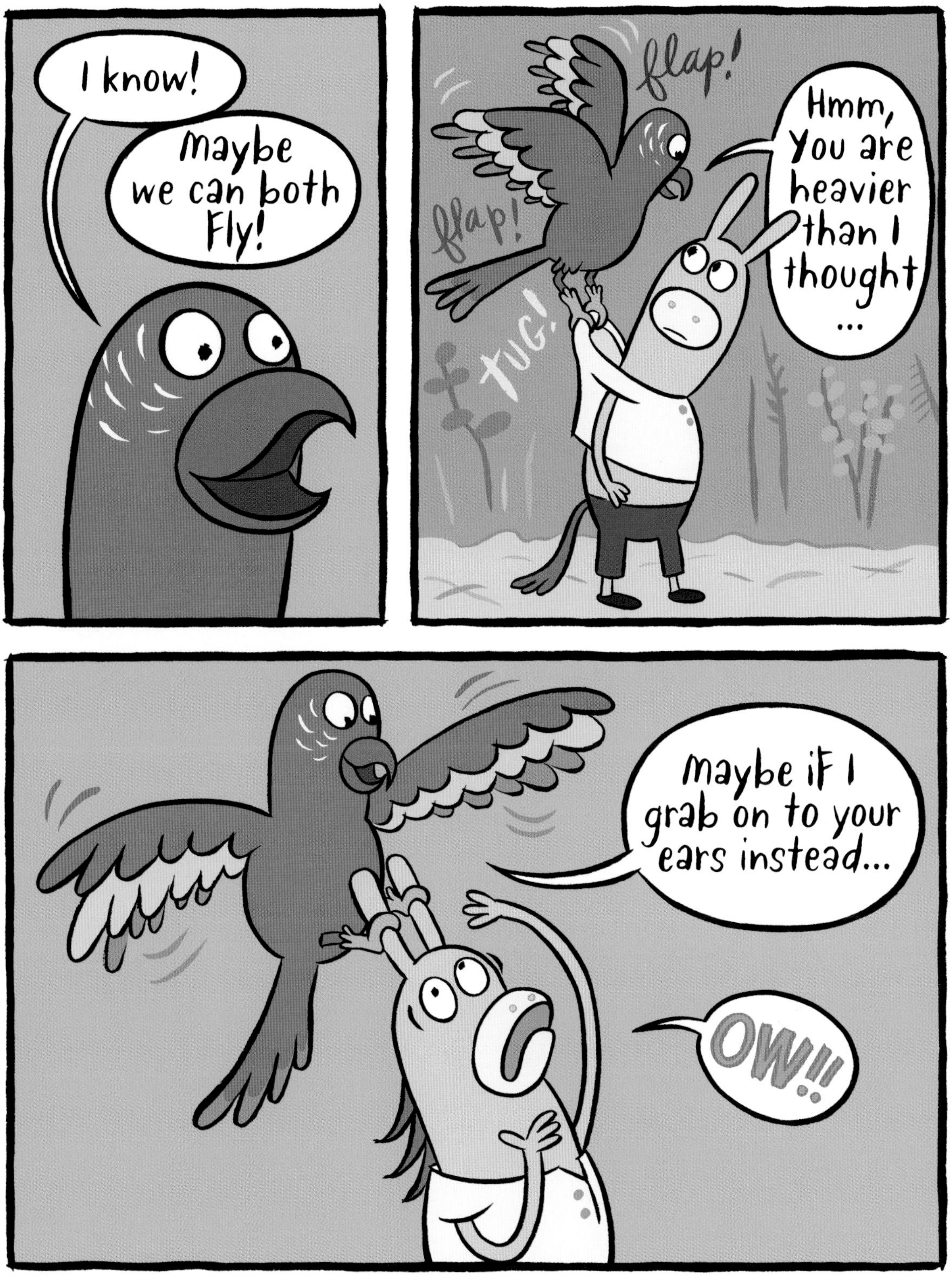
I know!
Maybe we can both Fly!
flap!
flap!
TUG!
Hmm, You are heavier than I thought ...
Maybe if I grab on to your ears instead...
OW!!

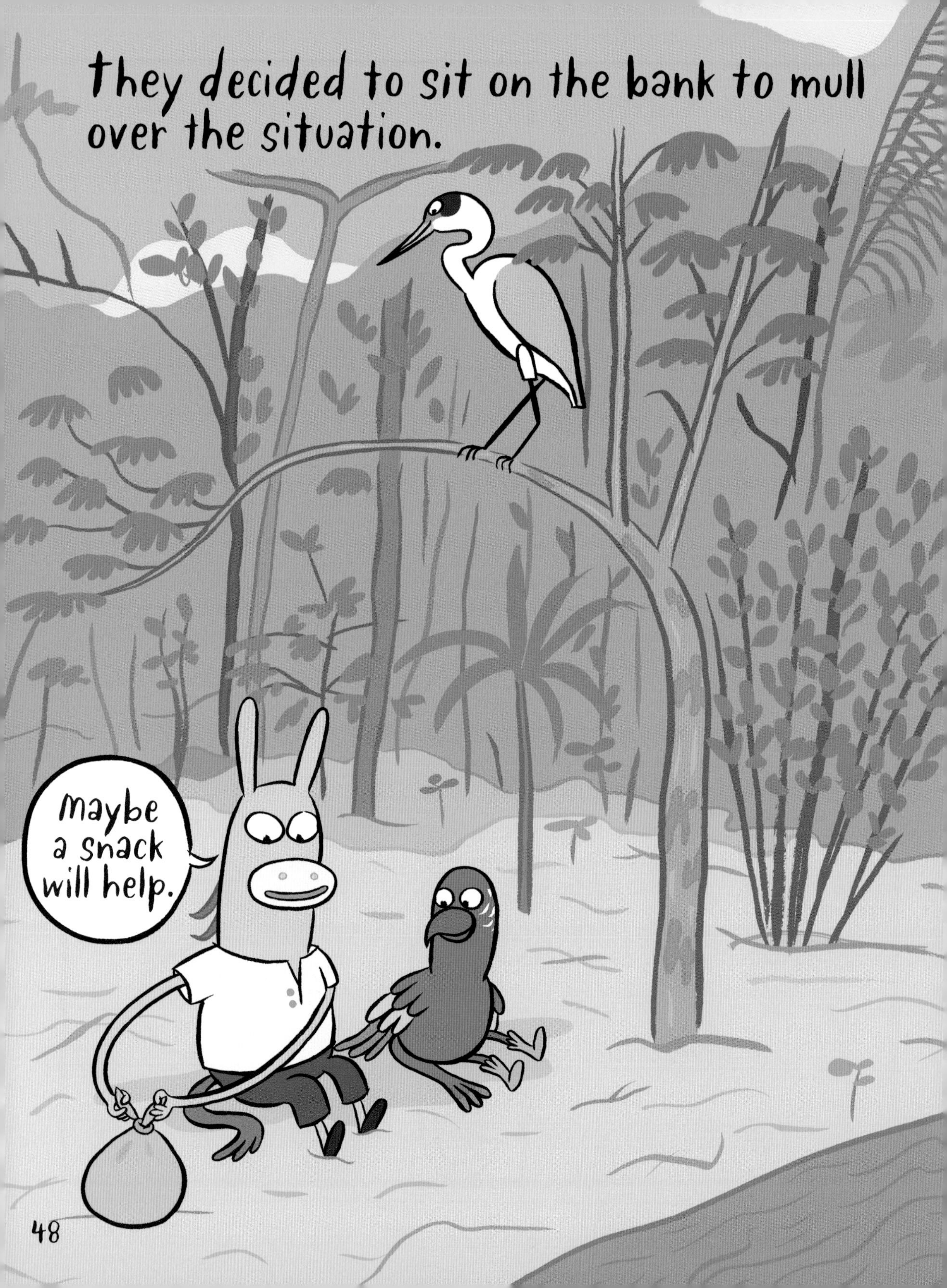
they decided to sit on the bank to mull over the situation.
maybe a snack will help.

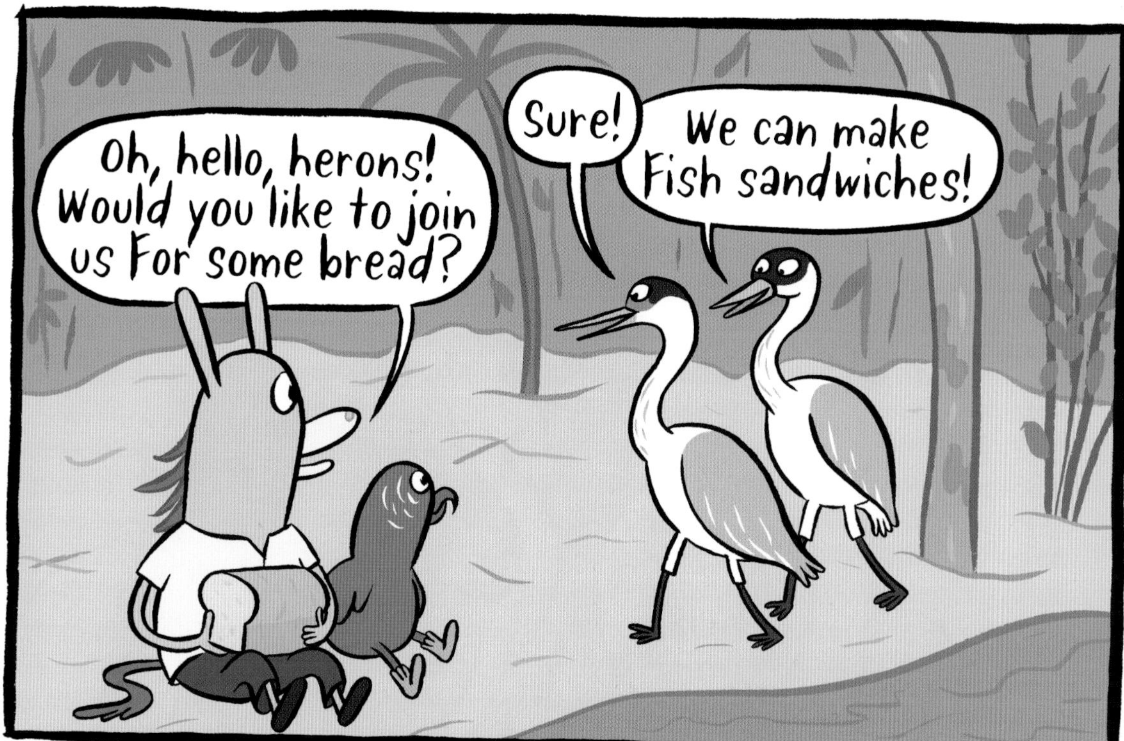
Oh, hello, herons! Would you like to join us For some bread?
Sure!
We can make Fish sandwiches!

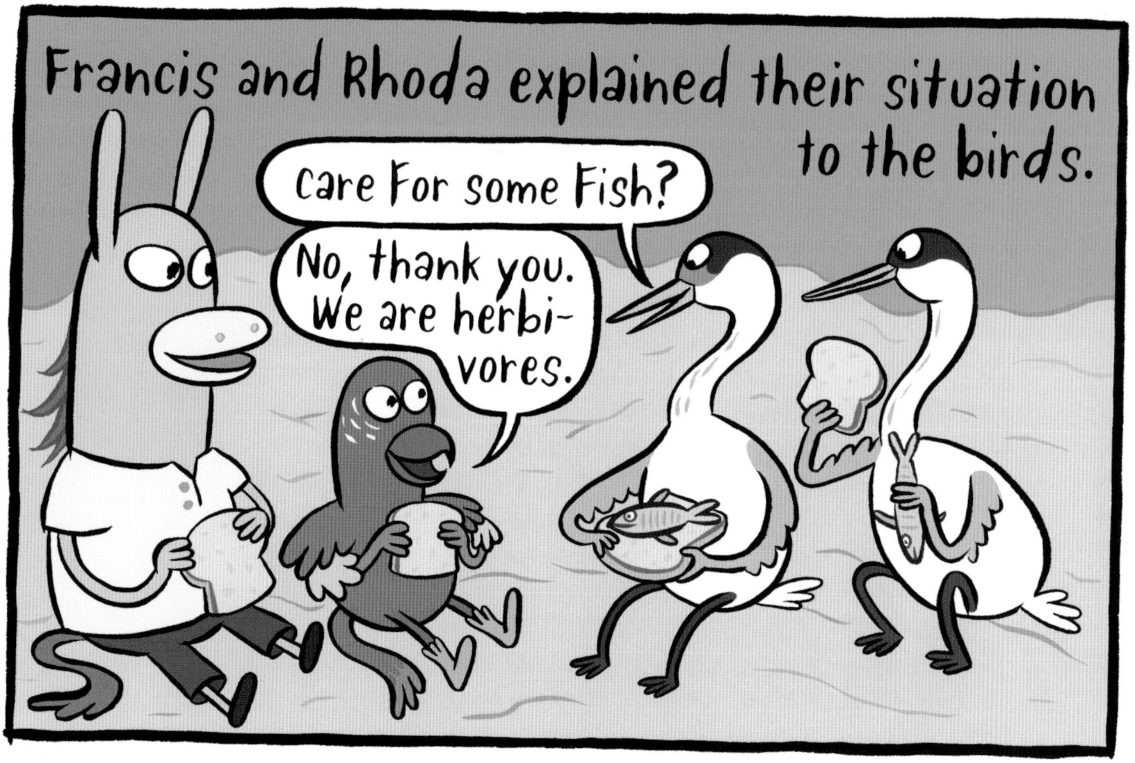
Francis and Rhoda explained their situation to the birds.
Care For some Fish?
No, thank you. We are herbi-vores.

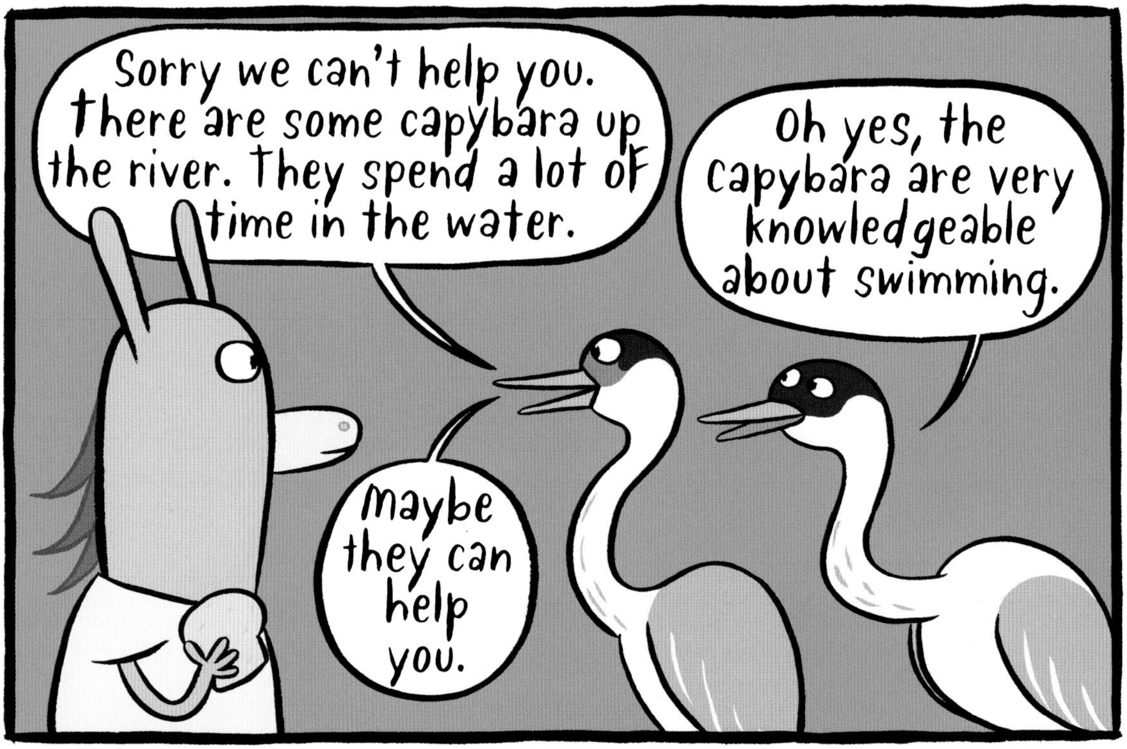
Sorry we can't help you. There are some capybara up the river. They spend a lot of time in the water.
Maybe they can help you.
Oh yes, the capybara are very knowledgeable about swimming.

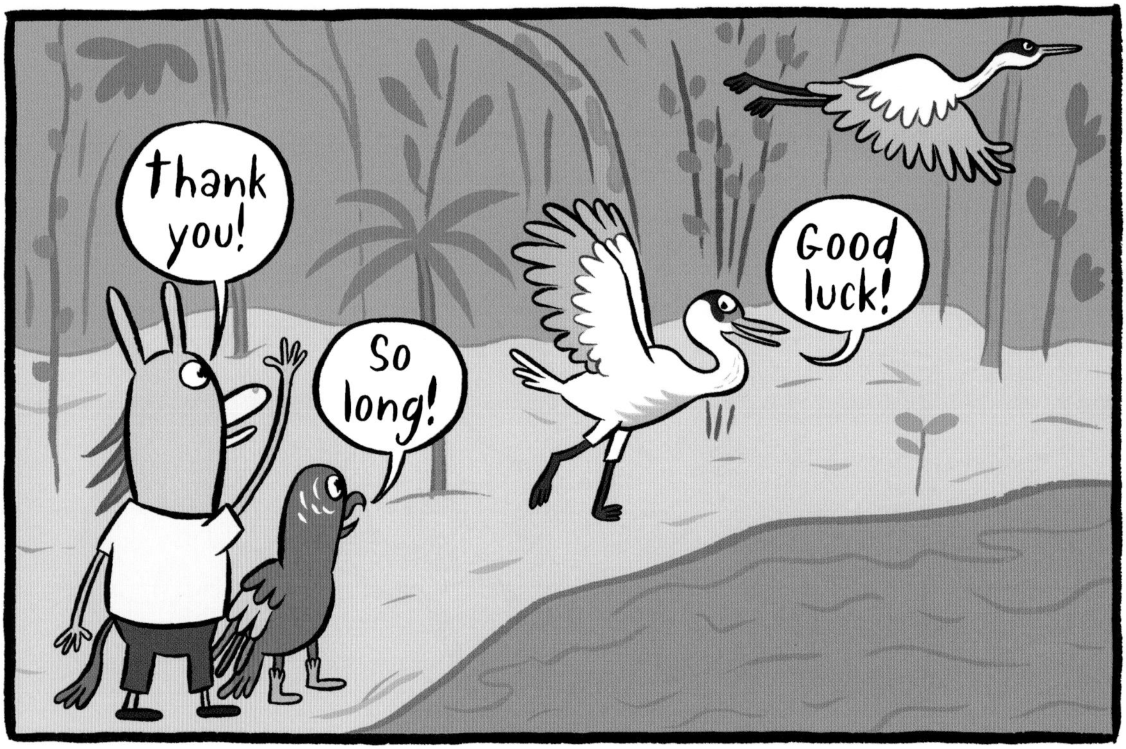
Thank you!
So long!
Good luck!

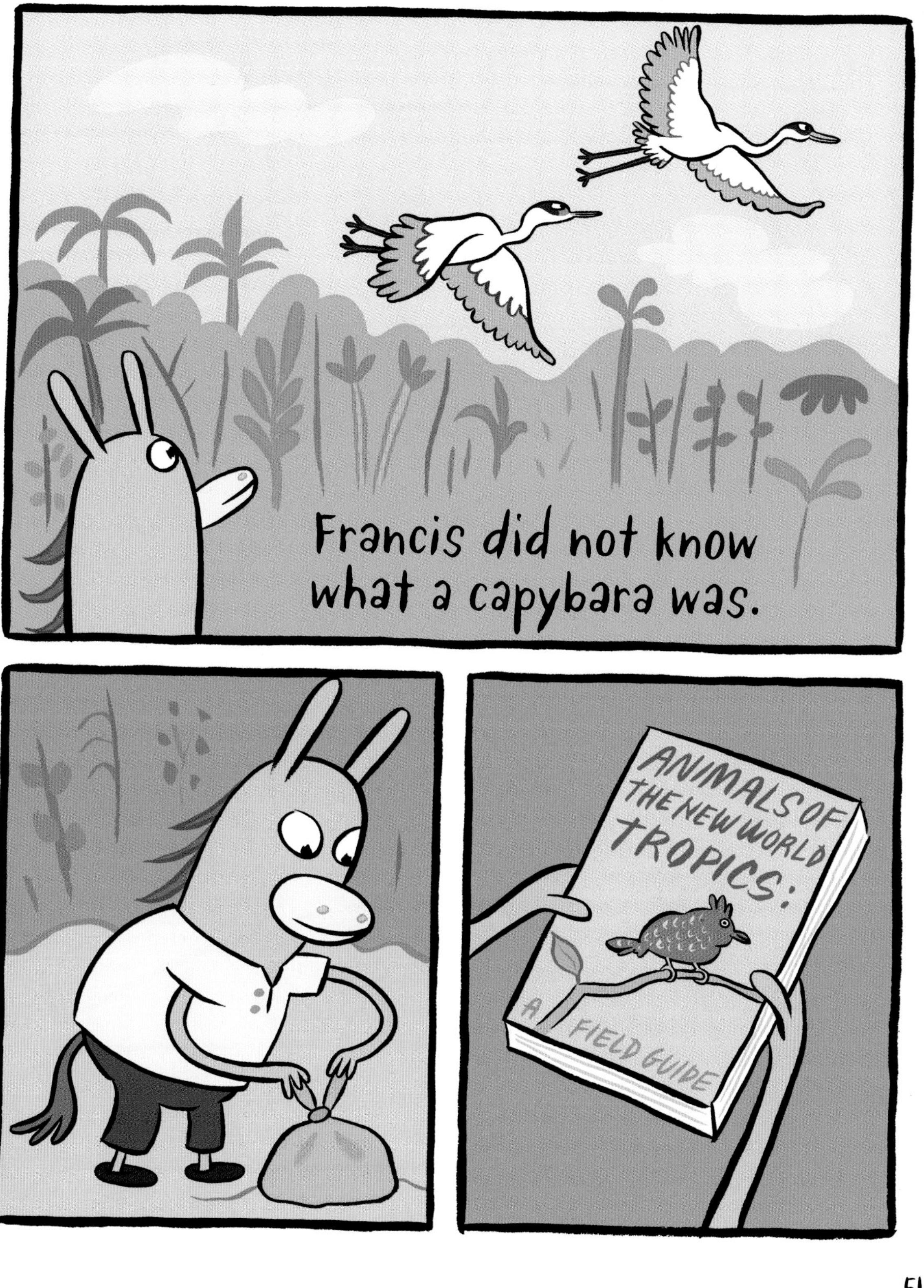
Francis did not know what a capybara was.
ANIMALS OF THE NEW WORLD TROPICS:
A FIELD GUIDE

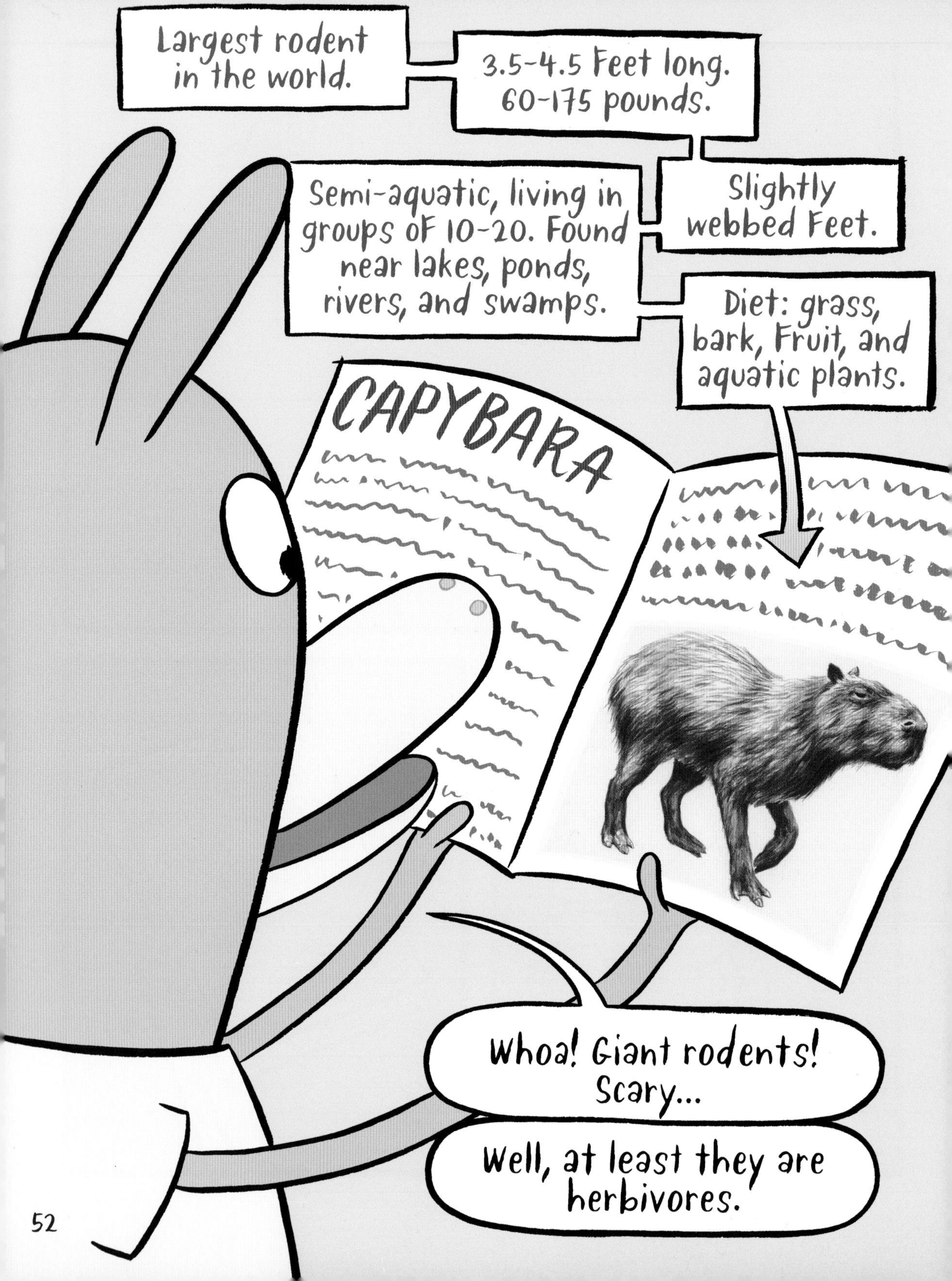
Largest rodent in the world.
3.5-4.5 Feet long. 60-175 pounds.
Semi-aquatic, living in groups of 10-20. Found near lakes, ponds, rivers, and swamps.
Slightly webbed Feet.
Diet: grass, bark, Fruit, and aquatic plants.
CAPYBARA
Whoa! Giant rodents! Scary...
Well, at least they are herbivores.

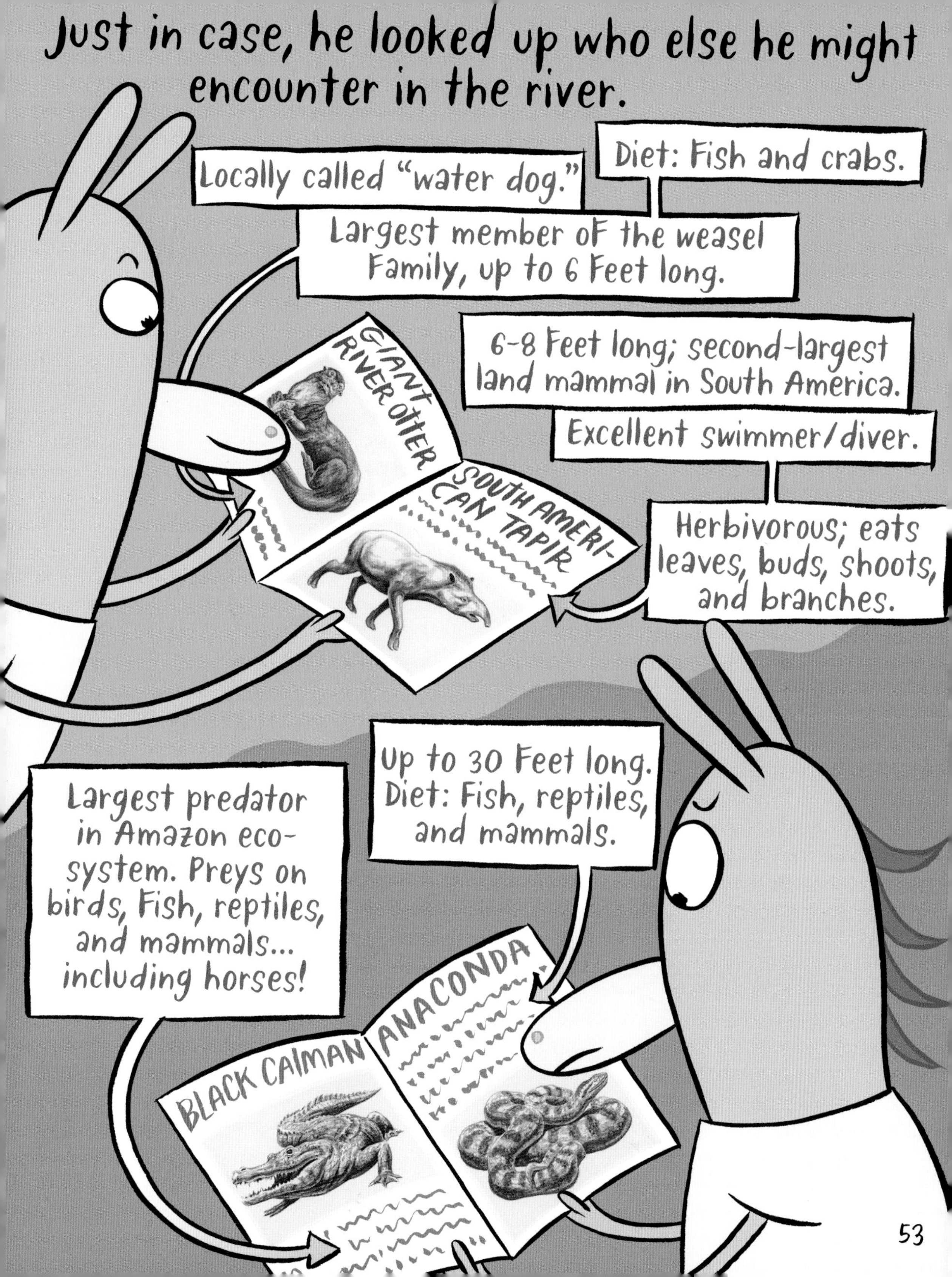
Just in case, he looked up who else he might encounter in the river.
Locally called "water dog."
Diet: Fish and crabs.
Largest member of the weasel family, up to 6 feet long.
GIANT RIVER OTTER
6-8 feet long; second-largest land mammal in South America.
Excellent swimmer/diver.
Herbivorous; eats leaves, buds, shoots, and branches.
SOUTH AMERICAN TAPIR
Largest predator in Amazon ecosystem. Preys on birds, fish, reptiles, and mammals... including horses!
Up to 30 feet long. Diet: Fish, reptiles, and mammals.
BLACK CAIMAN
ANACONDA

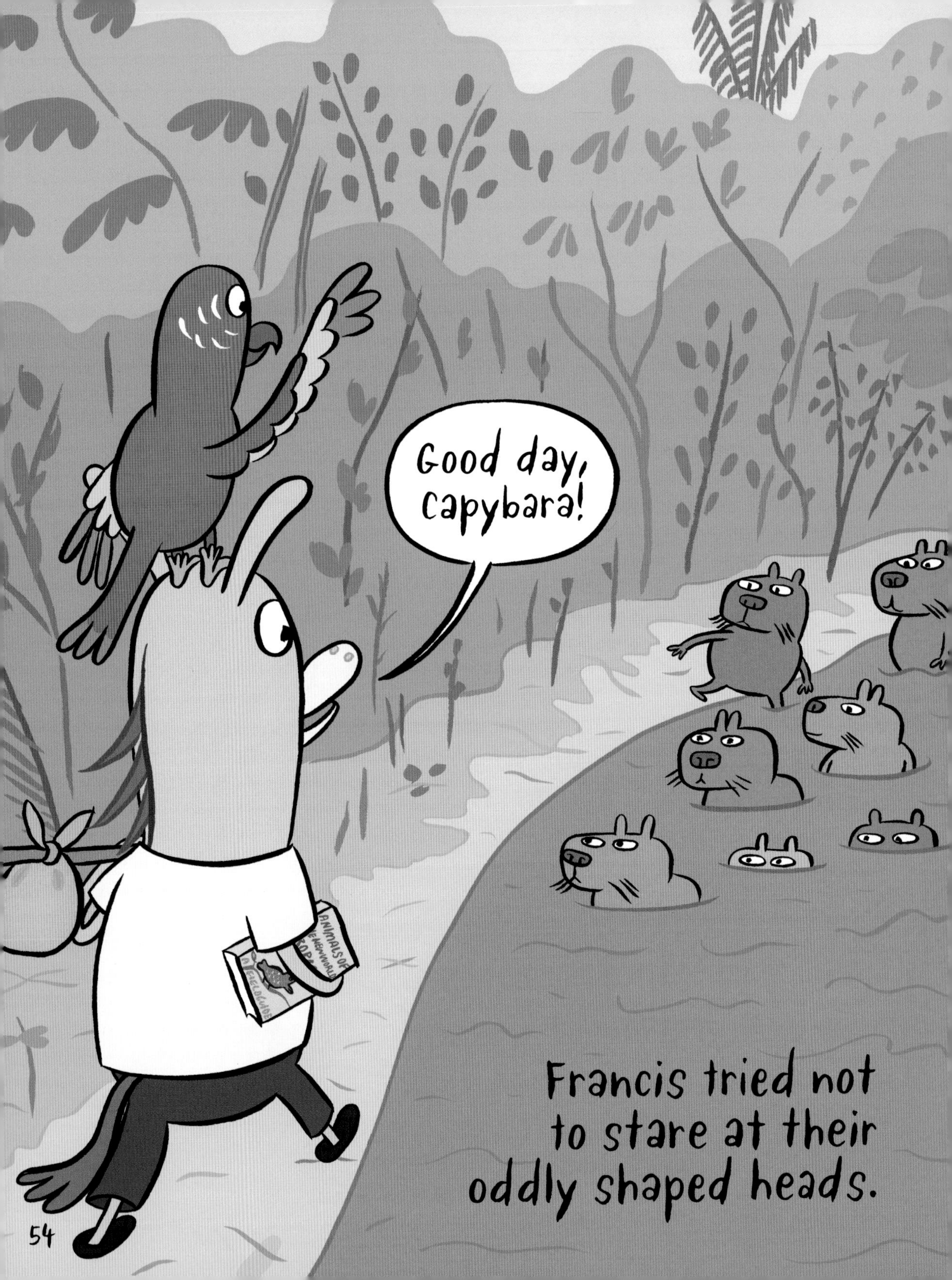
Good day, capybara!
Francis tried not to stare at their oddly shaped heads.

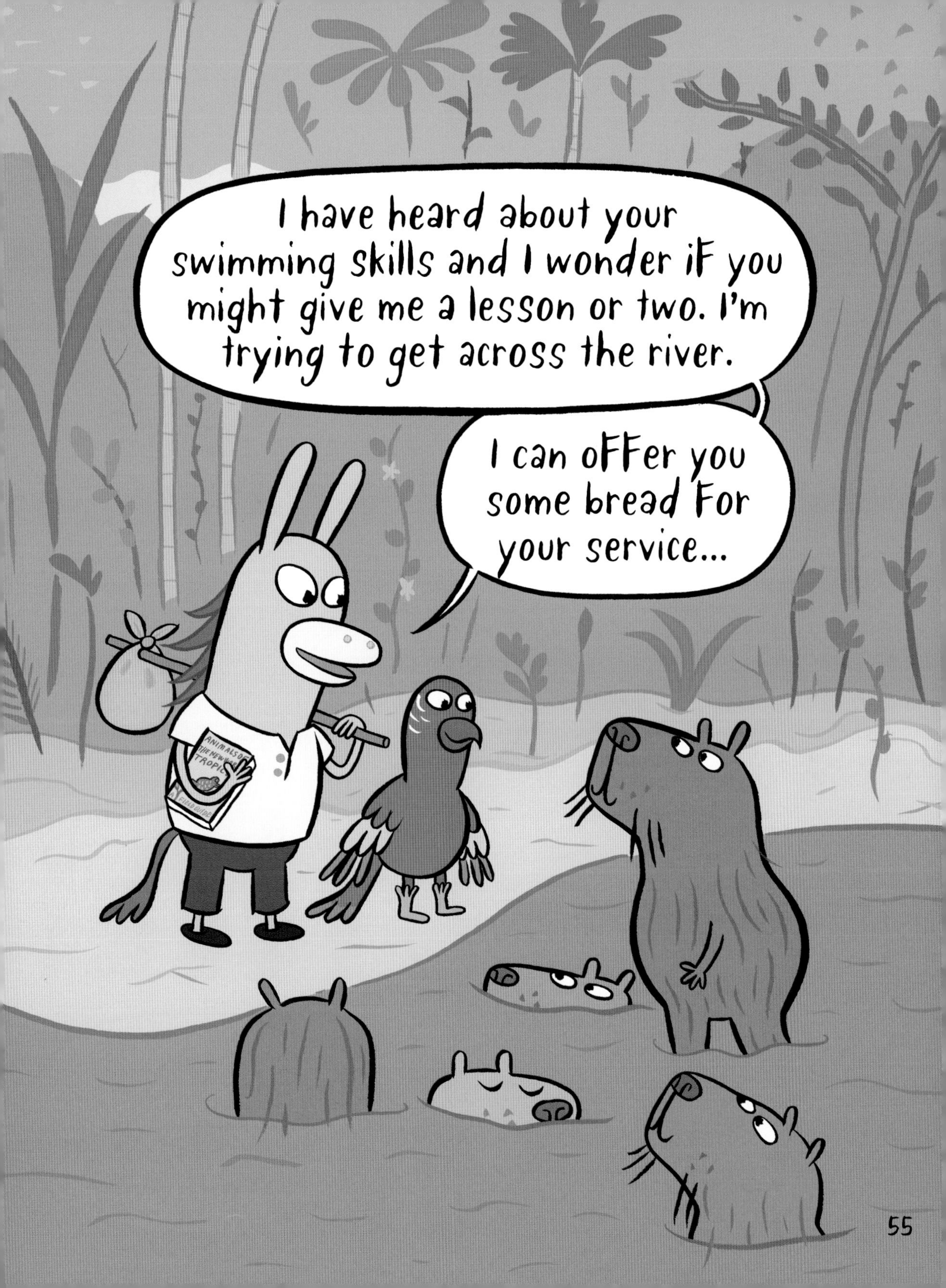
I have heard about your swimming skills and I wonder if you might give me a lesson or two. I'm trying to get across the river.
I can offer you some bread for your service...

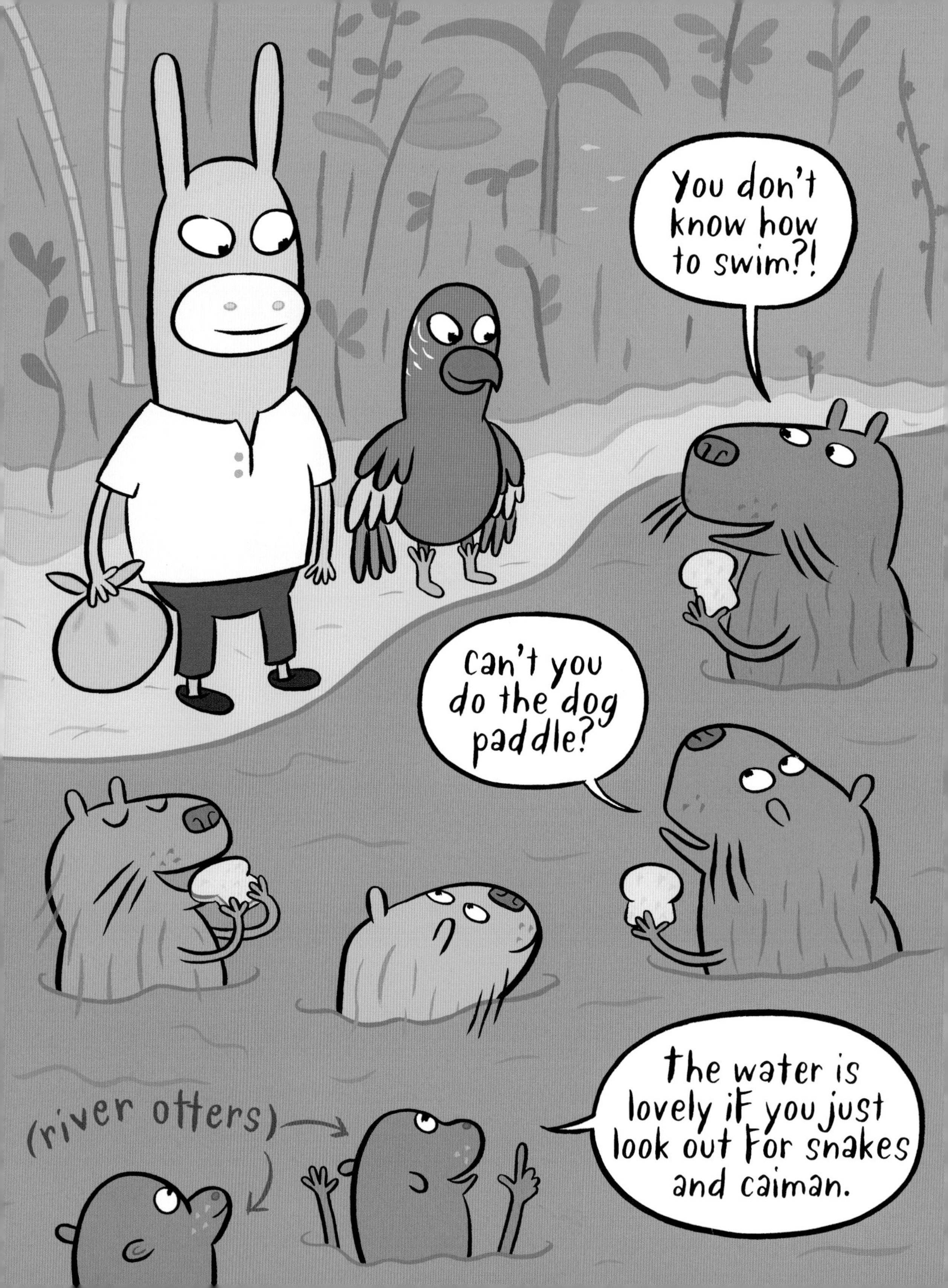
You don't know how to swim?!
Can't you do the dog paddle?
The water is lovely if you just look out for snakes and caiman.
(river otters)

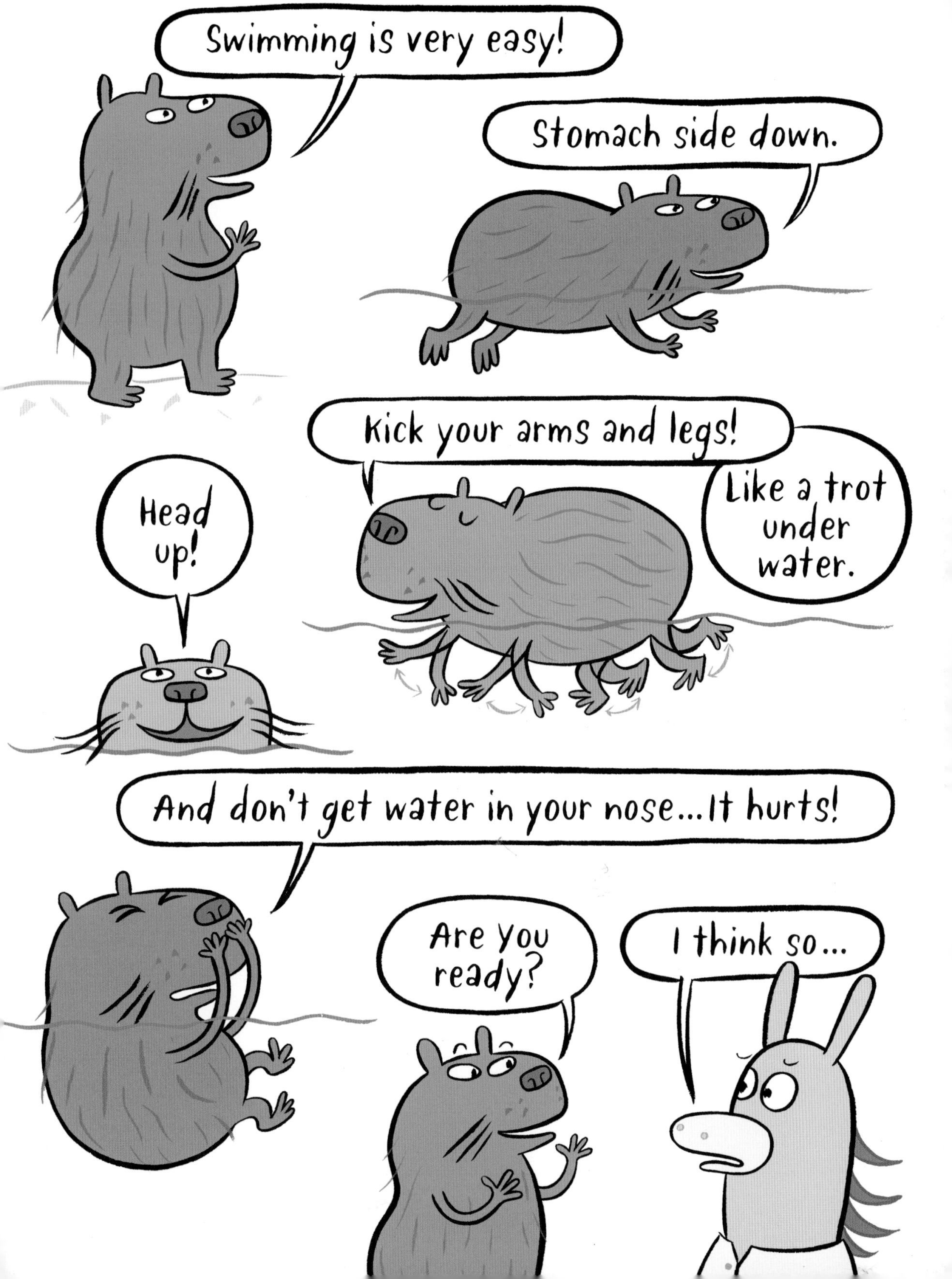
Swimming is very easy!
Stomach side down.
Kick your arms and legs!
Like a trot under water.
Head up!
And don't get water in your nose...It hurts!
Are you ready?
I think so...

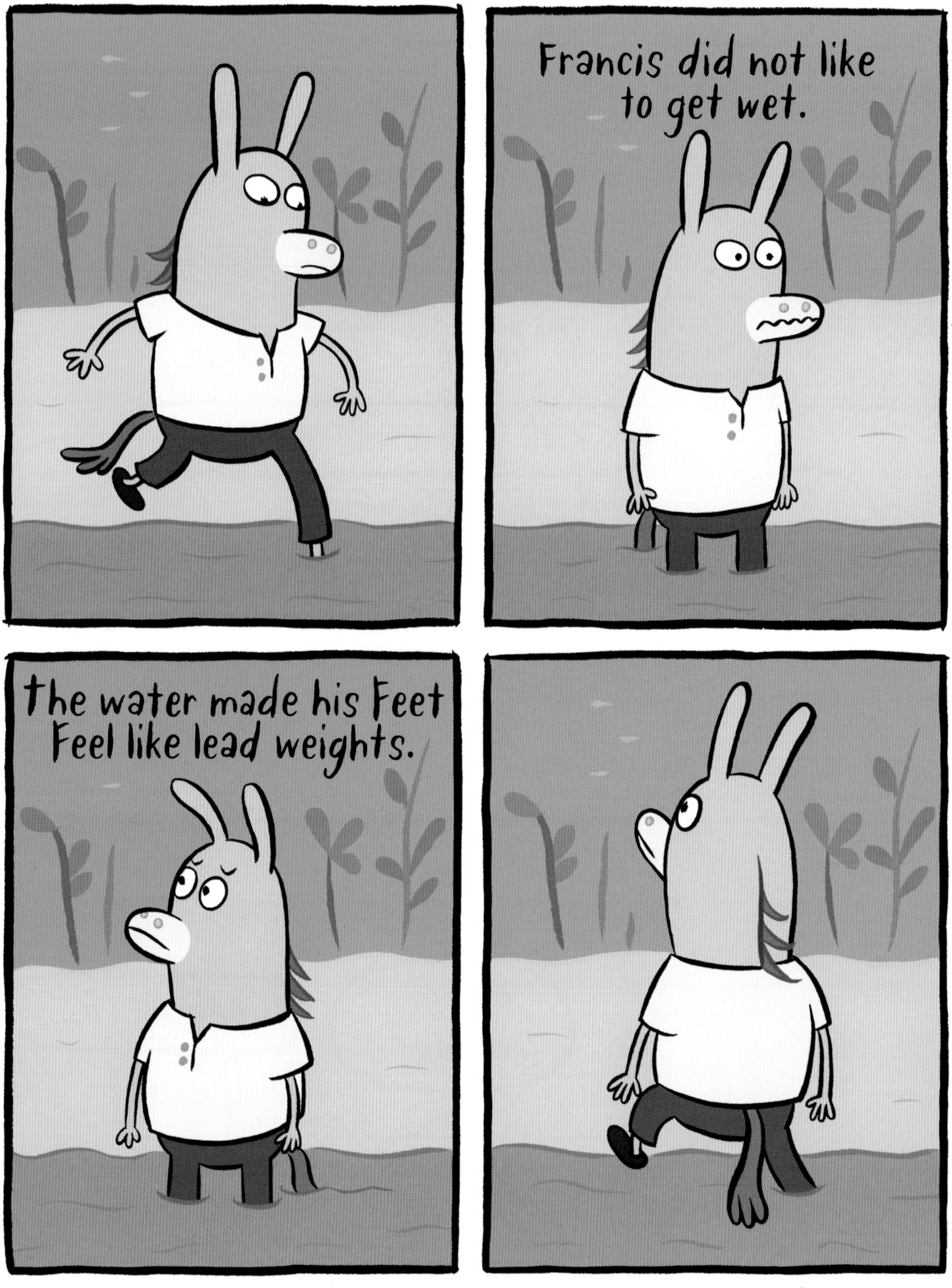
Francis did not like to get wet.
the water made his feet feel like lead weights.

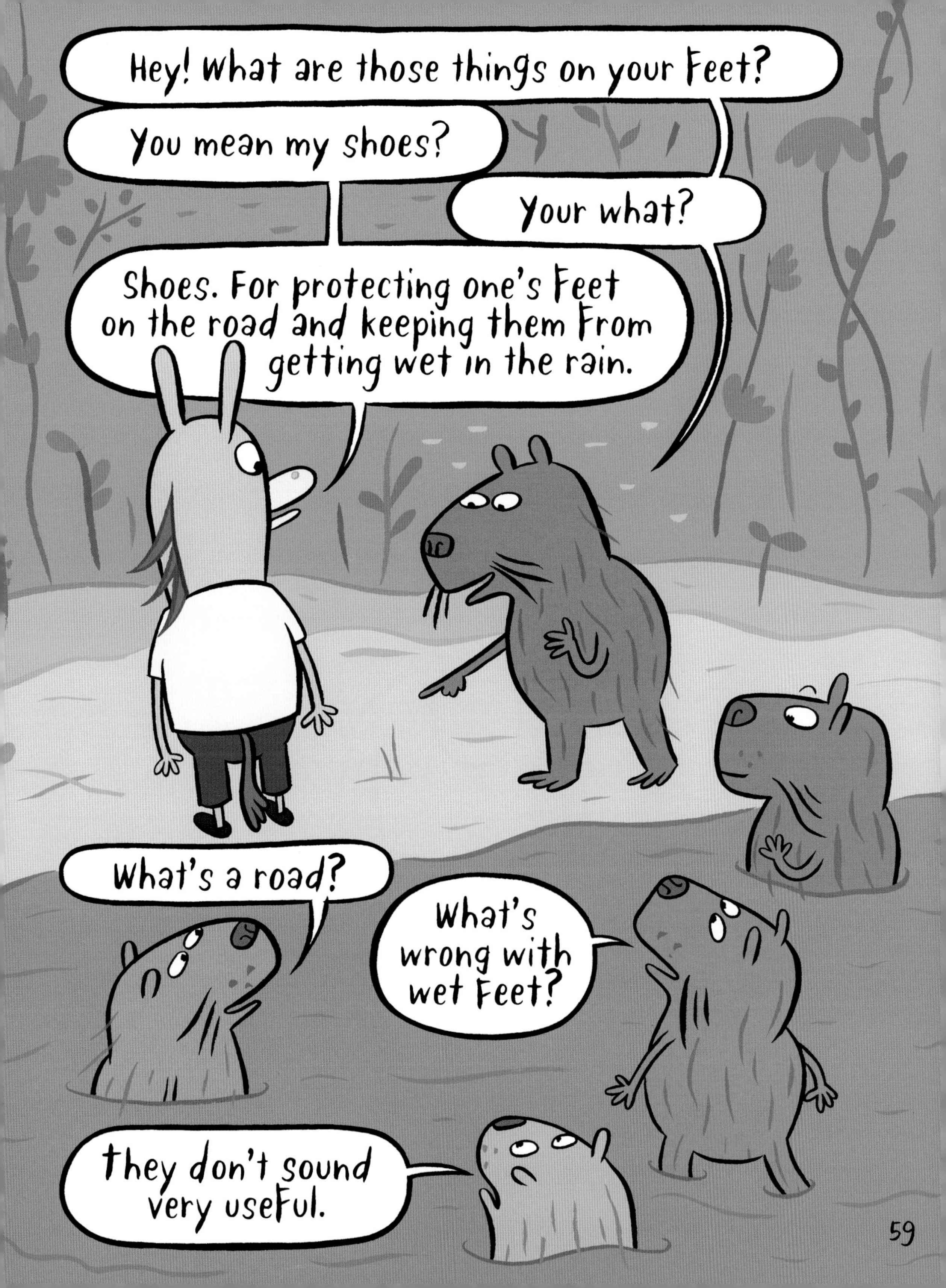
Hey! What are those things on your Feet?
You mean my shoes?
Your what?
Shoes. For protecting one's Feet on the road and keeping them From getting wet in the rain.
What's a road?
What's wrong with wet Feet?
They don't sound very useFul.

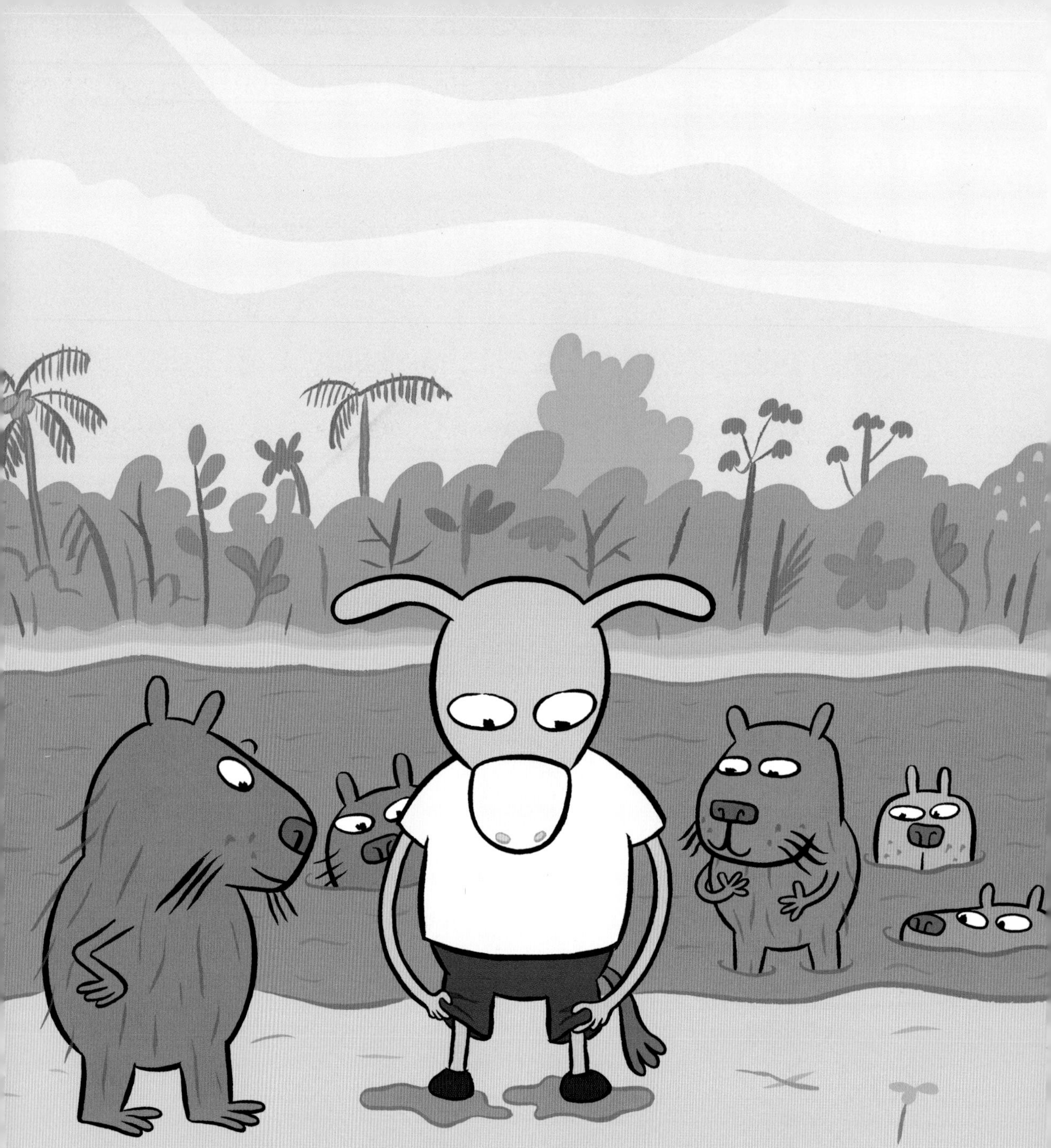

Perhaps shoes were not
good for swimming.

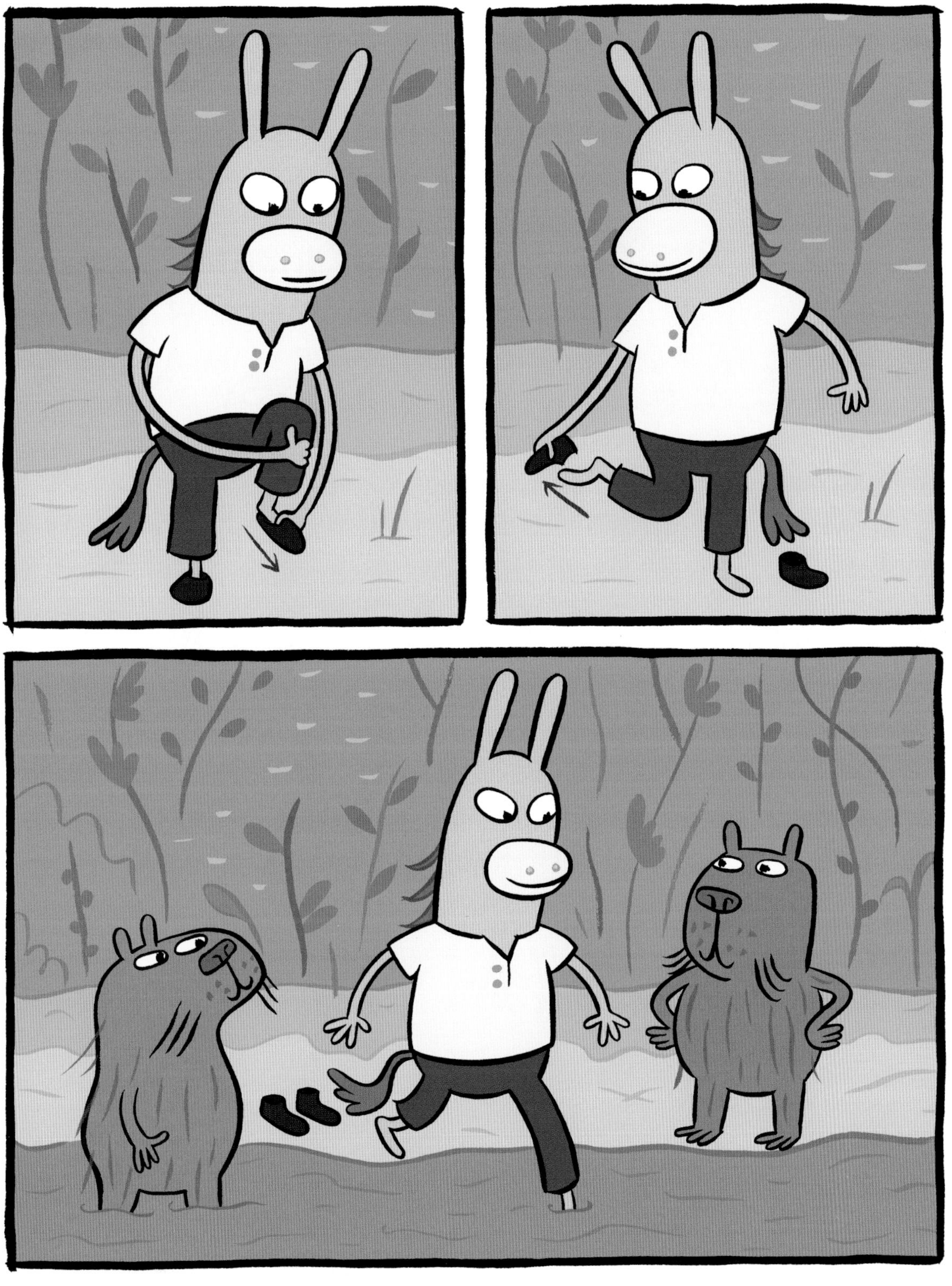

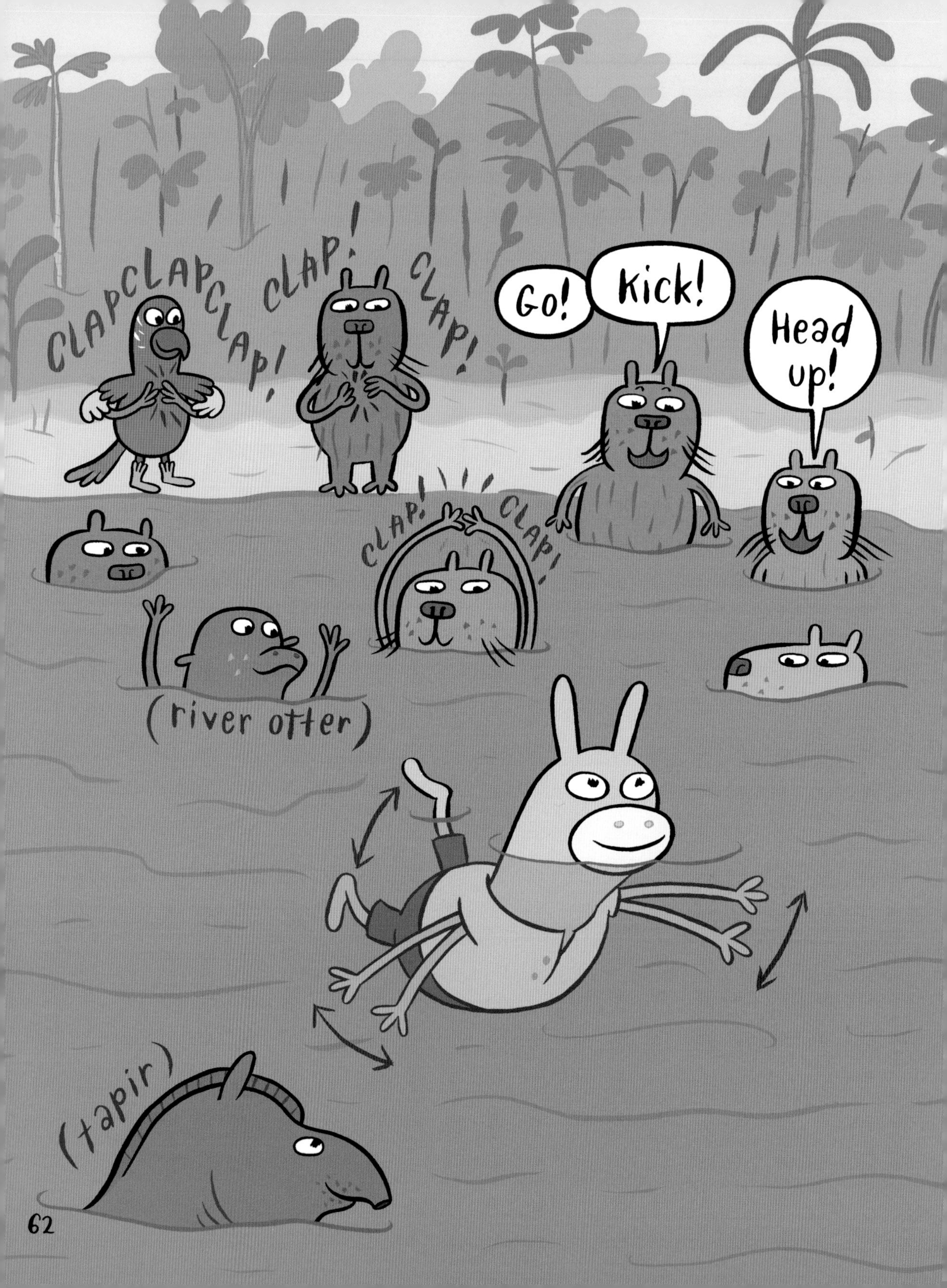
CLAPCLAPCLAP!
CLAP! CLAP!
Go!
Kick!
Head up!
CLAP! CLAP!
(river otter)
(tapir)

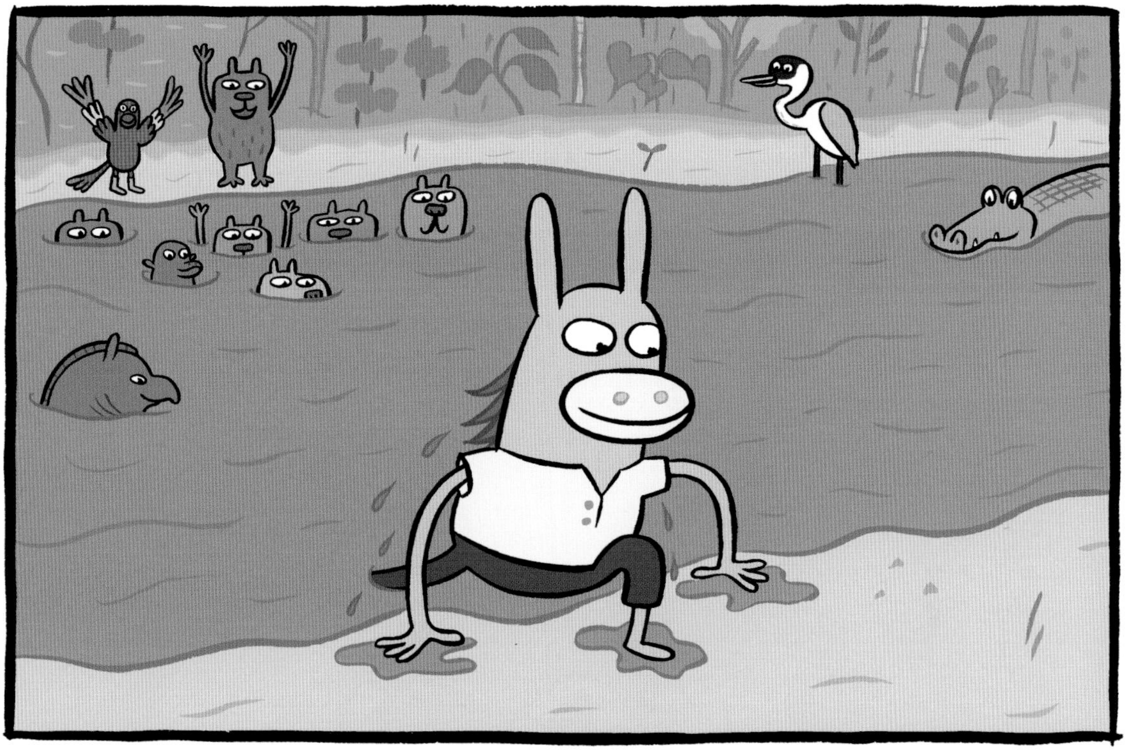
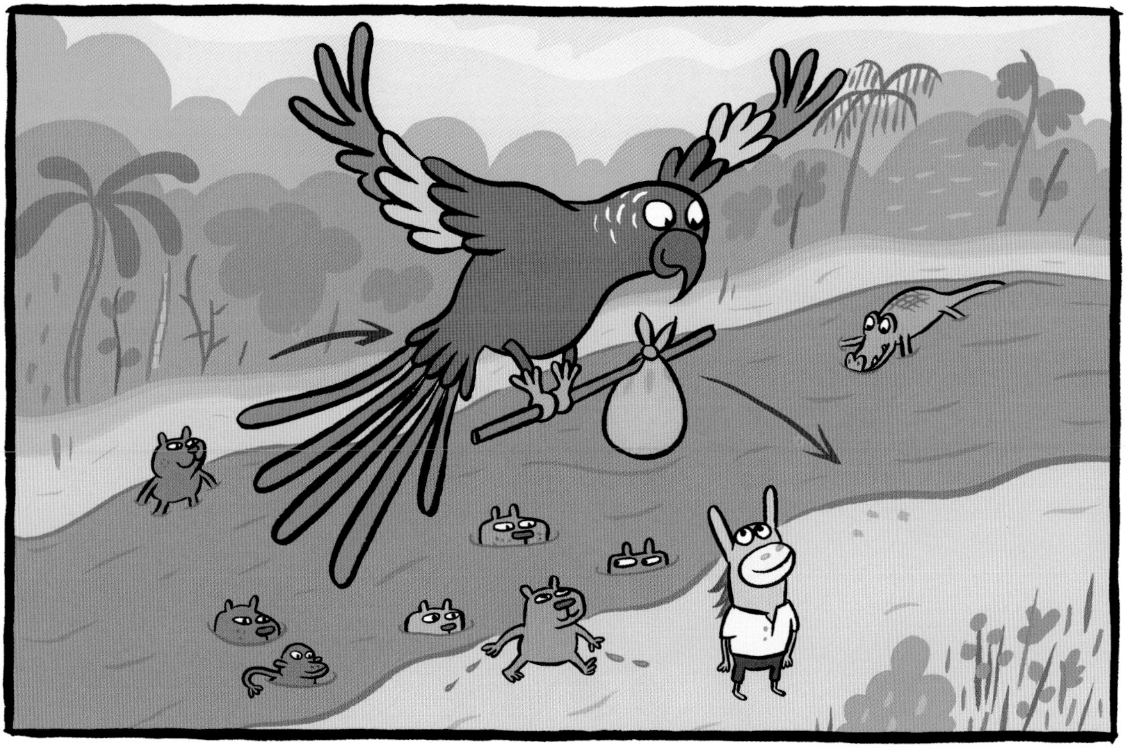

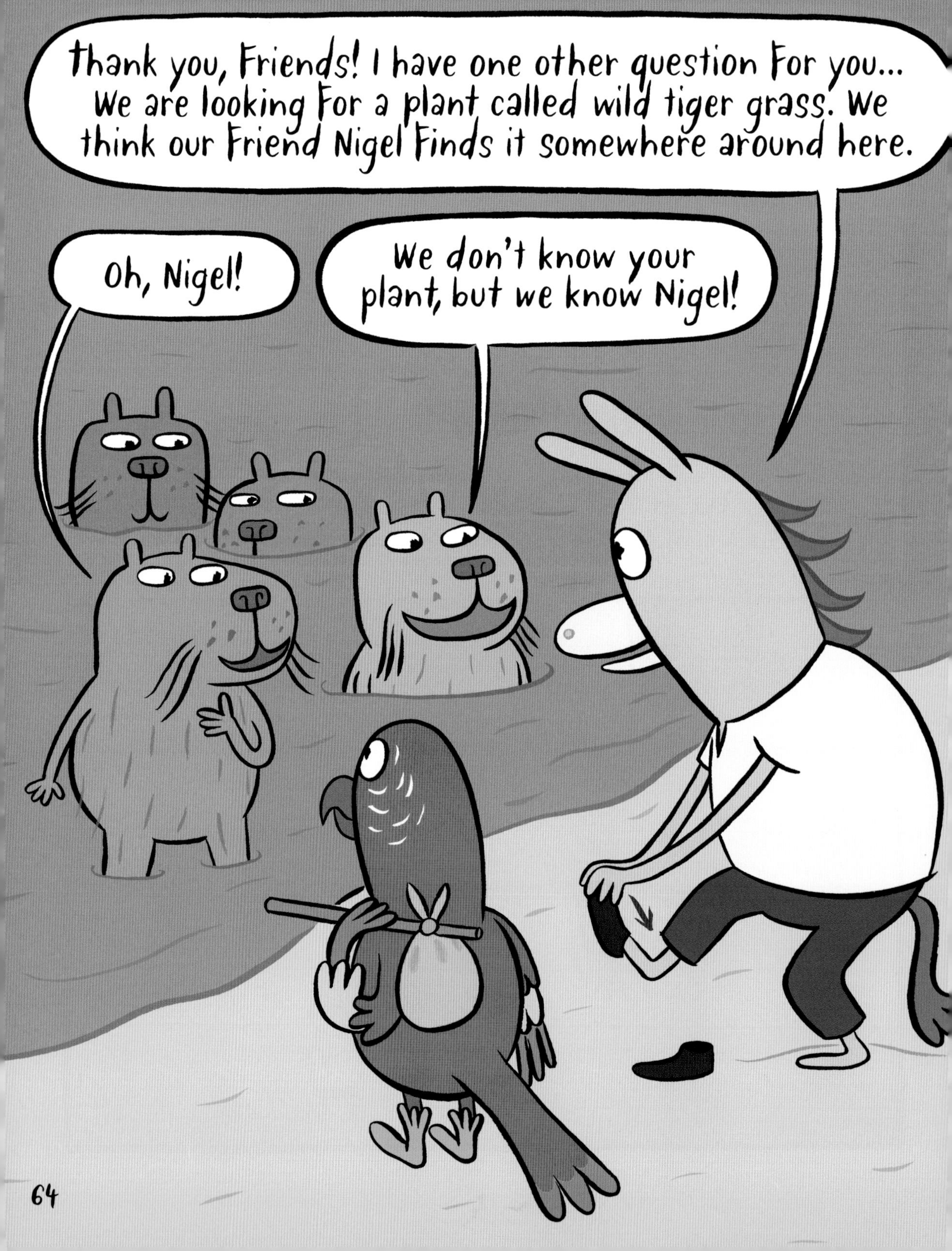
Thank you, Friends! I have one other question For you... We are looking For a plant called wild tiger grass. We think our Friend Nigel Finds it somewhere around here.
Oh, Nigel!
We don't know your plant, but we know Nigel!

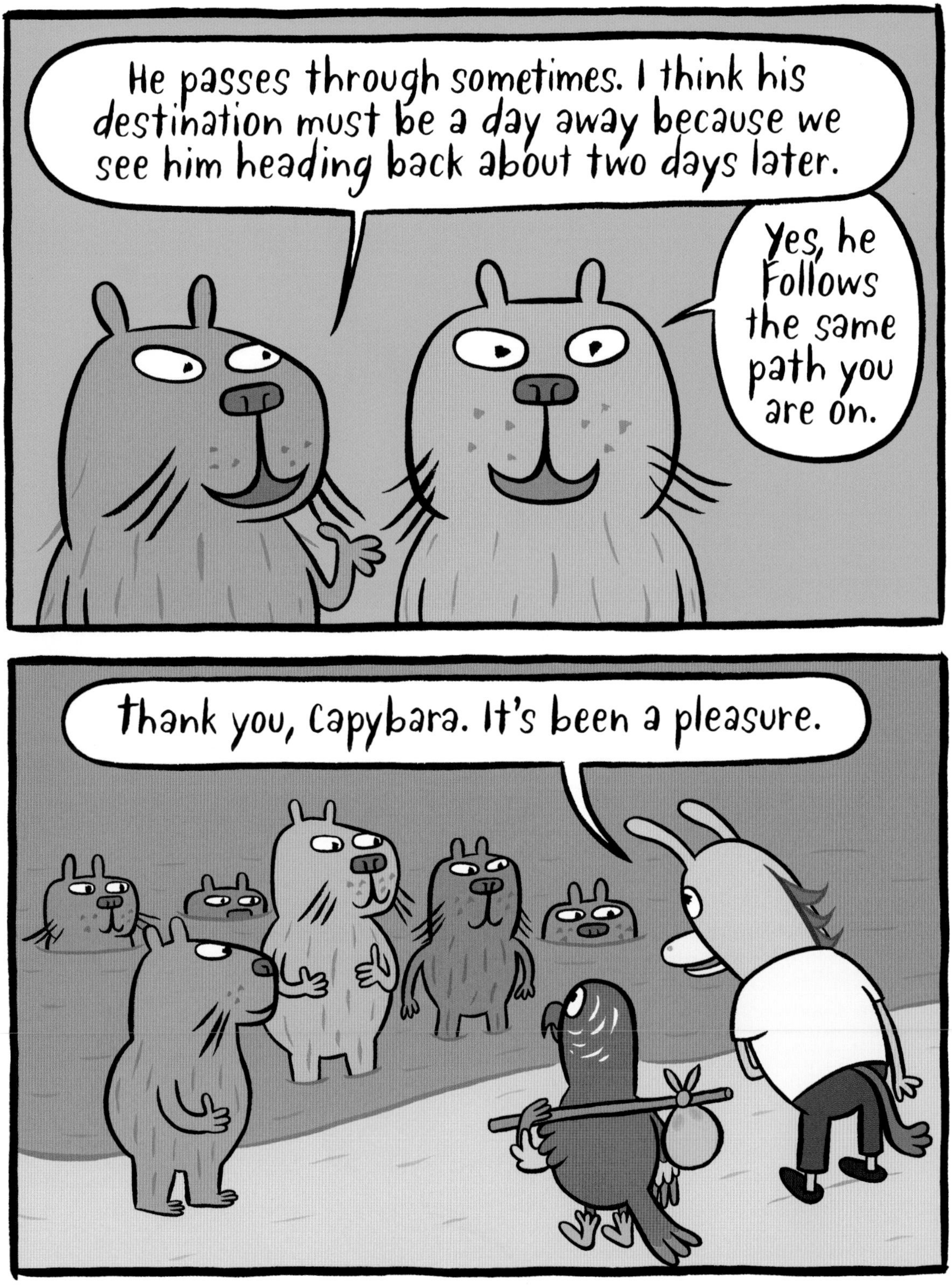
He passes through sometimes. I think his destination must be a day away because we see him heading back about two days later.
Yes, he Follows the same path you are on.
thank you, Capybara. It's been a pleasure.

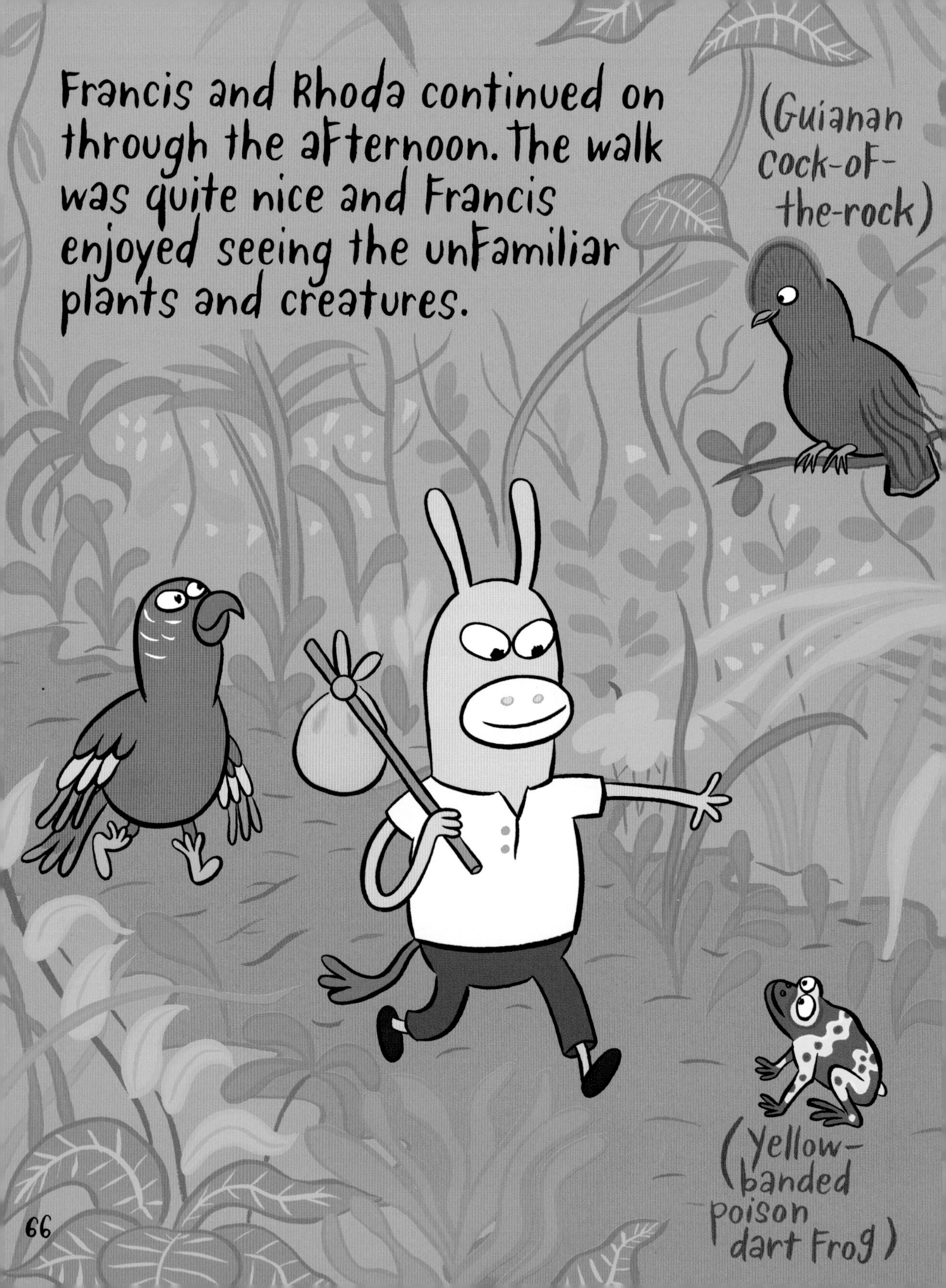
Francis and Rhoda continued on through the afternoon. The walk was quite nice and Francis enjoyed seeing the unfamiliar plants and creatures.
(Guianan cock-of-the-rock)
(Yellow-banded poison dart frog)

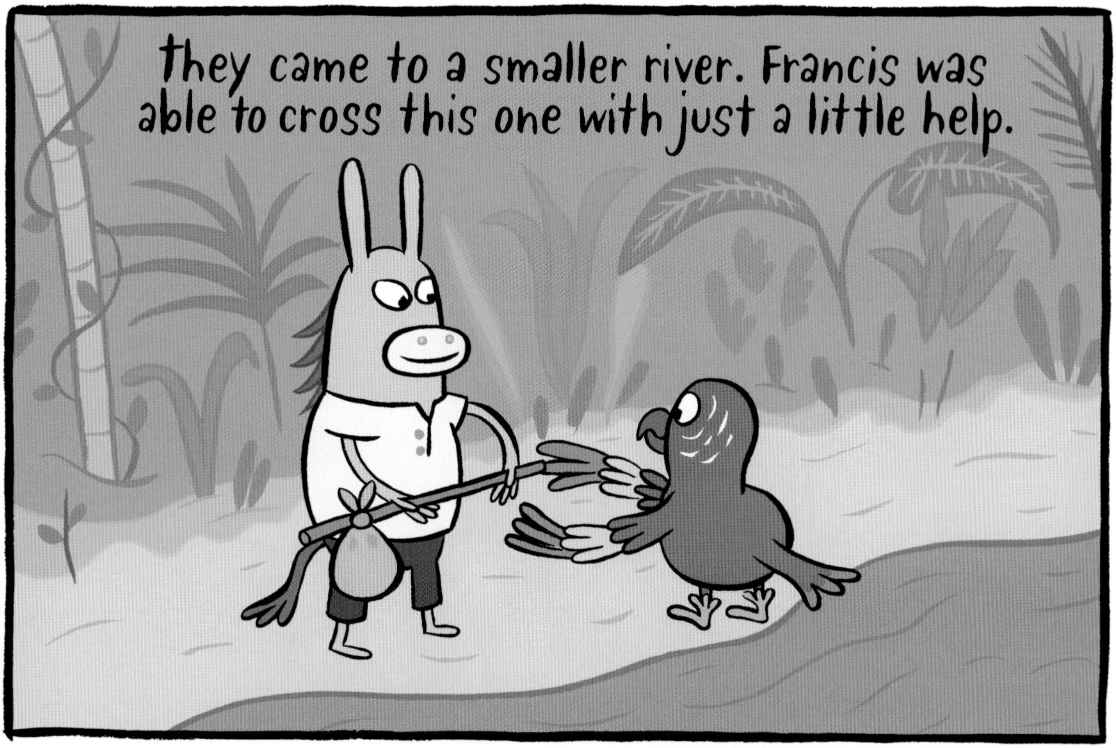
they came to a smaller river. Francis was able to cross this one with just a little help.

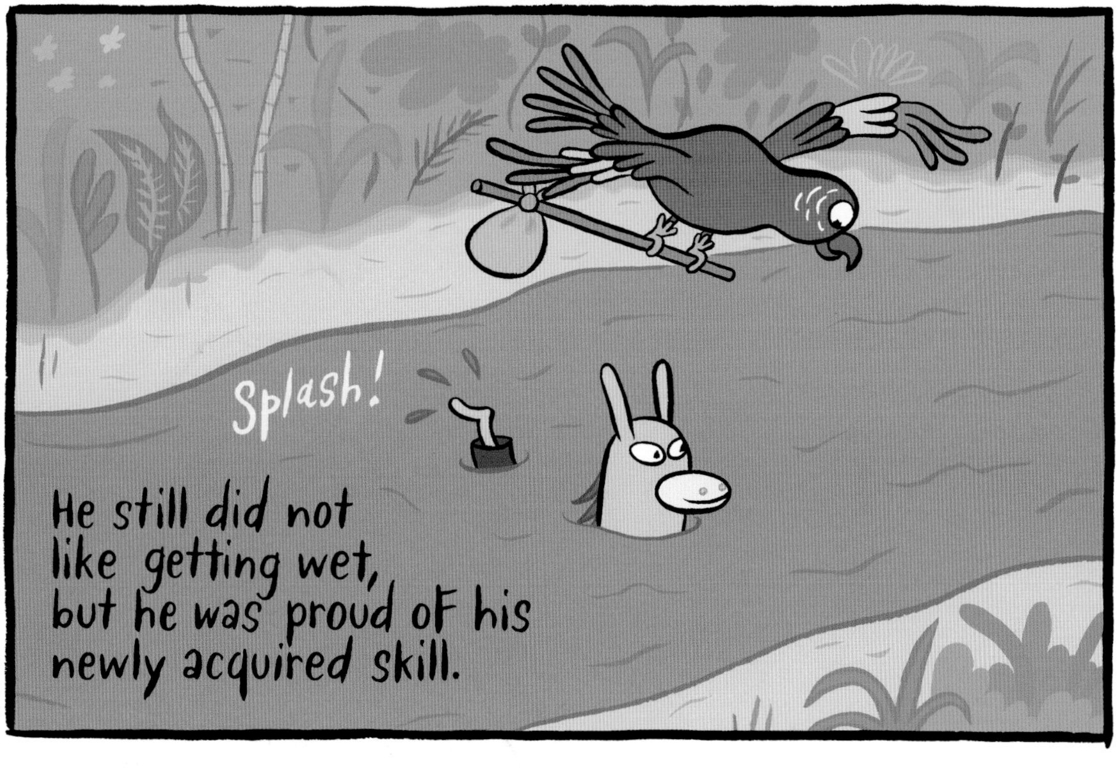
Splash!
He still did not like getting wet, but he was proud of his newly acquired skill.

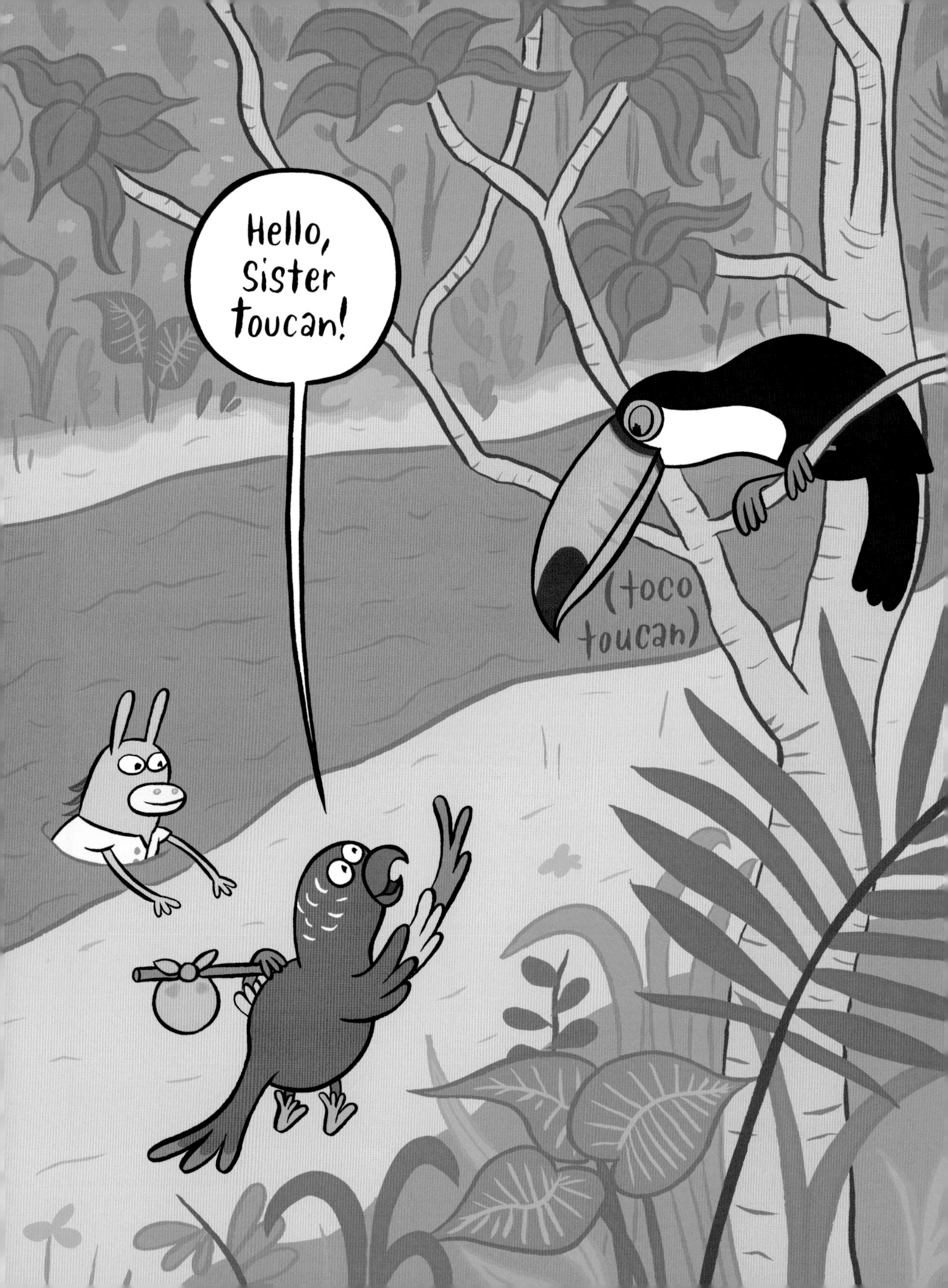
Hello, Sister toucan!
(toco toucan)

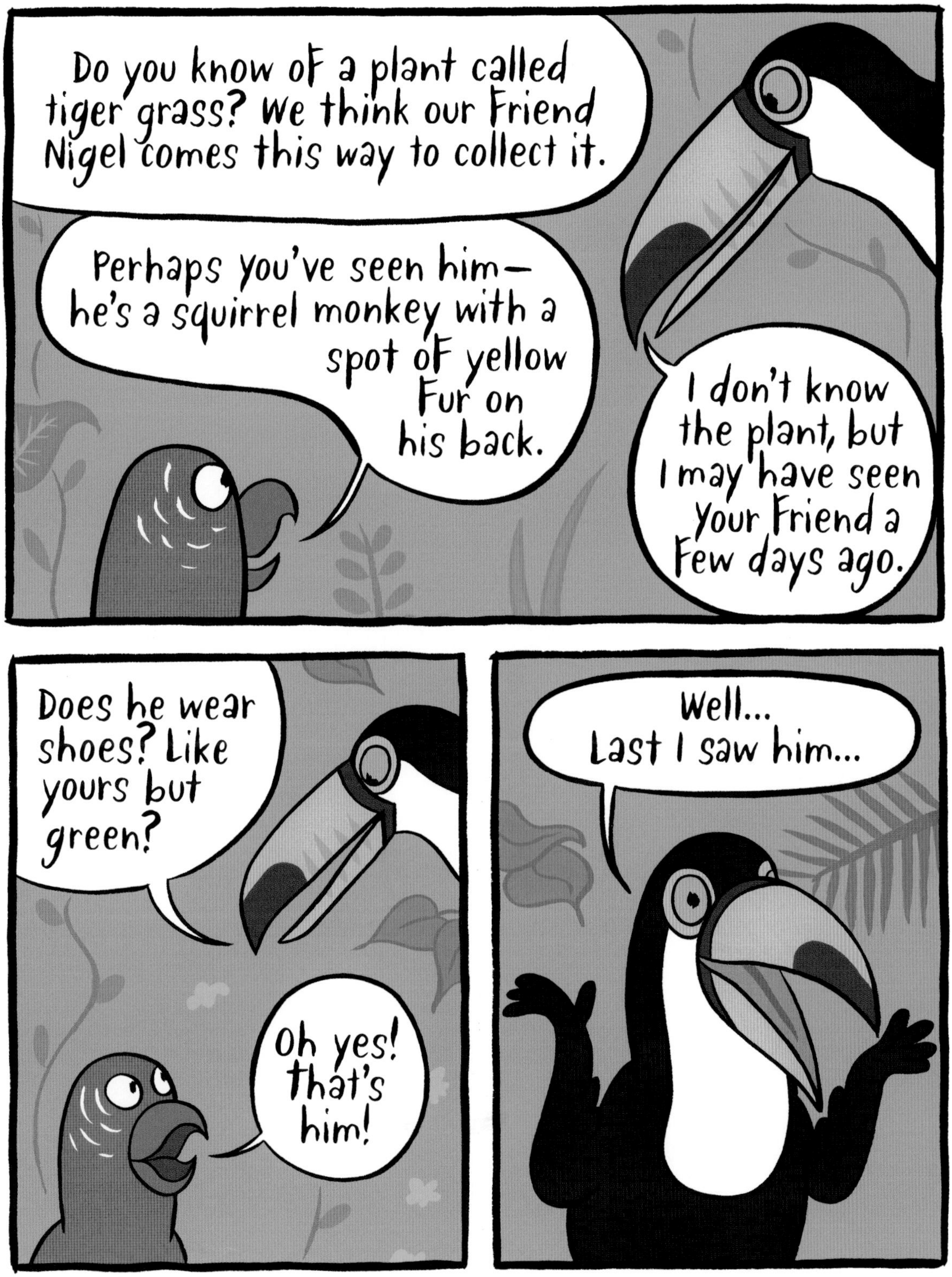
Do you know of a plant called tiger grass? We think our friend Nigel comes this way to collect it.
Perhaps you've seen him— he's a squirrel monkey with a spot of yellow fur on his back.
I don't know the plant, but I may have seen your friend a few days ago.
Does he wear shoes? Like yours but green?
Oh yes! that's him!
Well... Last I saw him...

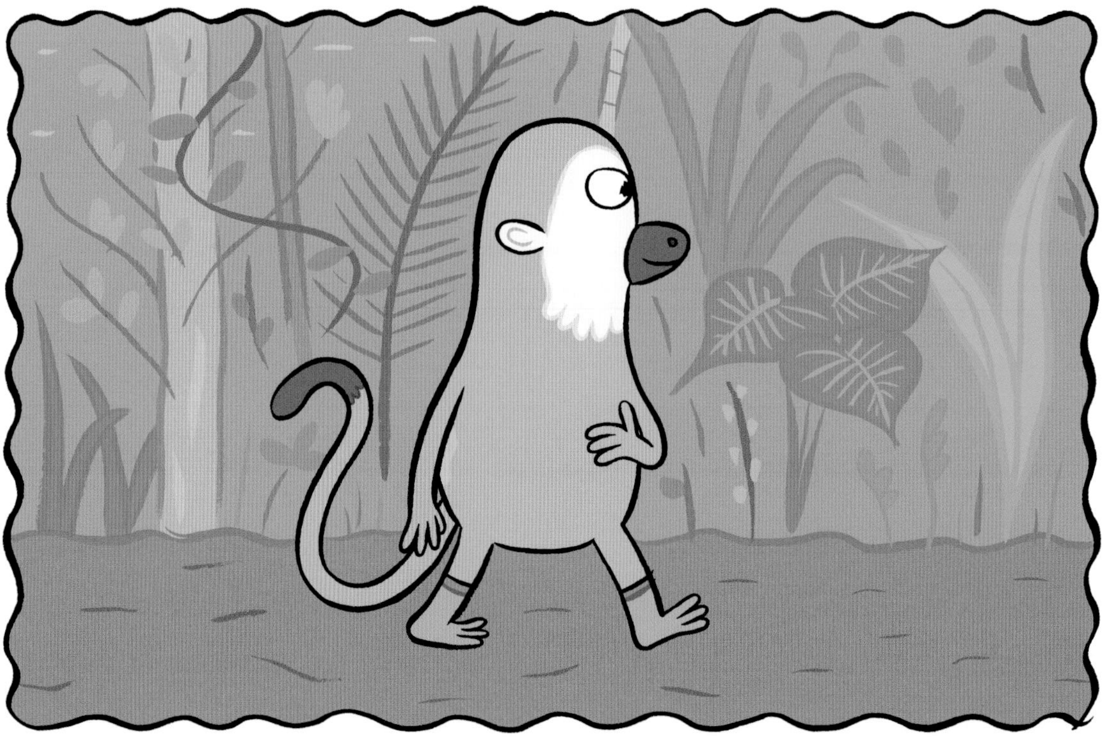

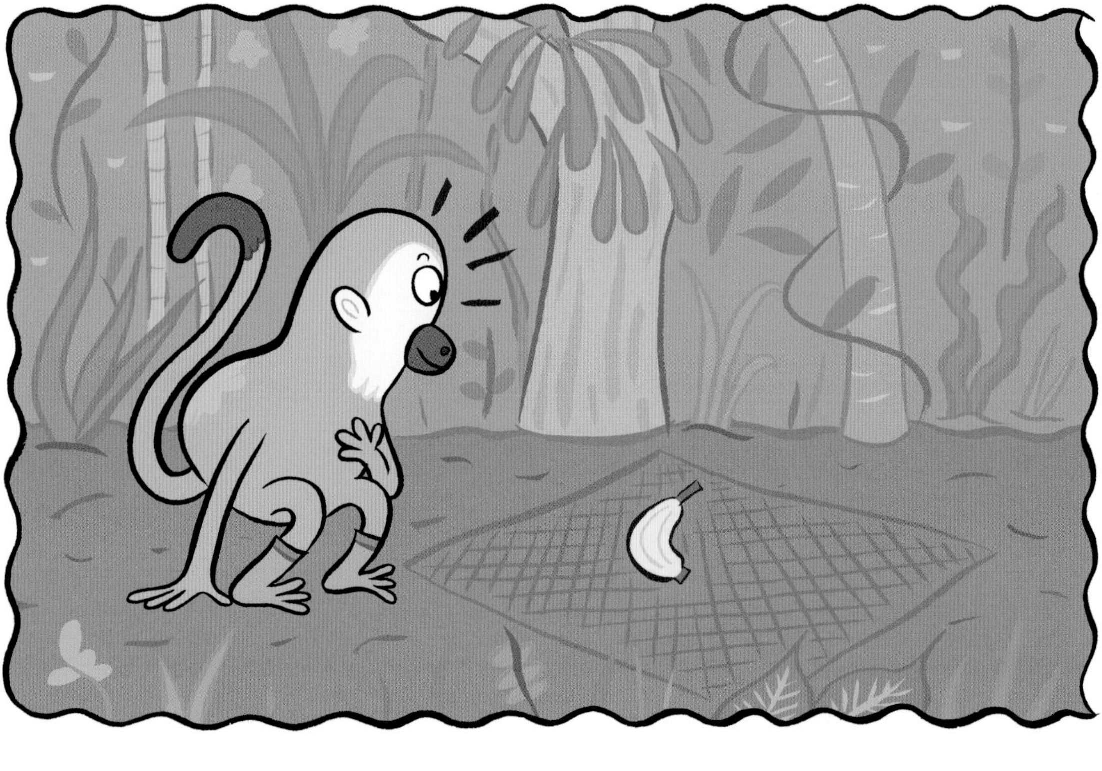

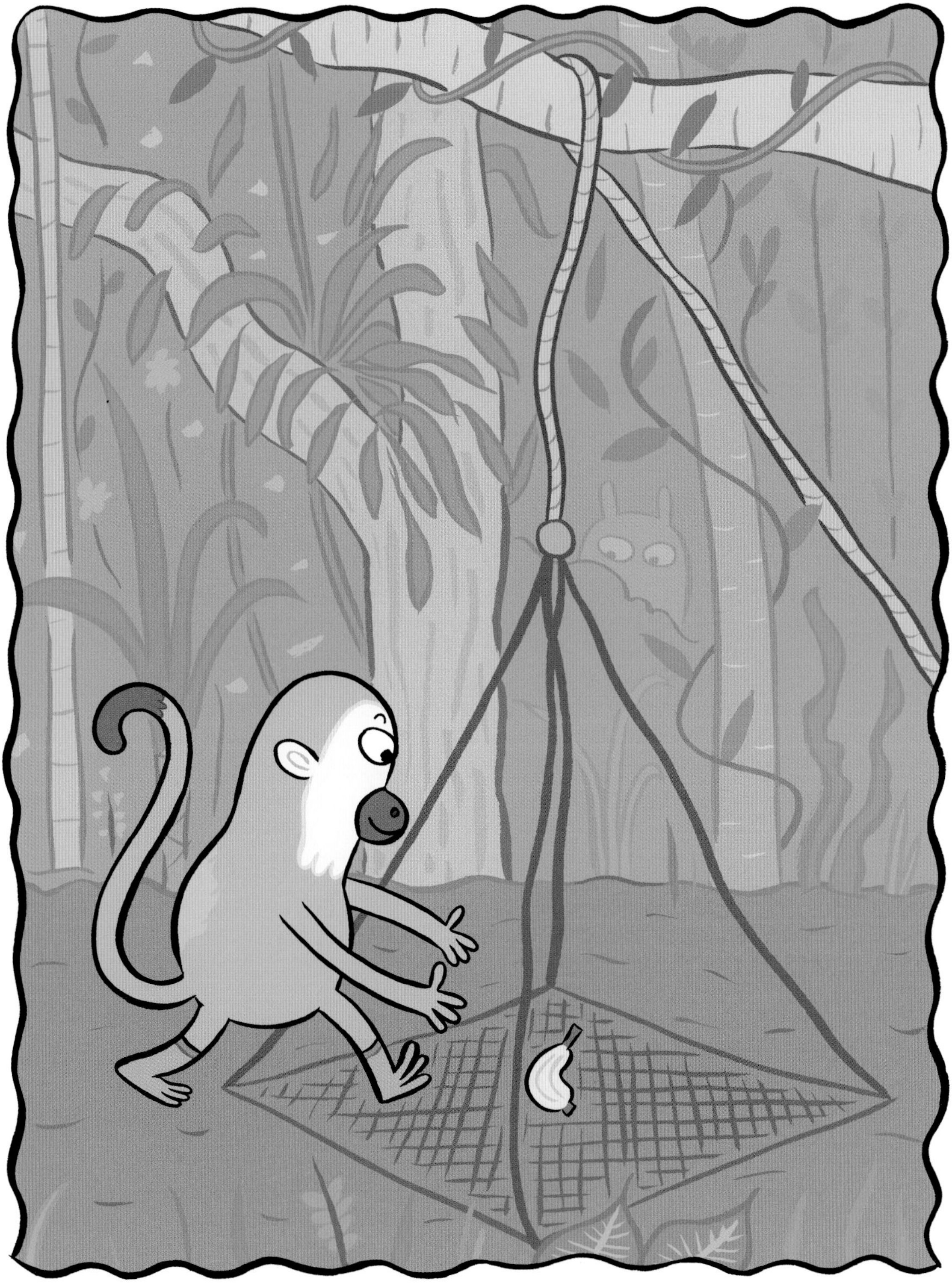

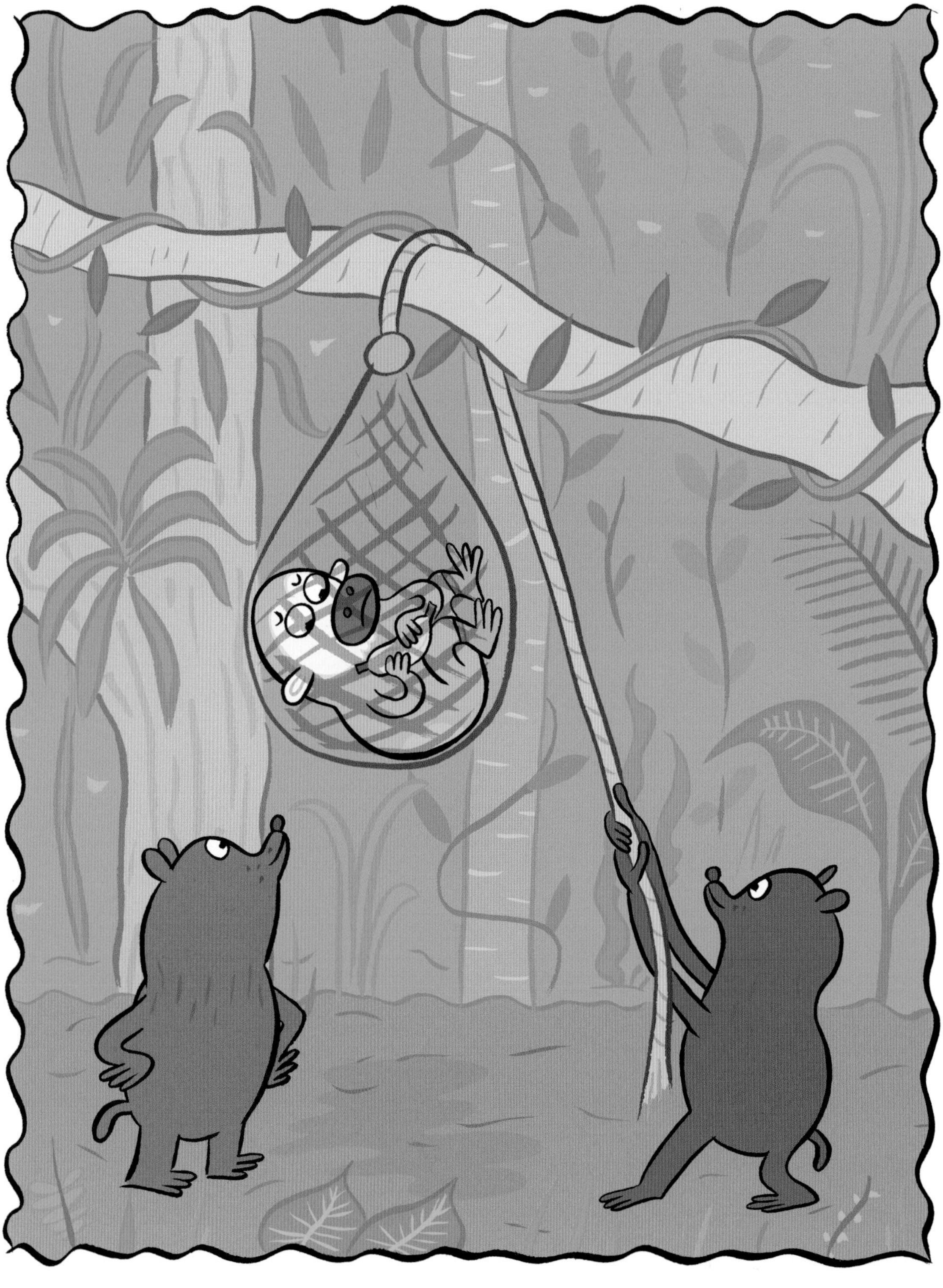

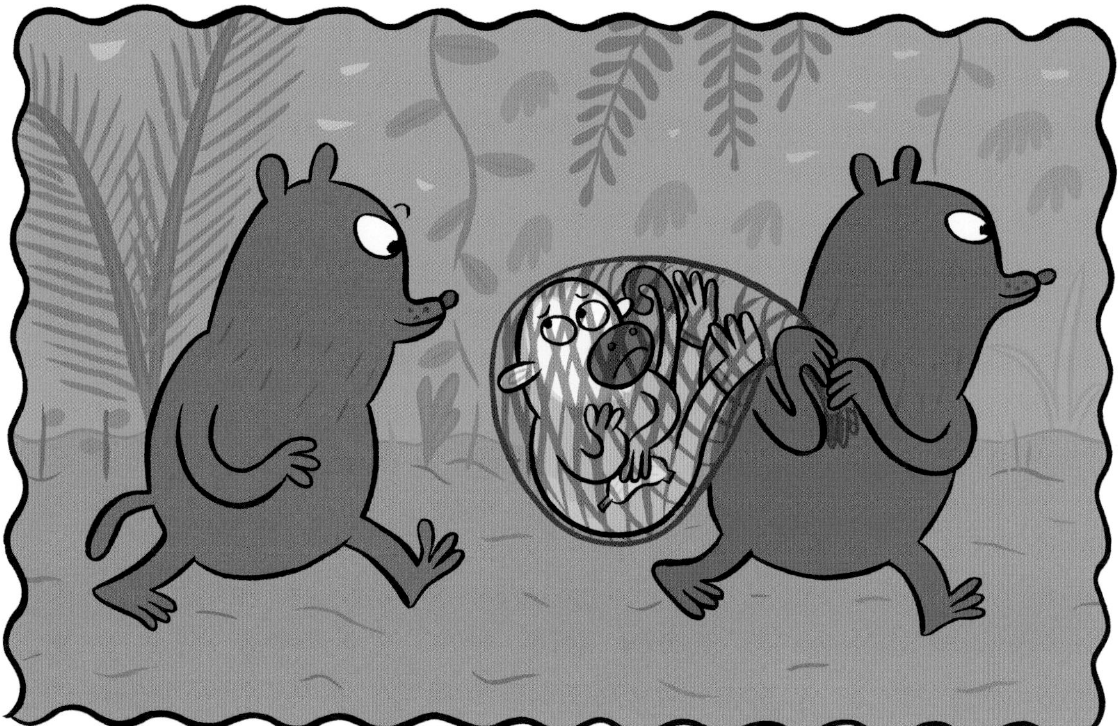

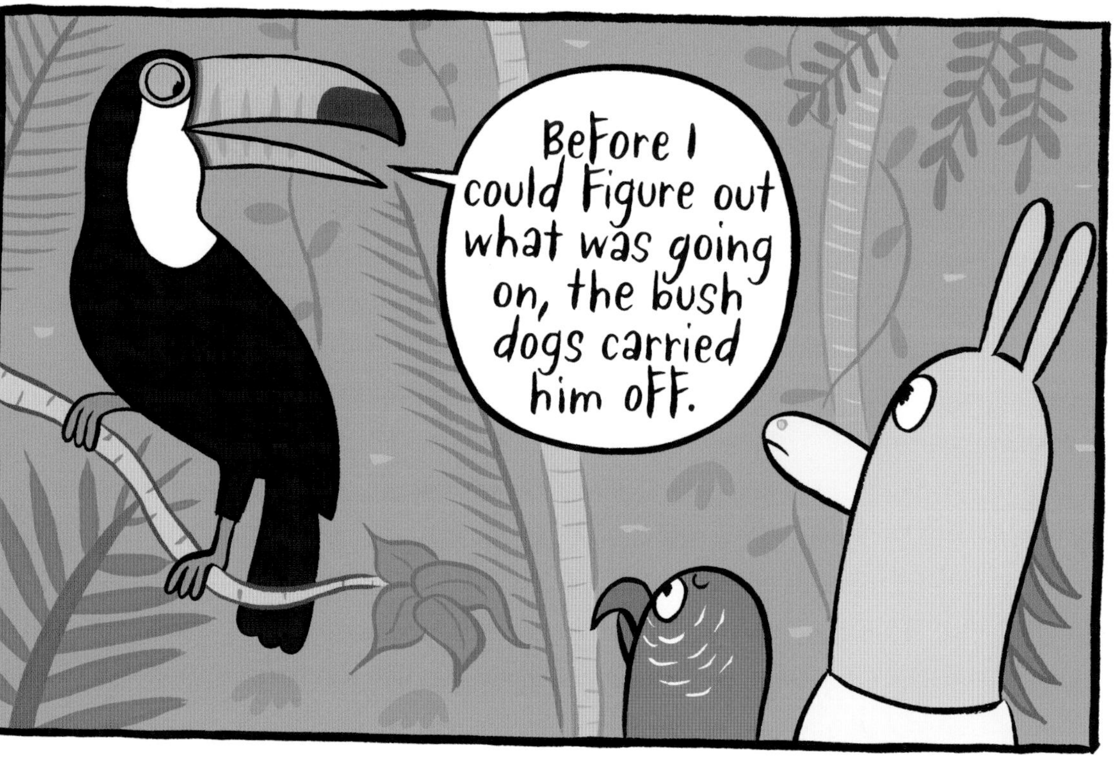
Before I could figure out what was going on, the bush dogs carried him off.

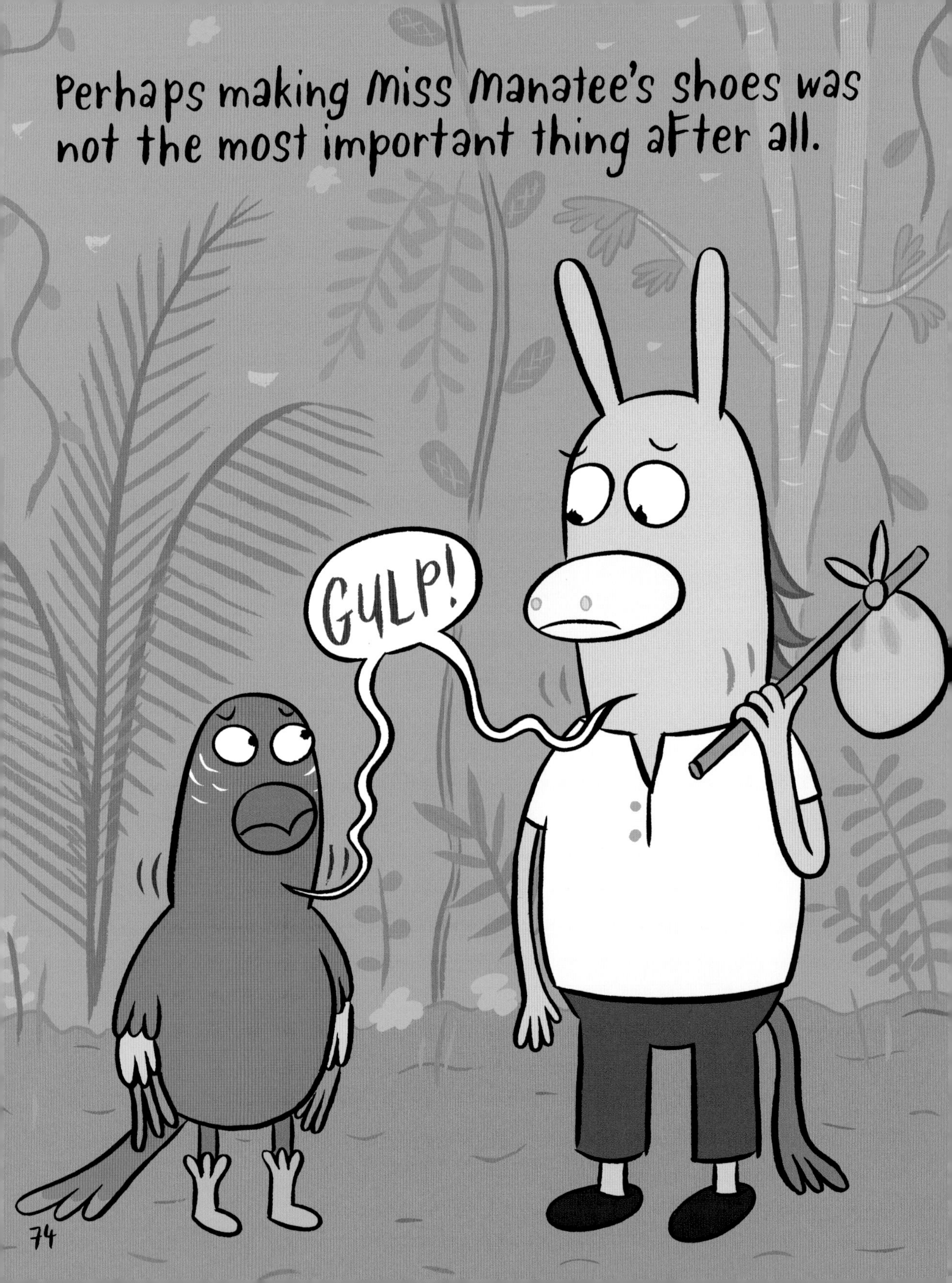
Perhaps making Miss Manatee's shoes was not the most important thing after all.
GULP!

chapter Four

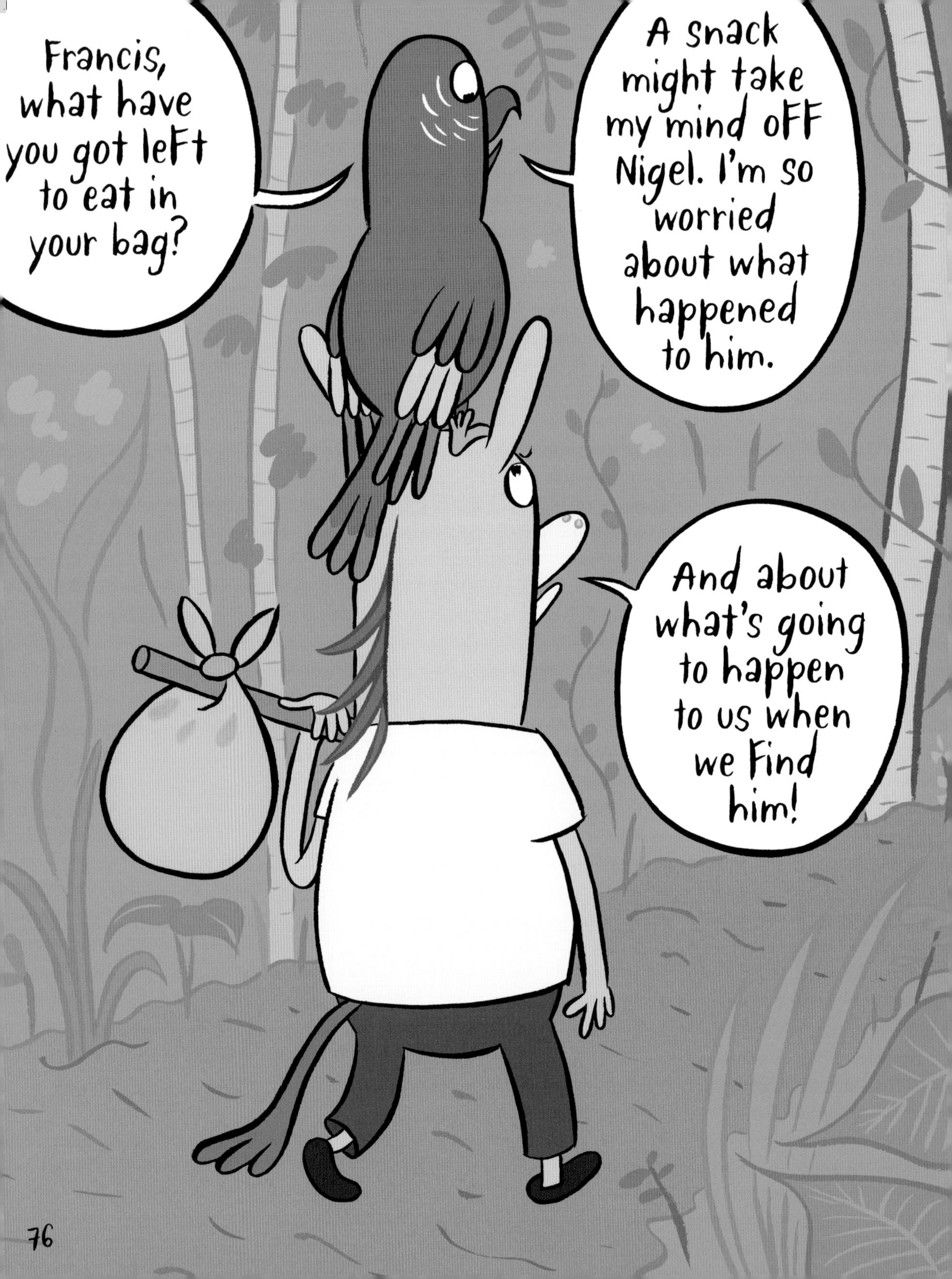
Francis, what have you got leFt to eat in your bag?
A snack might take my mind oFF Nigel. I'm so worried about what happened to him.
And about what's going to happen to us when we Find him!

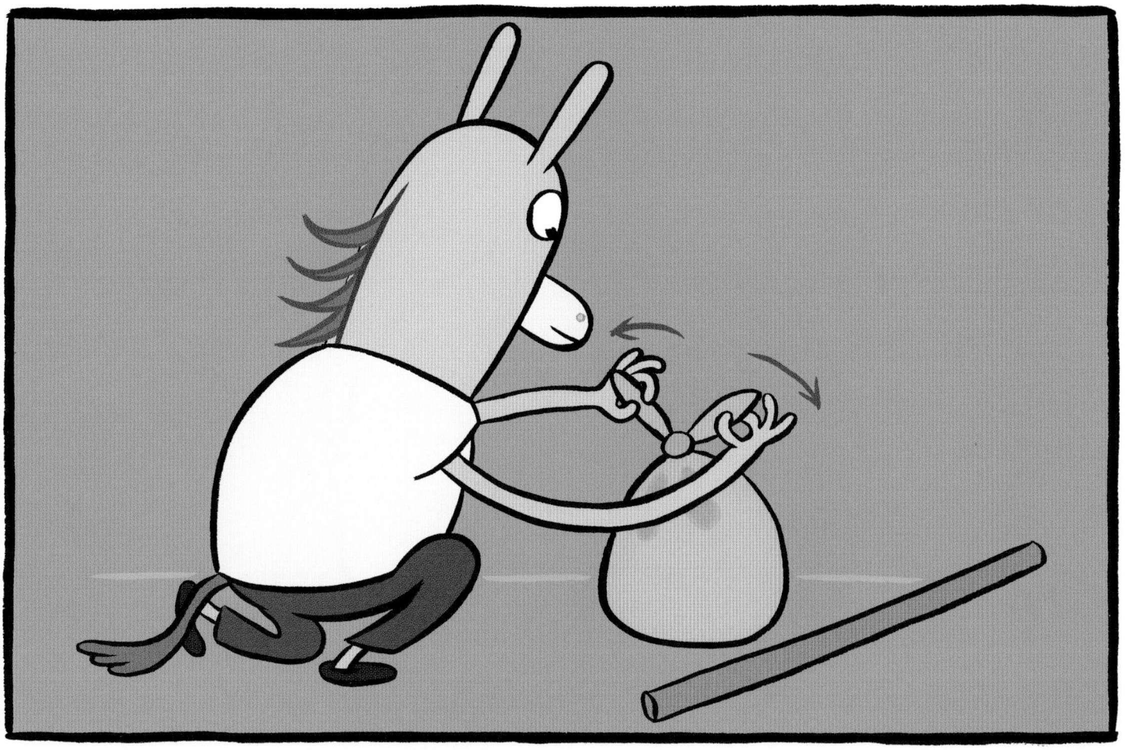

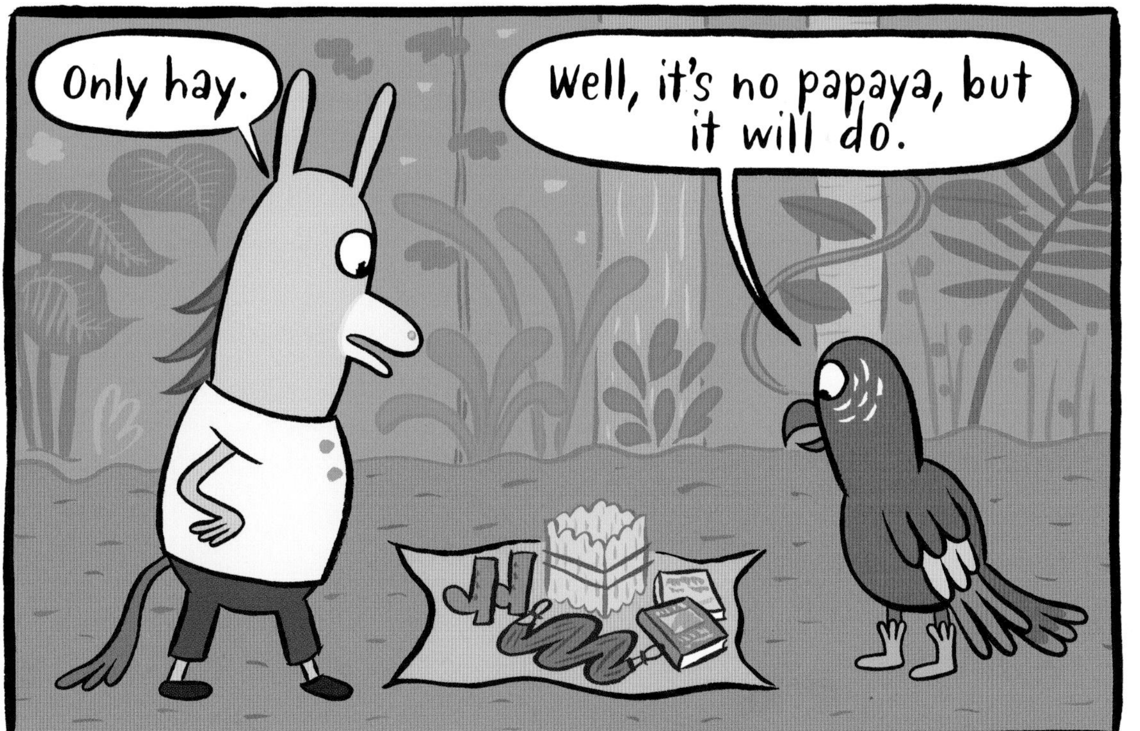
Only hay.
Well, it's no papaya, but it will do.

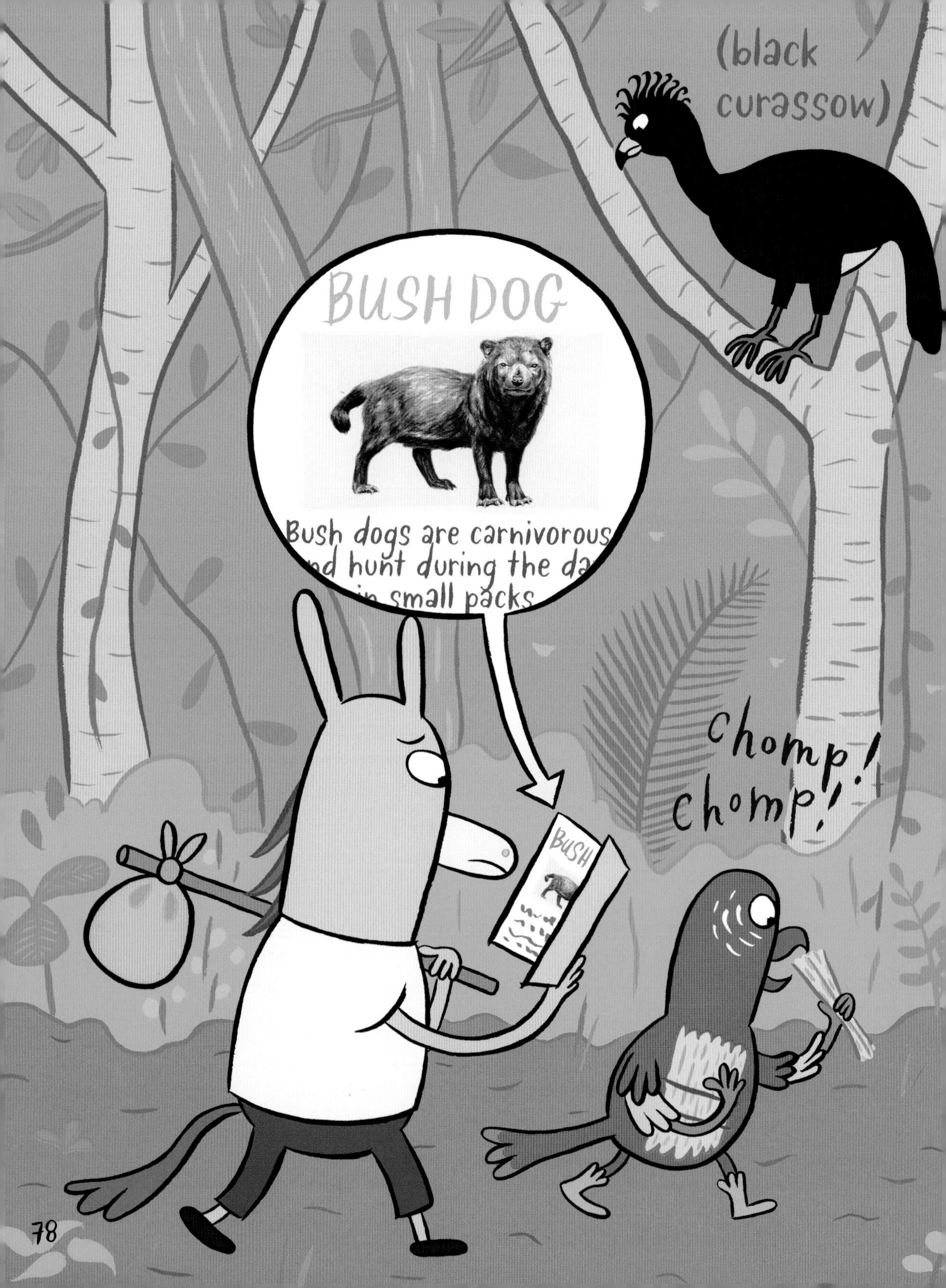
(black curassow)
BUSH DOG
Bush dogs are carnivorous
nd hunt during the da
in small packs
BUSH
Chomp! Chomp!

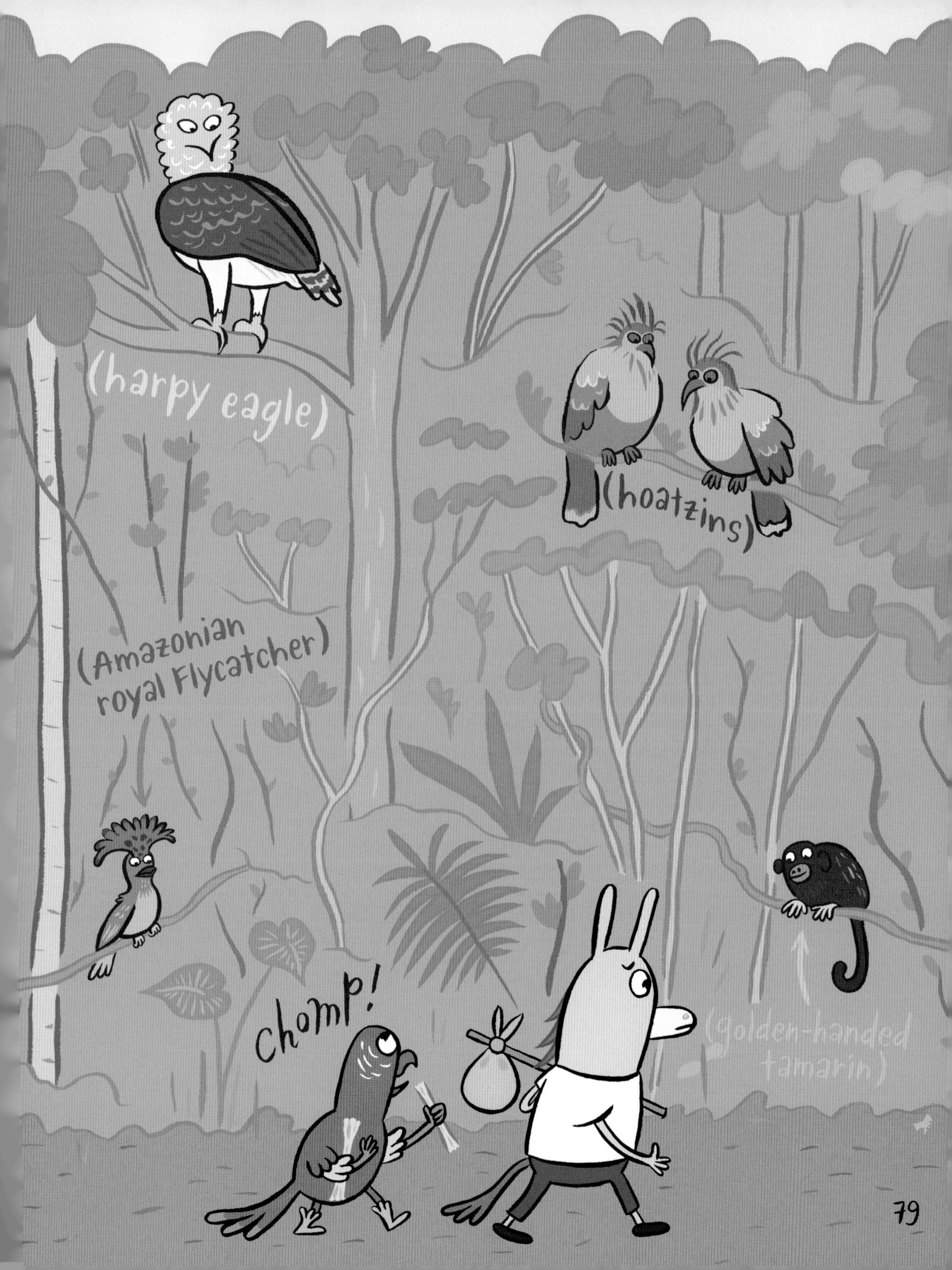
(harpy eagle)
(hoatzins)
(Amazonian royal Flycatcher)
Chomp!
(golden-handed tamarin)

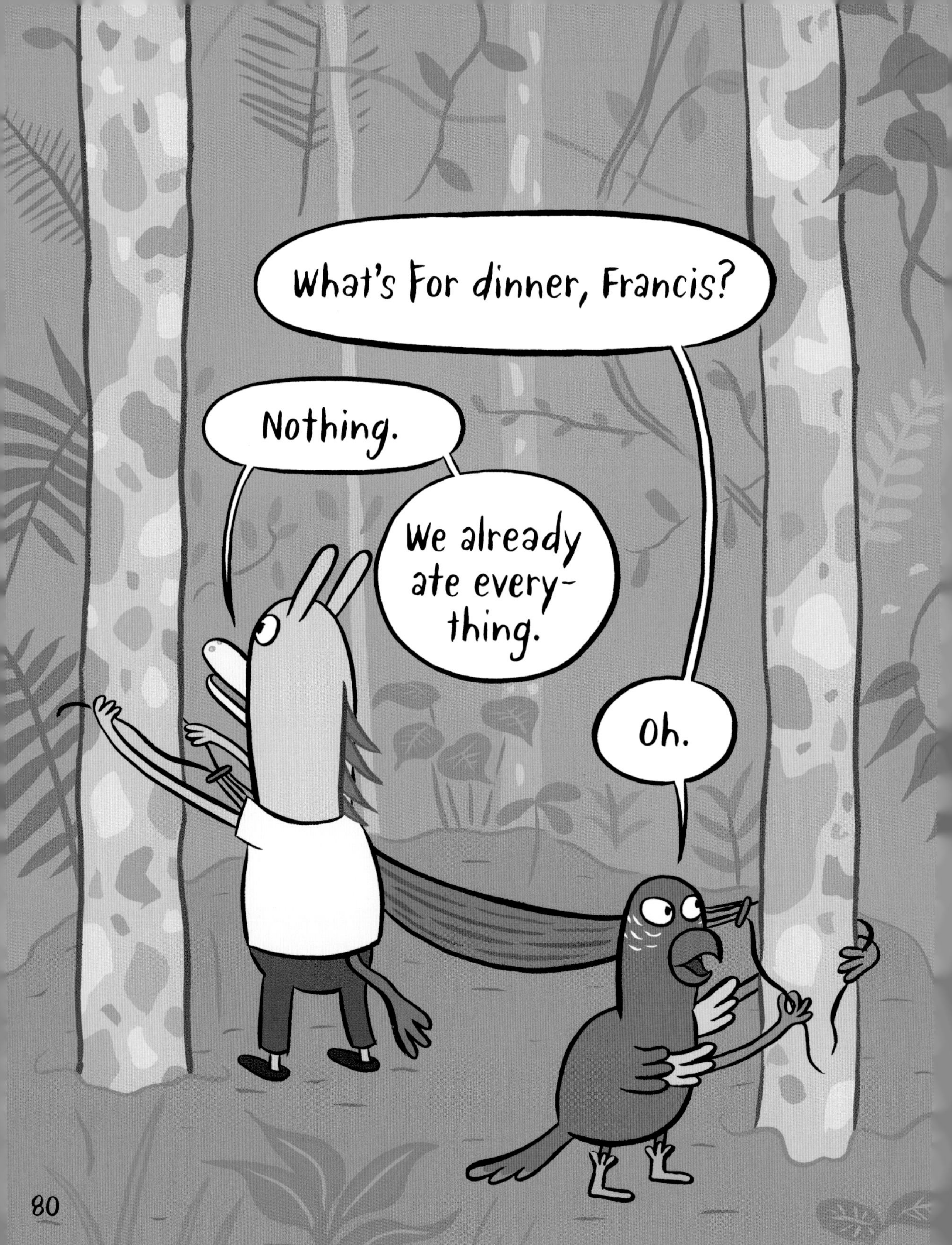
What's For dinner, Francis?
Nothing.
We already ate every-thing.
Oh.

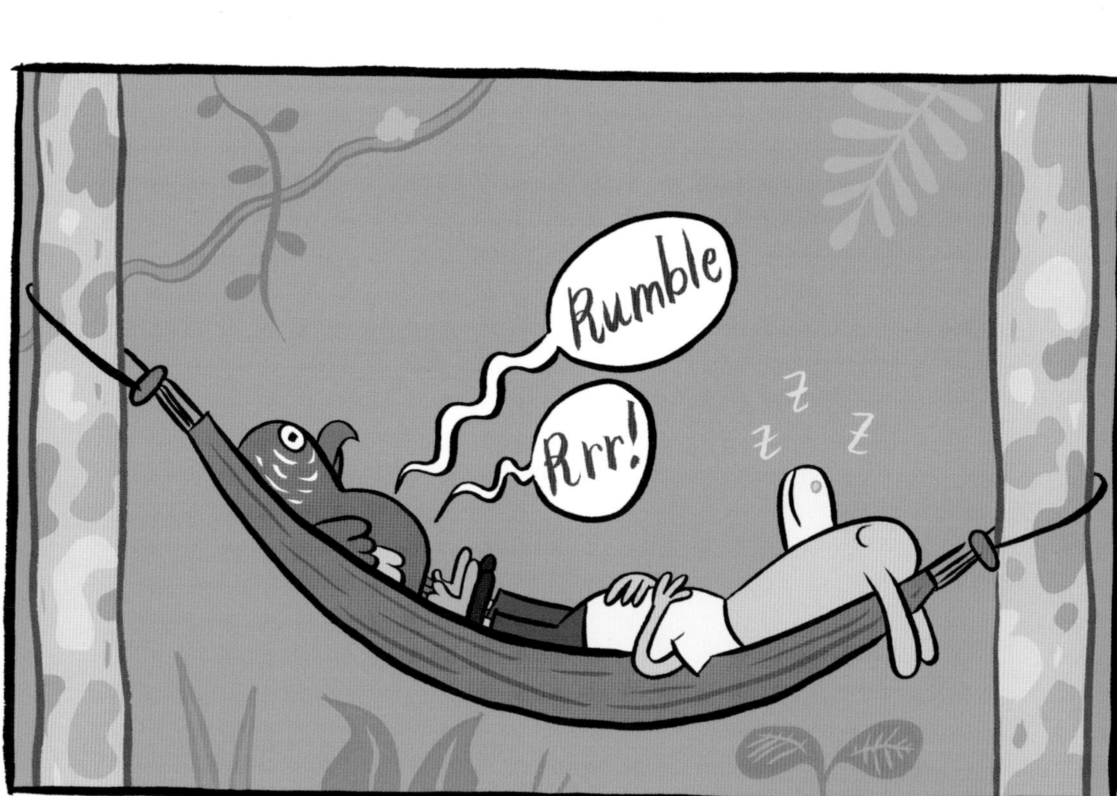
Rumble
Rrr!
Z Z Z

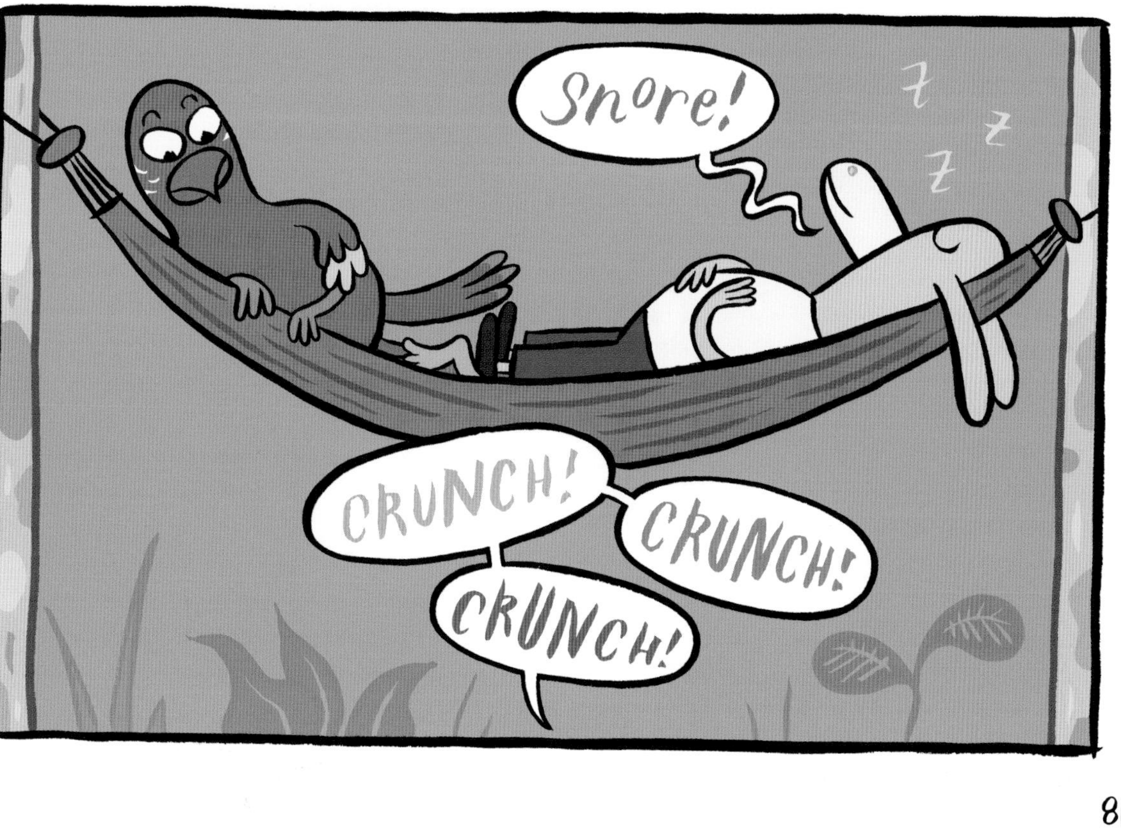
Snore!
Z Z Z
CRUNCH!
CRUNCH!
CRUNCH!

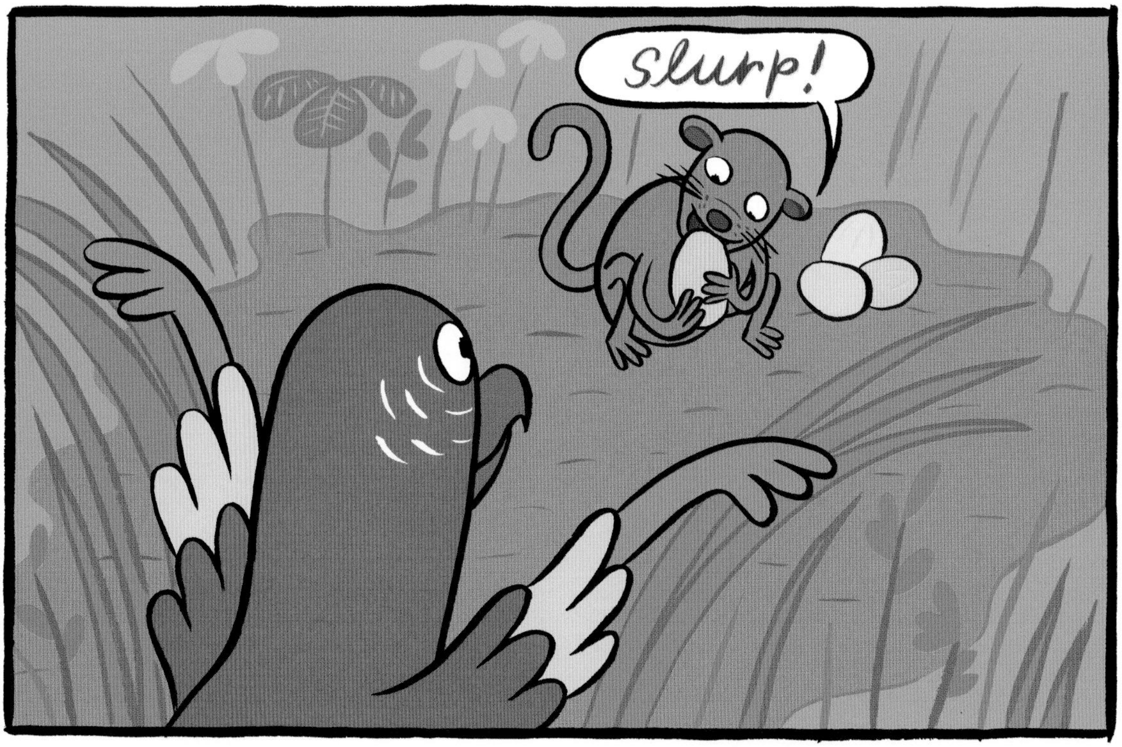
Slurp!

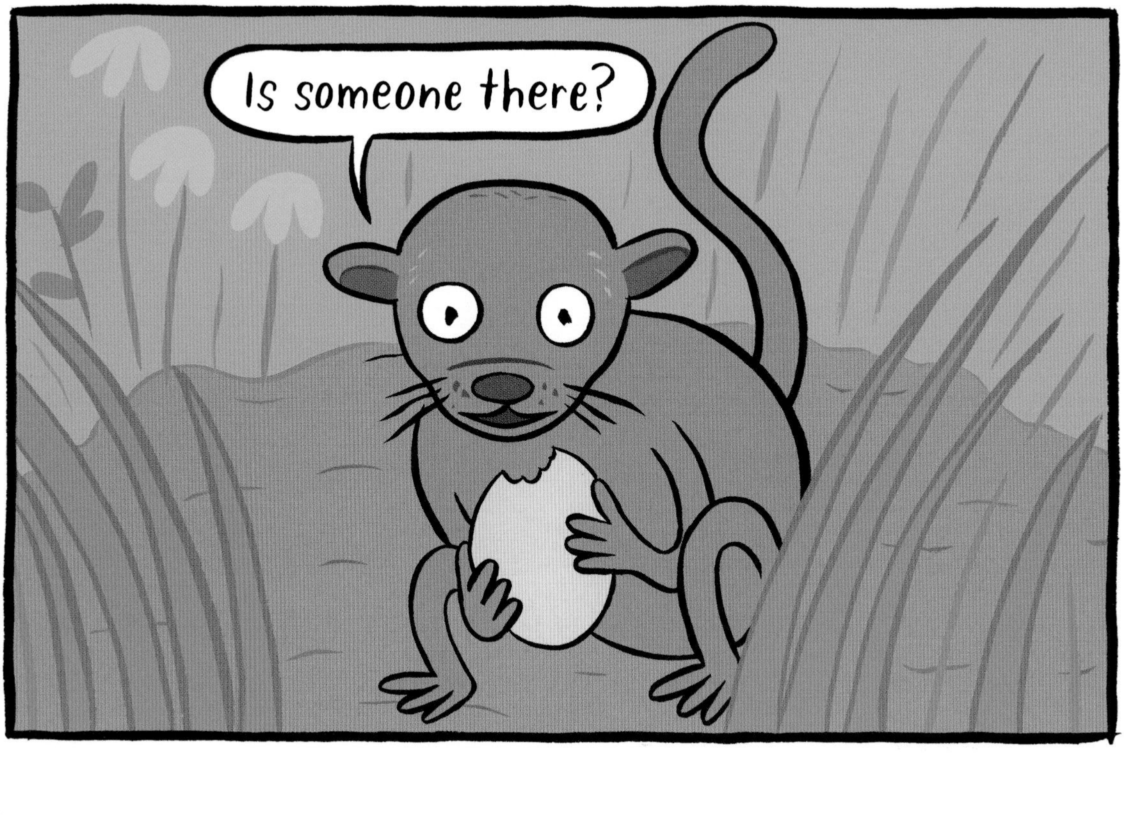
Is someone there?

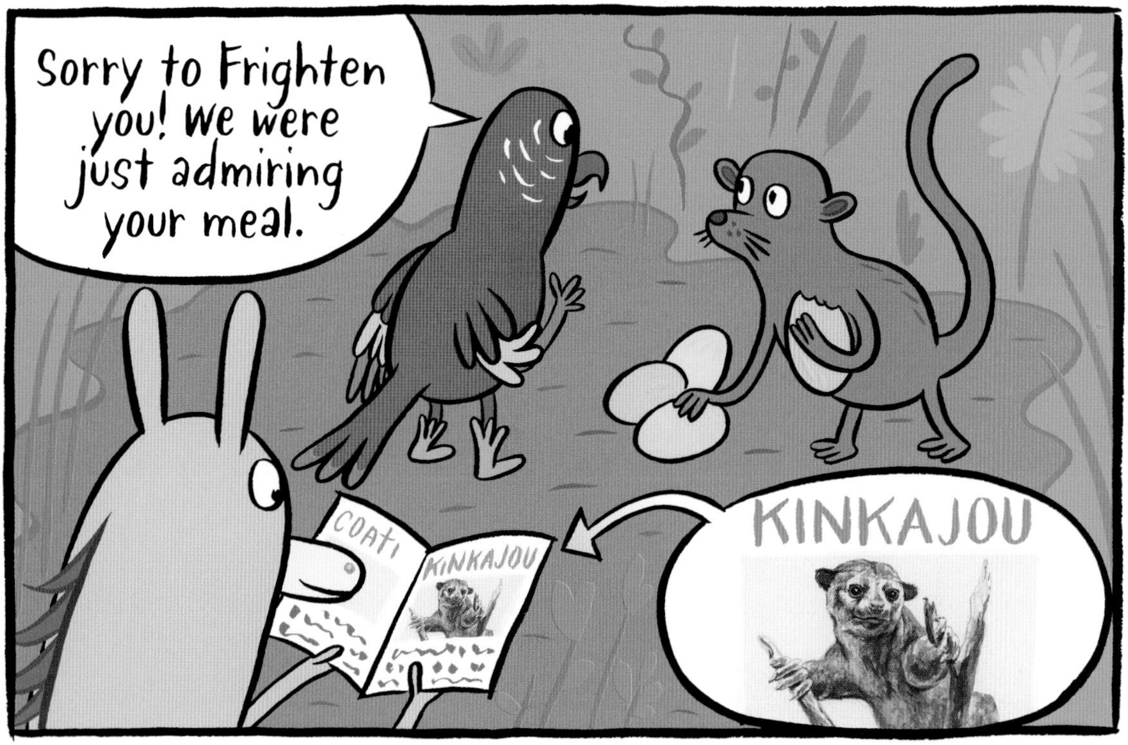

Sorry to Frighten you! We were just admiring your meal.
COATI
KINKAJOU
KINKAJOU

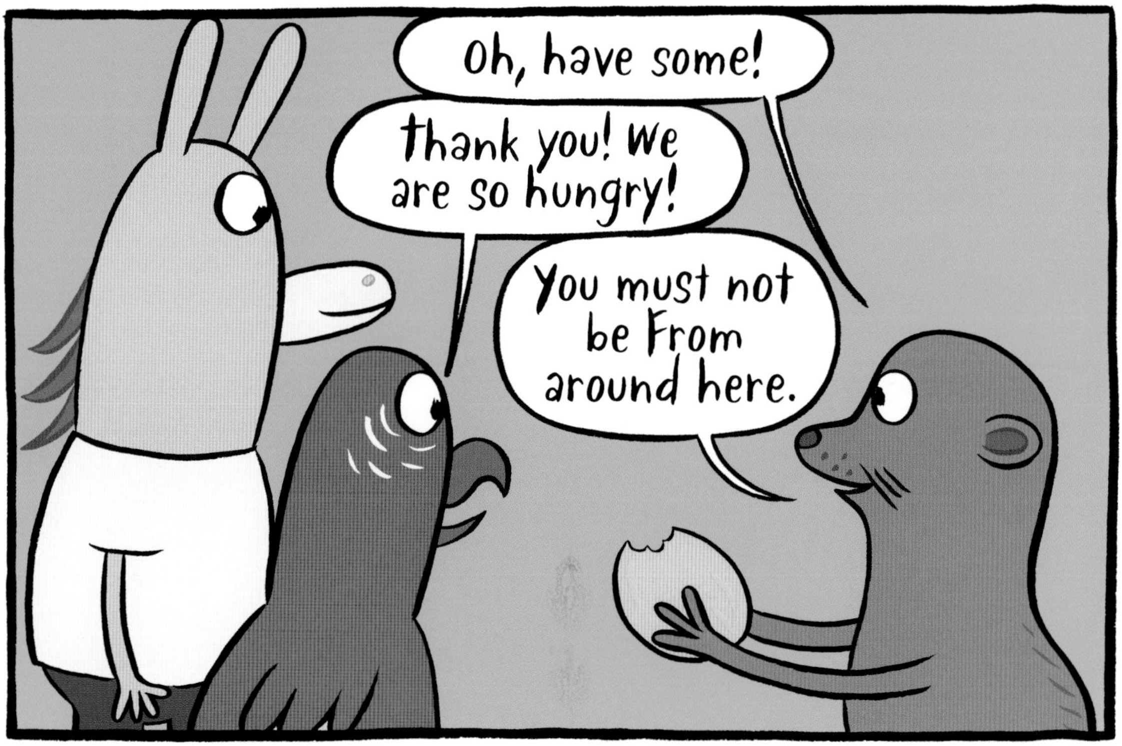

Oh, have some!
Thank you! We are so hungry!
You must not be From around here.

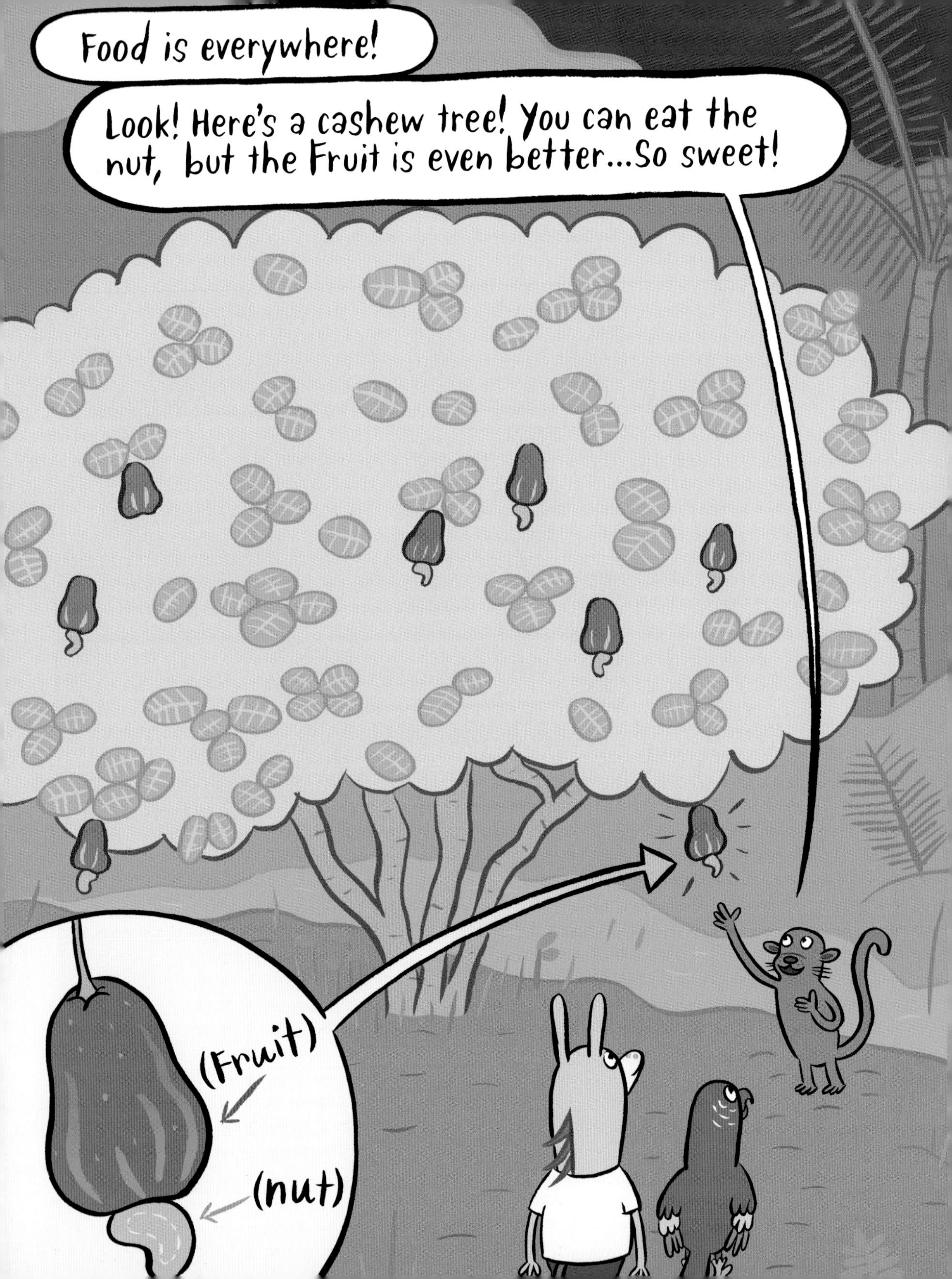
Food is everywhere!
Look! Here's a cashew tree! You can eat the nut, but the Fruit is even better...So sweet!
(Fruit)
(nut)

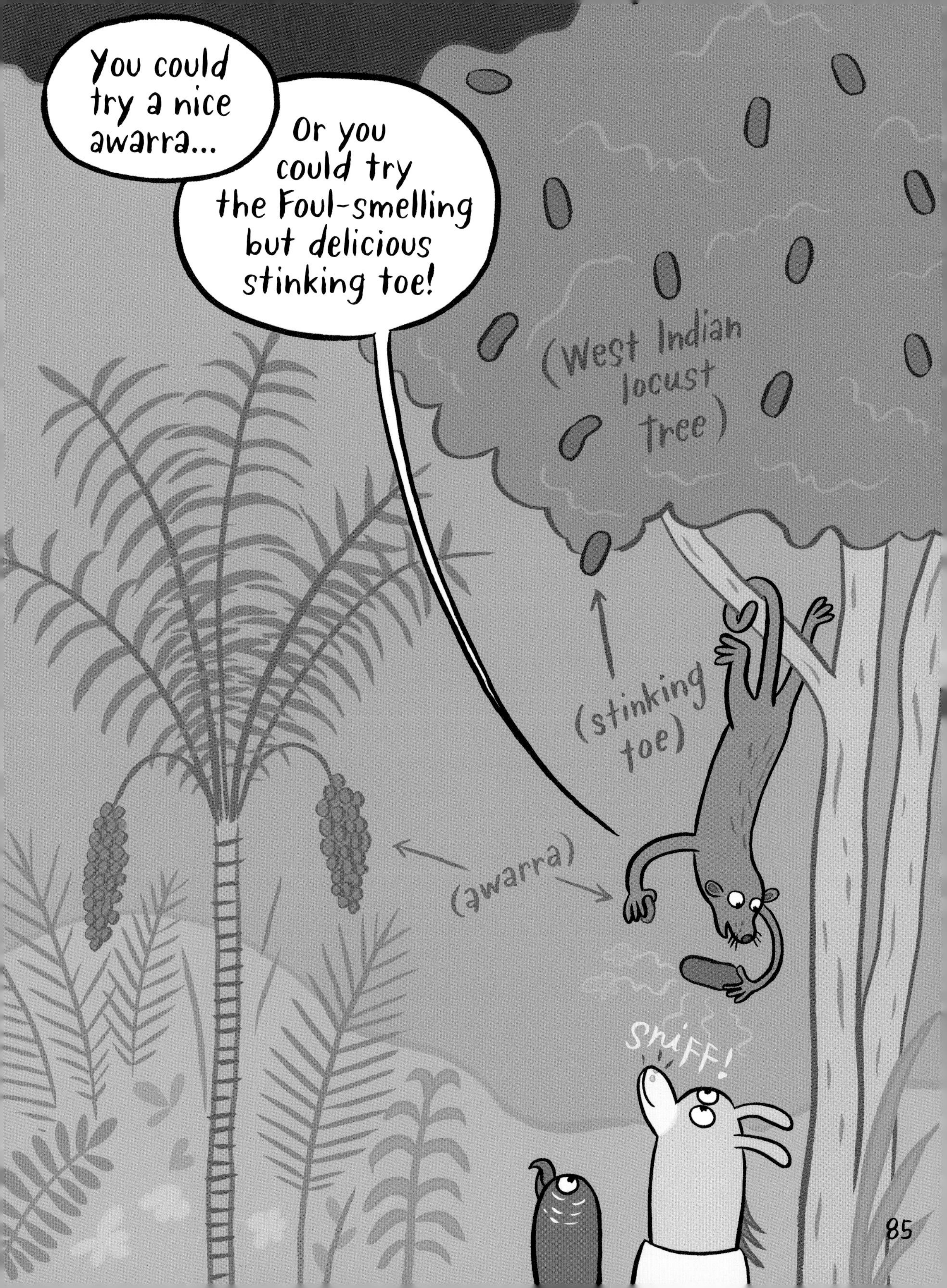
You could try a nice awarra...
Or you could try the Foul-smelling but delicious stinking toe!
(West Indian locust tree)
(stinking toe)
(awarra)
SNiFF!

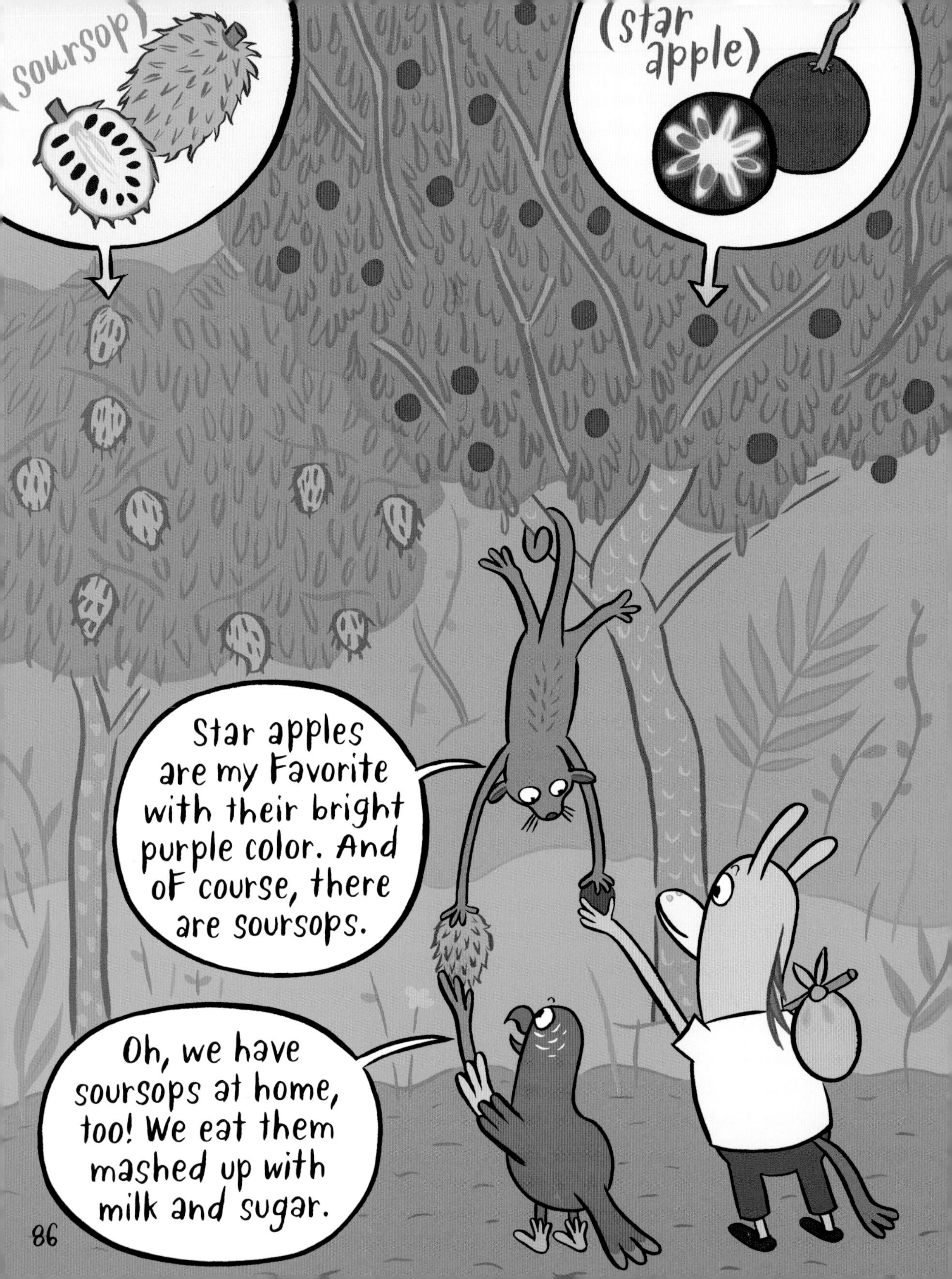
(soursop)
(star apple)
Star apples are my Favorite with their bright purple color. And oF course, there are soursops.
Oh, we have soursops at home, too! We eat them mashed up with milk and sugar.

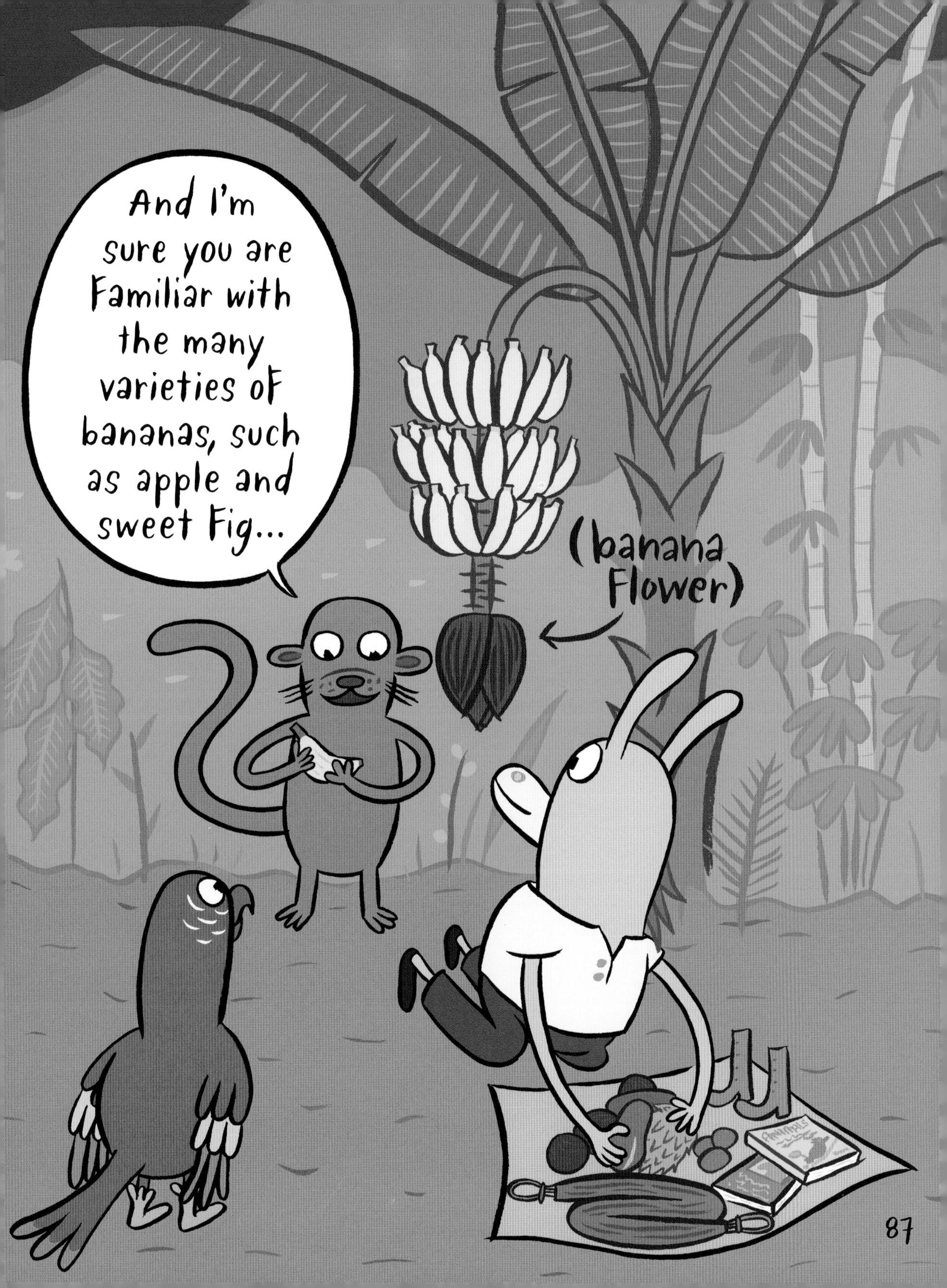
And I'm sure you are Familiar with the many varieties of bananas, such as apple and sweet Fig...
(banana Flower)

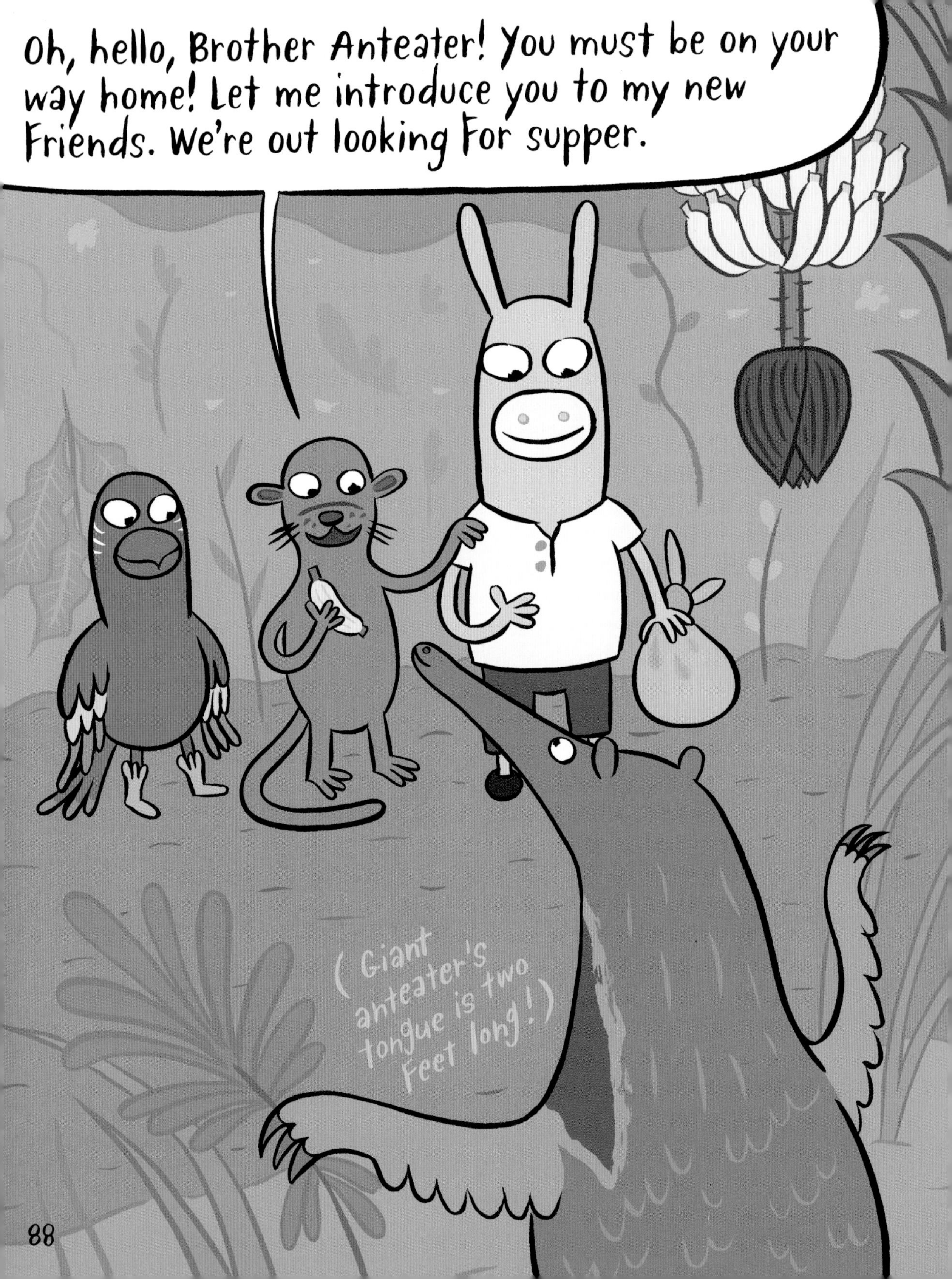
Oh, hello, Brother Anteater! You must be on your way home! Let me introduce you to my new Friends. We're out looking For supper.
(Giant anteater's tongue is two Feet long!)

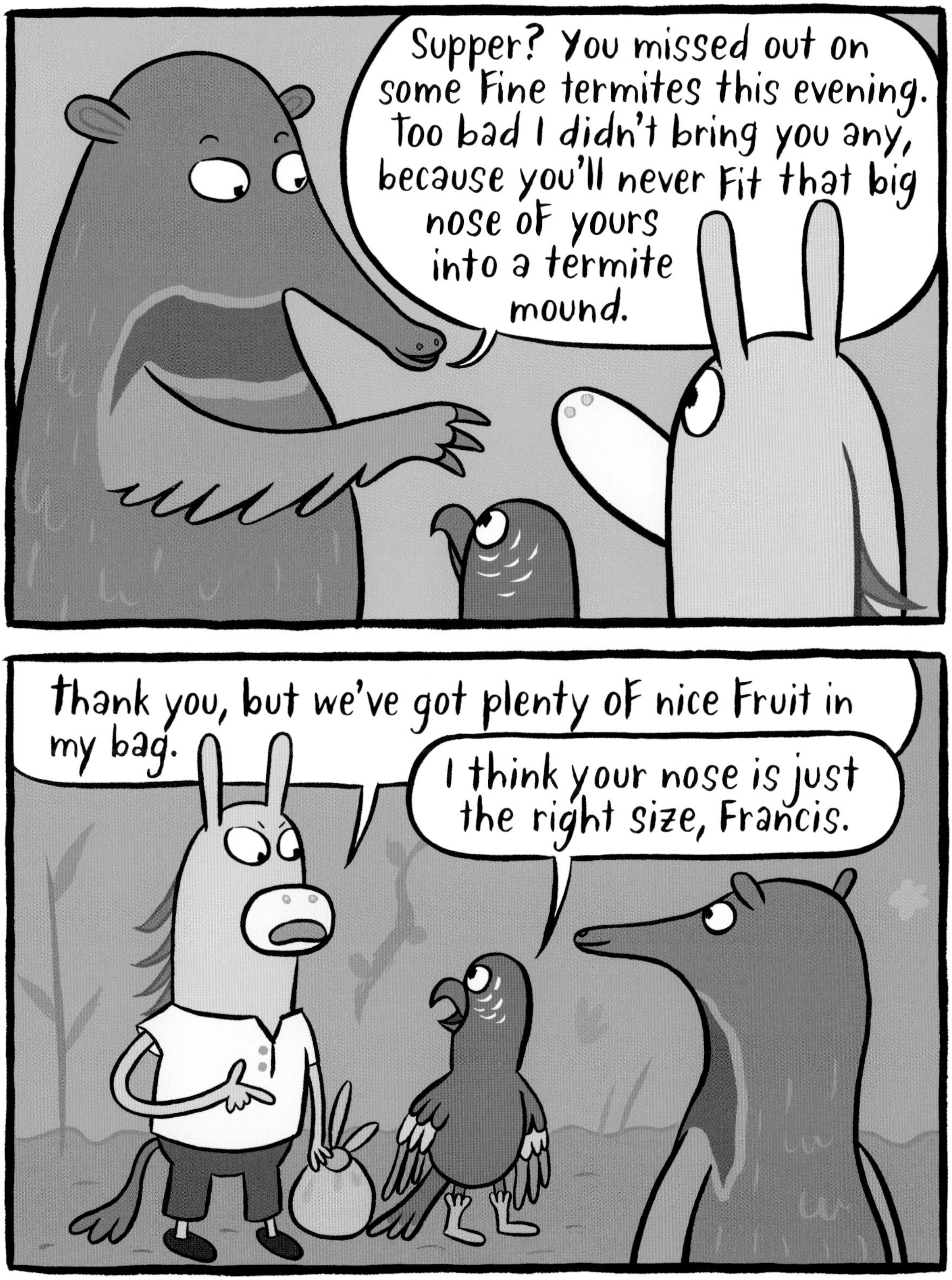
Supper? You missed out on some Fine termites this evening. Too bad I didn't bring you any, because you'll never Fit that big nose of yours into a termite mound.
thank you, but we've got plenty of nice Fruit in my bag.
I think your nose is just the right size, Francis.

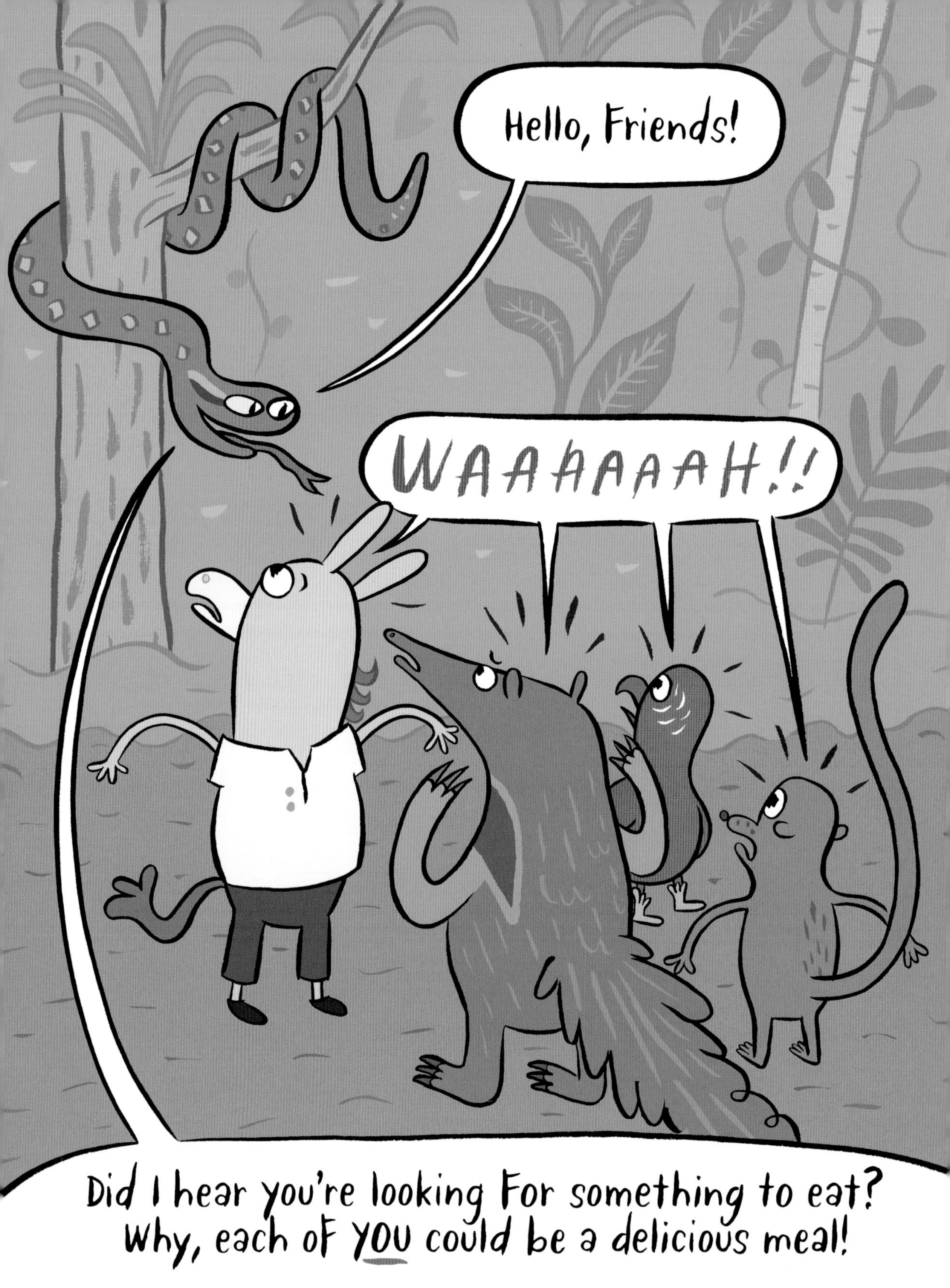
Hello, Friends!
WAAAAAAH!!
Did I hear you're looking For something to eat?
Why, each oF YOU could be a delicious meal!

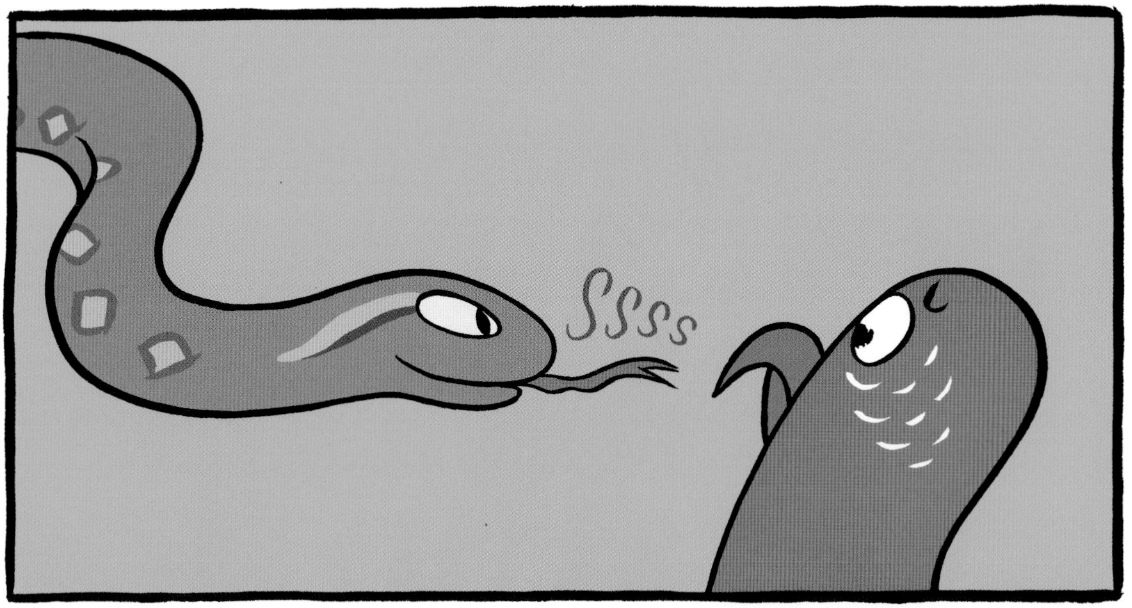
Ssss

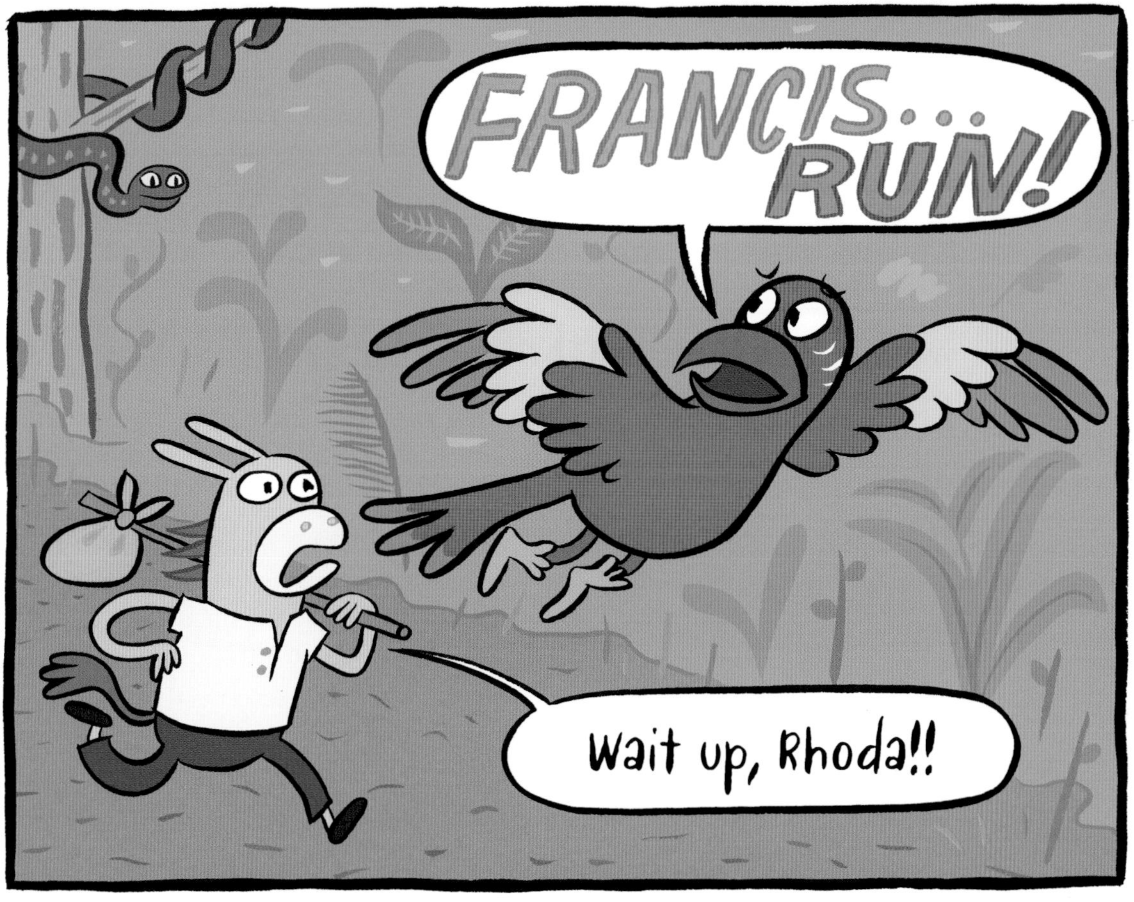
FRANCIS... RUN!
Wait up, Rhoda!!

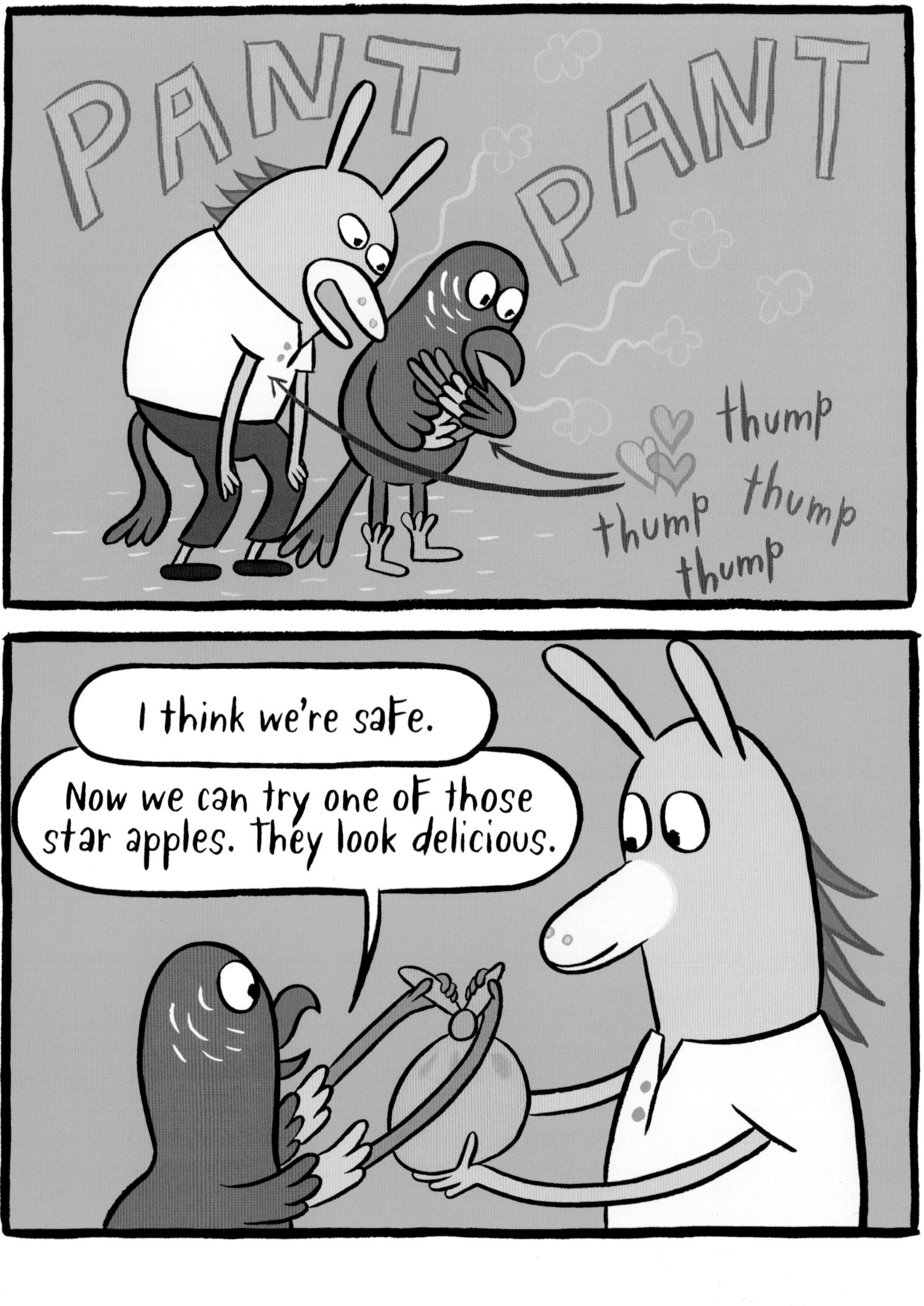
PANT PANT
thump
thump thump
thump
I think we're safe.
Now we can try one of those star apples. They look delicious.

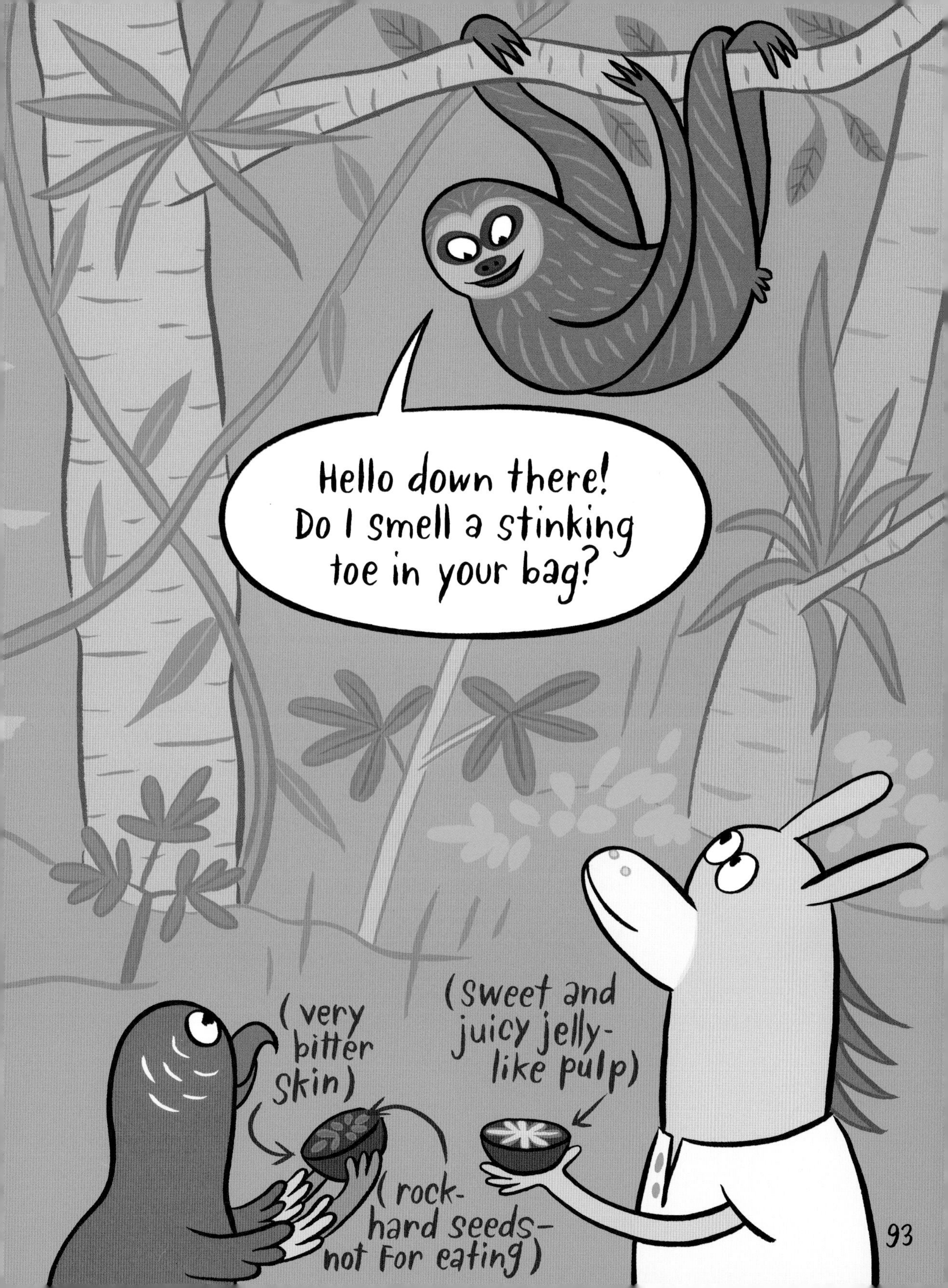
Hello down there! Do I smell a stinking toe in your bag?
(very bitter skin)
(sweet and juicy jelly-like pulp)
(rock-hard seeds-not for eating)

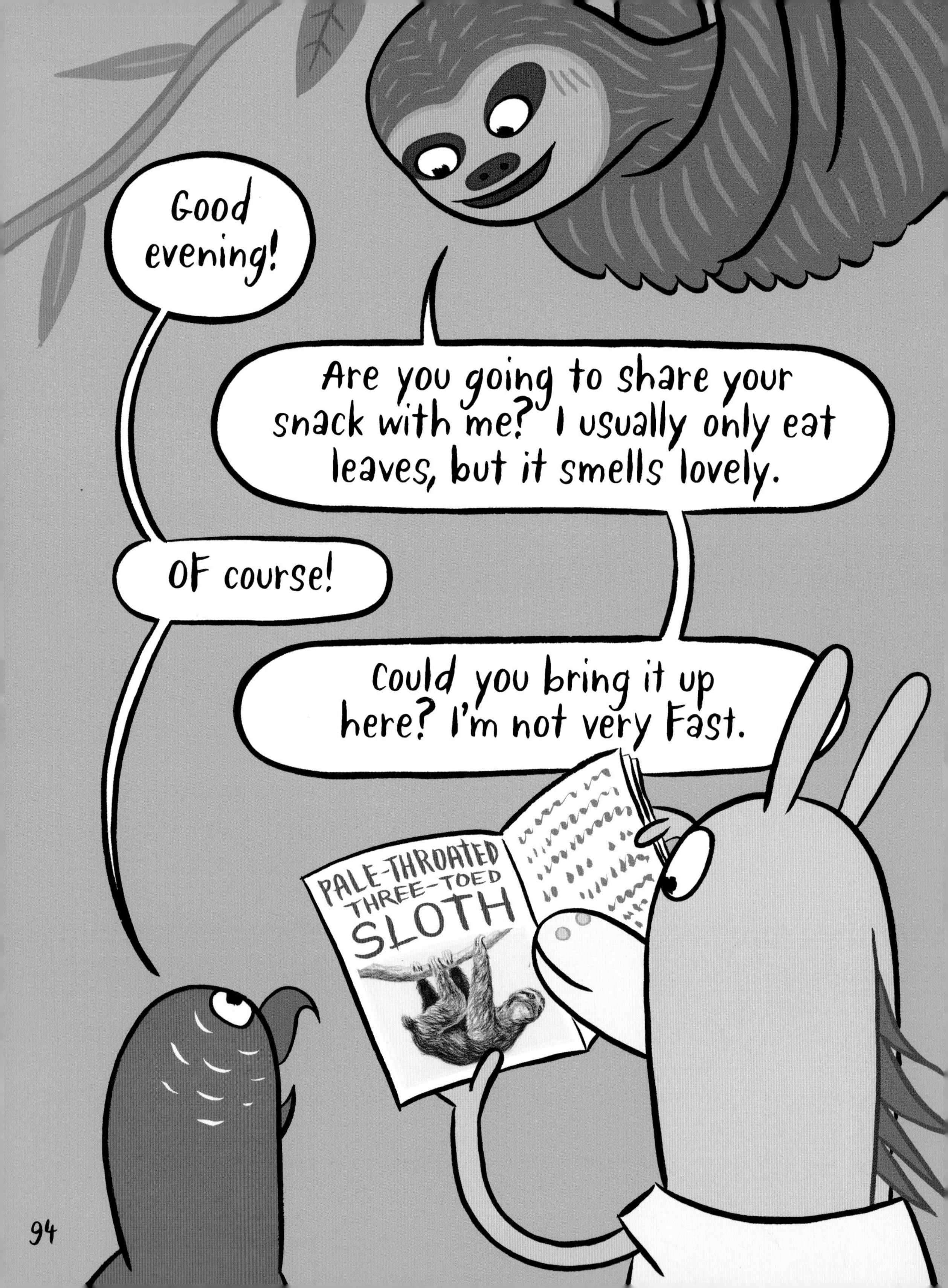
Good evening!
Are you going to share your snack with me? I usually only eat leaves, but it smells lovely.
OF course!
Could you bring it up here? I'm not very Fast.
PALE-THROATED THREE-TOED SLOTH

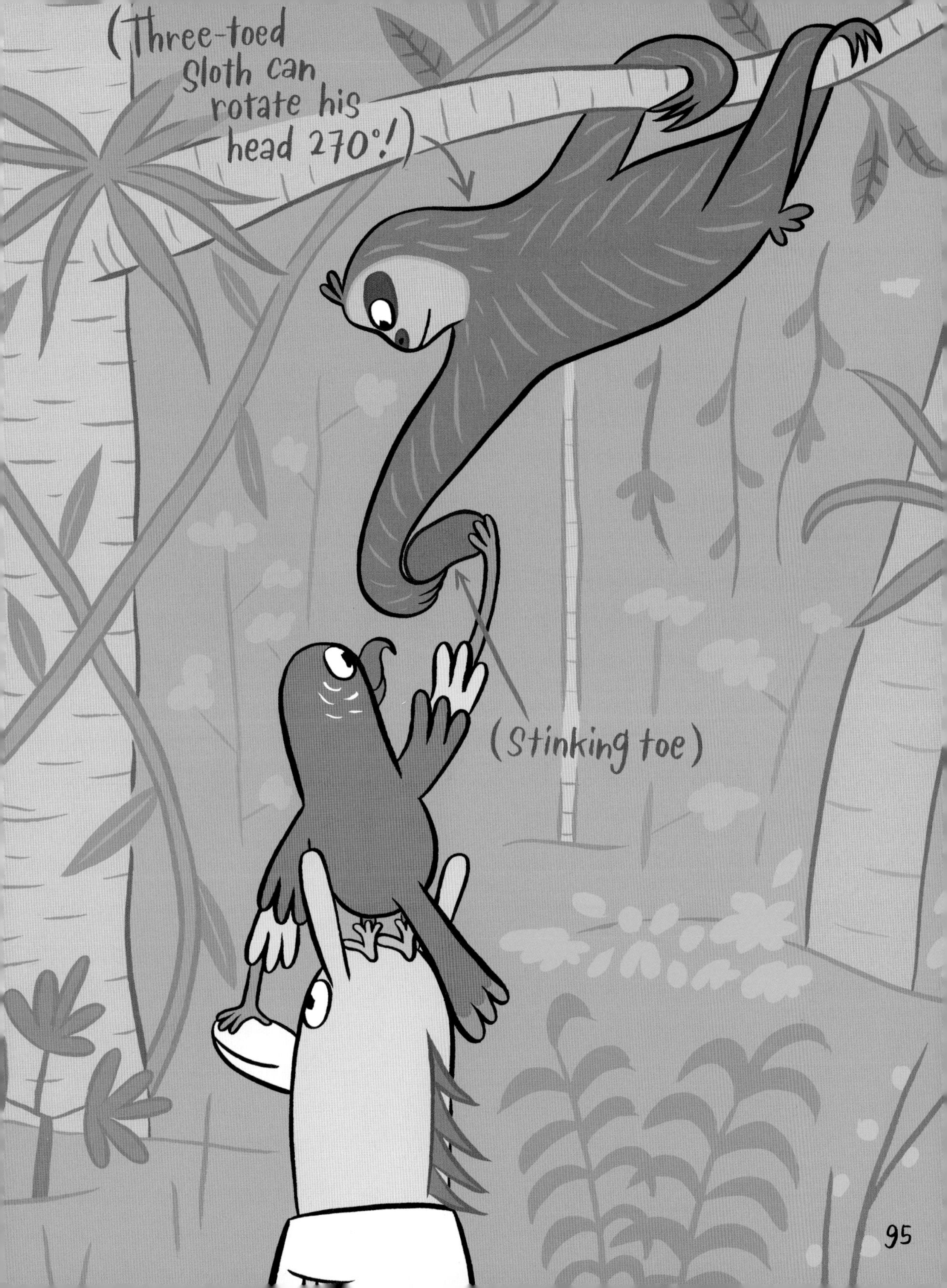
(Three-toed Sloth can rotate his head 270°!)
(Stinking toe)

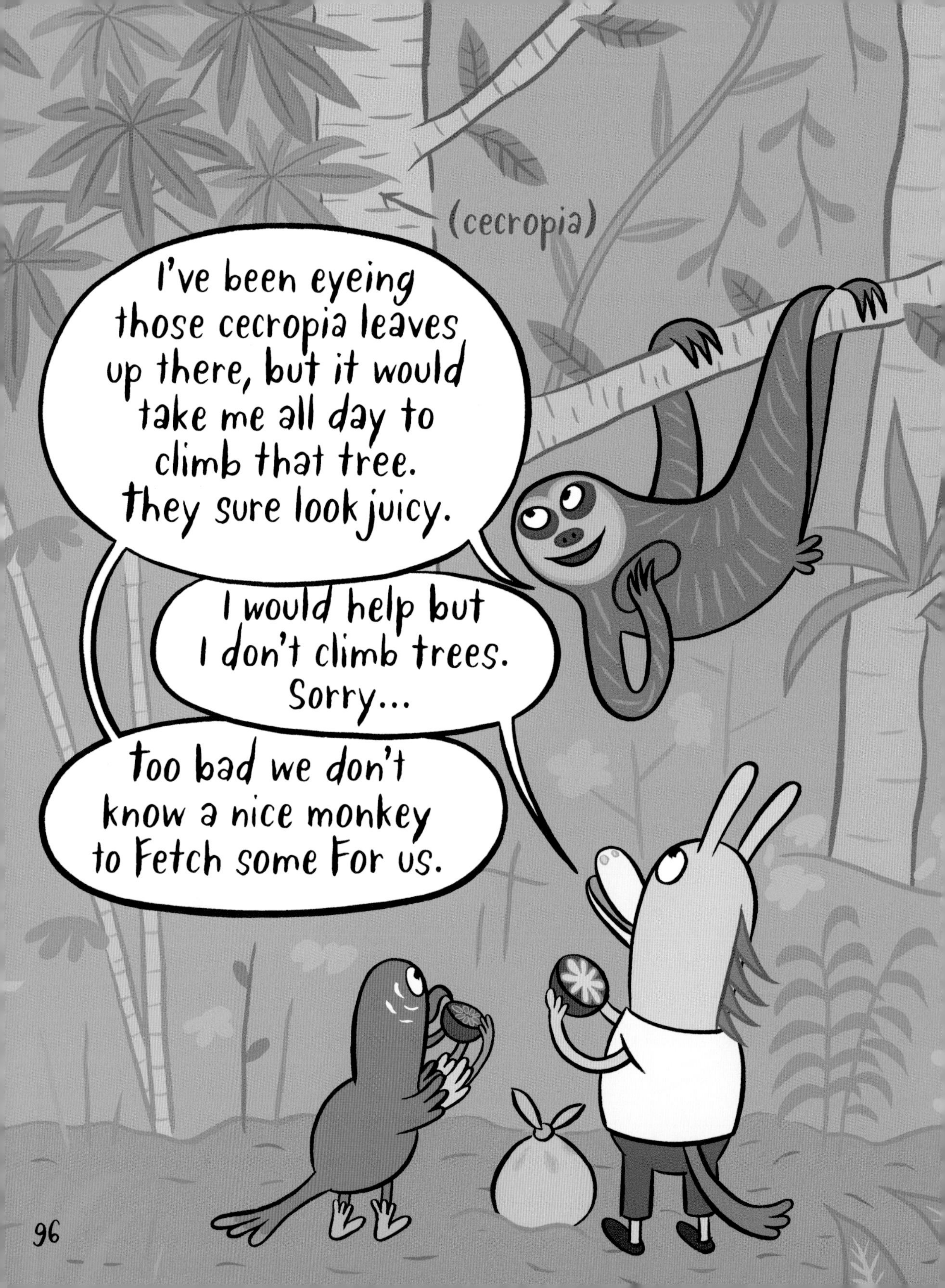
(cecropia)
I've been eyeing those cecropia leaves up there, but it would take me all day to climb that tree. They sure look juicy.
I would help but I don't climb trees. Sorry...
Too bad we don't know a nice monkey to fetch some for us.

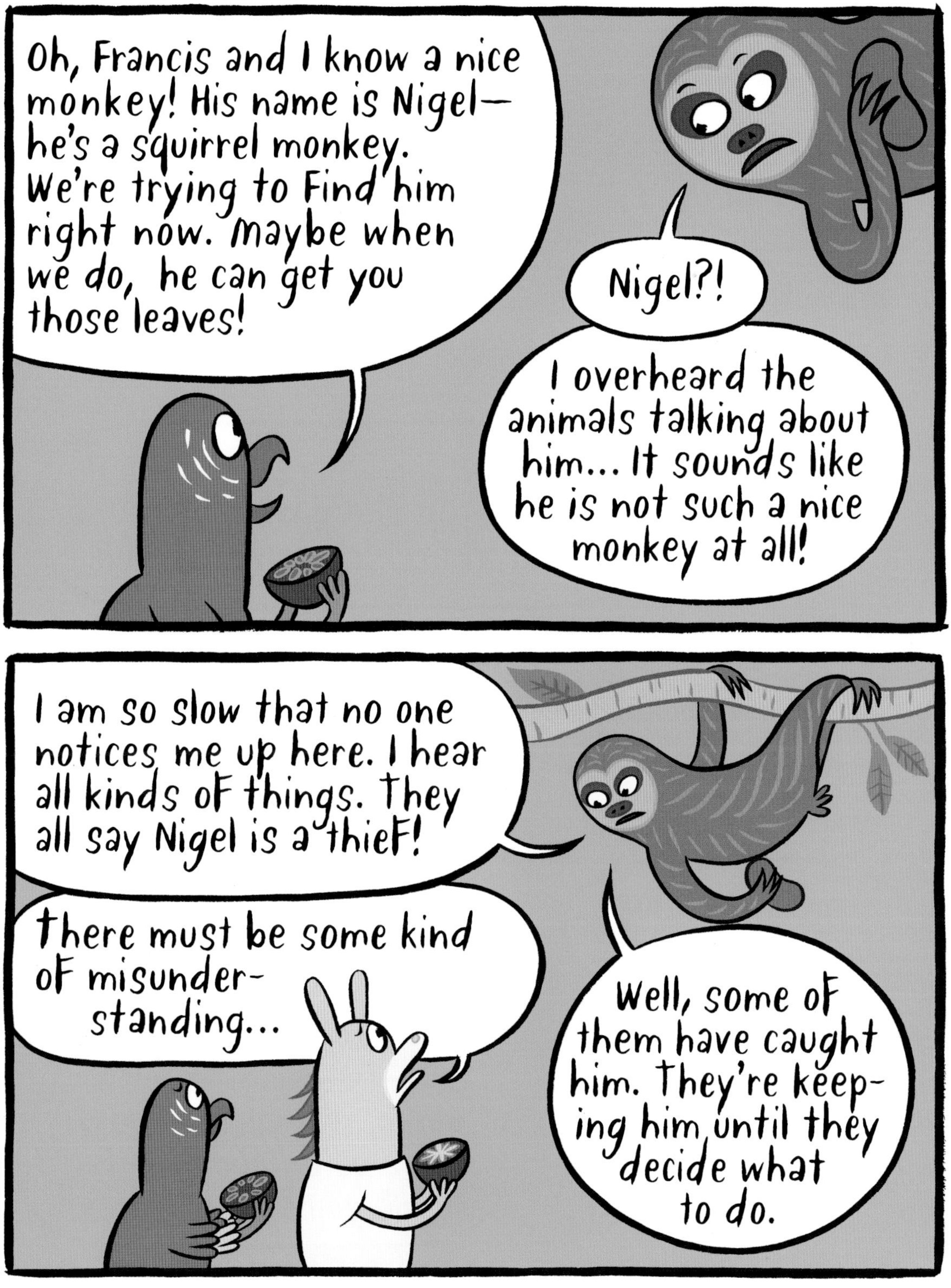
Oh, Francis and I know a nice monkey! His name is Nigel— he's a squirrel monkey. We're trying to find him right now. Maybe when we do, he can get you those leaves!
Nigel?!
I overheard the animals talking about him... It sounds like he is not such a nice monkey at all!
I am so slow that no one notices me up here. I hear all kinds of things. They all say Nigel is a thief!
There must be some kind of misunder-standing...
Well, some of them have caught him. They're keep-ing him until they decide what to do.

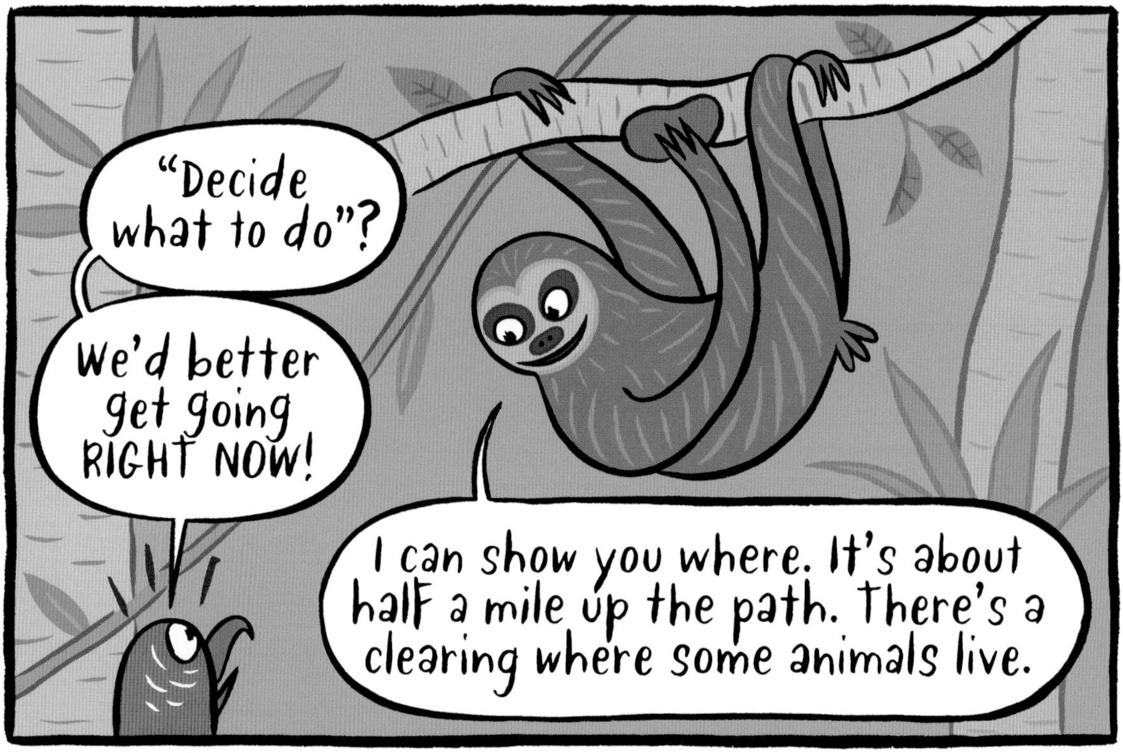
"Decide what to do"?
We'd better get going RIGHT NOW!
I can show you where. It's about half a mile up the path. There's a clearing where some animals live.

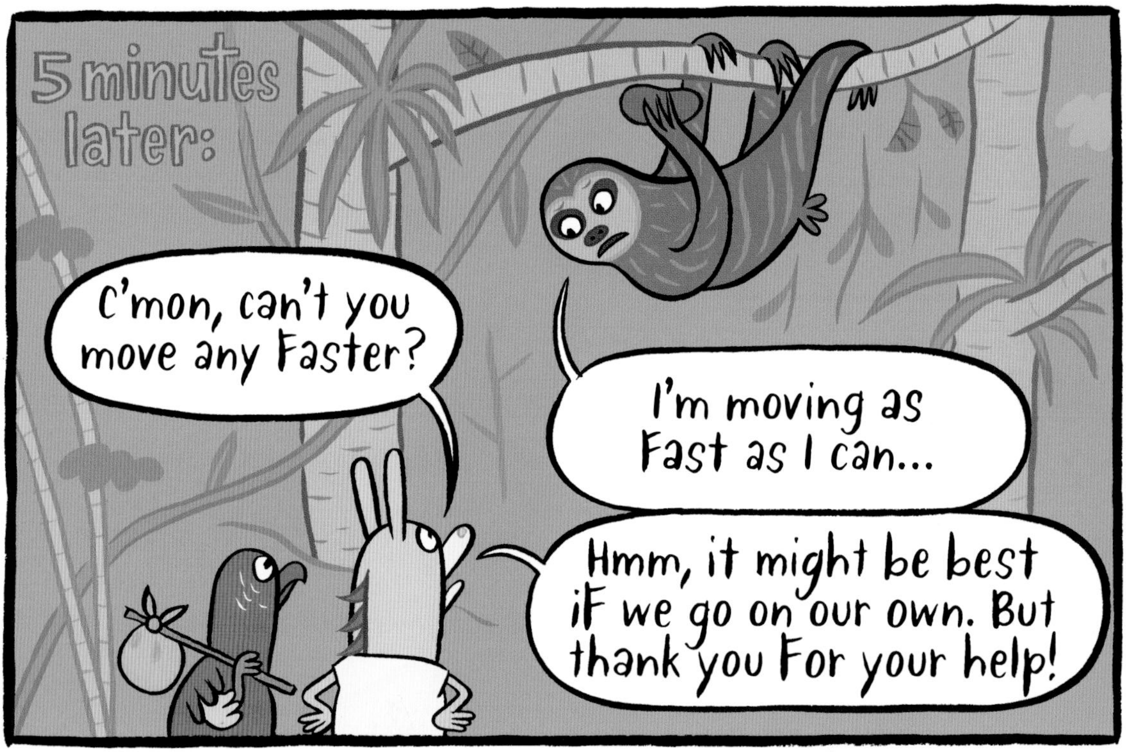
5 minutes later:
C'mon, can't you move any faster?
I'm moving as fast as I can...
Hmm, it might be best if we go on our own. But thank you for your help!

Francis and Rhoda hustled up the path.

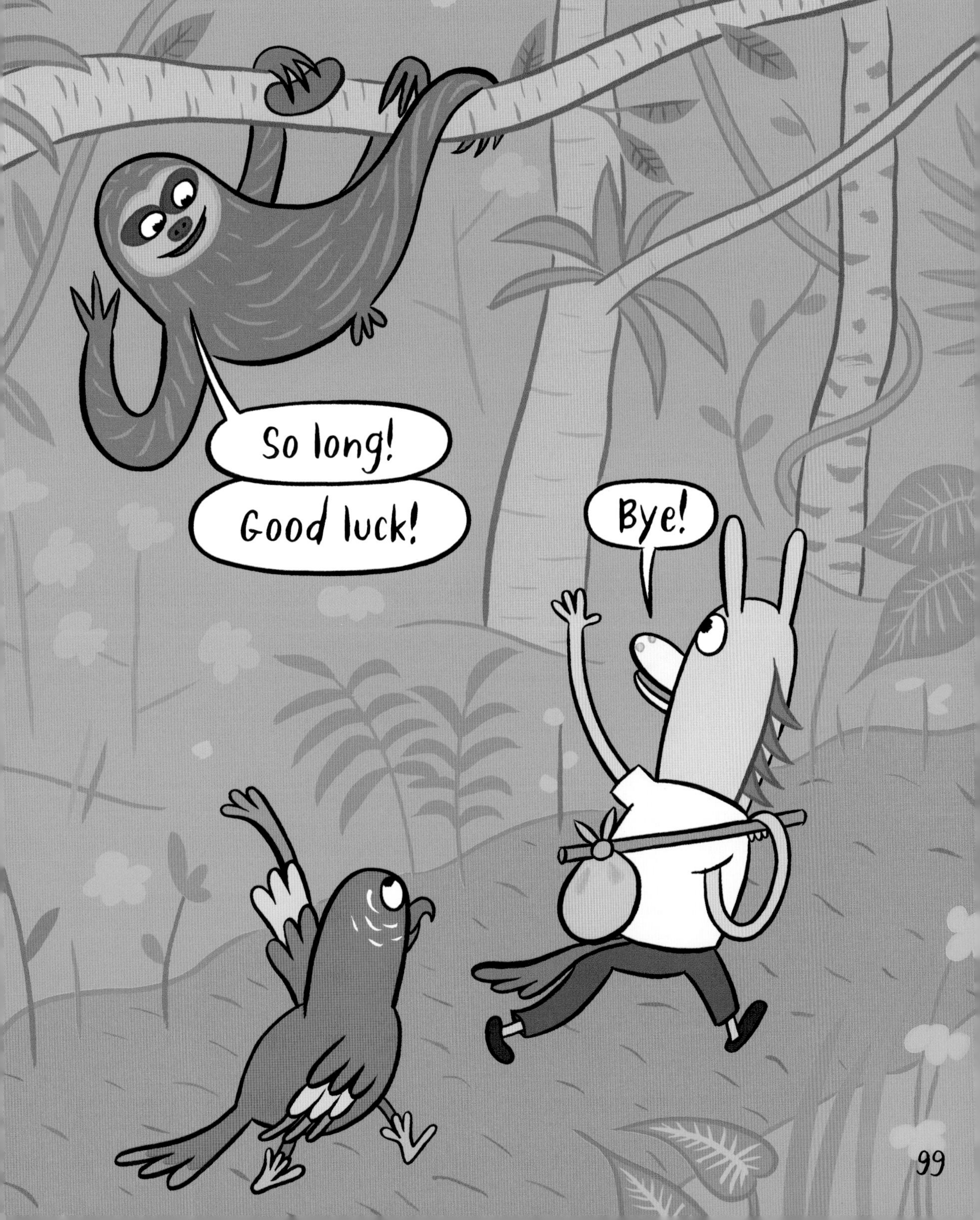
So long!
Good luck!
Bye!

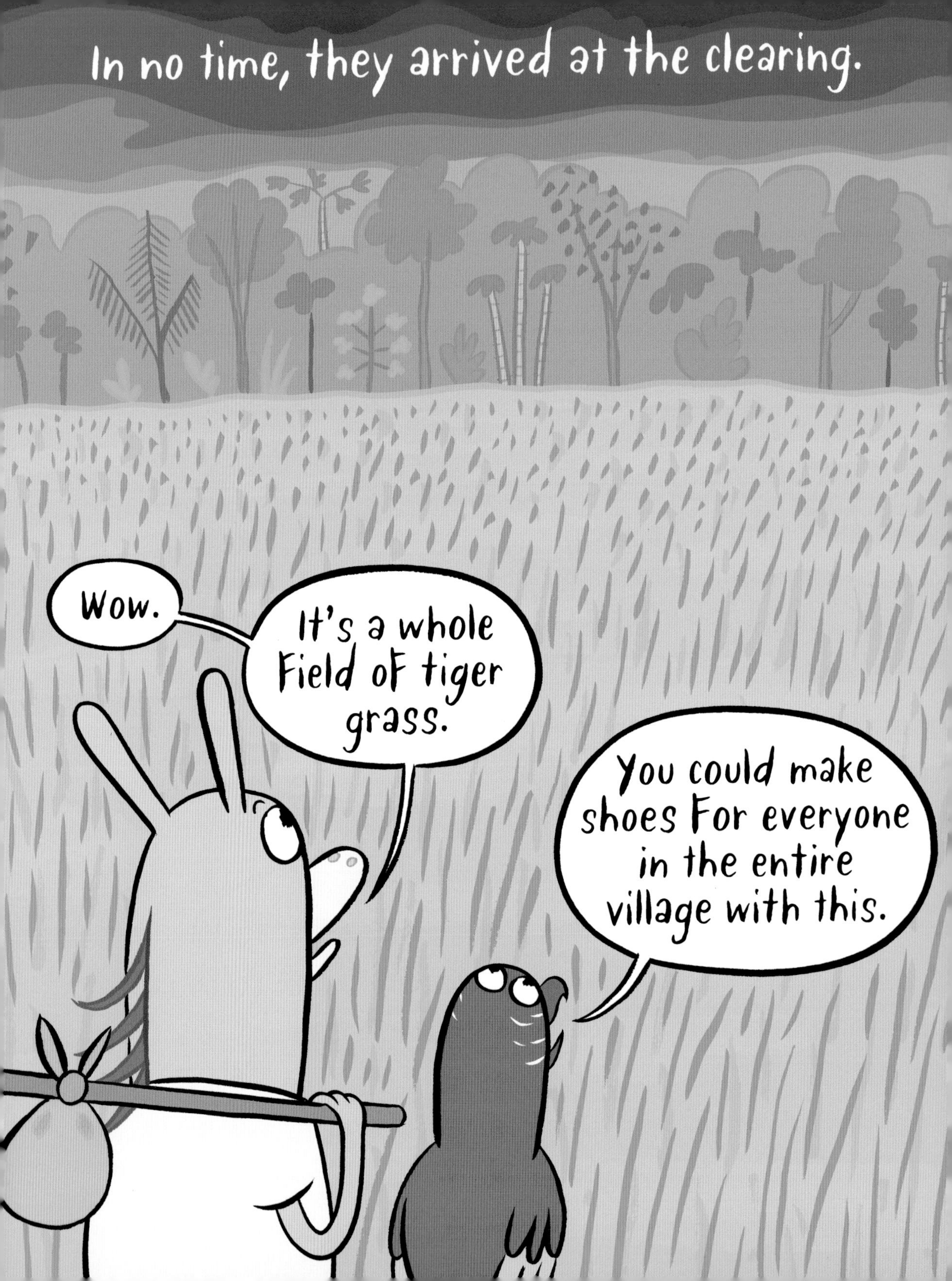
In no time, they arrived at the clearing.
Wow.
It's a whole Field of tiger grass.
You could make shoes For everyone in the entire village with this.

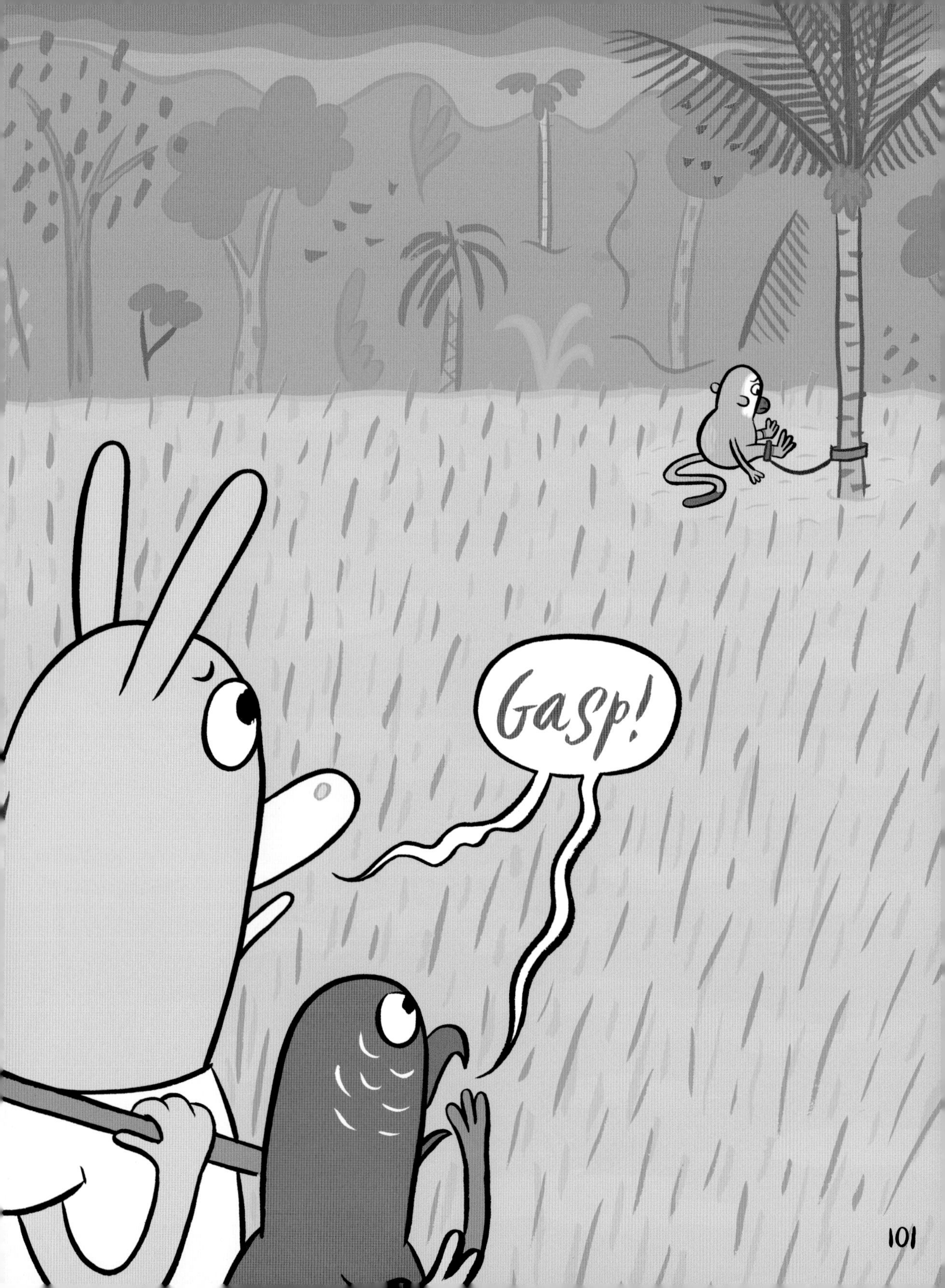
Gasp!

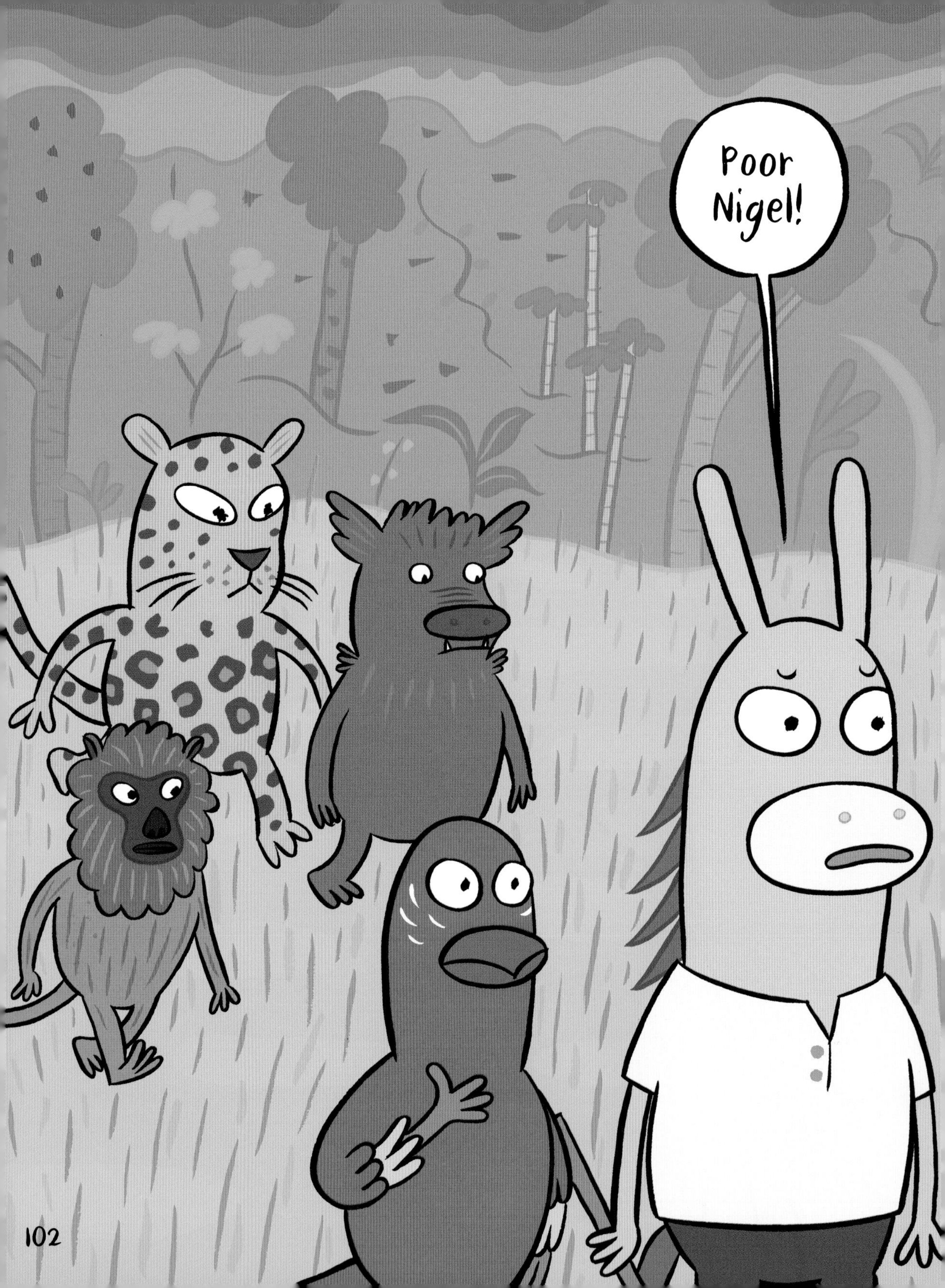
Poor Nigel!

Chapter Five

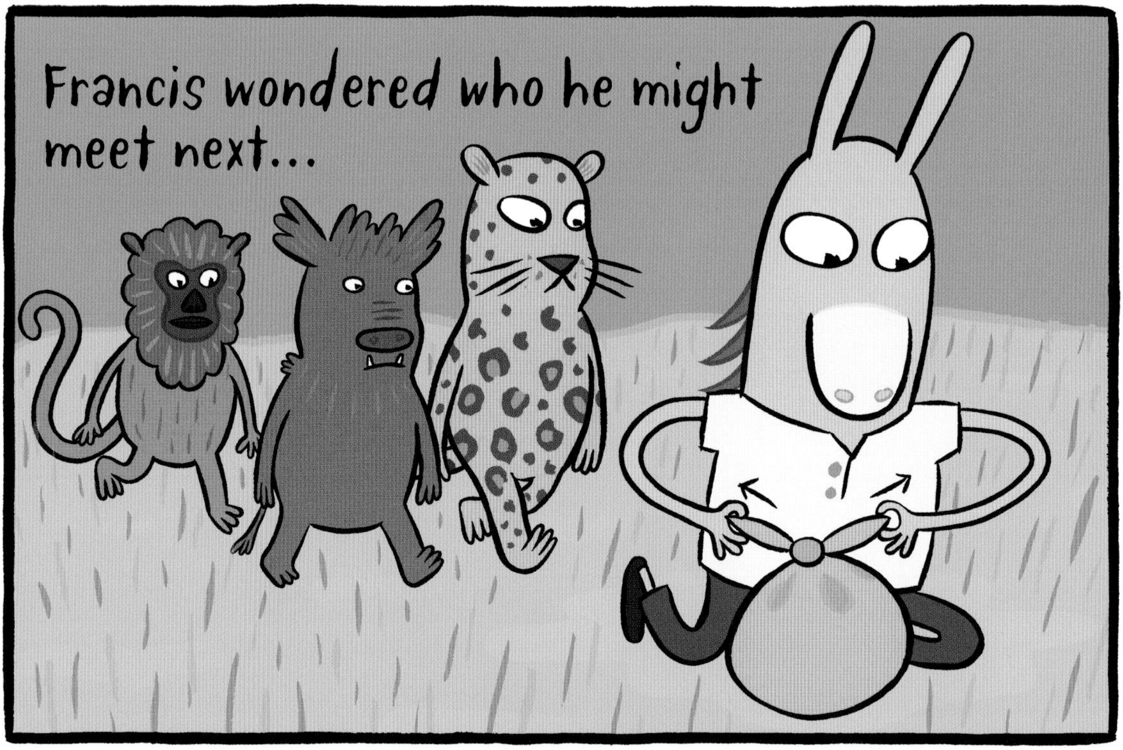
Francis wondered who he might meet next...

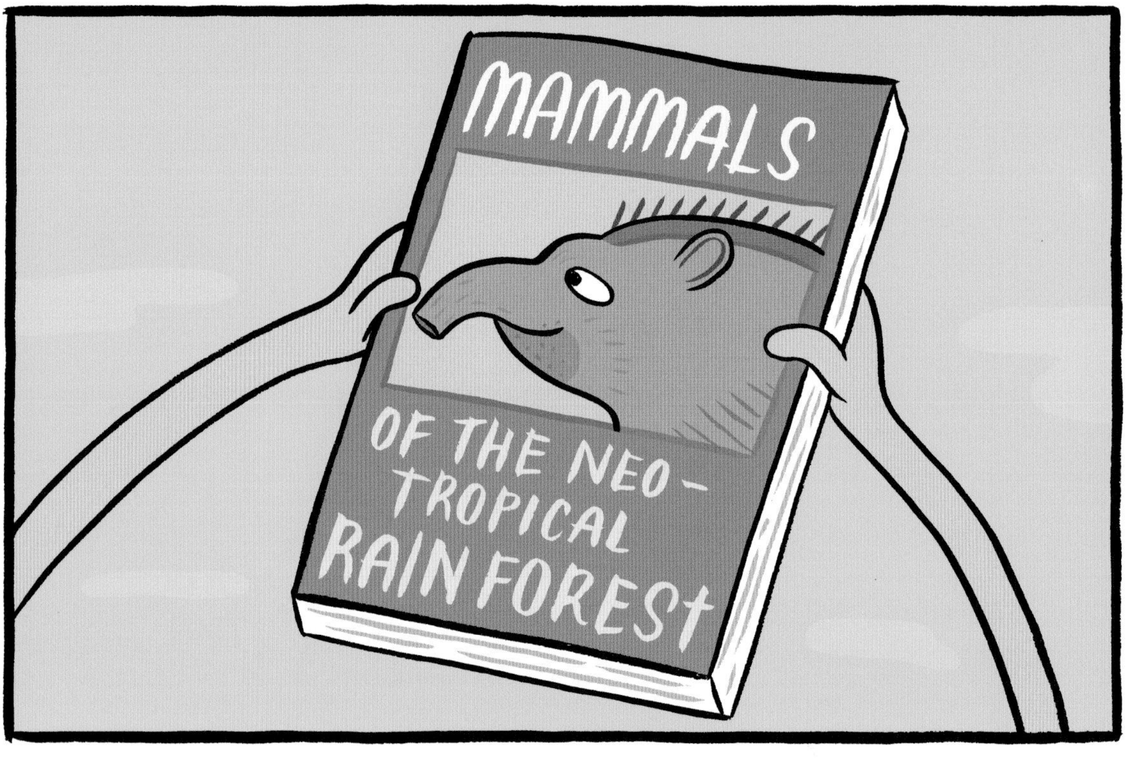
MAMMALS
OF THE NEO-TROPICAL RAIN FOREST

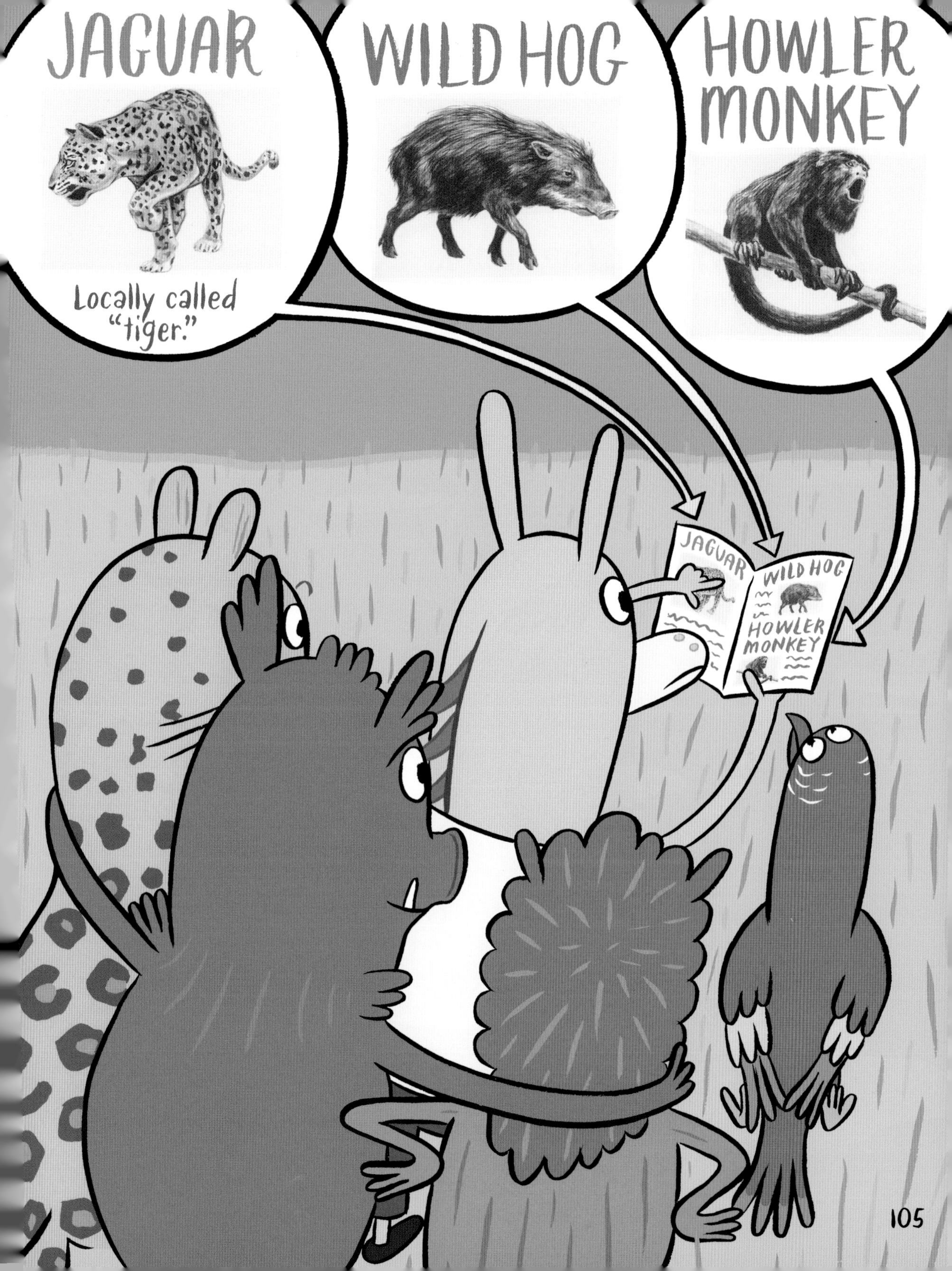
JAGUAR
Locally called "tiger."
WILD HOG
HOWLER MONKEY
JAGUAR
WILD HOG
HOWLER MONKEY

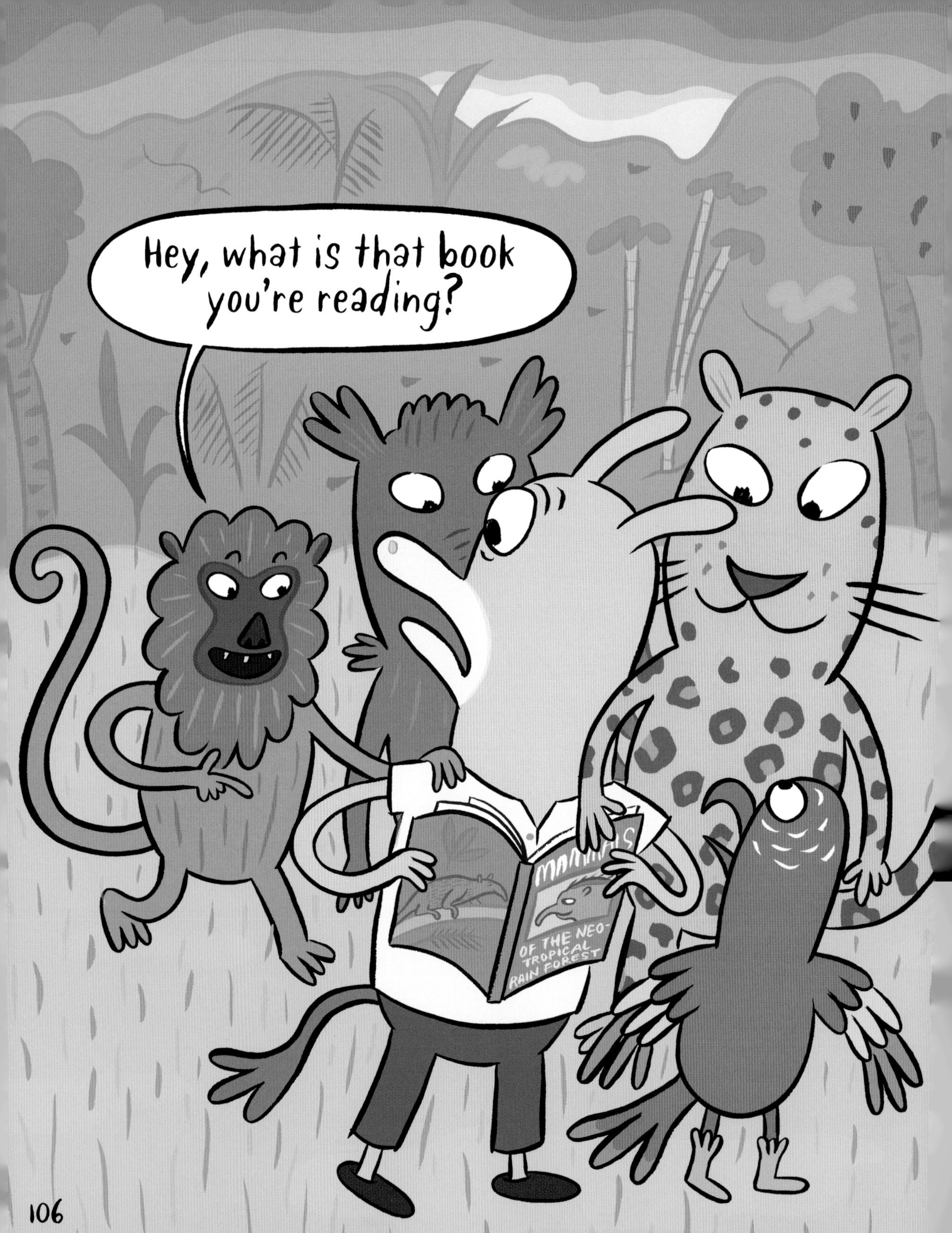
Hey, what is that book you're reading?
OF THE NEO-TROPICAL RAIN FOREST

Rhoda thought she was going to have a heart attack, but instead just passed out. Not wanting to leave her, Francis fell over and played dead.

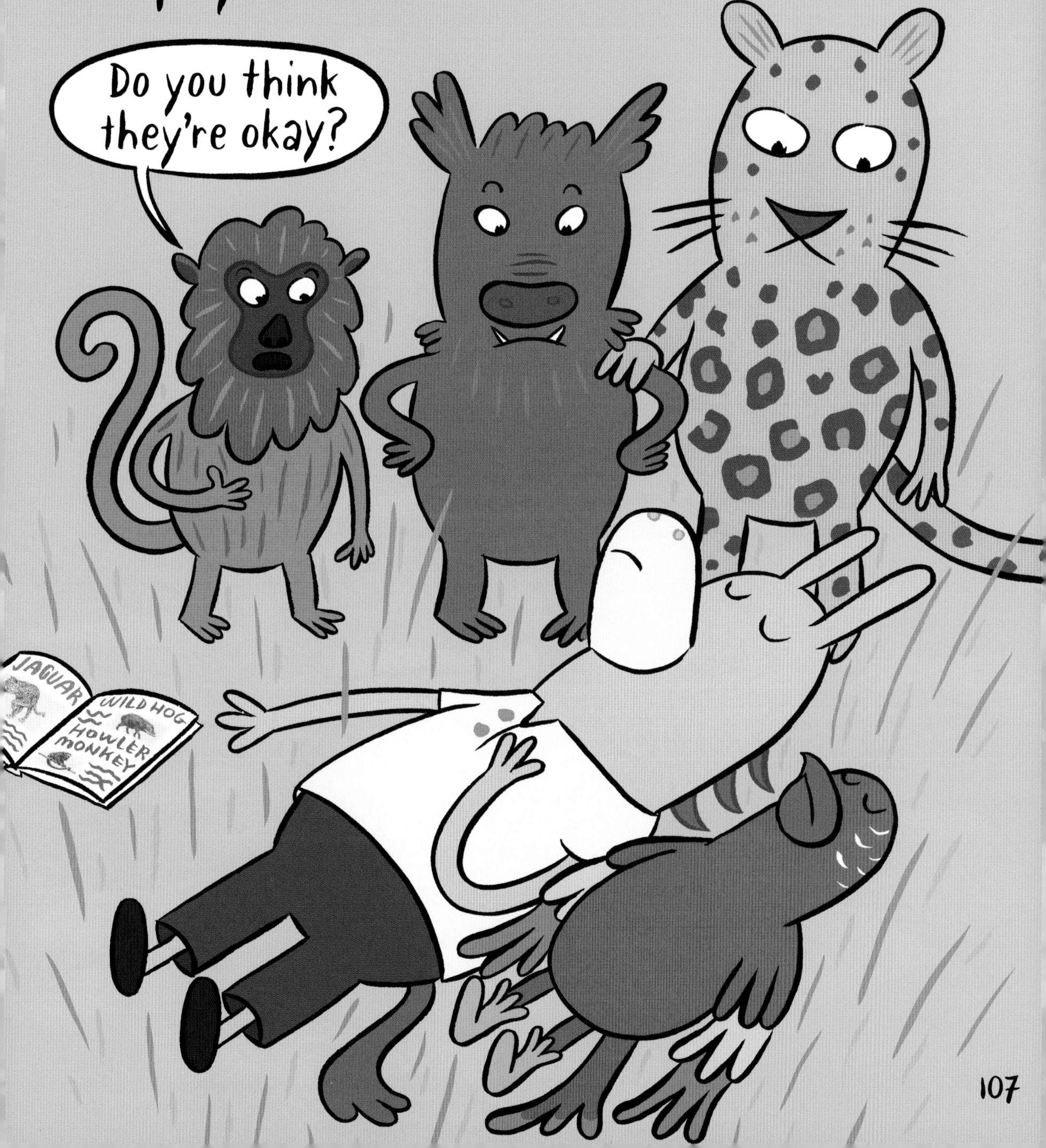
Do you think they're okay?
JAGUAR
WILD HOG
HOWLER MONKEY

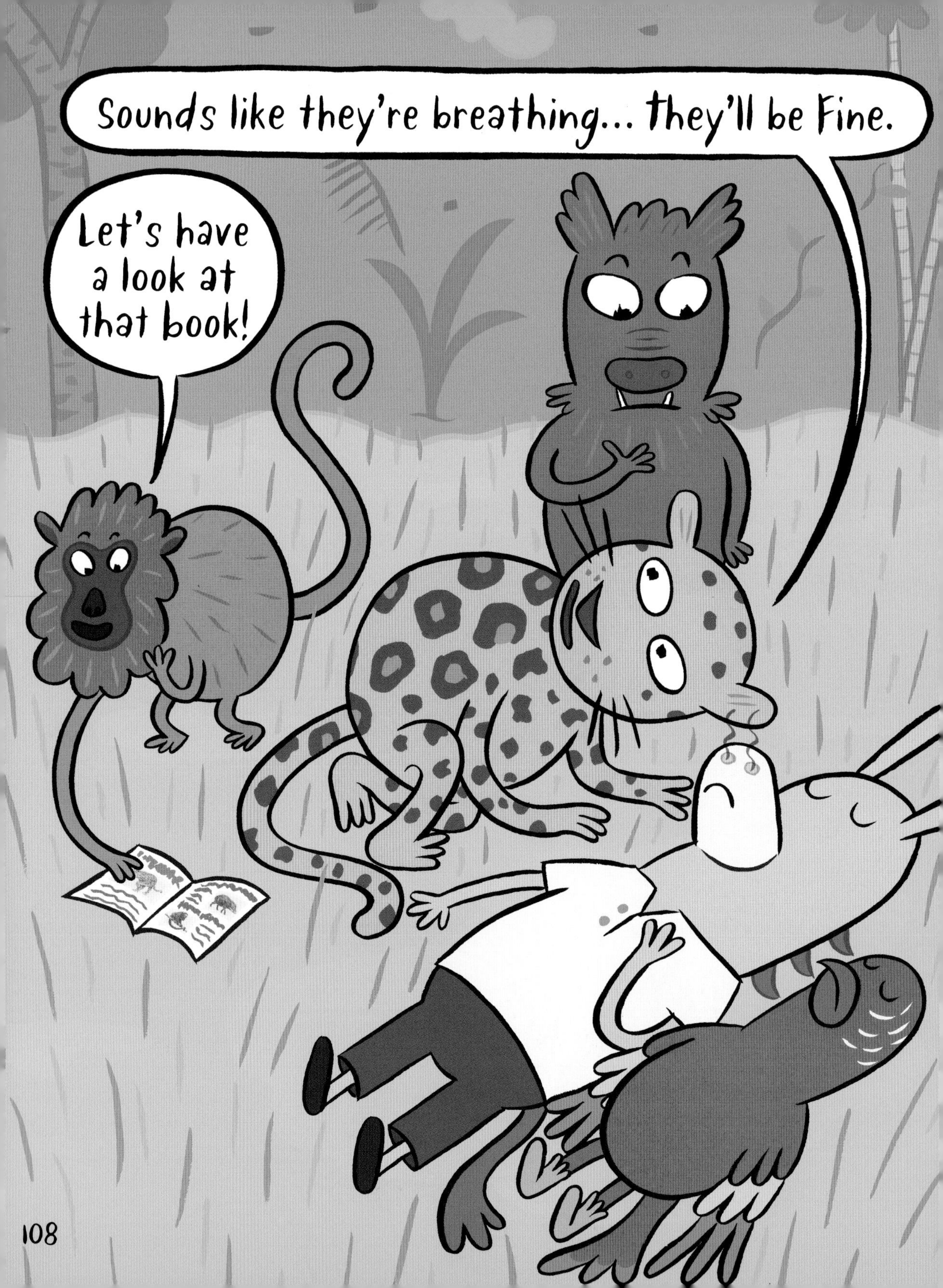
Let's have a look at that book!
Sounds like they're breathing... they'll be fine.

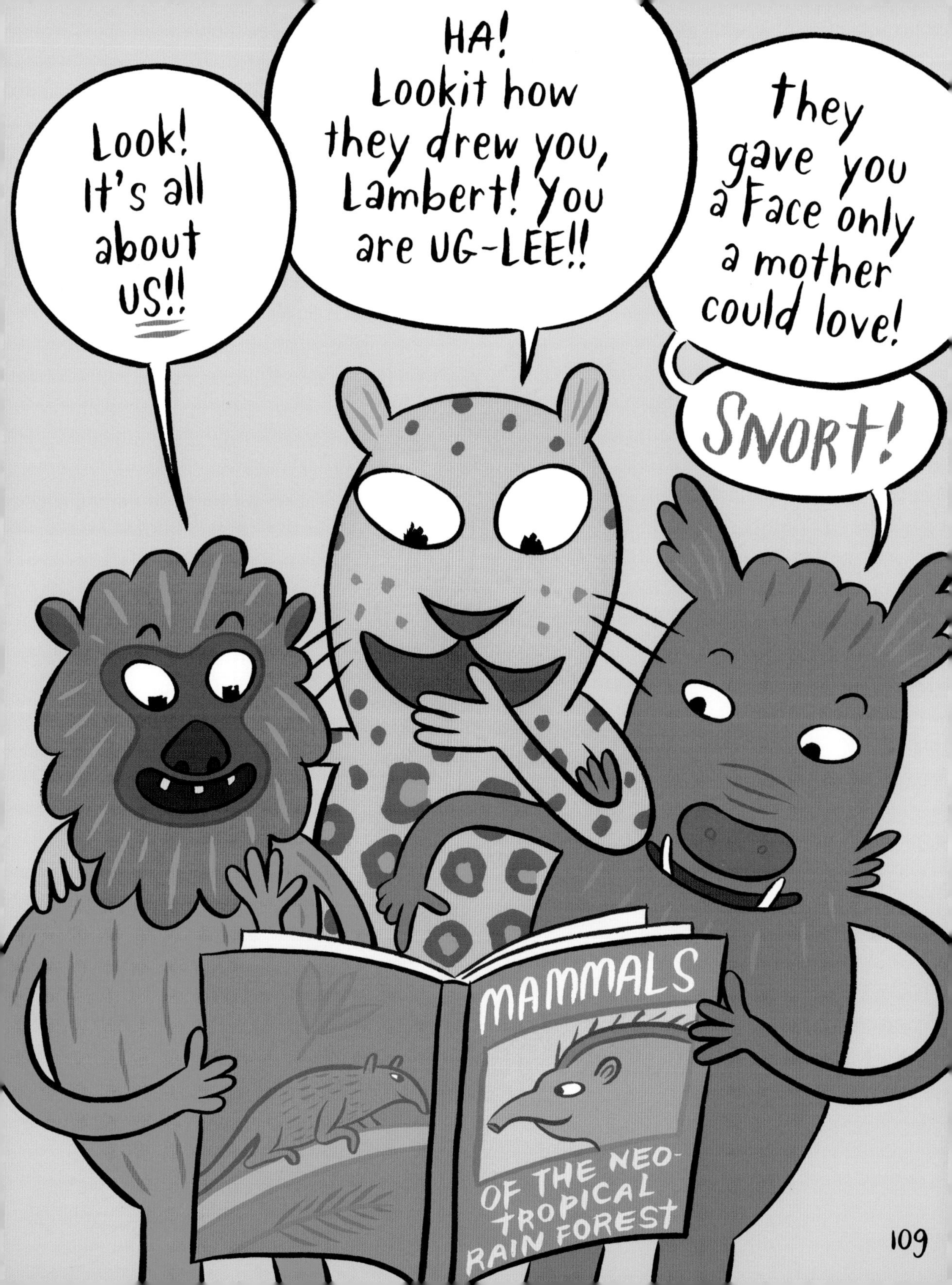
Look! It's all about US!!
HA! Lookit how they drew you, Lambert! You are UG-LEE!!
they gave you a Face only a mother could love!
SNORT!
MAMMALS OF THE NEO-TROPICAL RAIN FOREST

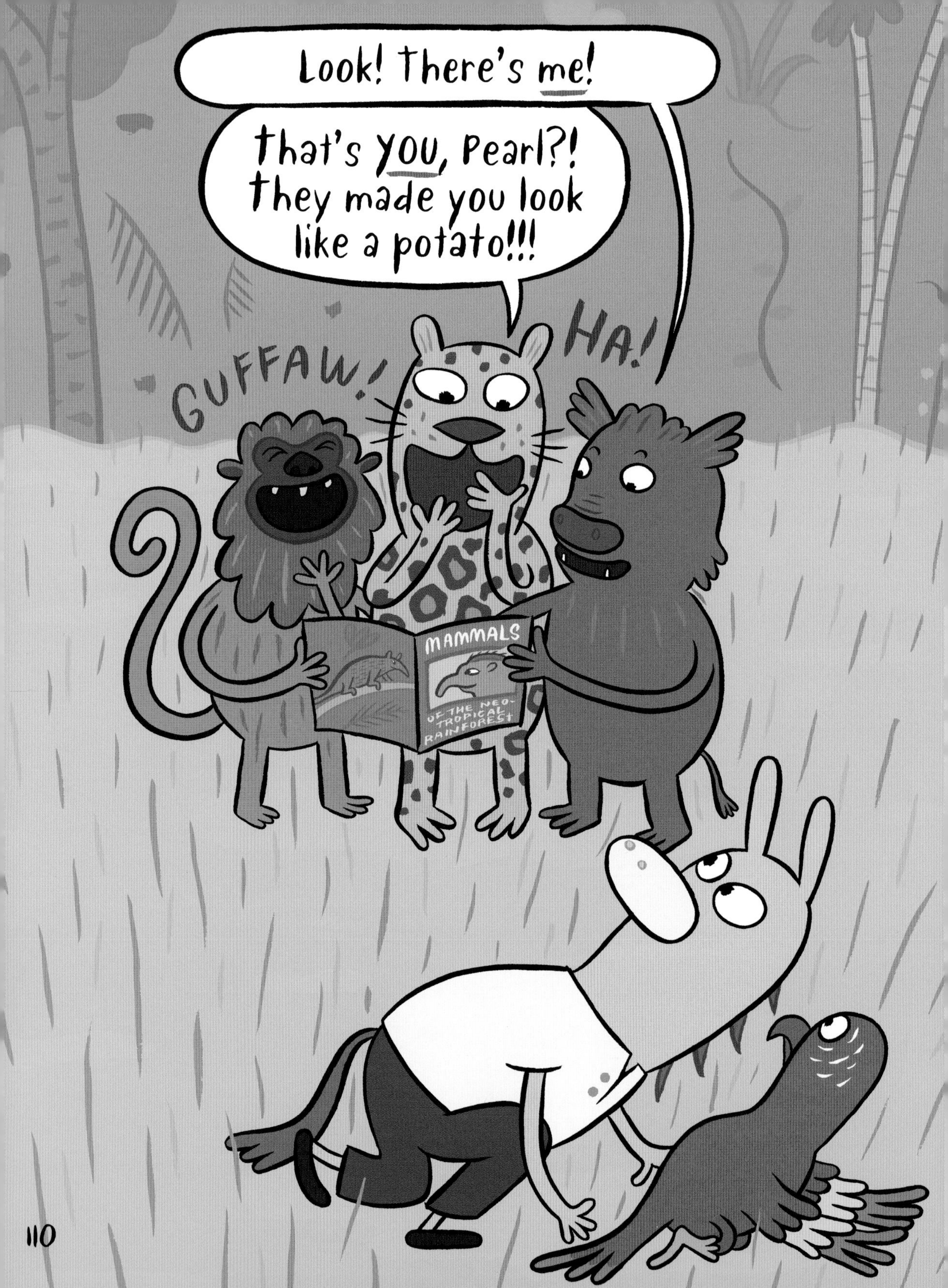
Look! There's me!
That's YOU, Pearl?! They made you look like a potato!!!
GUFFAW!
HA!
MAMMALS OF THE NEO-TROPICAL RAINFOREST

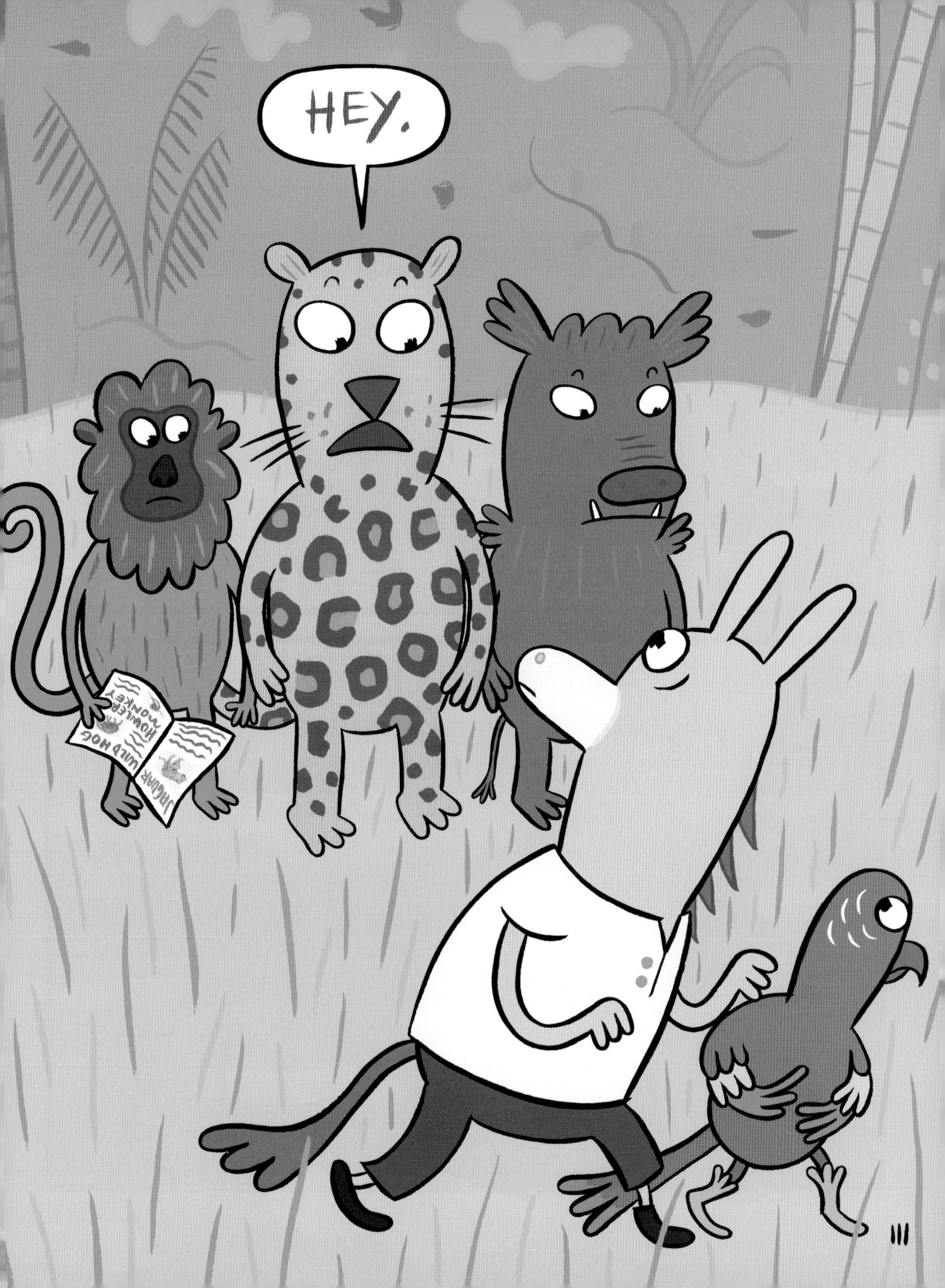
HEY.
WILD HOG
HOWLER MONKEY
JAGUAR

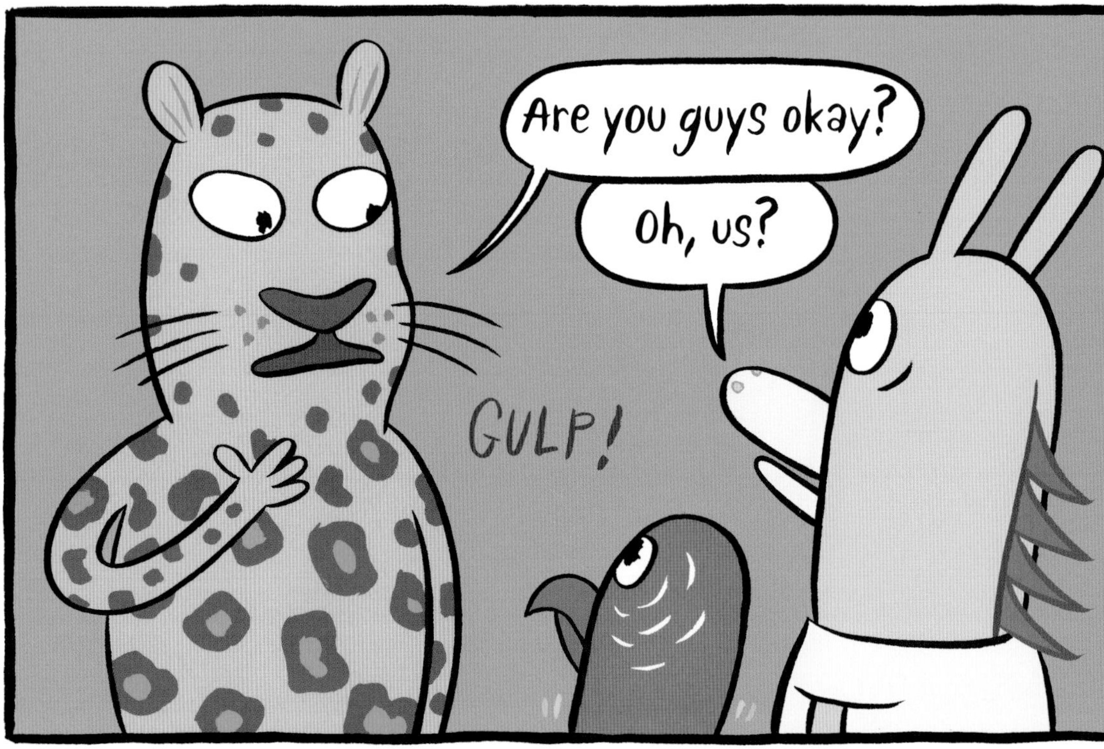
Are you guys okay?
Oh, us?
GULP!

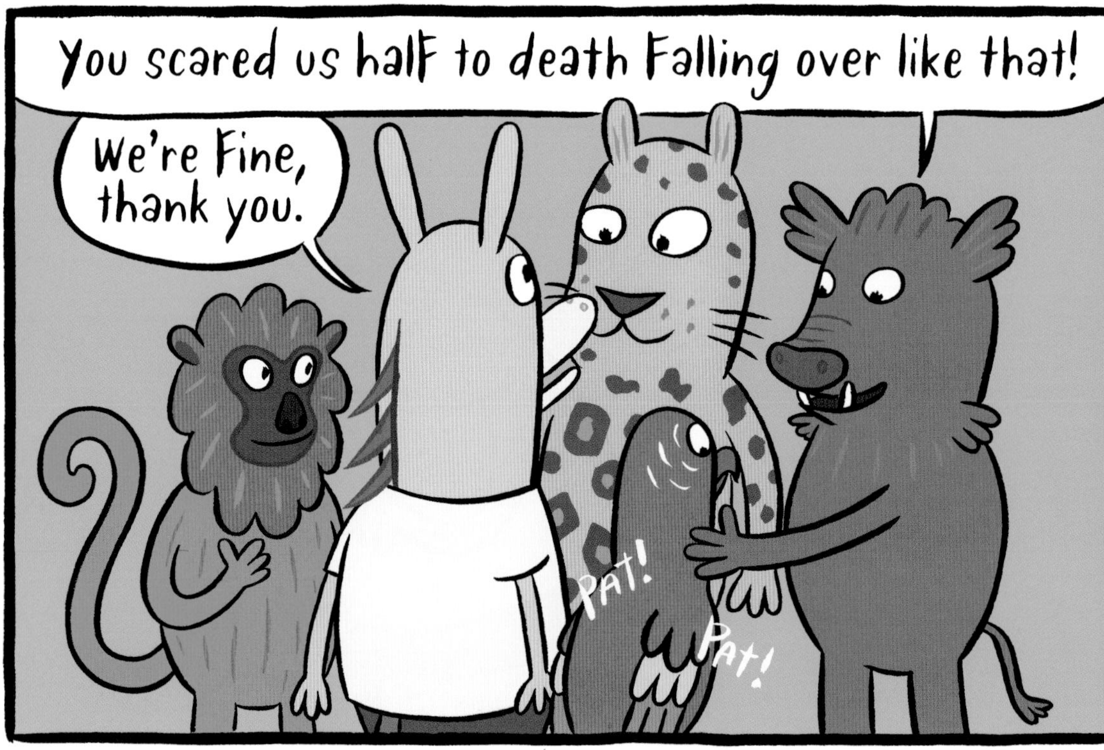
You scared us half to death falling over like that!
We're fine, thank you.
PAT!
PAT!

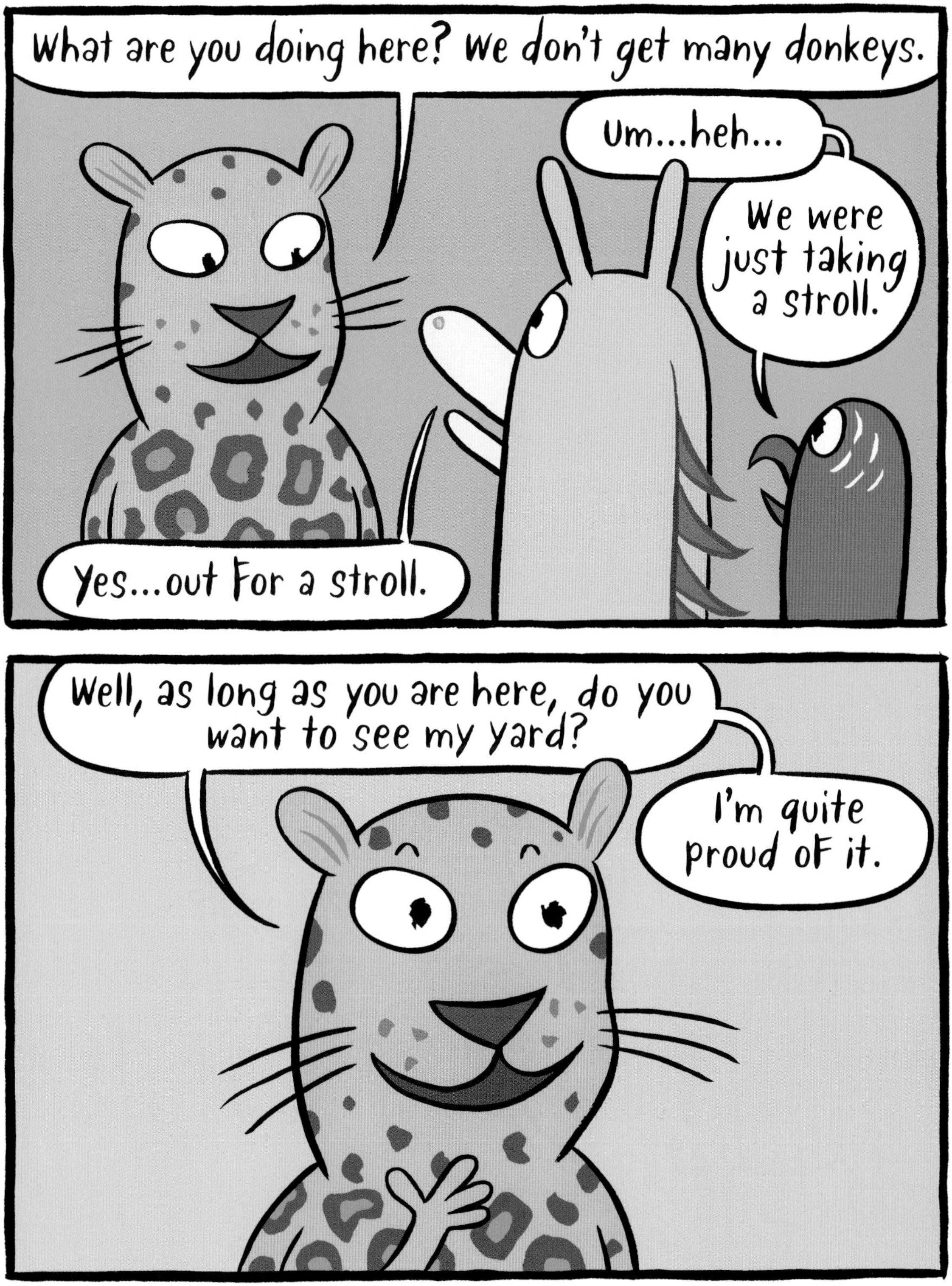
What are you doing here? We don't get many donkeys.
Um...heh...
We were just taking a stroll.
Yes...out for a stroll.
Well, as long as you are here, do you want to see my yard?
I'm quite proud of it.

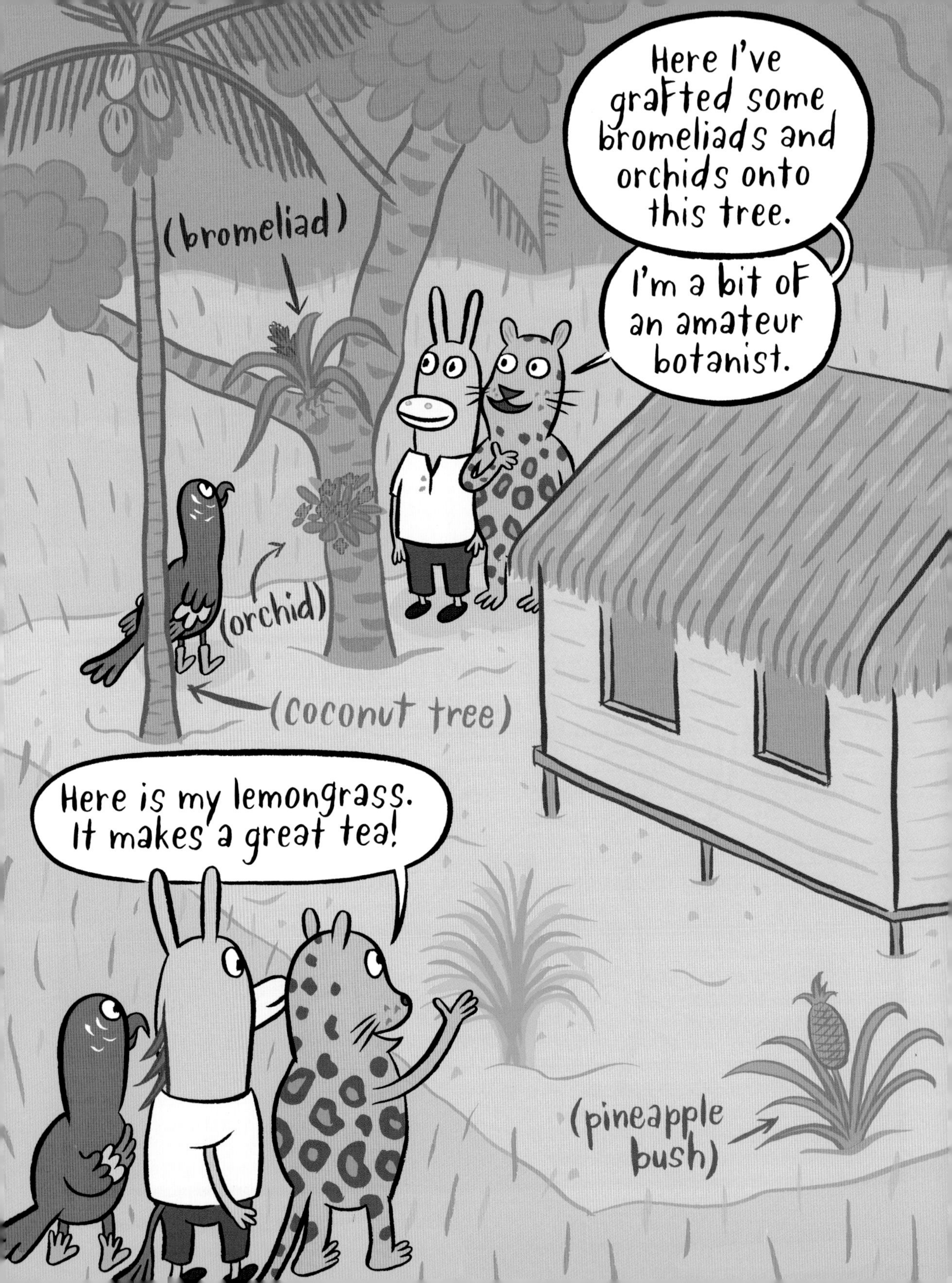
Here I've grafted some bromeliads and orchids onto this tree.
I'm a bit of an amateur botanist.
(bromeliad)
(orchid)
(coconut tree)
Here is my lemongrass. It makes a great tea!
(pineapple bush)

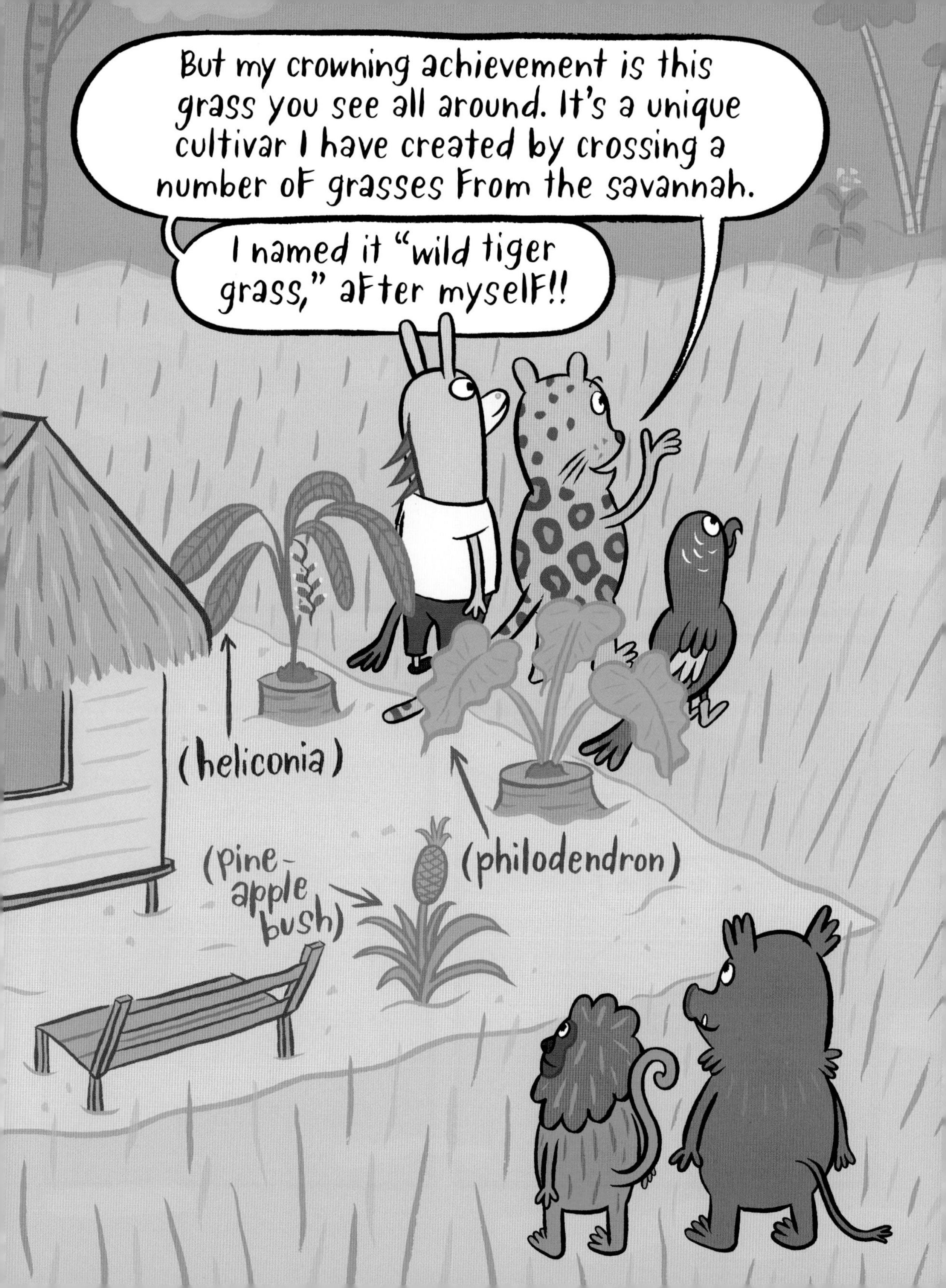
But my crowning achievement is this grass you see all around. It's a unique cultivar I have created by crossing a number of grasses from the savannah.
I named it "wild tiger grass," after myself!!
(heliconia)
(philodendron)
(pine-apple bush)

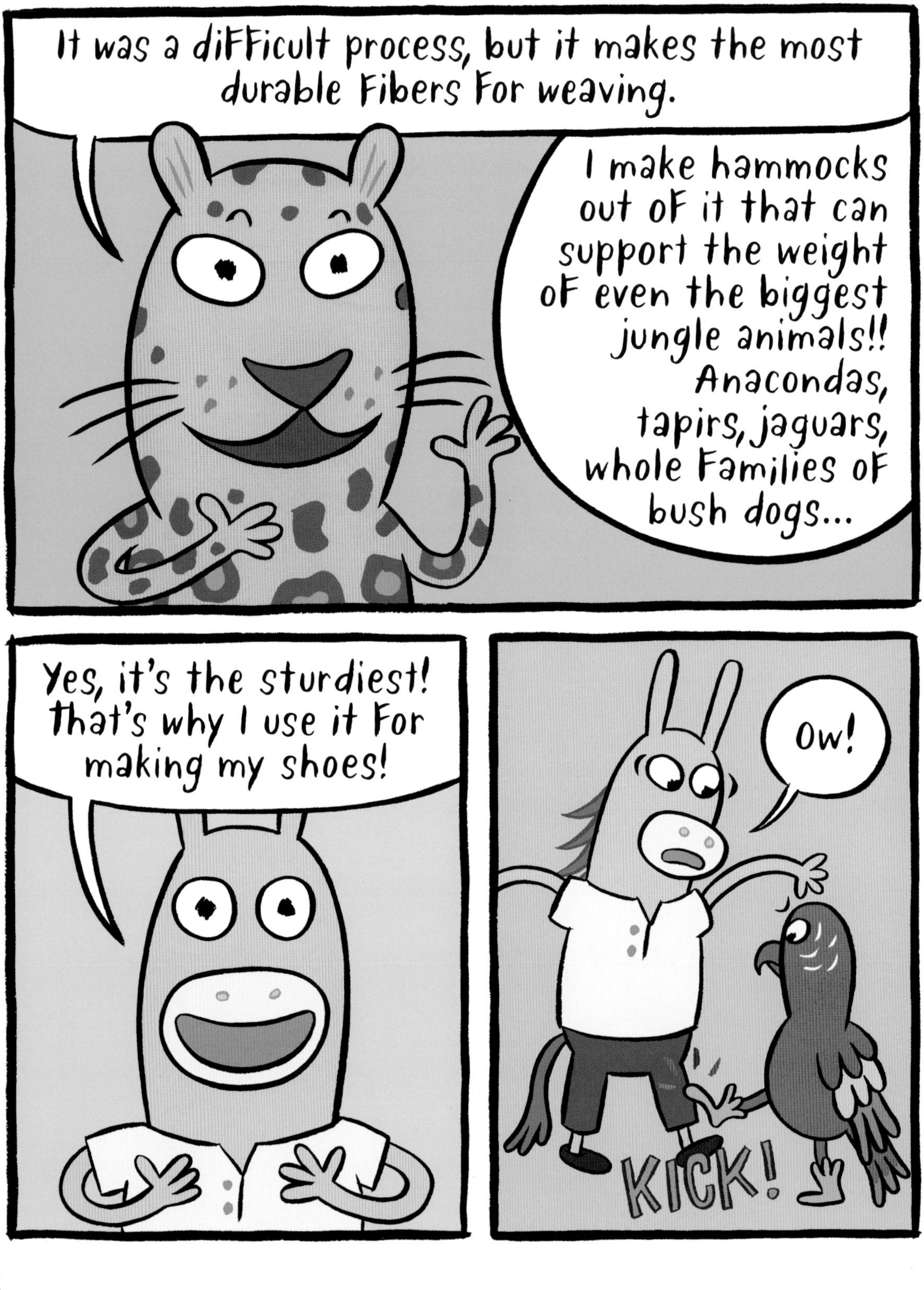
It was a difficult process, but it makes the most durable fibers for weaving.
I make hammocks out of it that can support the weight of even the biggest jungle animals!! Anacondas, tapirs, jaguars, whole families of bush dogs...
Yes, it's the sturdiest! That's why I use it for making my shoes!
Ow!
KICK!

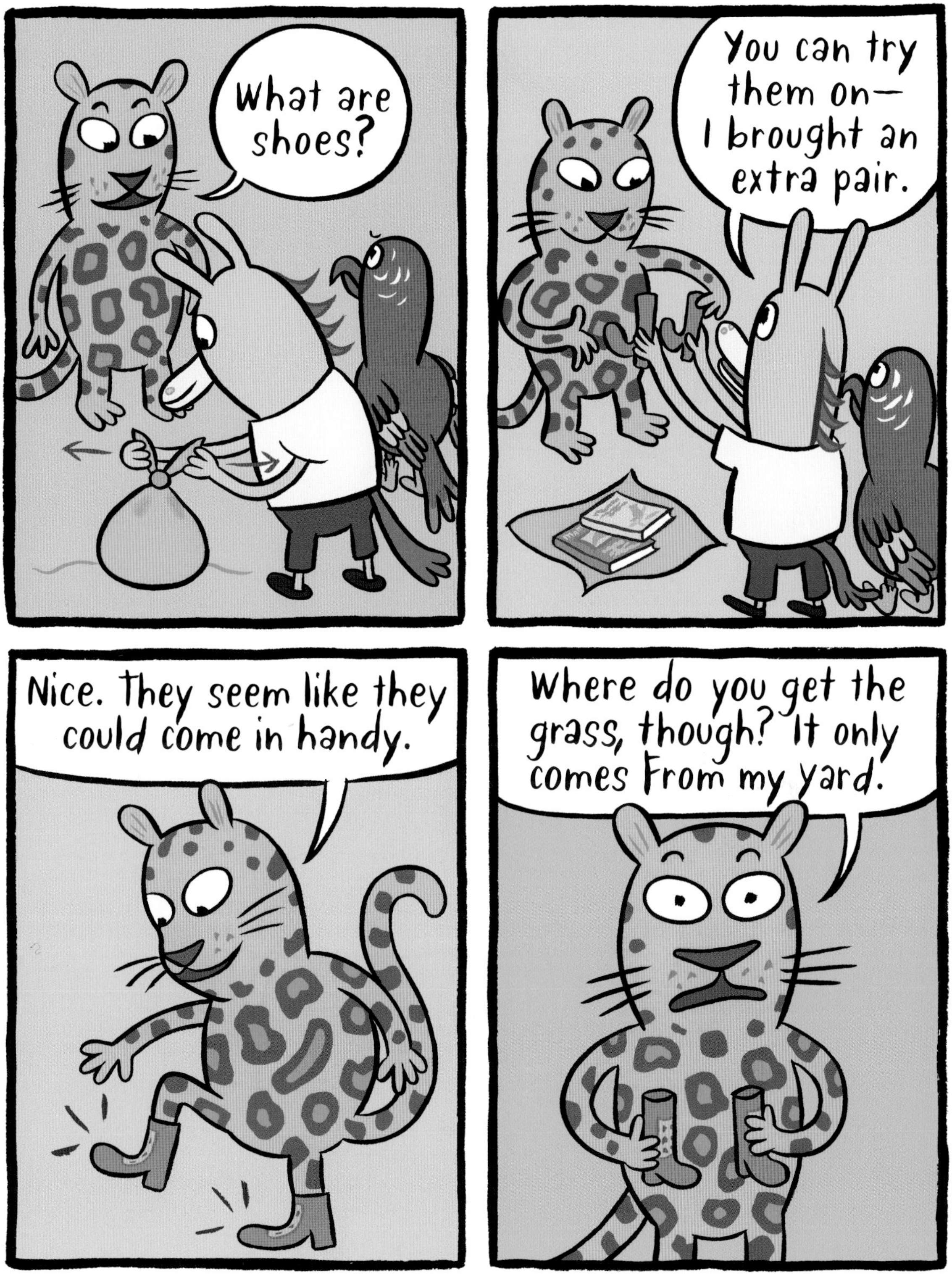
What are shoes?
You can try them on— I brought an extra pair.
Nice. They seem like they could come in handy.
Where do you get the grass, though? It only comes from my yard.

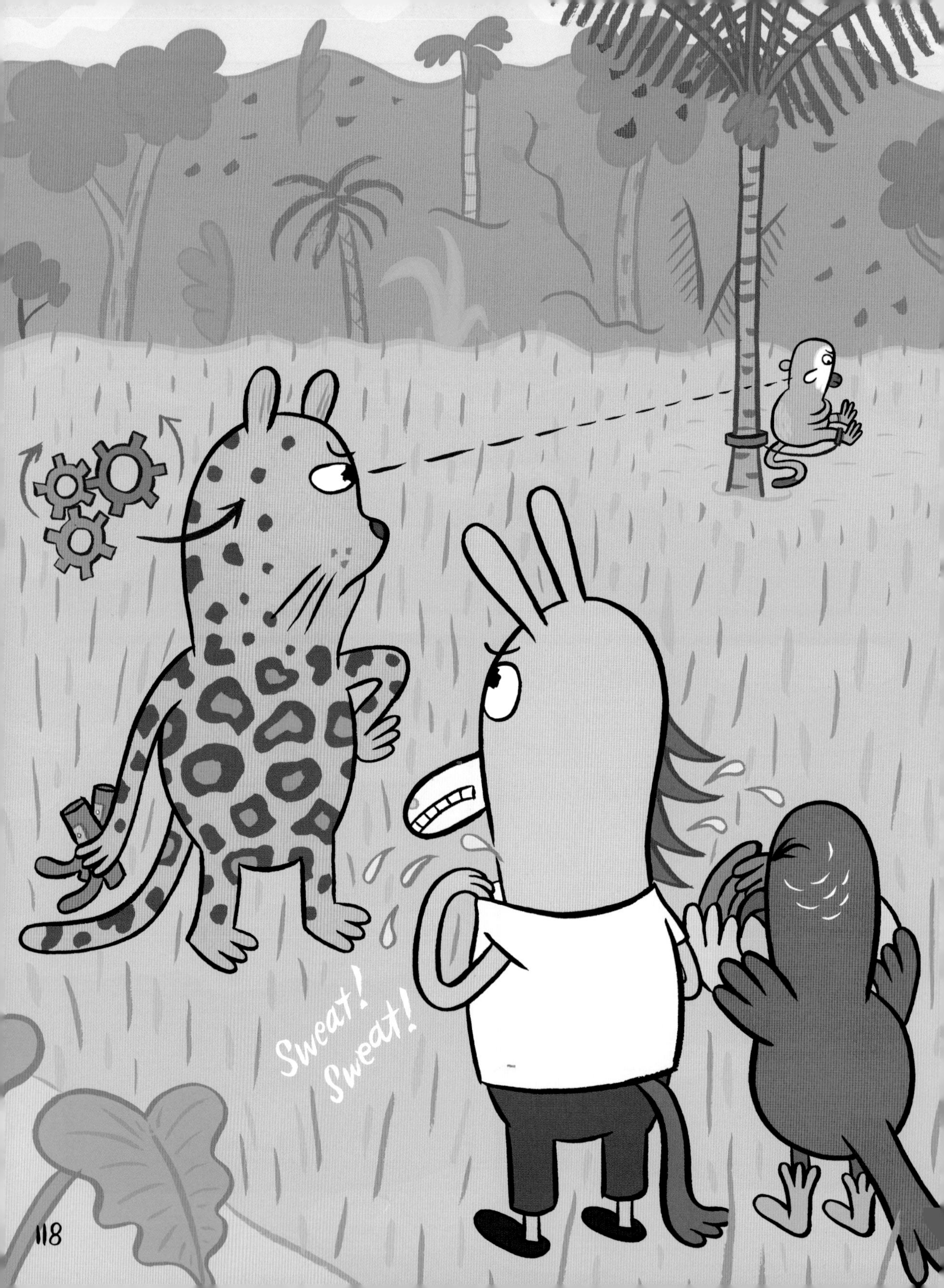
Sweat!
Sweat!

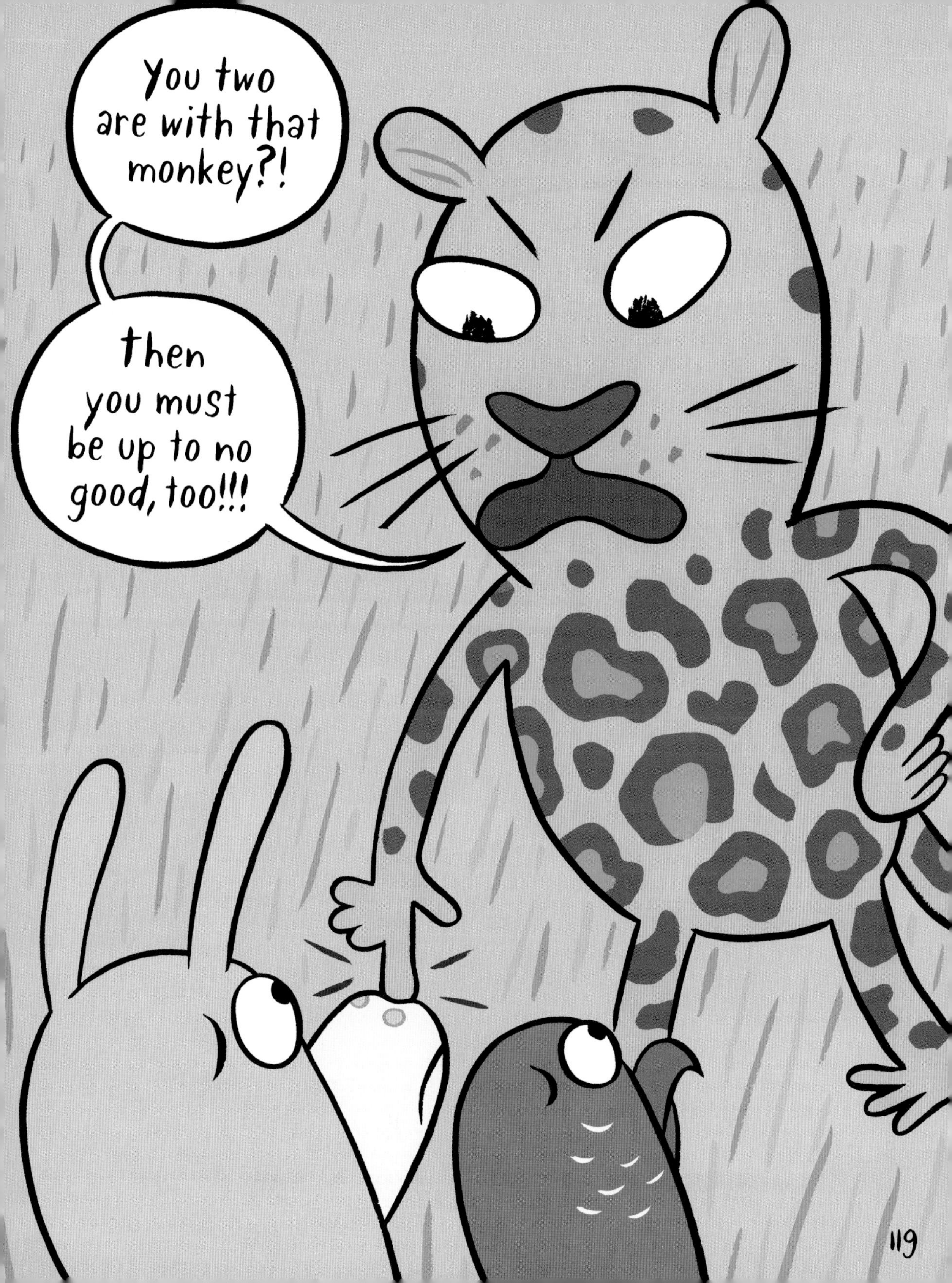
You two are with that monkey?!
then you must be up to no good, too!!!

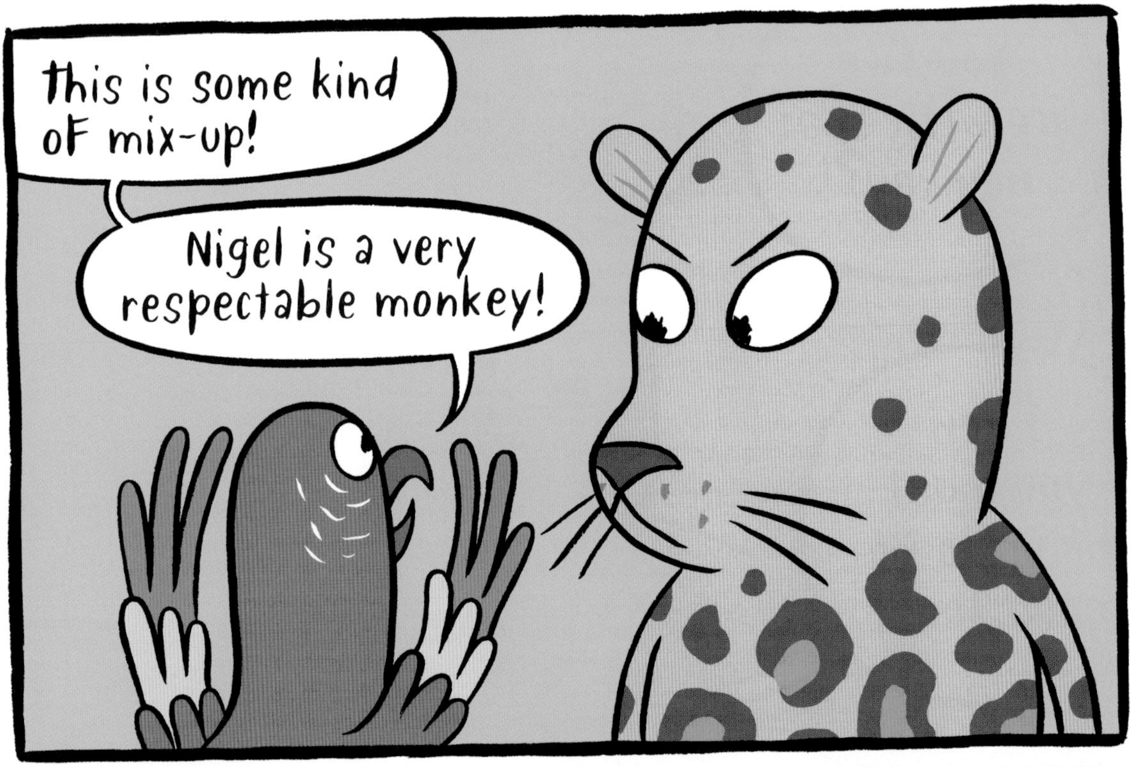
This is some kind of mix-up!
Nigel is a very respectable monkey!

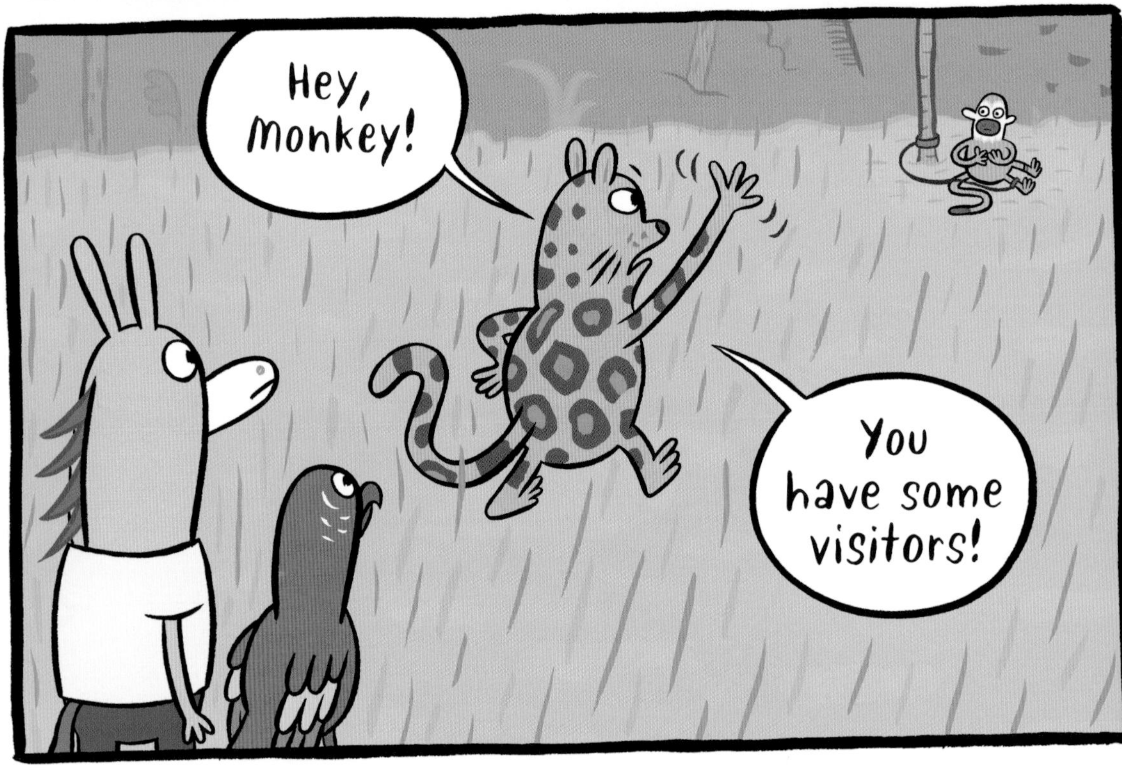
Hey, monkey!
You have some visitors!

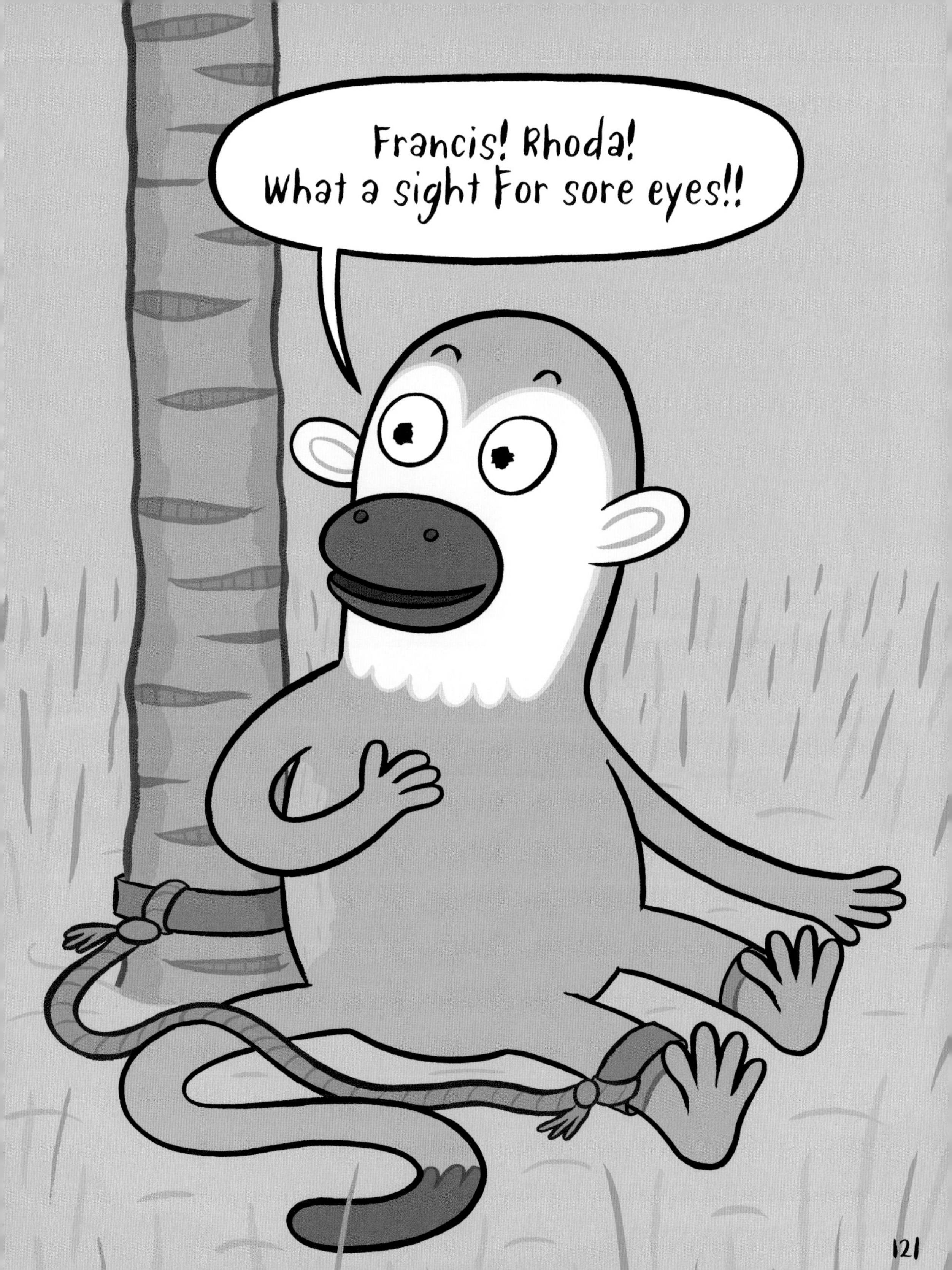
Francis! Rhoda!
What a sight For sore eyes!!

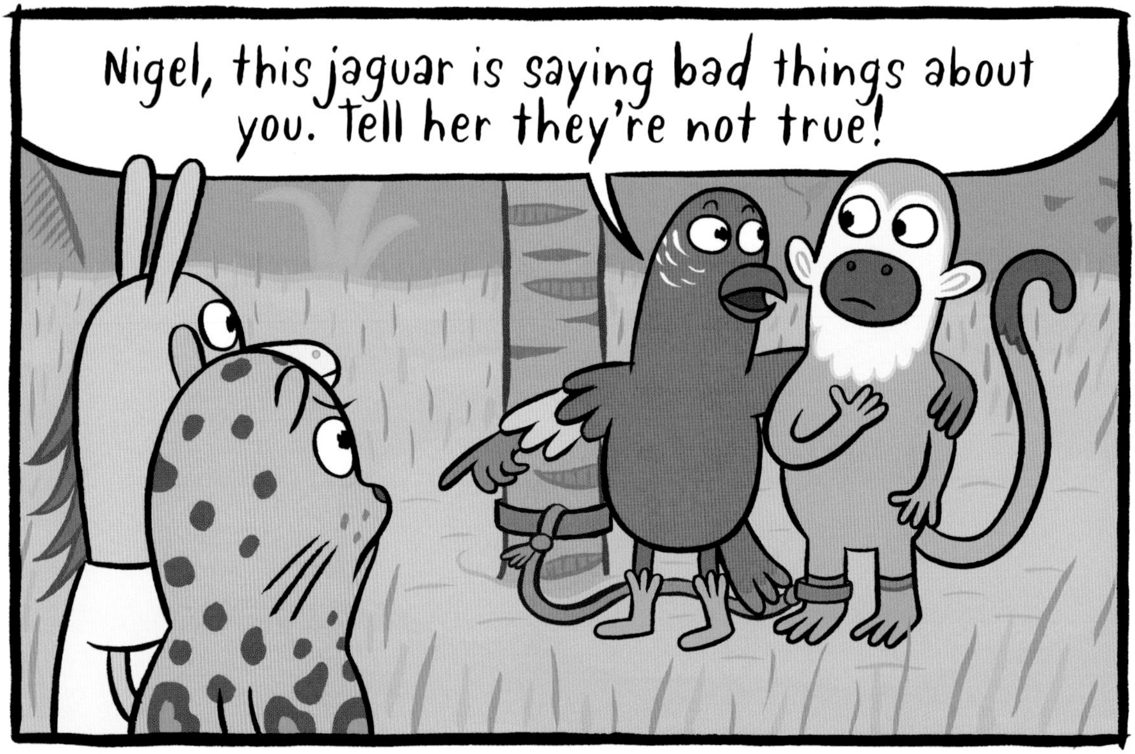
Nigel, this jaguar is saying bad things about you. Tell her they're not true!

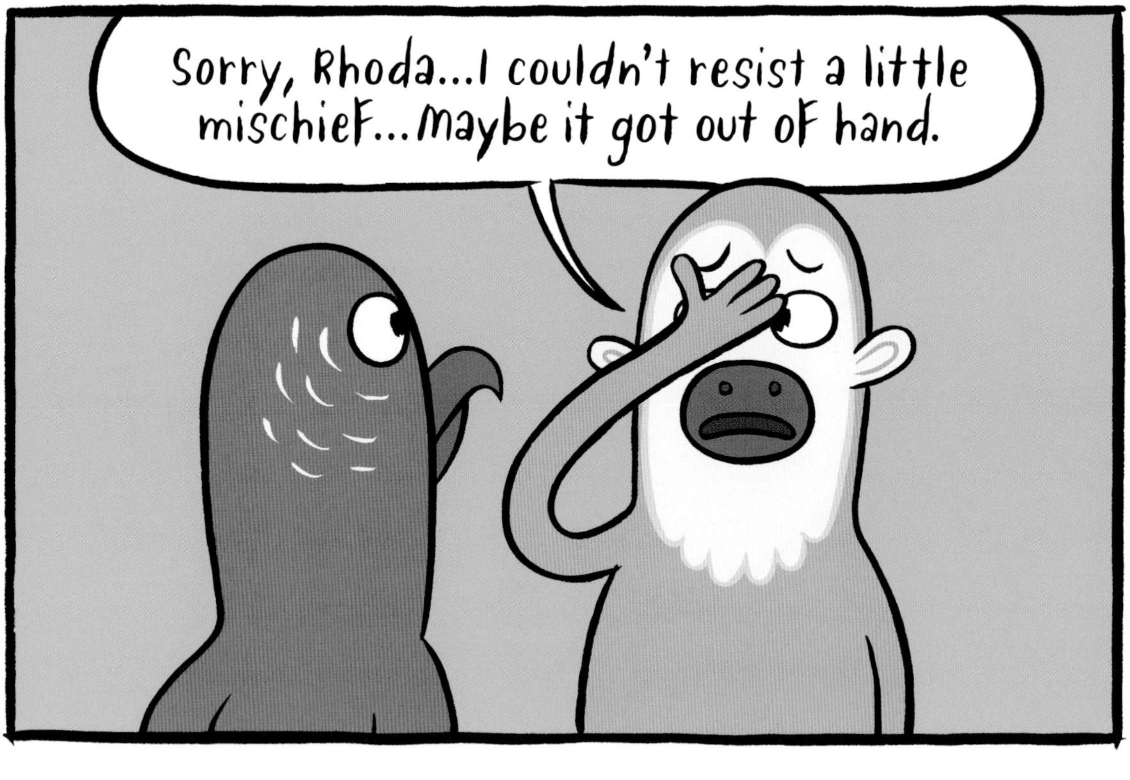
Sorry, Rhoda...I couldn't resist a little mischief...Maybe it got out of hand.

"You see, I used to come here each week with a basket of duck eggs to trade for tiger grass...

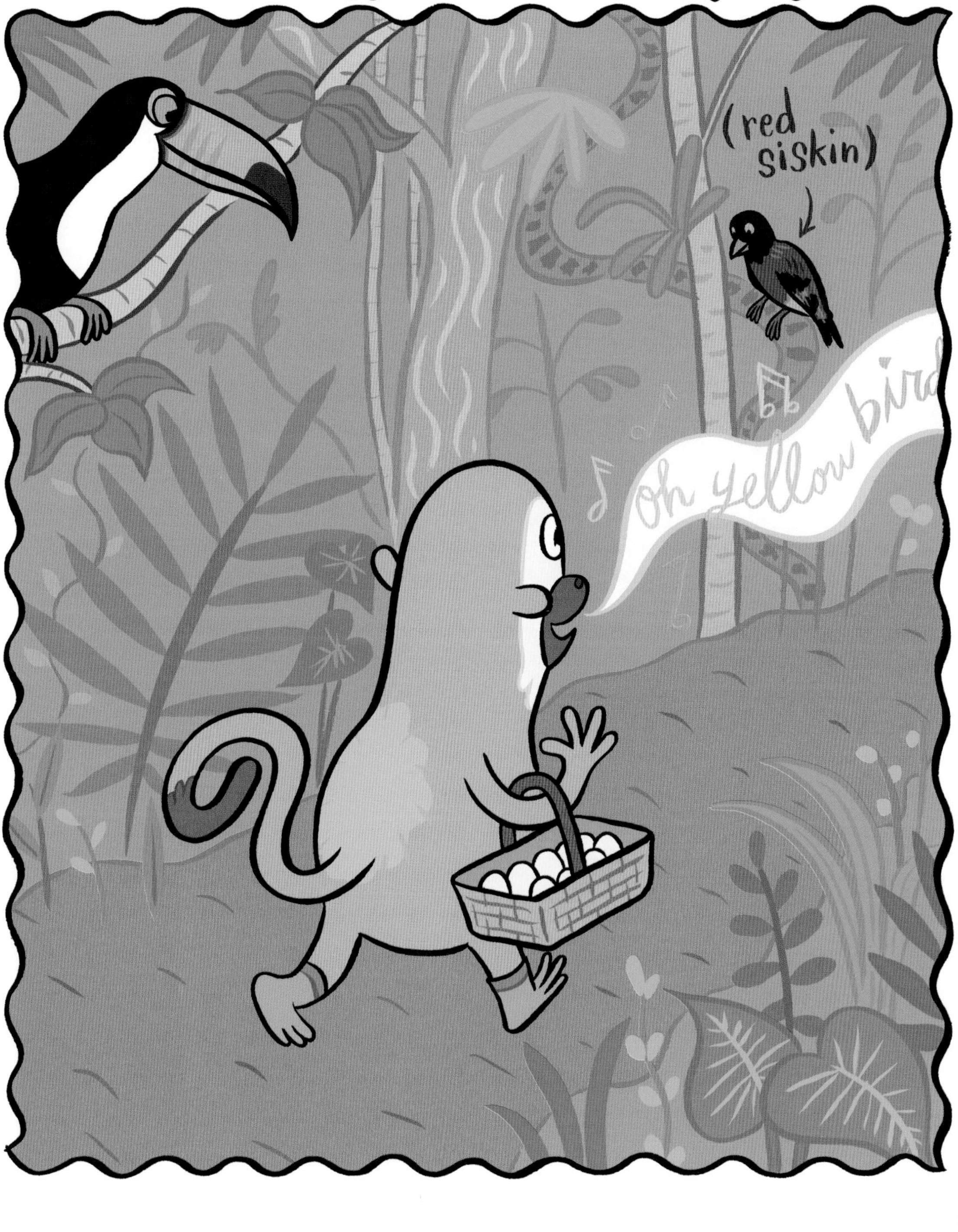

(red siskin)
Oh yellow bird

But one time, I was almost here when...

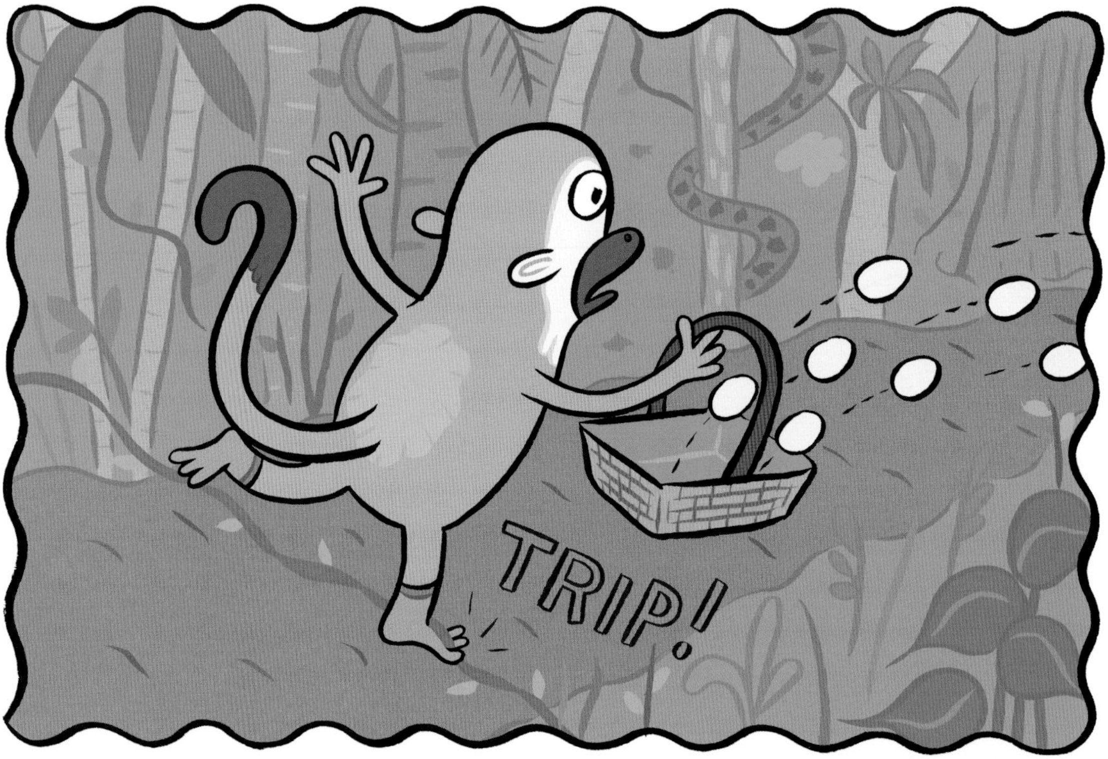
TRIP!

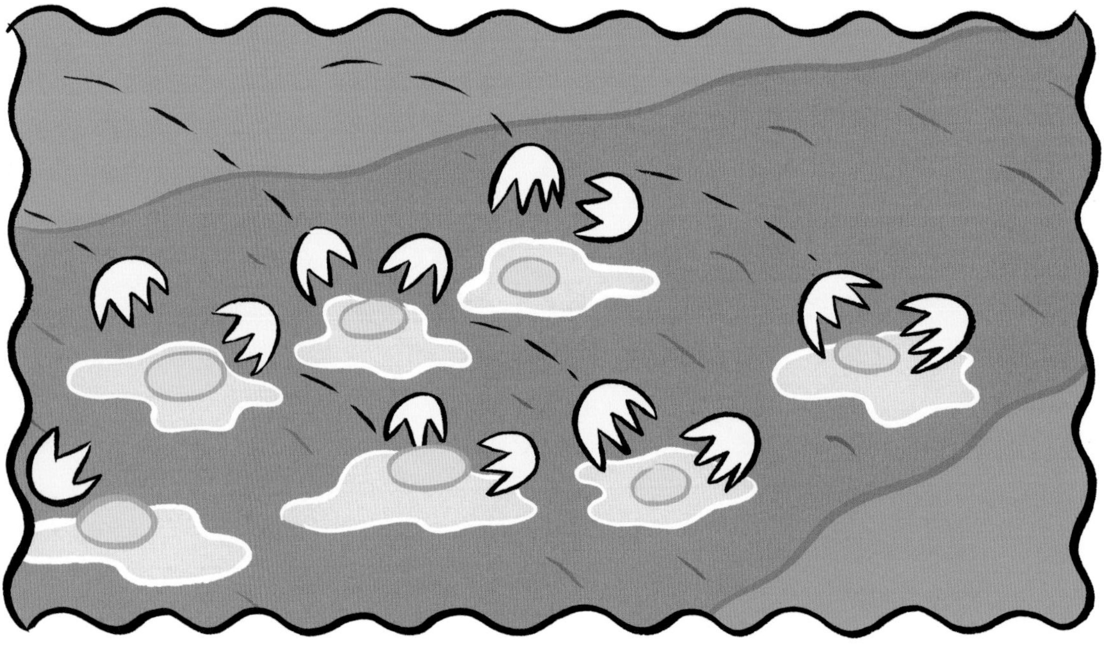

I didn't want to go all the way home empty-handed.

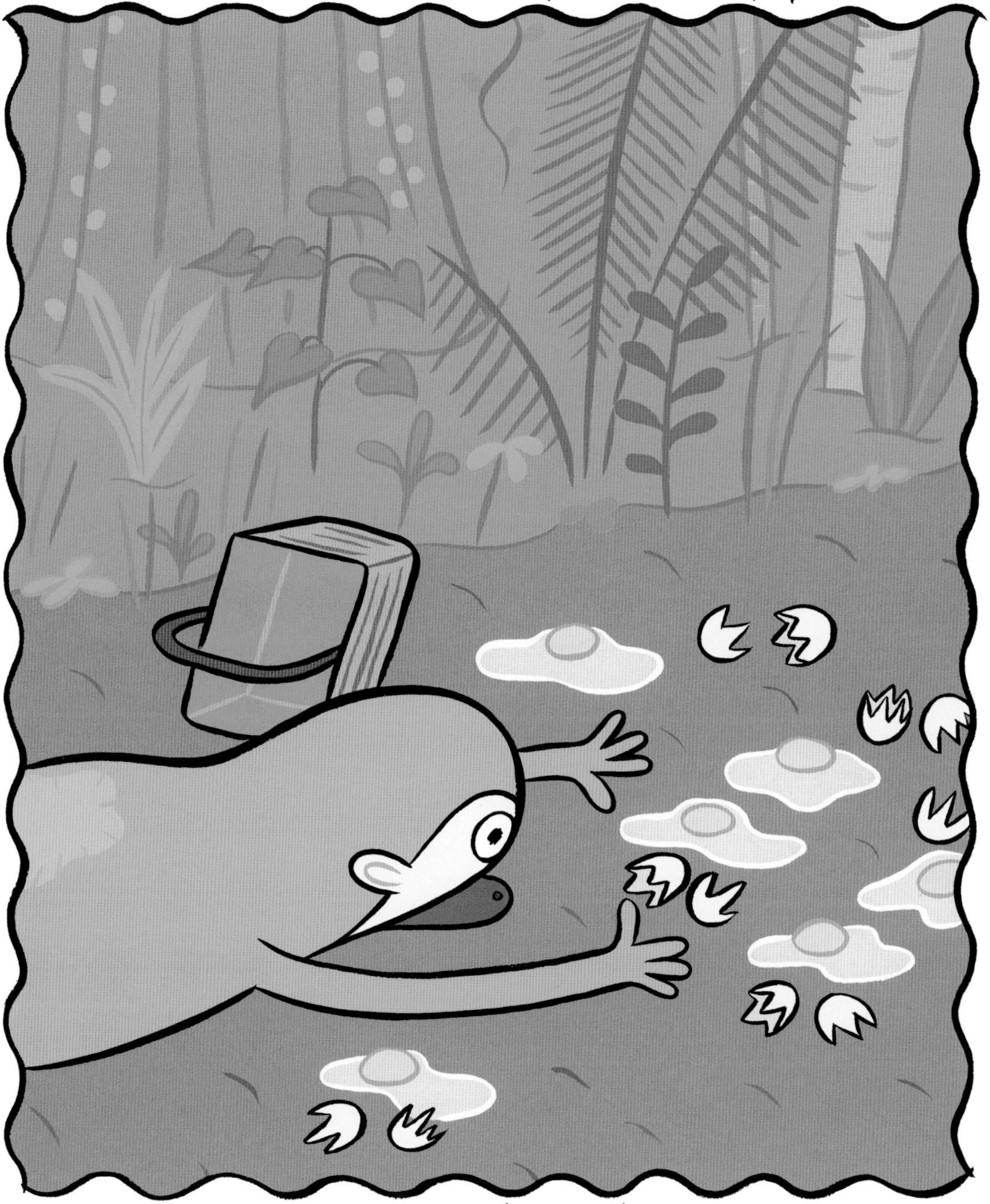

then, I had an idea...

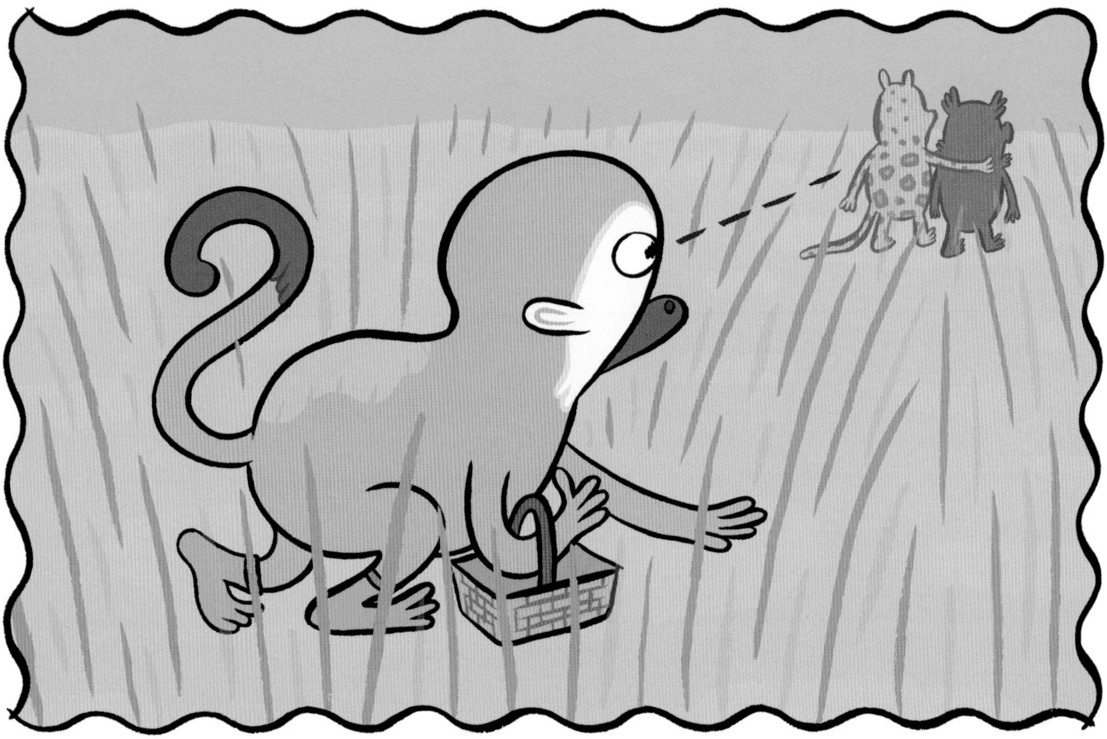

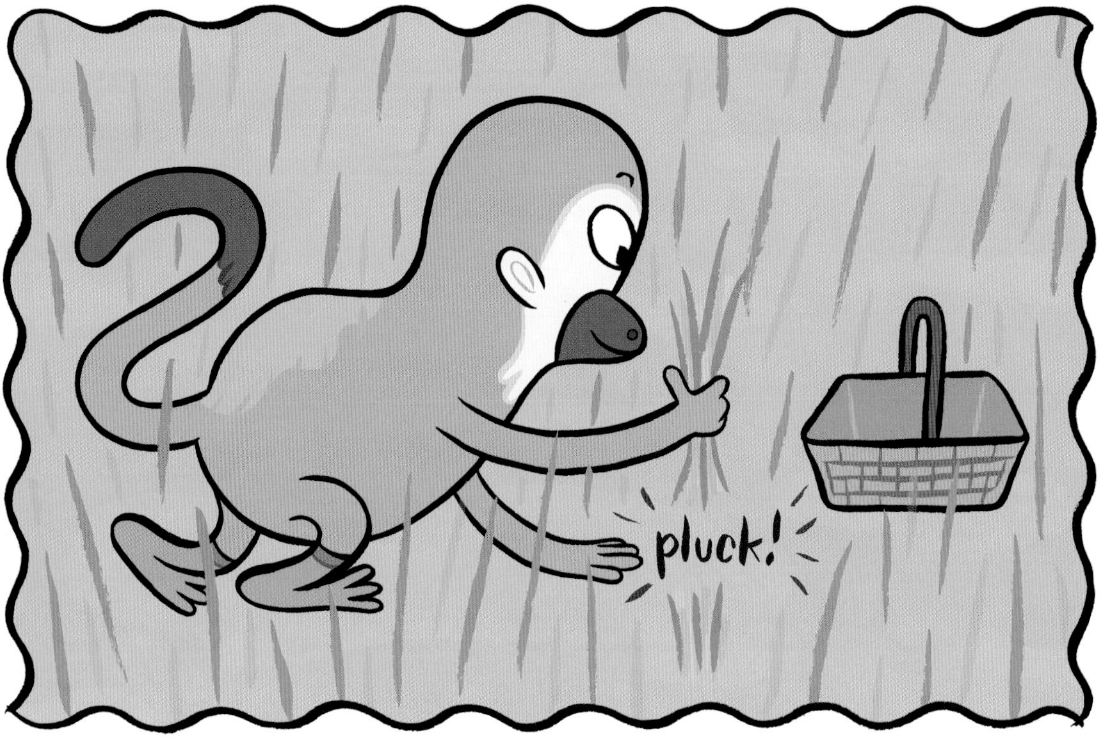
pluck!

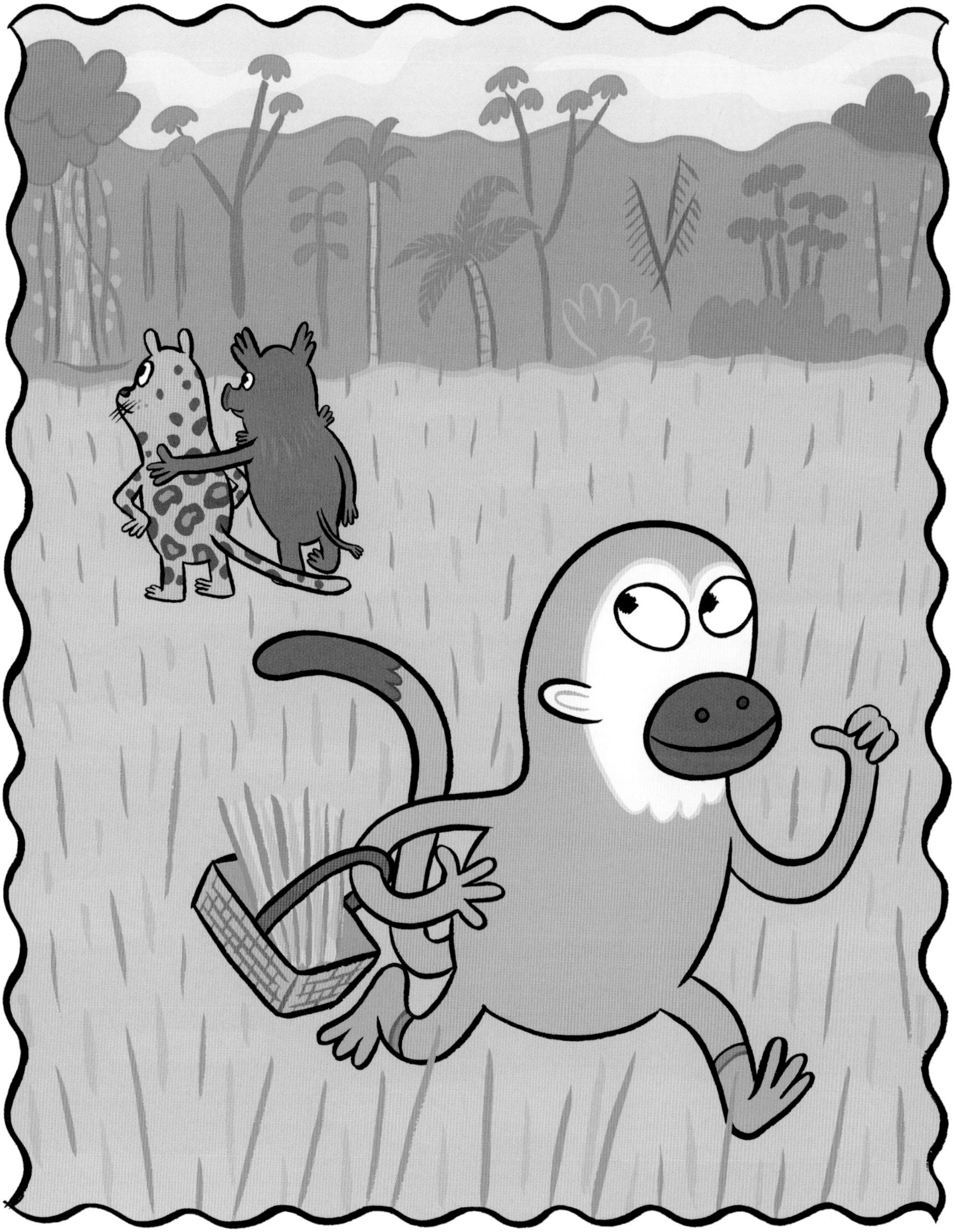

It was a piece of cake!"

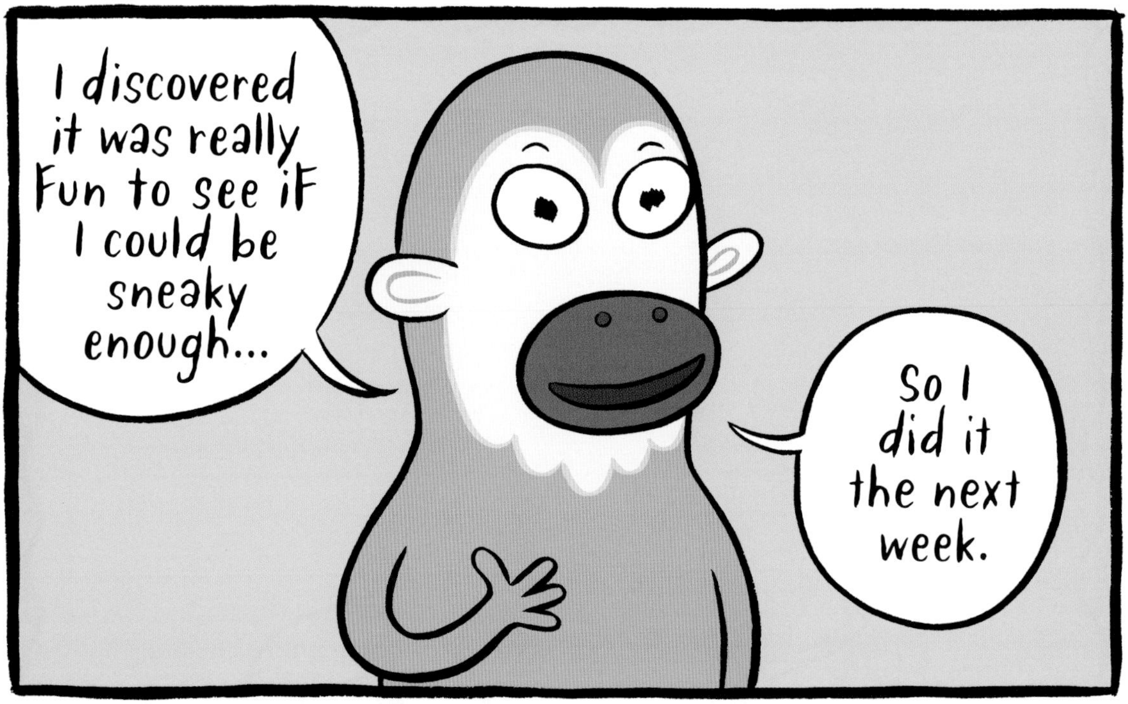
I discovered it was really fun to see if I could be sneaky enough...
So I did it the next week.

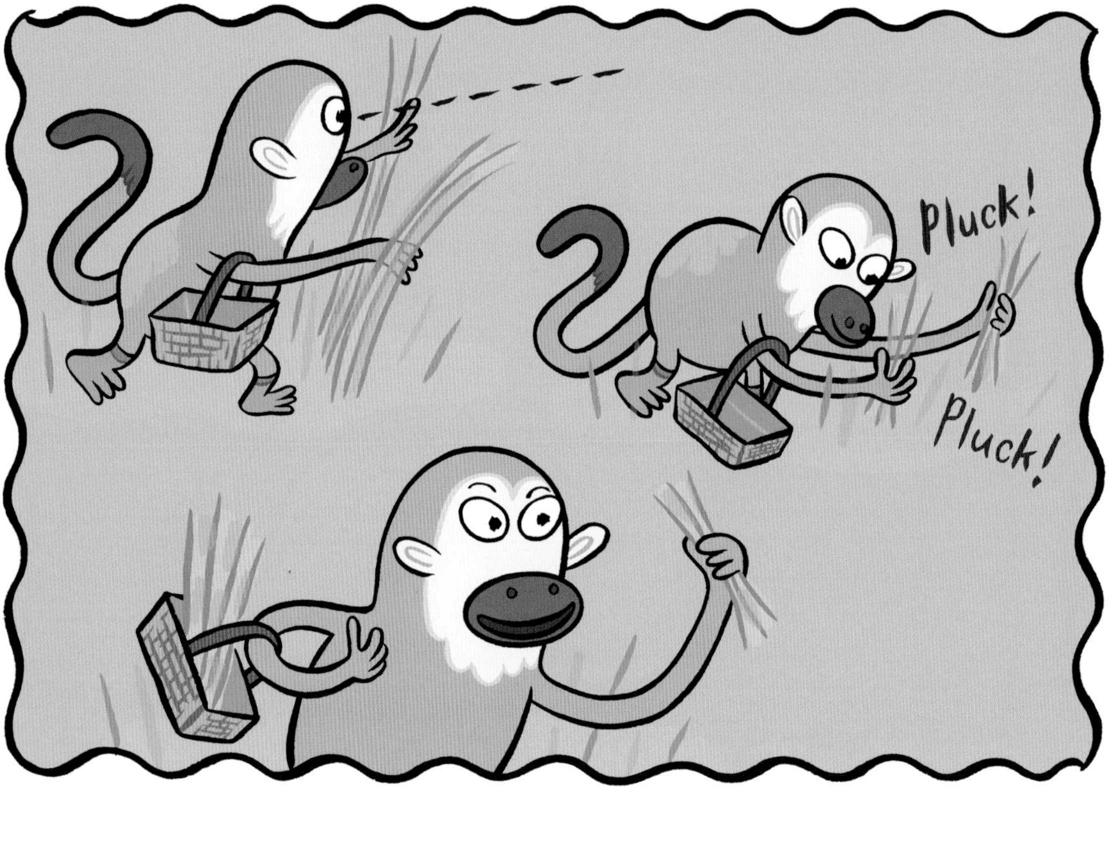
Pluck!
Pluck!

"AFter a Few times, they spotted me...

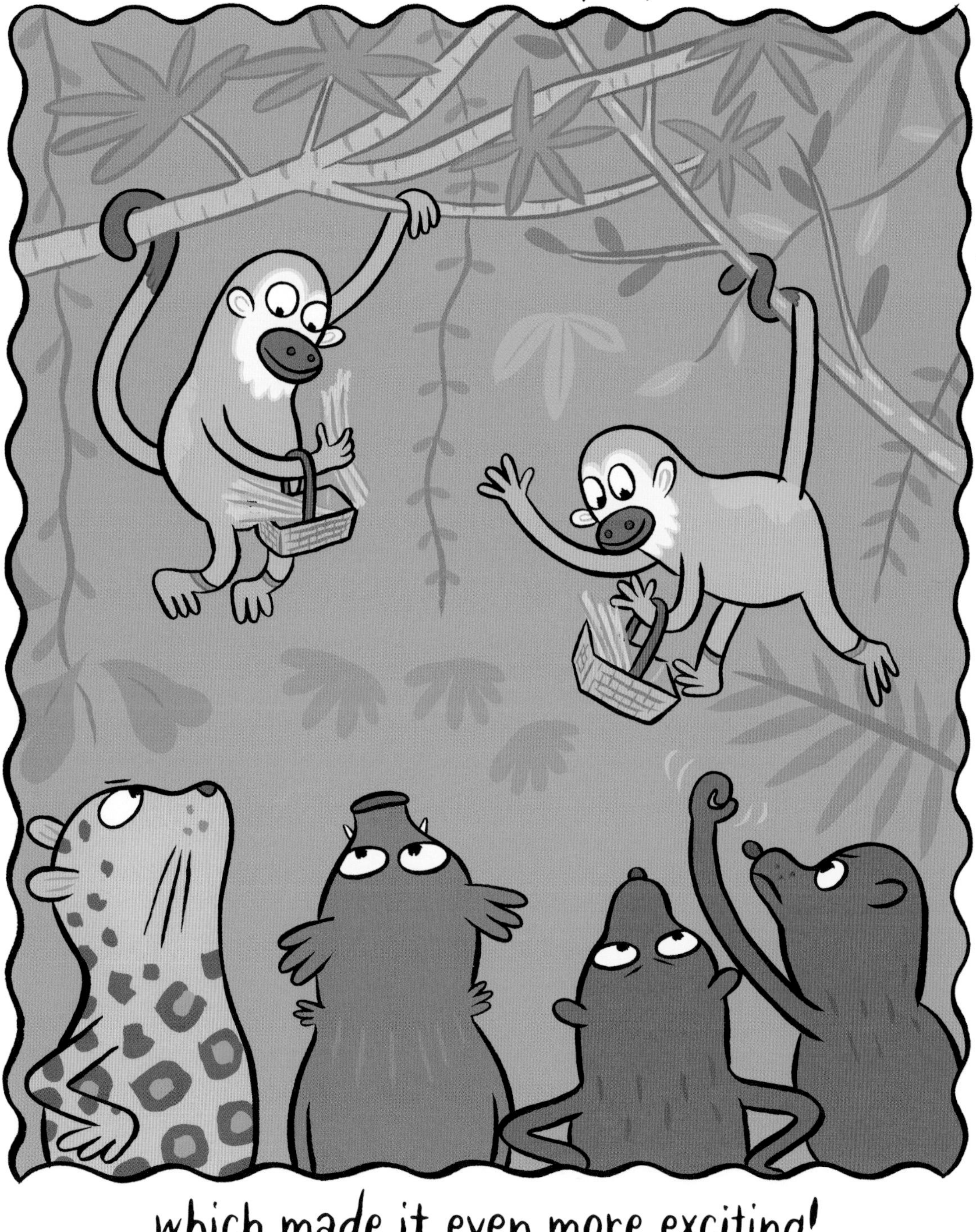

which made it even more exciting!

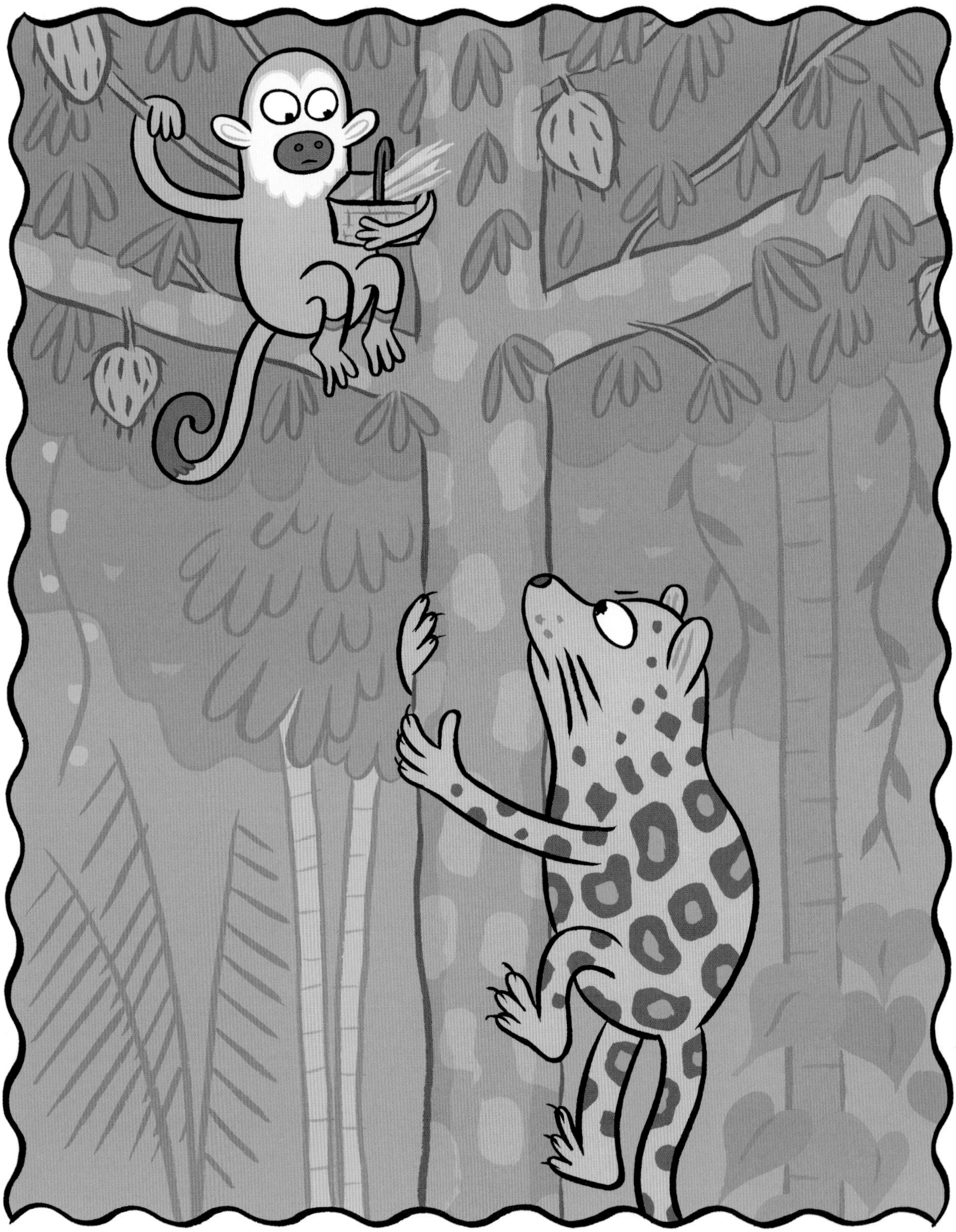

I almost got caught once...

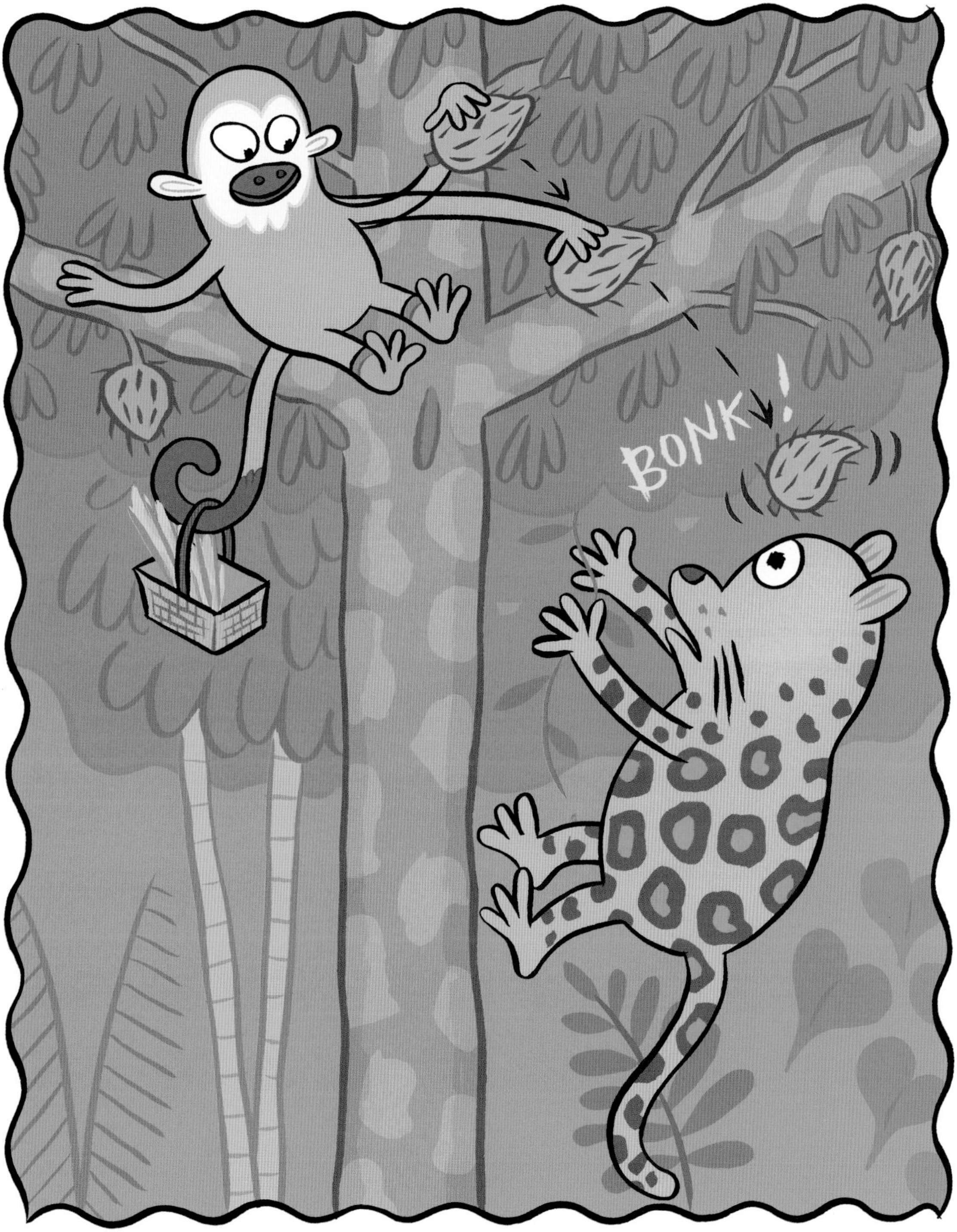
BONK!

but I drove them away with soursops!"

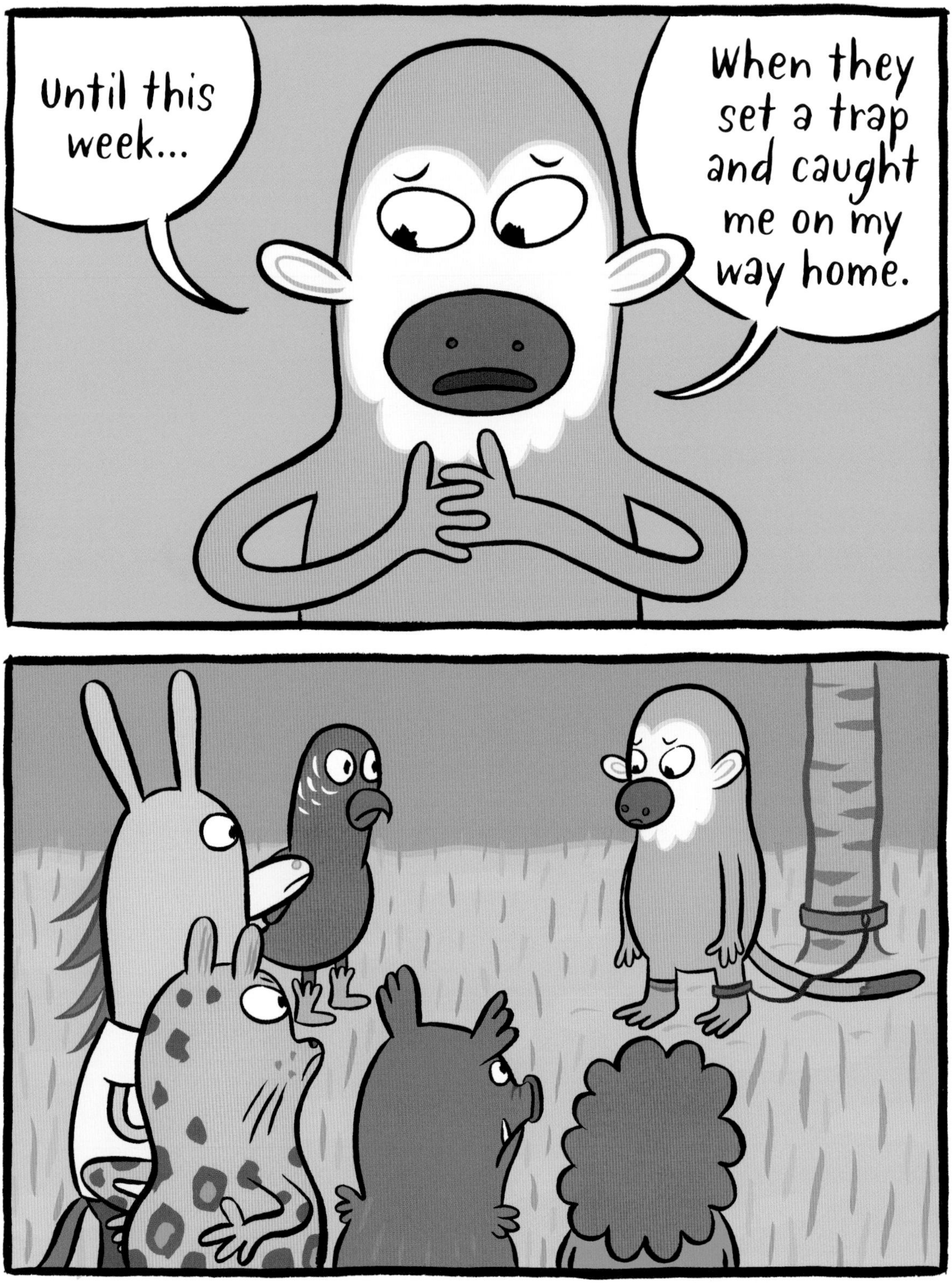
Until this week...
When they set a trap and caught me on my way home.

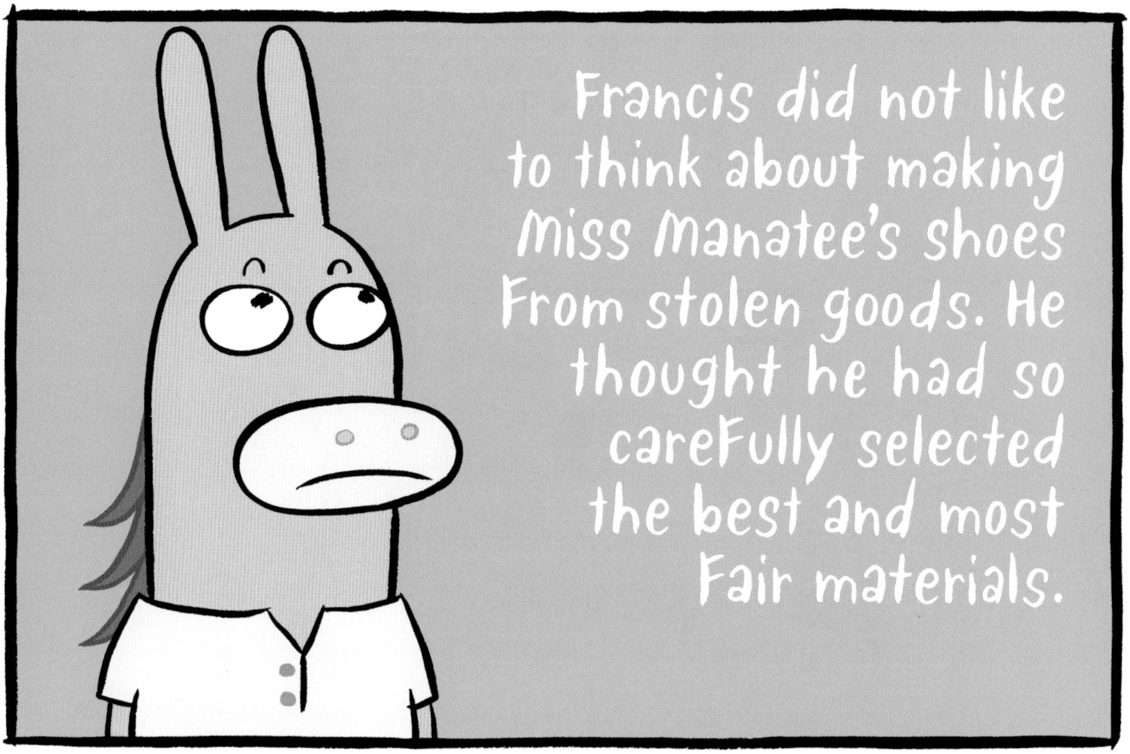
Francis did not like to think about making Miss Manatee's shoes From stolen goods. He thought he had so careFully selected the best and most Fair materials.

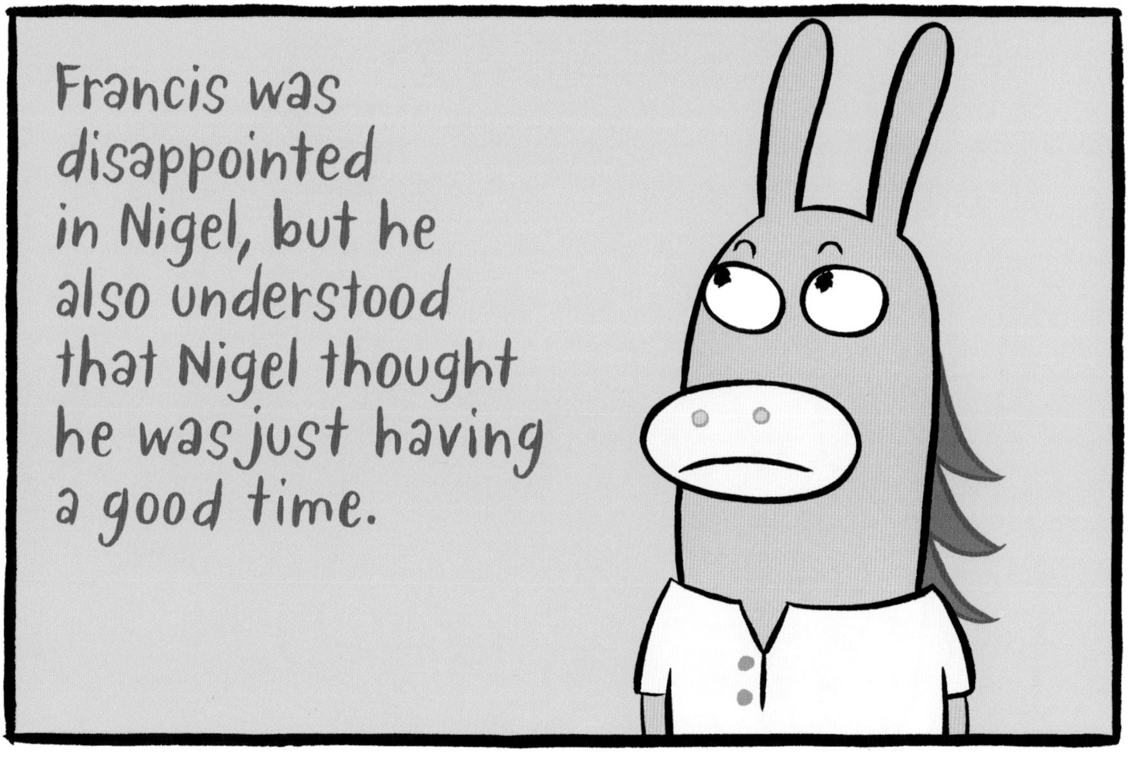
Francis was disappointed in Nigel, but he also understood that Nigel thought he was just having a good time.

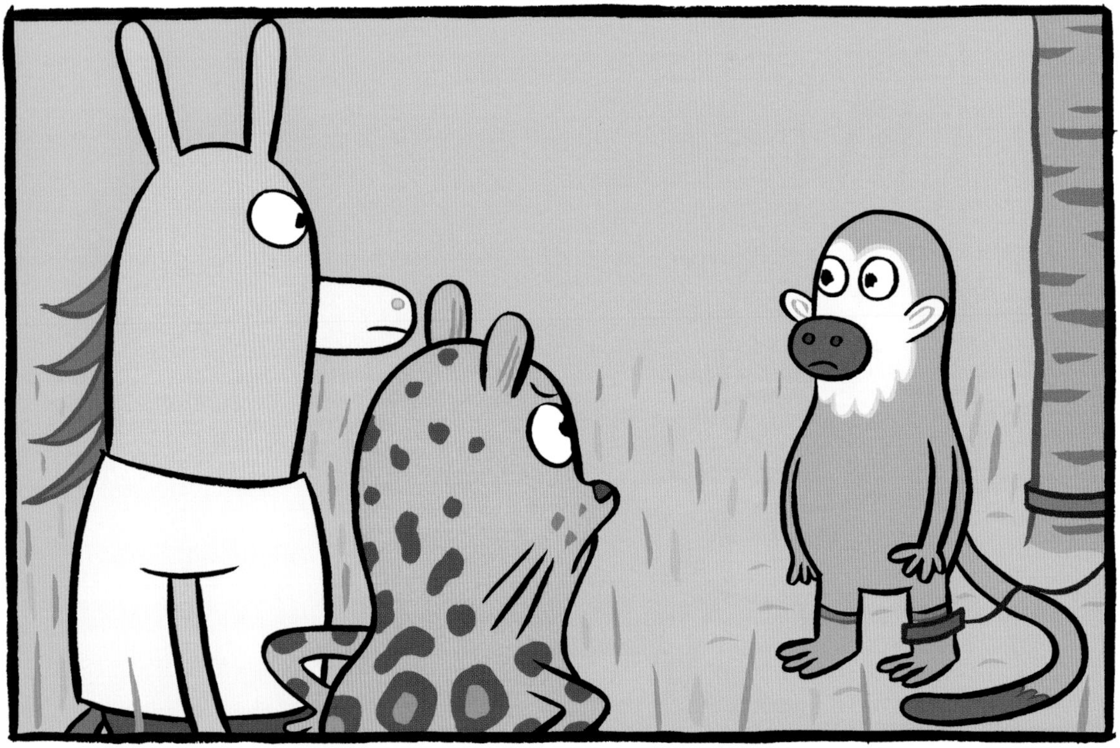

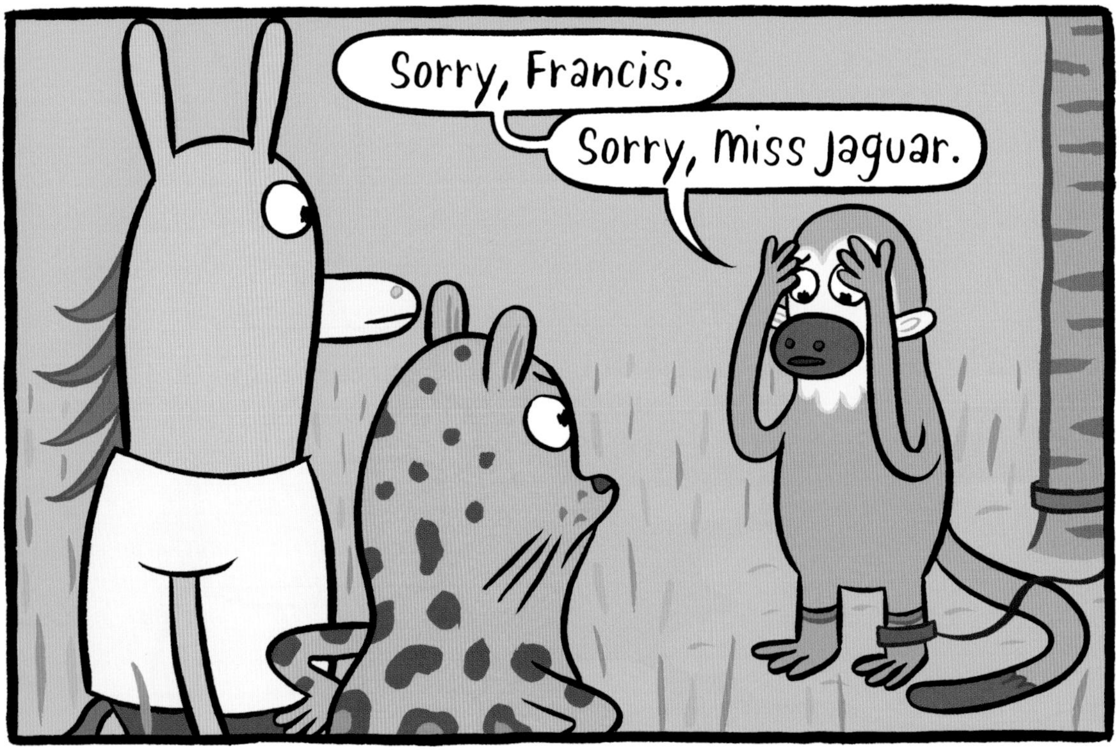
Sorry, Francis.
Sorry, Miss Jaguar.

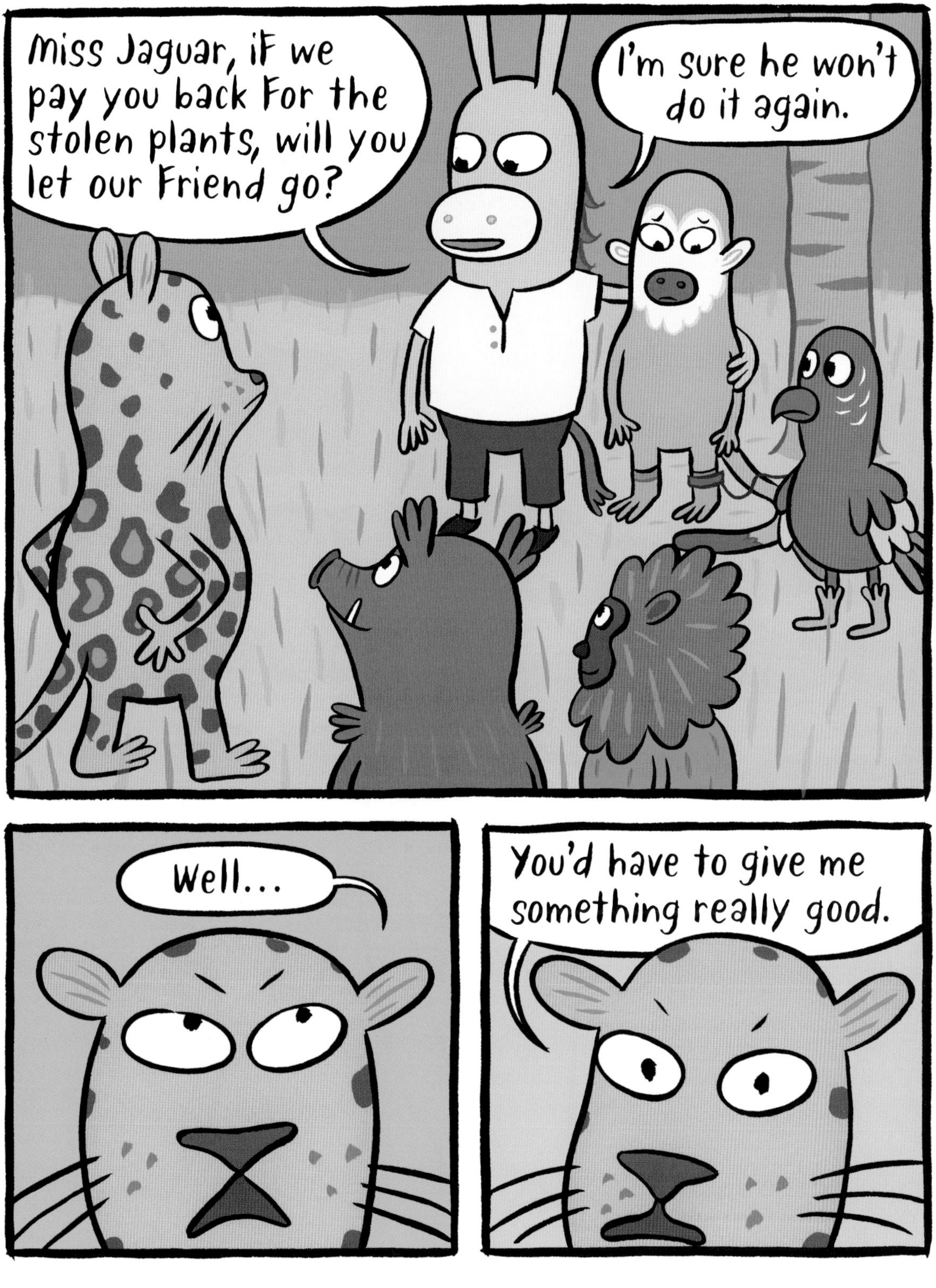
Miss Jaguar, if we pay you back for the stolen plants, will you let our friend go?
I'm sure he won't do it again.
Well...
You'd have to give me something really good.

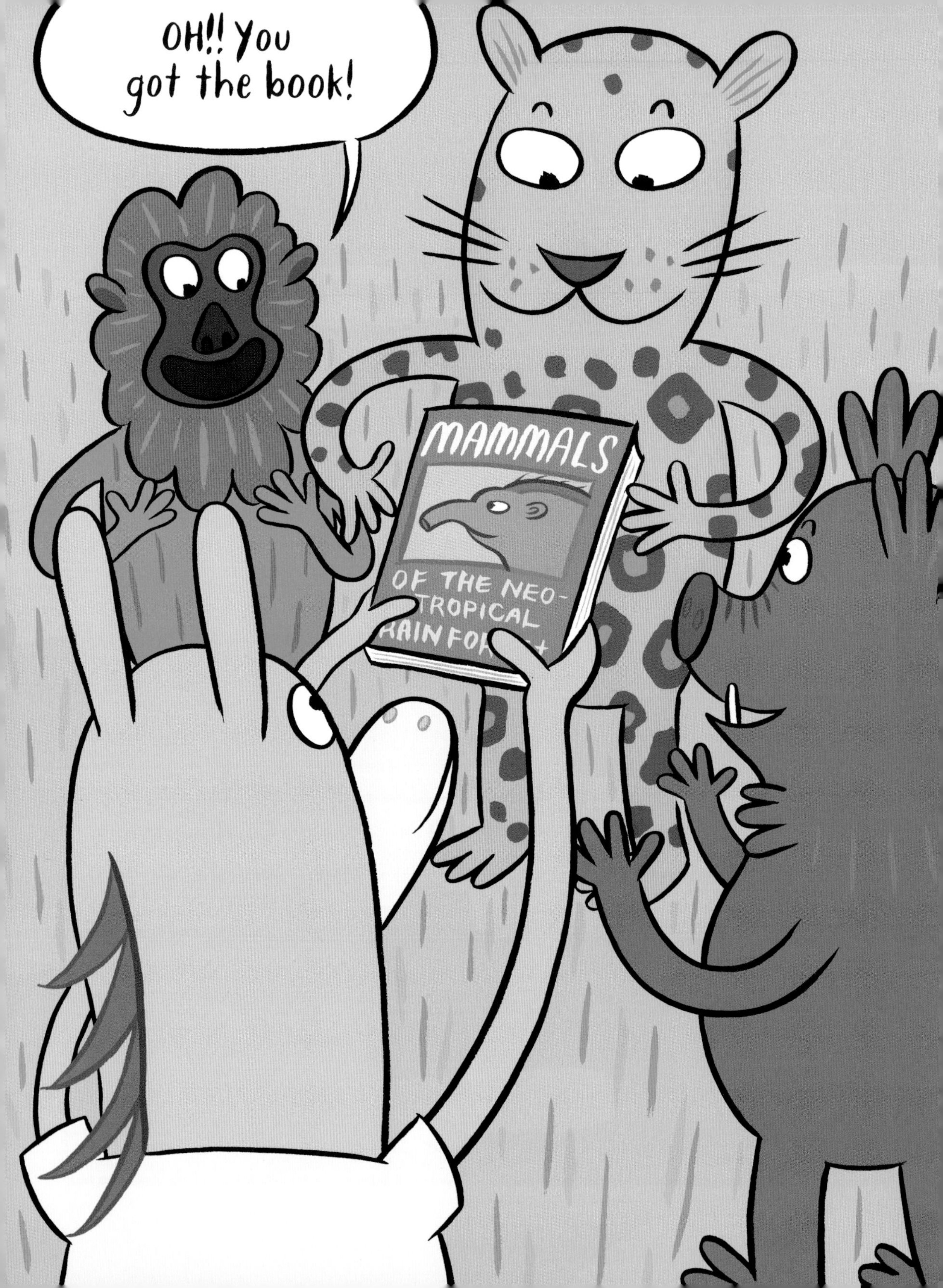
OH!! You got the book!
MAMMALS
OF THE NEO-TROPICAL

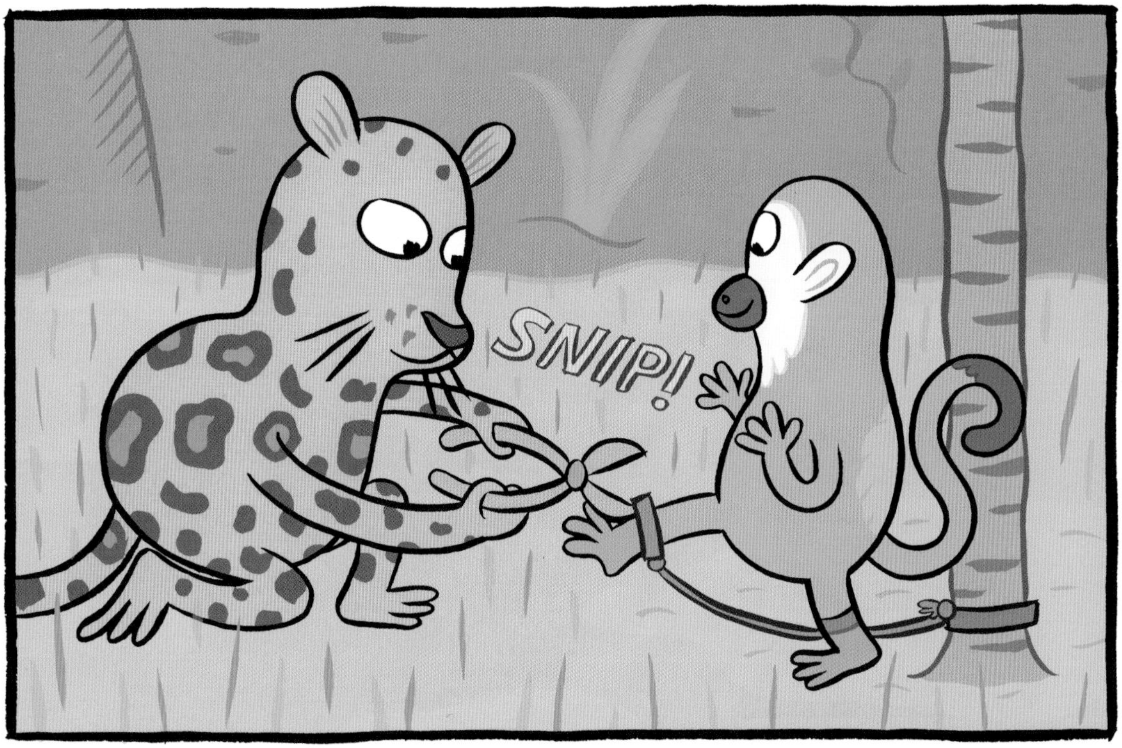
SNIP!

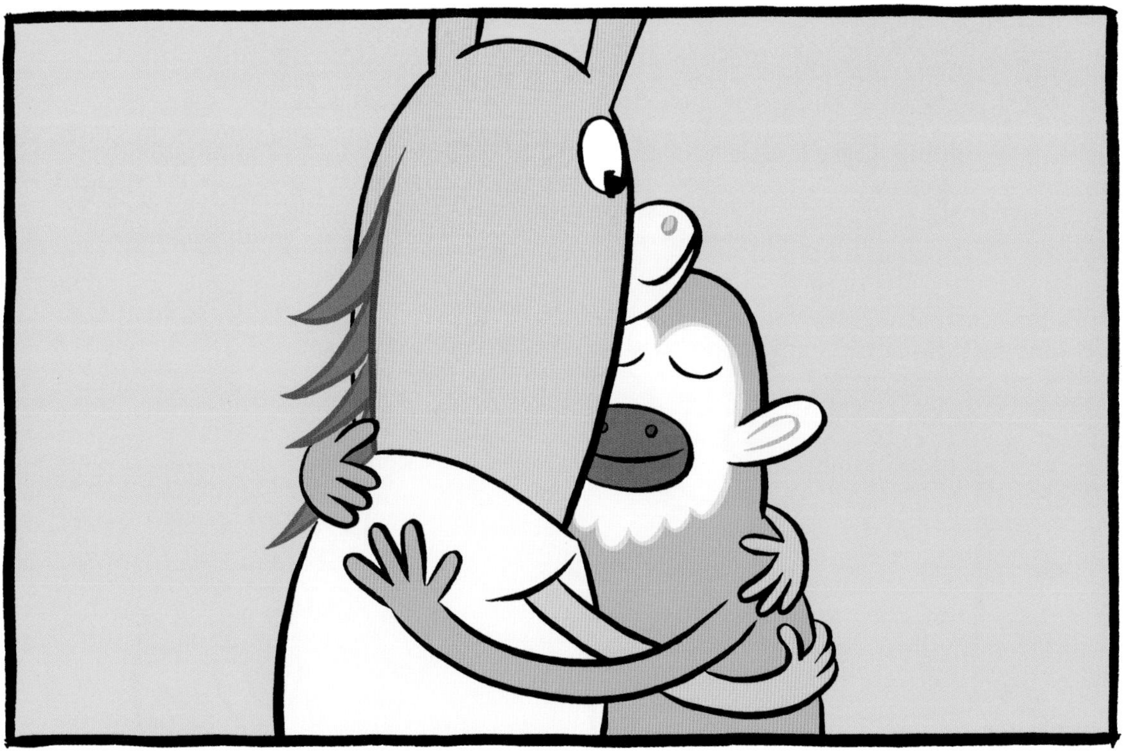

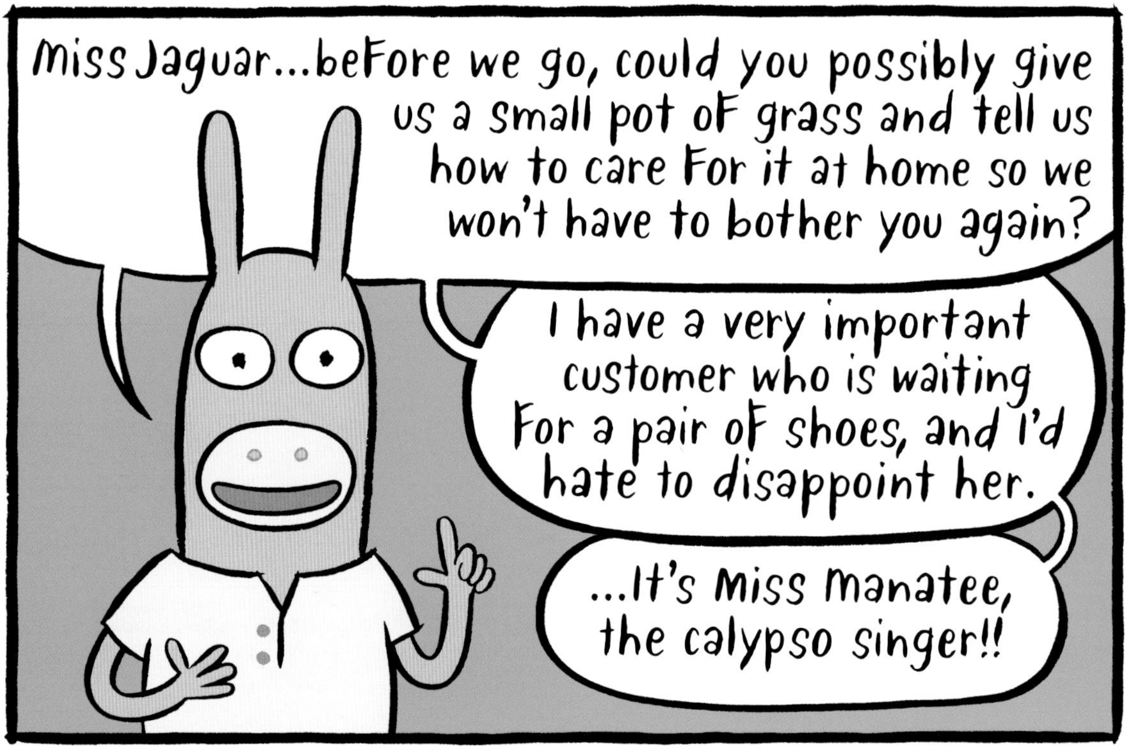
Miss Jaguar...before we go, could you possibly give us a small pot of grass and tell us how to care for it at home so we won't have to bother you again?
I have a very important customer who is waiting for a pair of shoes, and I'd hate to disappoint her.
...It's Miss Manatee, the calypso singer!!

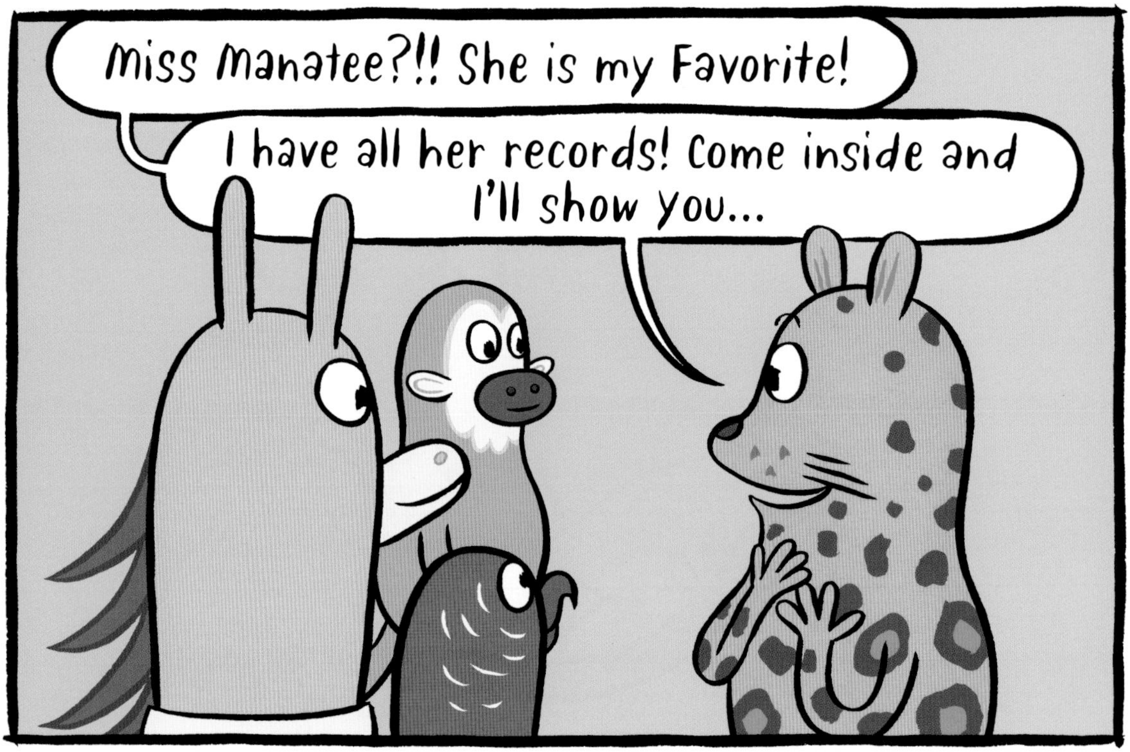
Miss Manatee?!! She is my favorite!
I have all her records! Come inside and I'll show you...

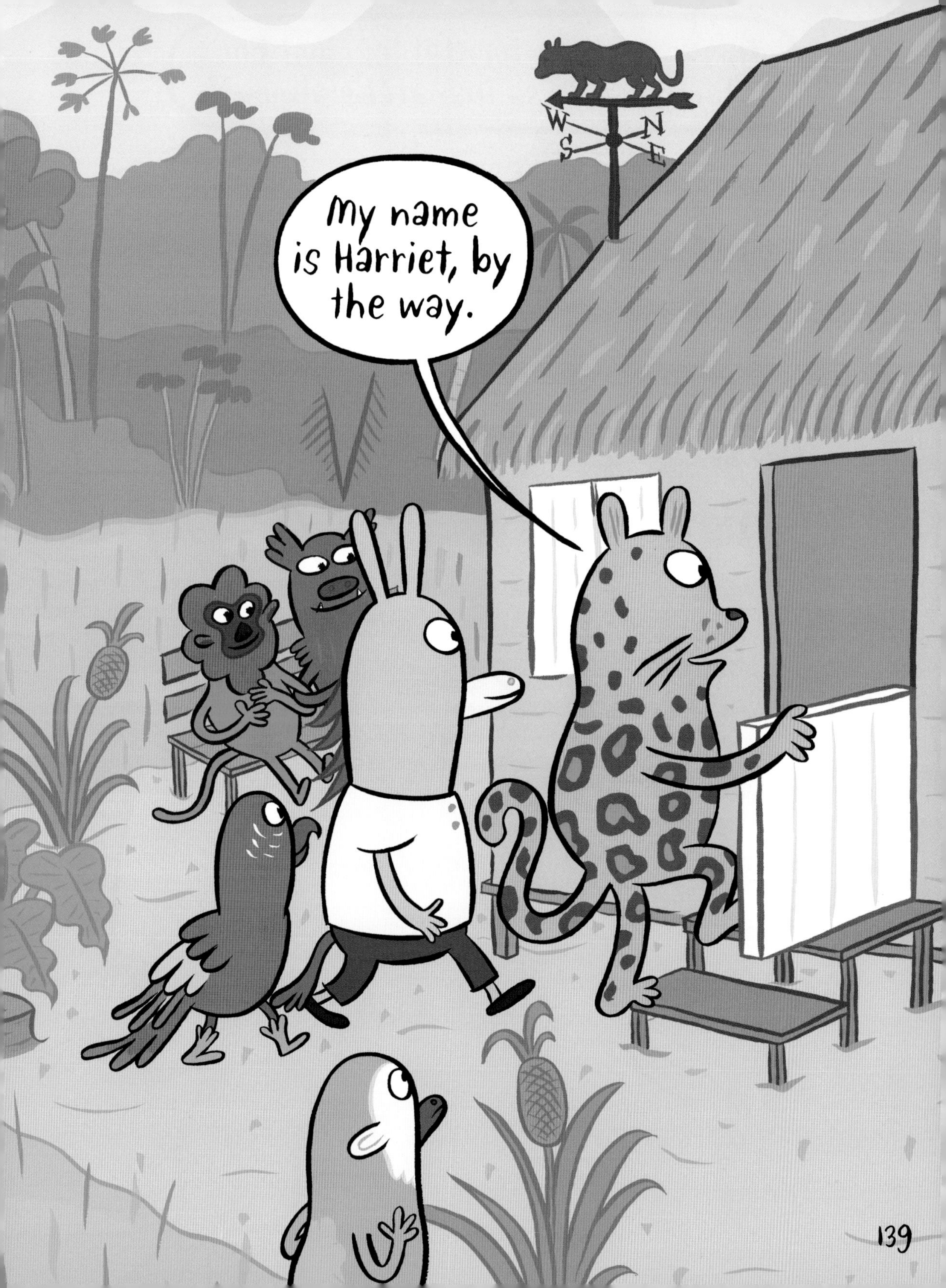
W S N E
My name is Harriet, by the way.

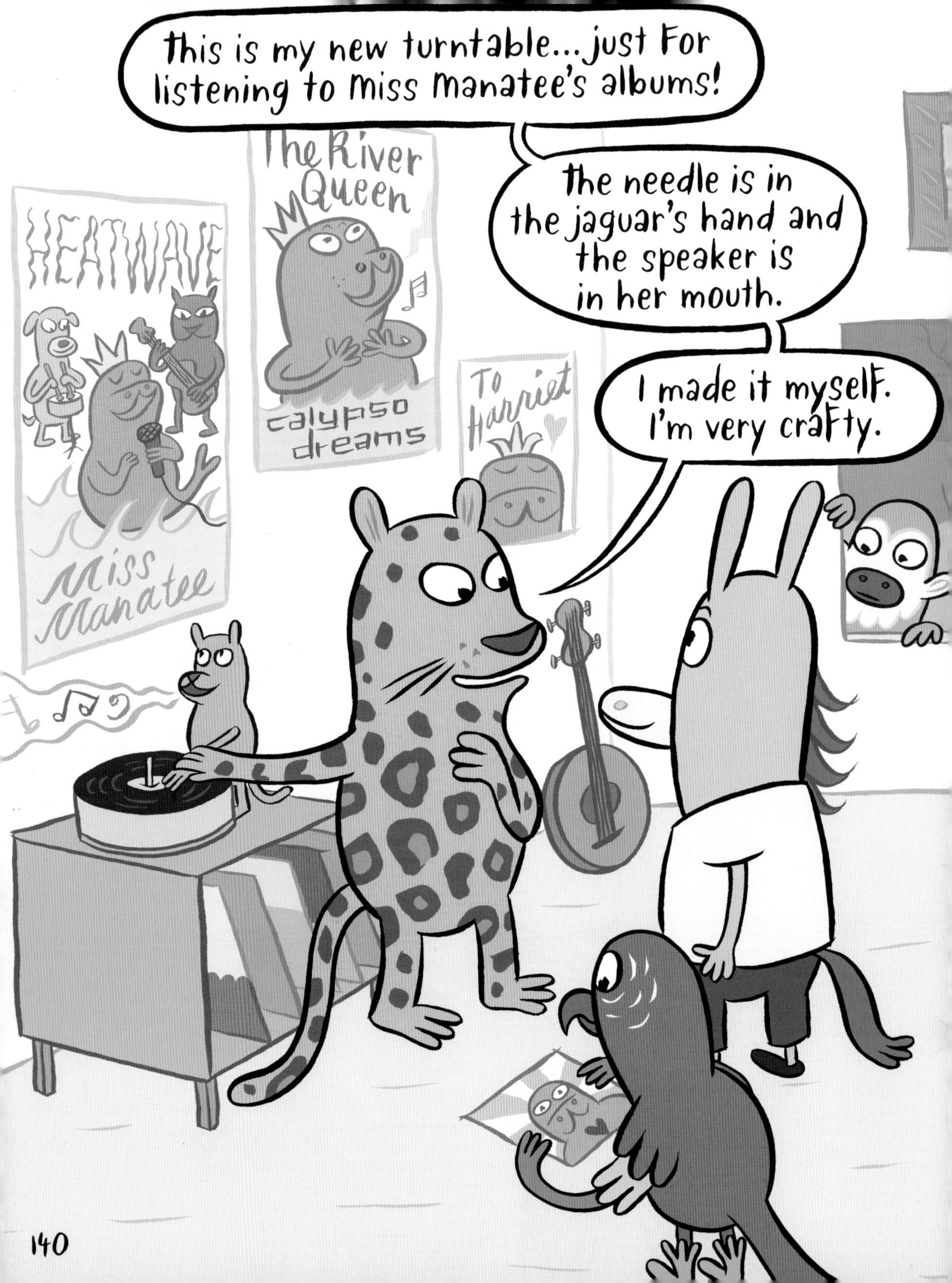
this is my new turntable... just for listening to Miss Manatee's albums!
The River Queen
HEATWAVE
Miss Manatee
calypso dreams
To Harriet
the needle is in the jaguar's hand and the speaker is in her mouth.
I made it myself. I'm very crafty.

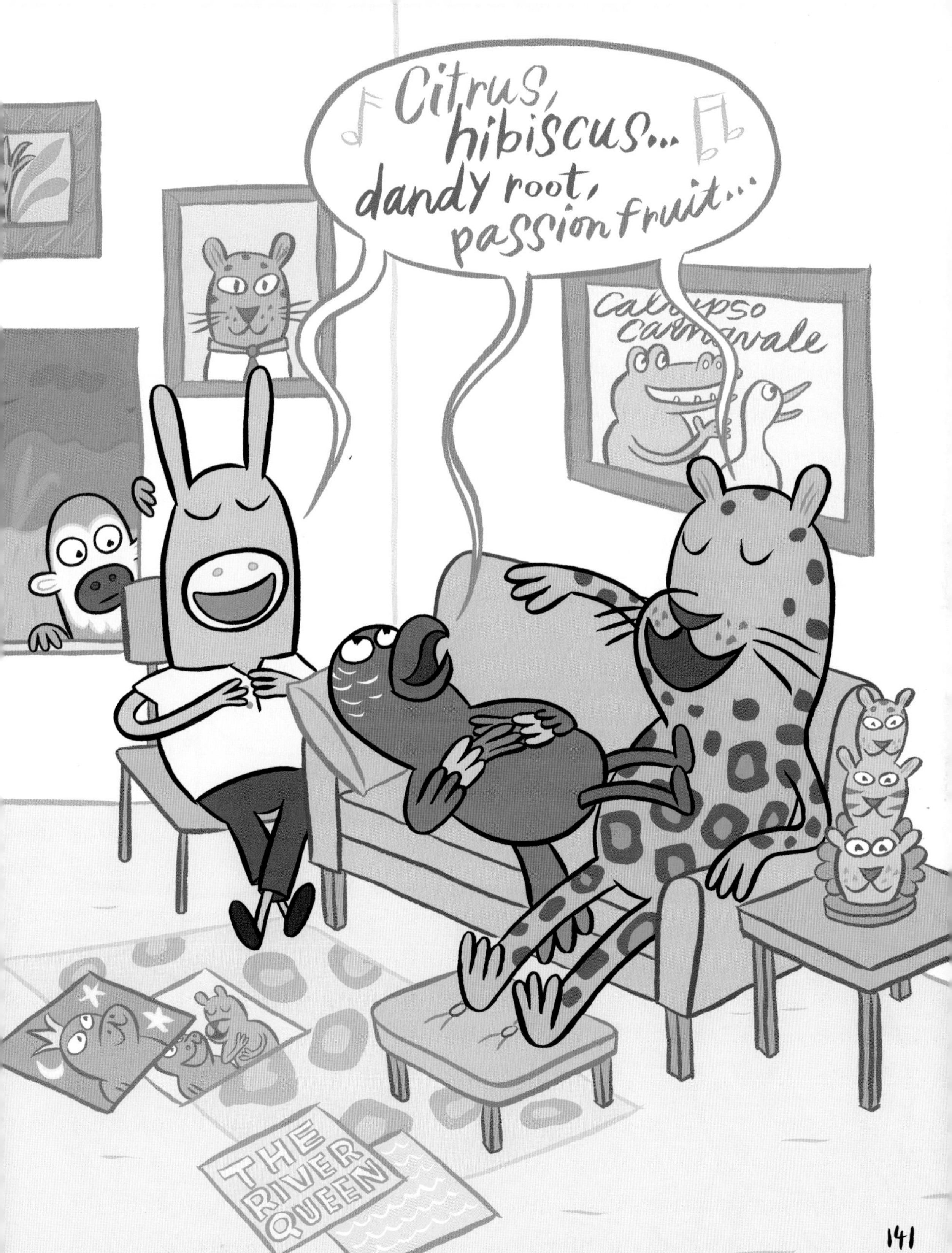
Citrus, hibiscus... dandy root, passion fruit...
THE RIVER QUEEN

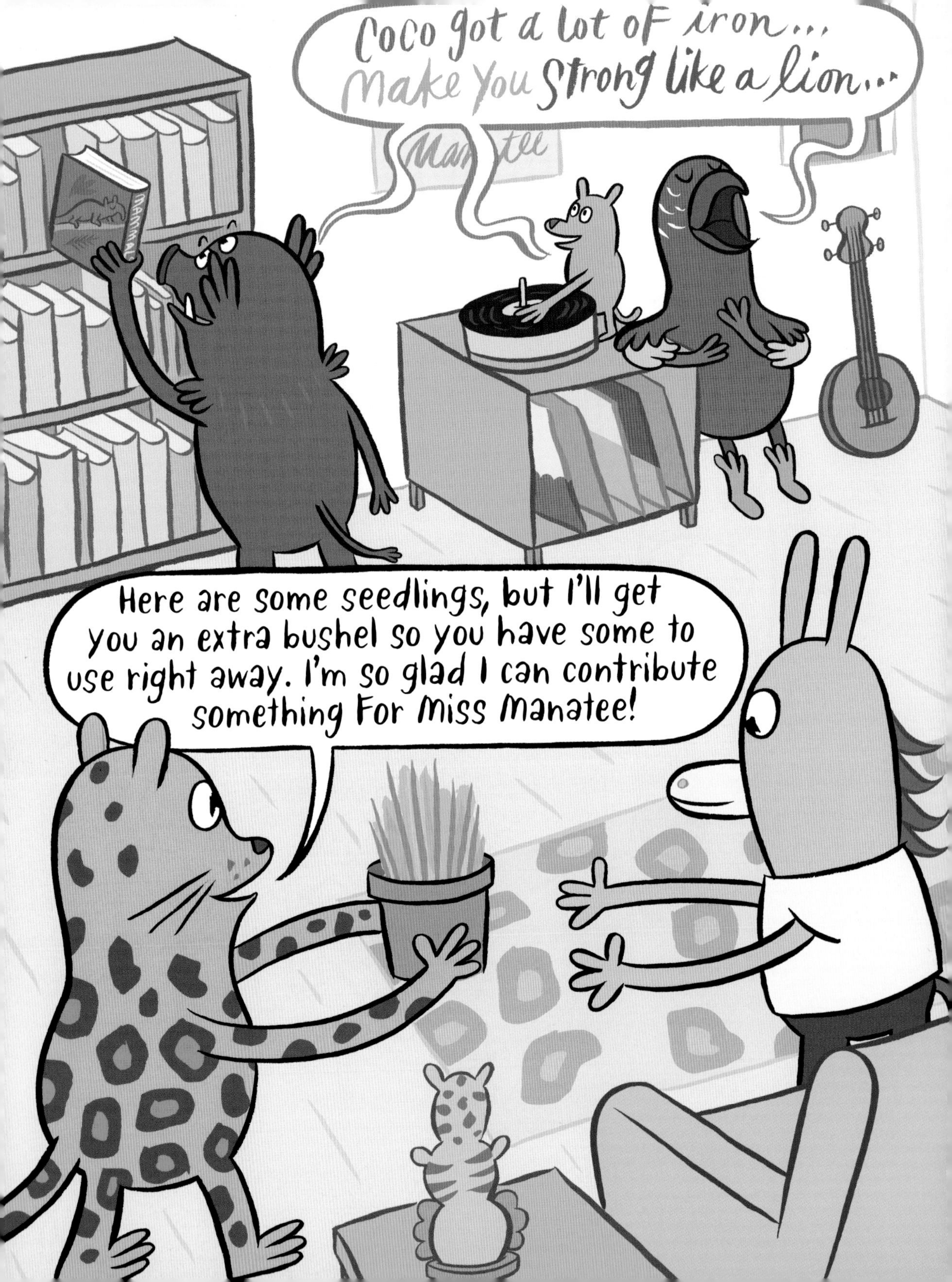
Coco got a lot of iron... Make you strong like a lion...
Manatee
MAMMAL
Here are some seedlings, but I'll get you an extra bushel so you have some to use right away. I'm so glad I can contribute something for Miss Manatee!

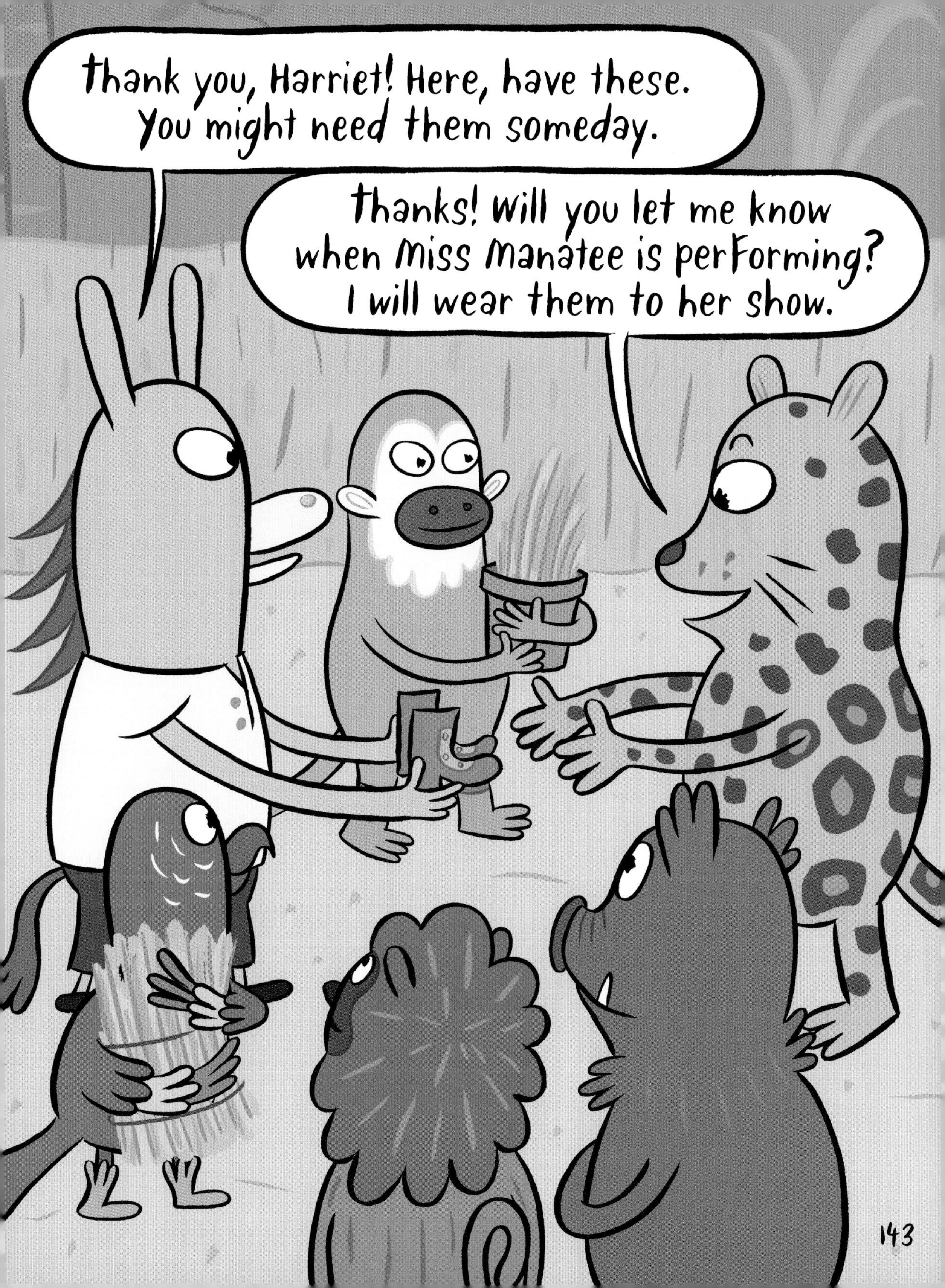
thank you, Harriet! Here, have these. You might need them someday.
thanks! Will you let me know when Miss Manatee is performing? I will wear them to her show.

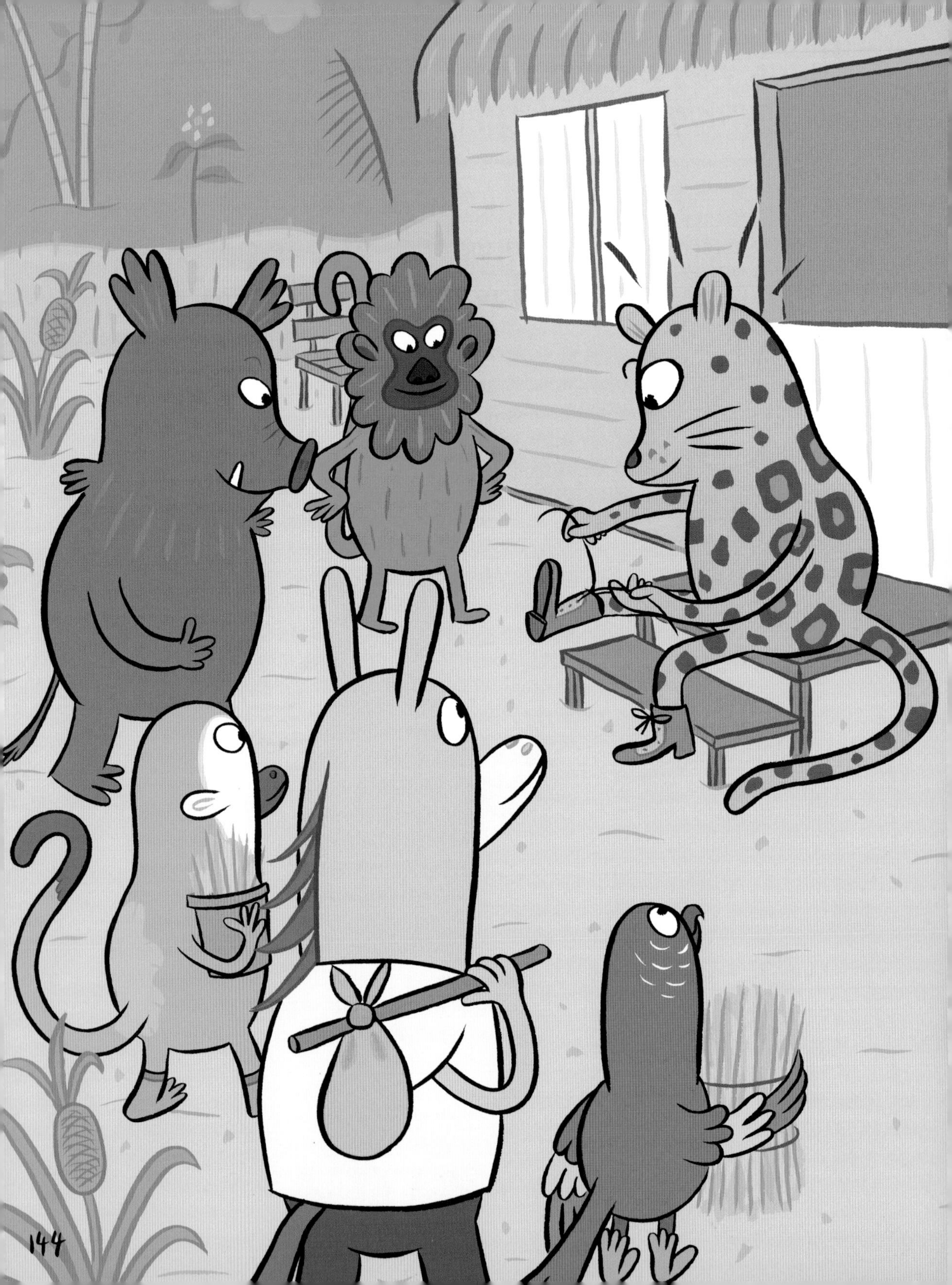

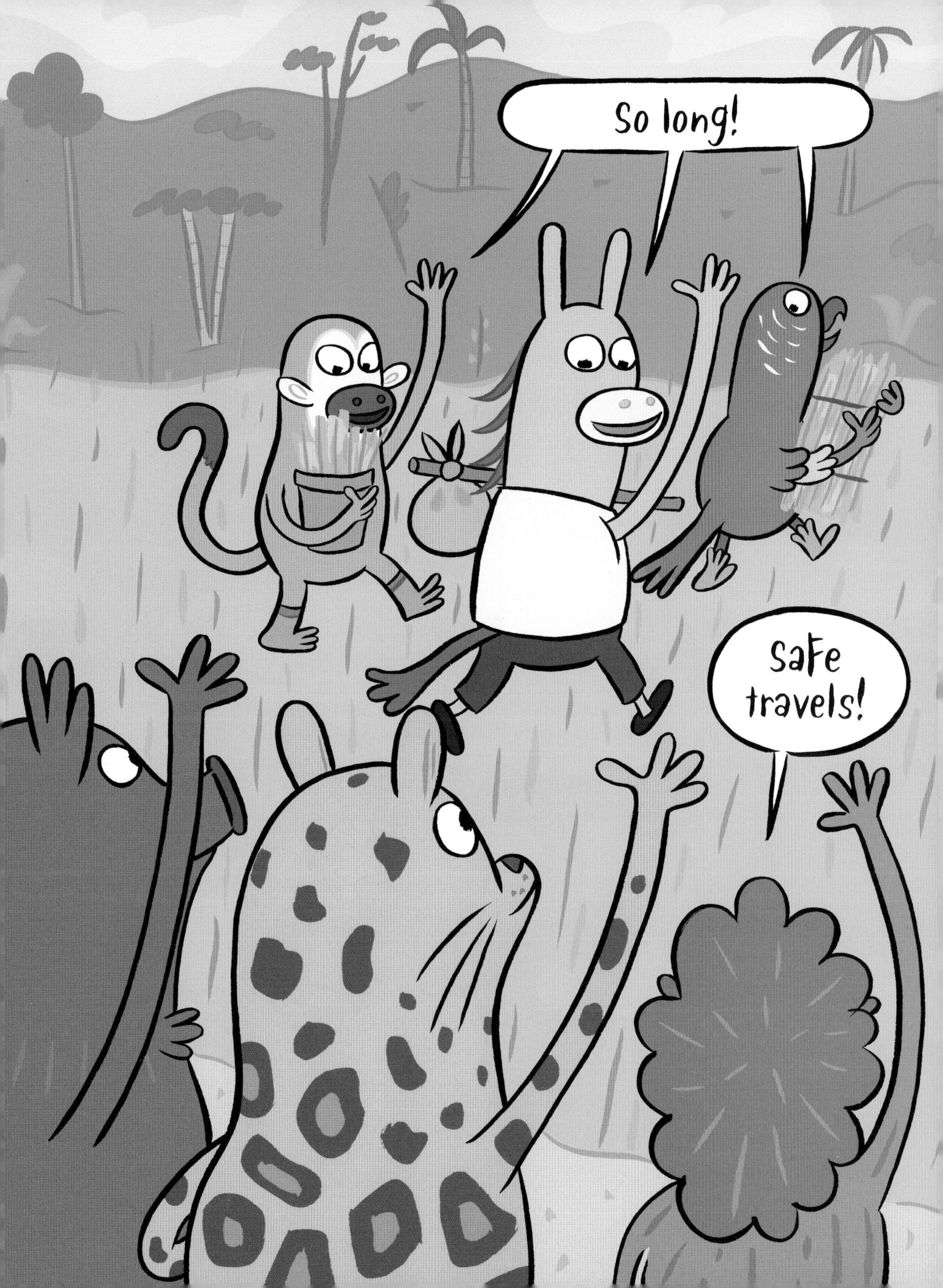
So long!
Safe travels!

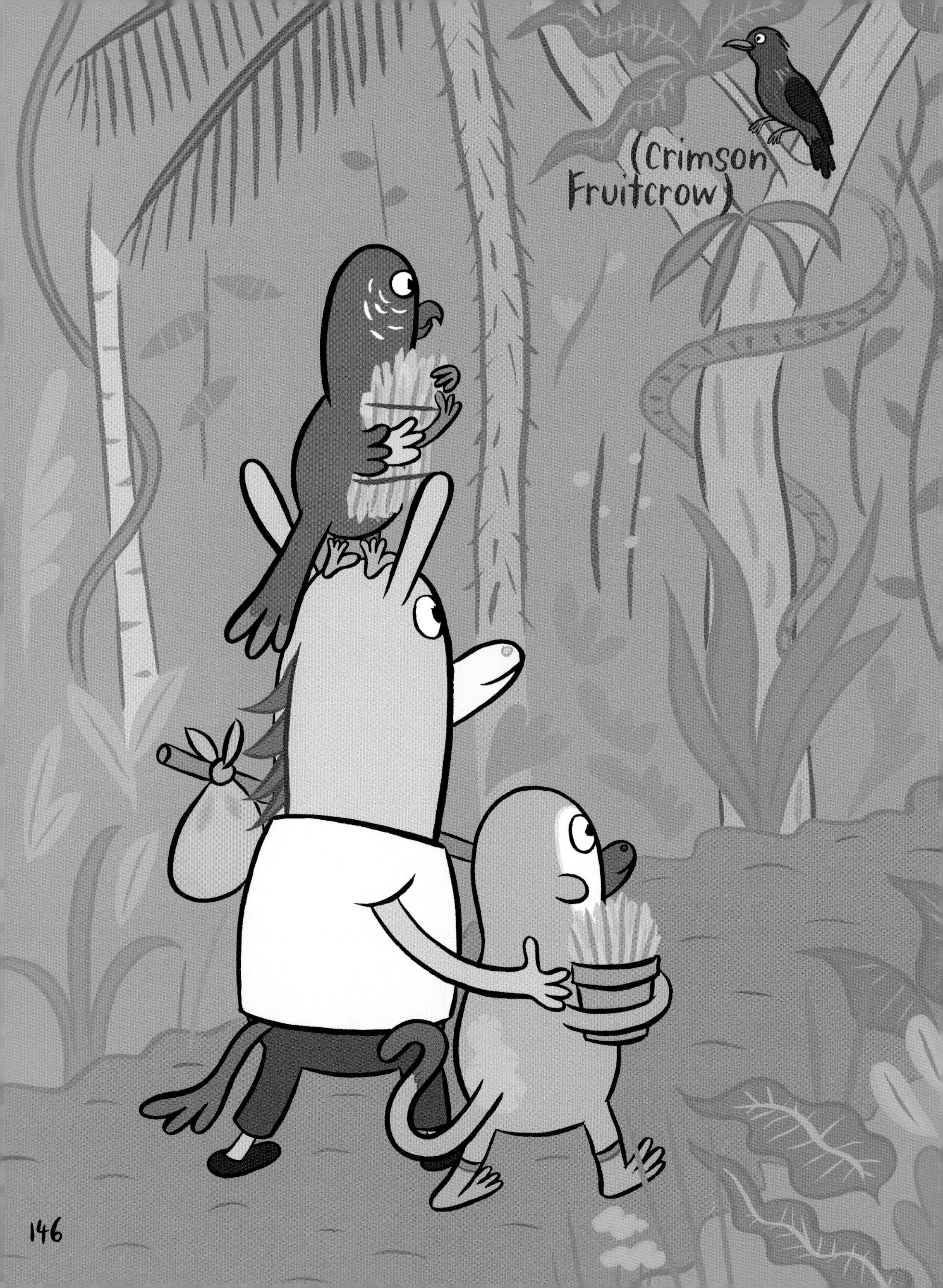
(Crimson
Fruitcrow)

chapter six

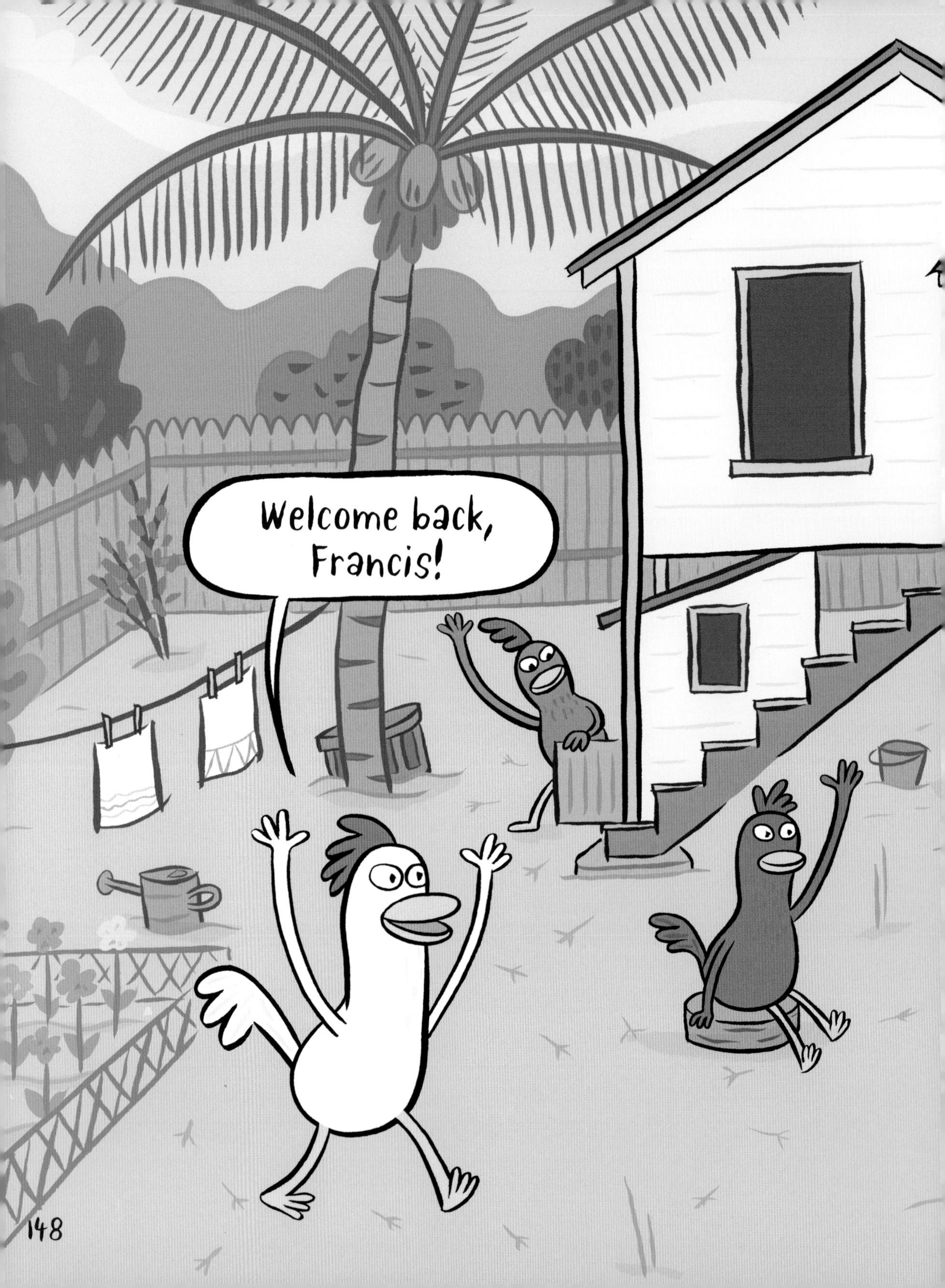
Welcome back, Francis!

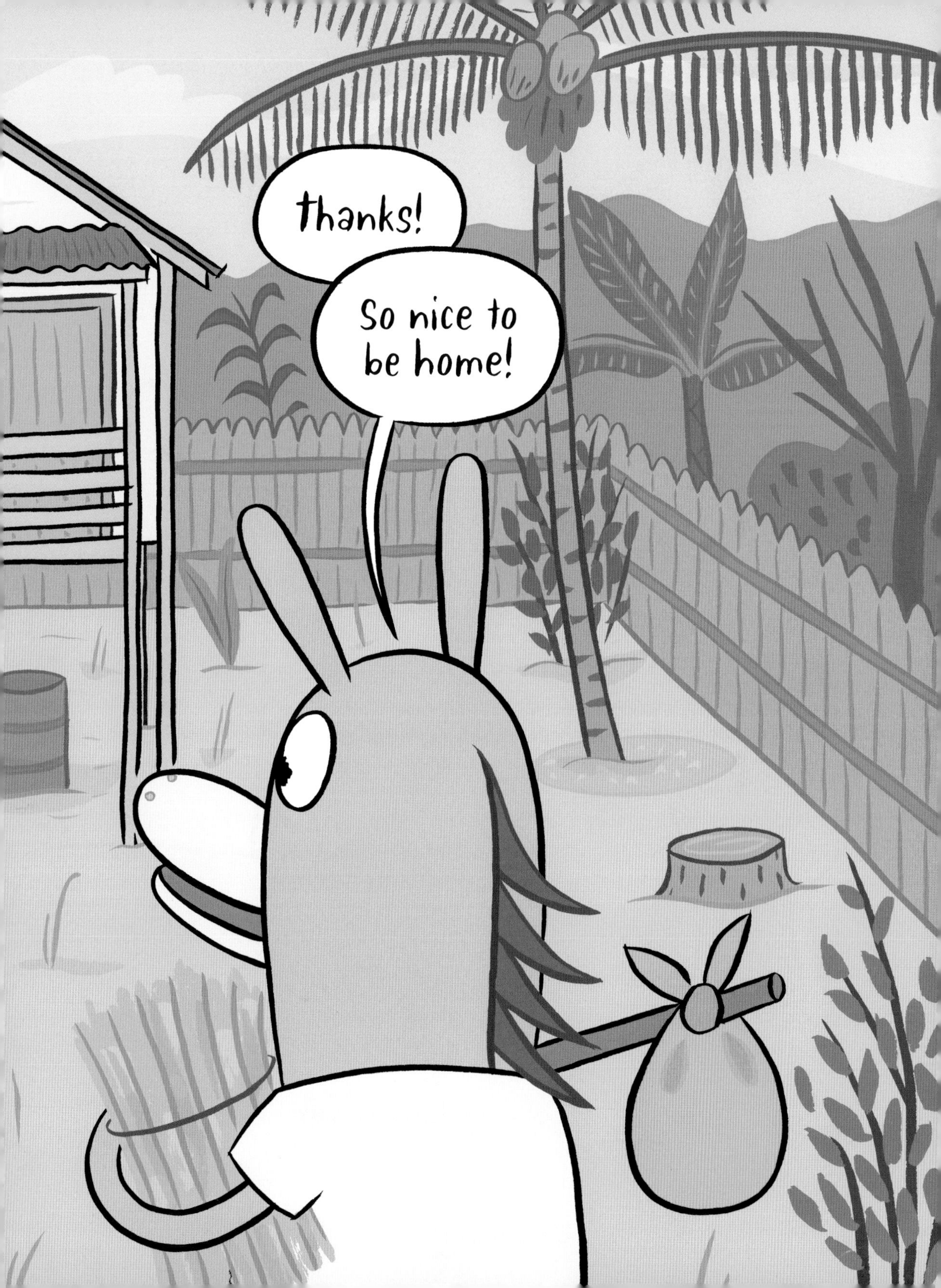
thanks!
So nice to be home!

The First thing Francis did when he got home was deliver the tiger grass to the downstairs chickens.

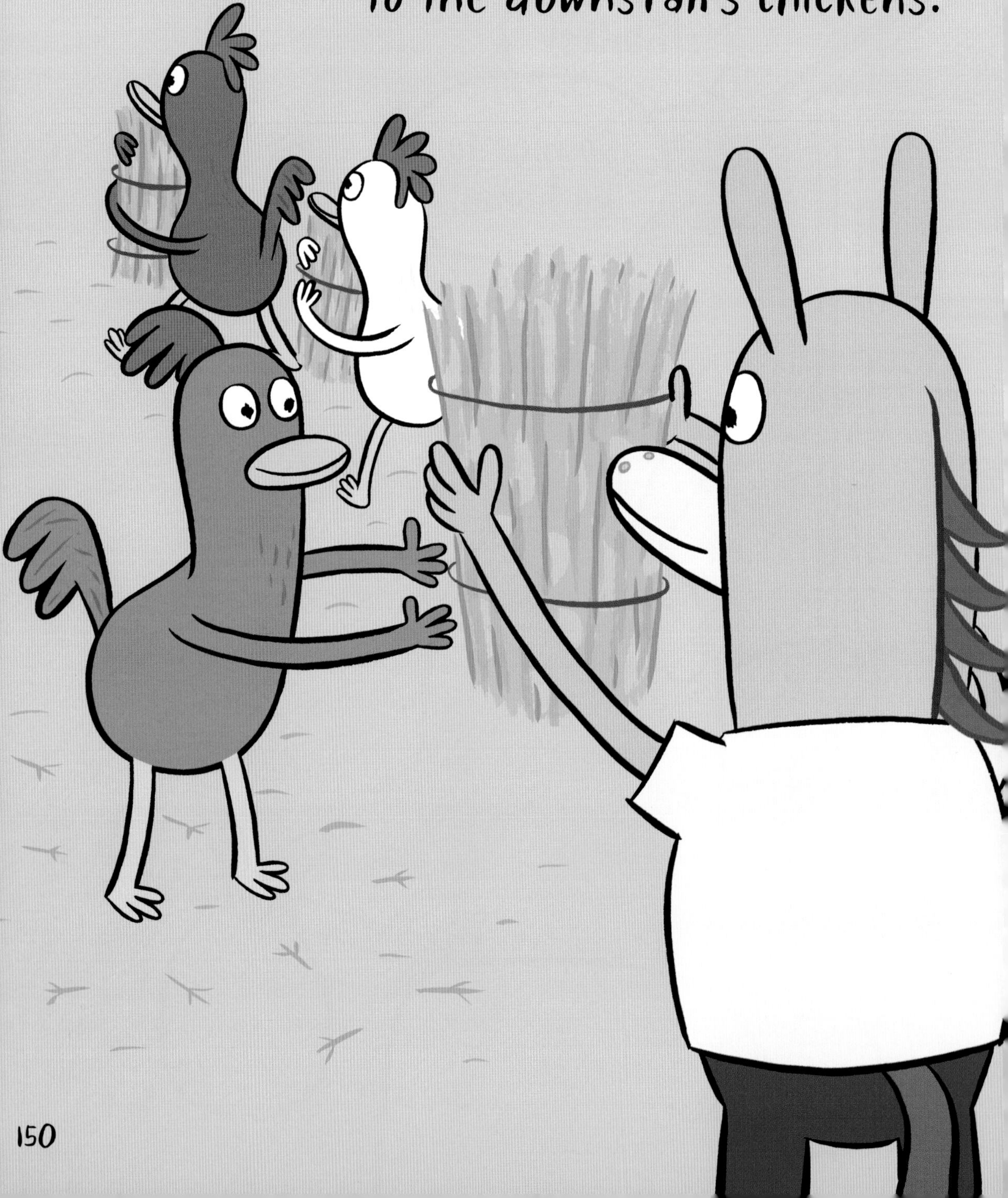

He then helped
Nigel plant the seedlings
Harriet had given him.

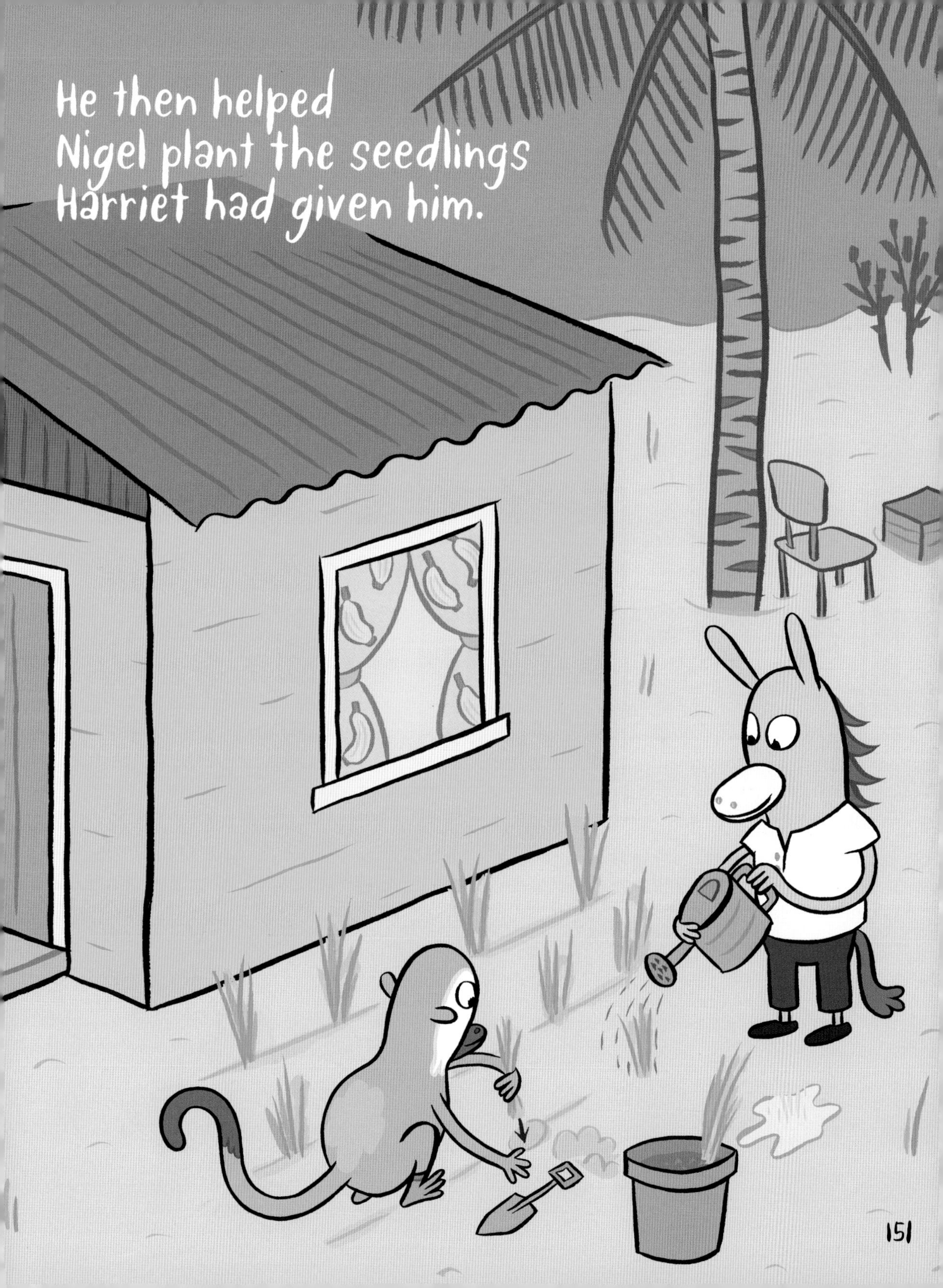

Nigel promised to take proper care of the new plants so that soon he could supply Francis with tiger grass grown in his very own yard.

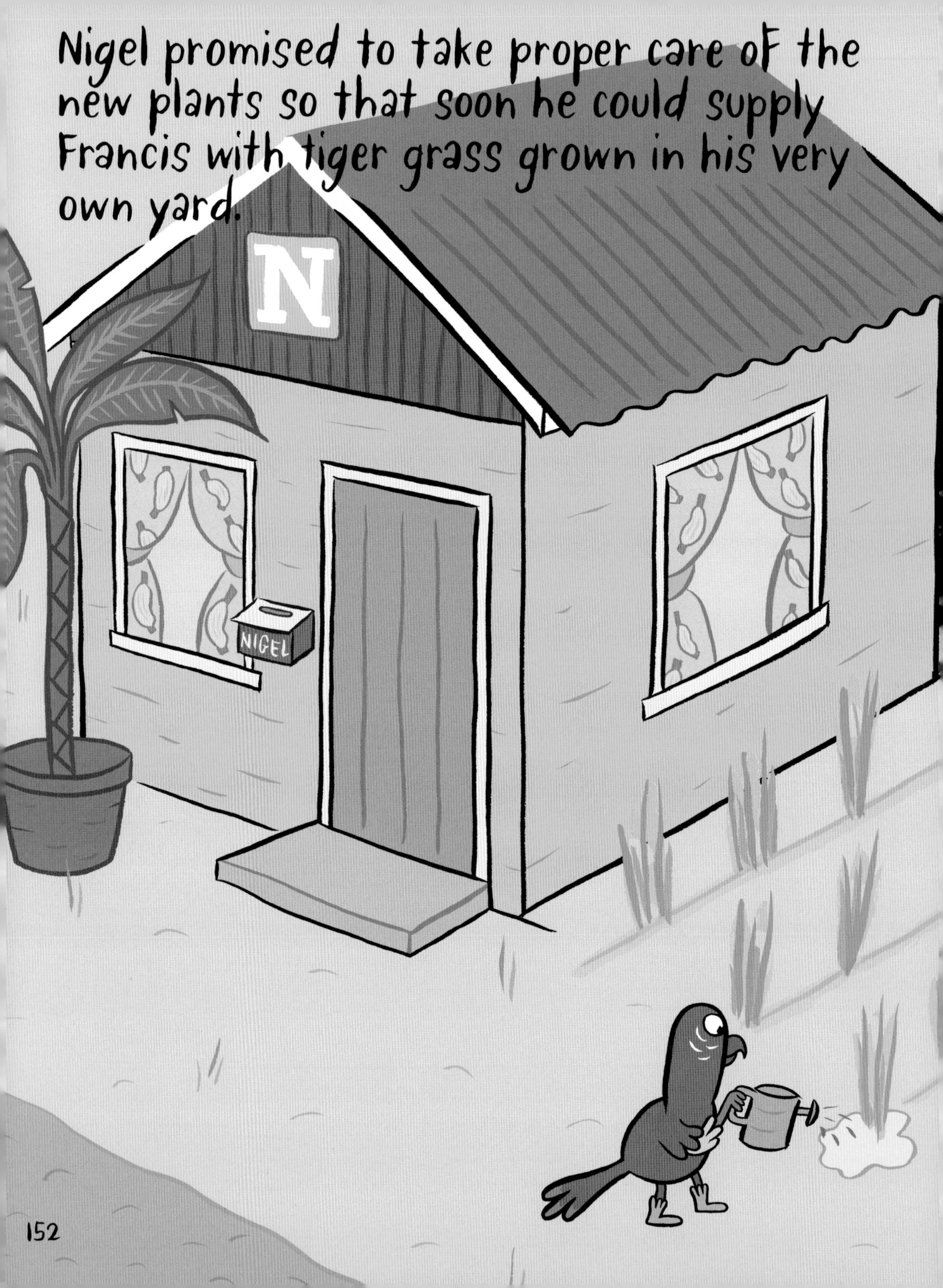
N
NIGEL

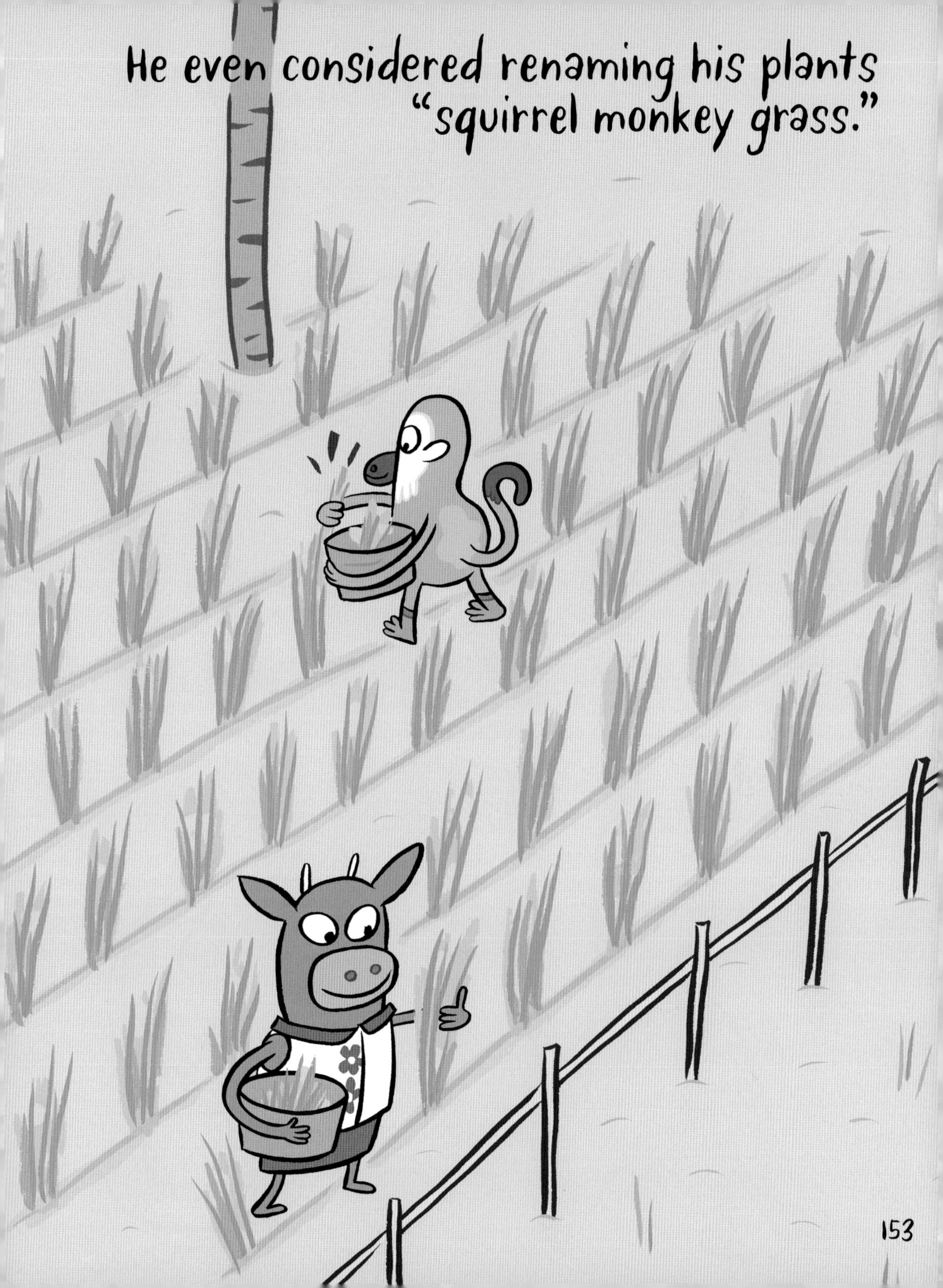
He even considered renaming his plants "squirrel monkey grass."

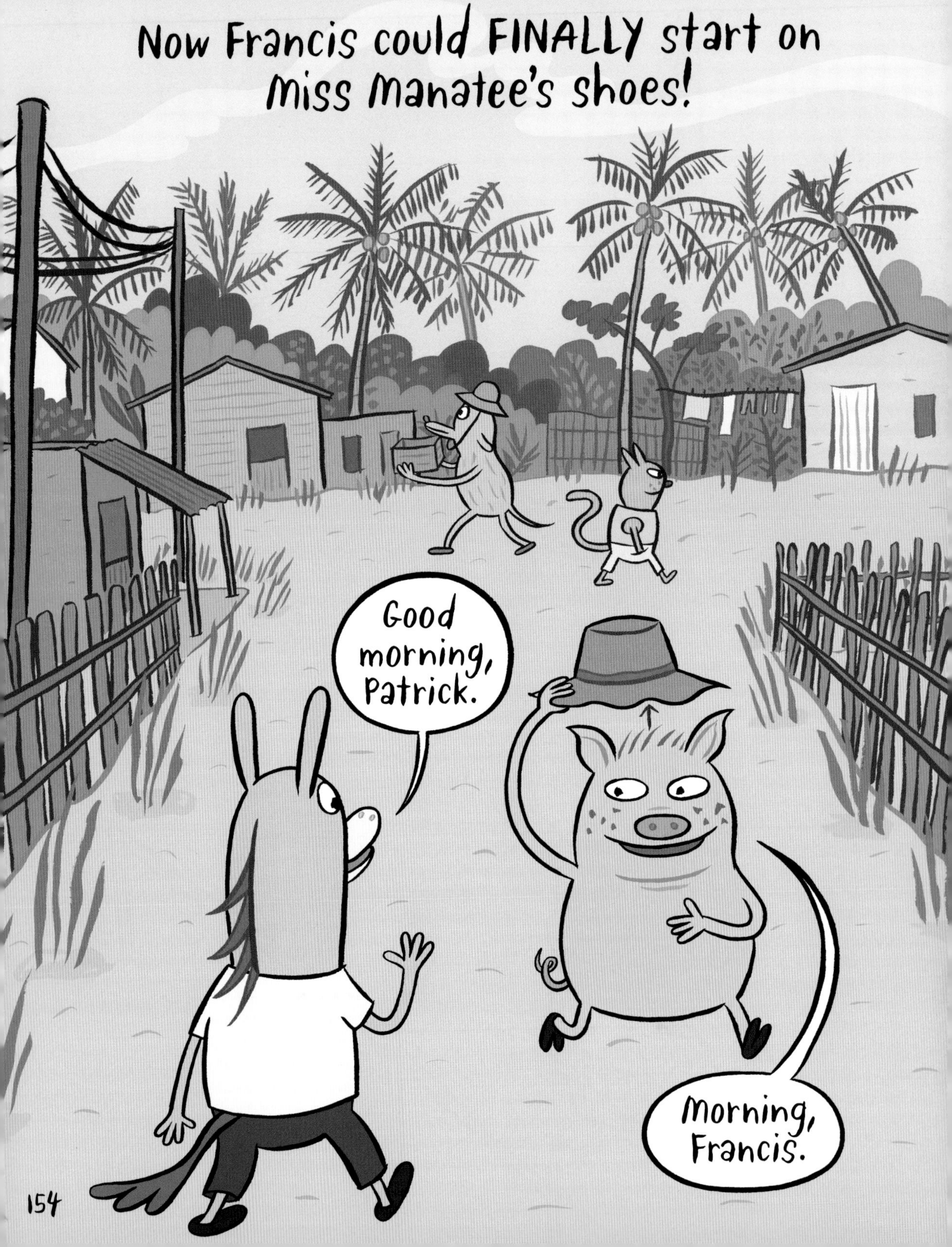
Now Francis could FINALLY start on Miss Manatee's shoes!
Good morning, Patrick.
Morning, Francis.

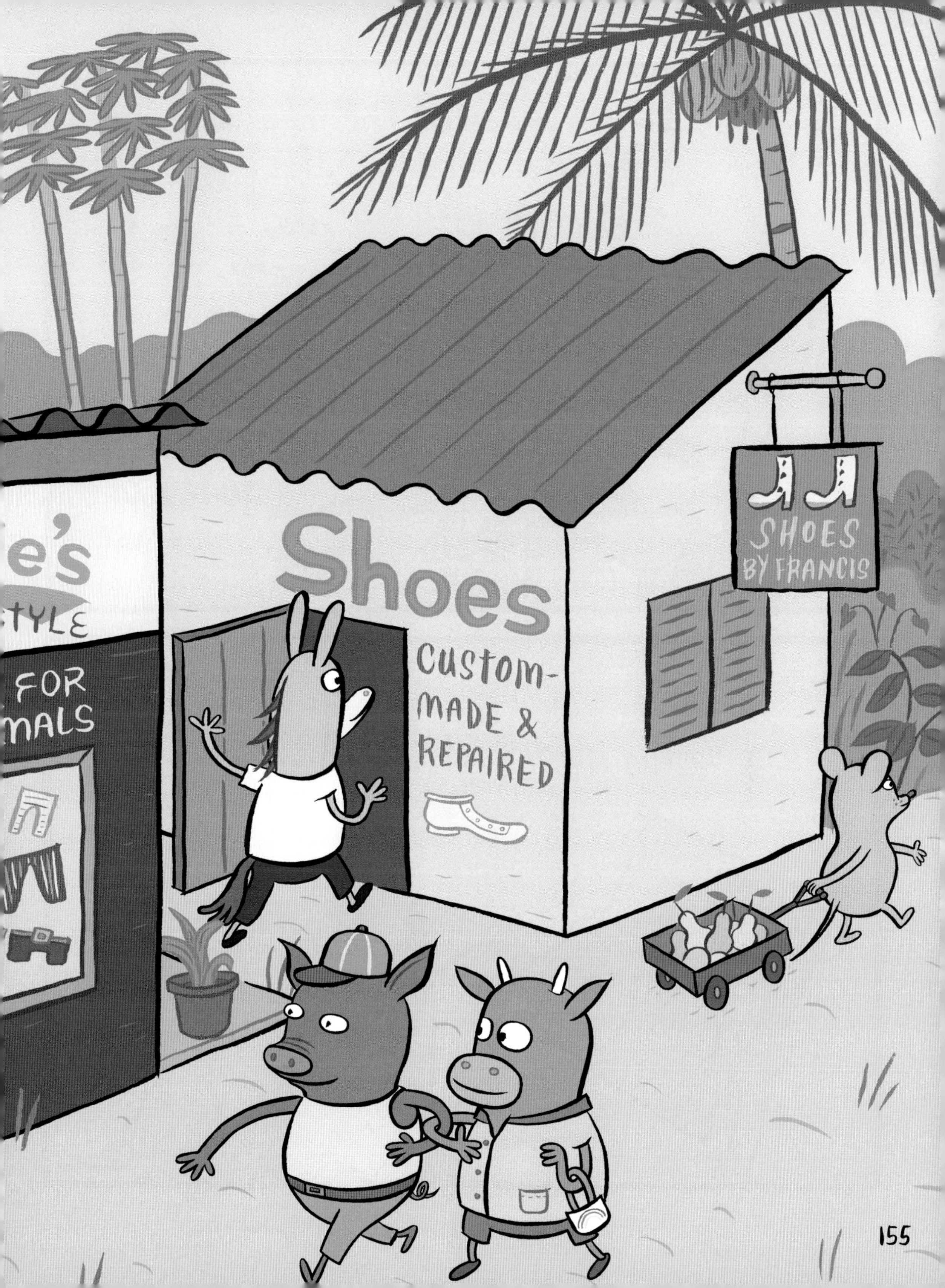
e's
TYLE
FOR
MALS
Shoes
CUSTOM-
MADE &
REPAIRED
SHOES
BY FRANCIS

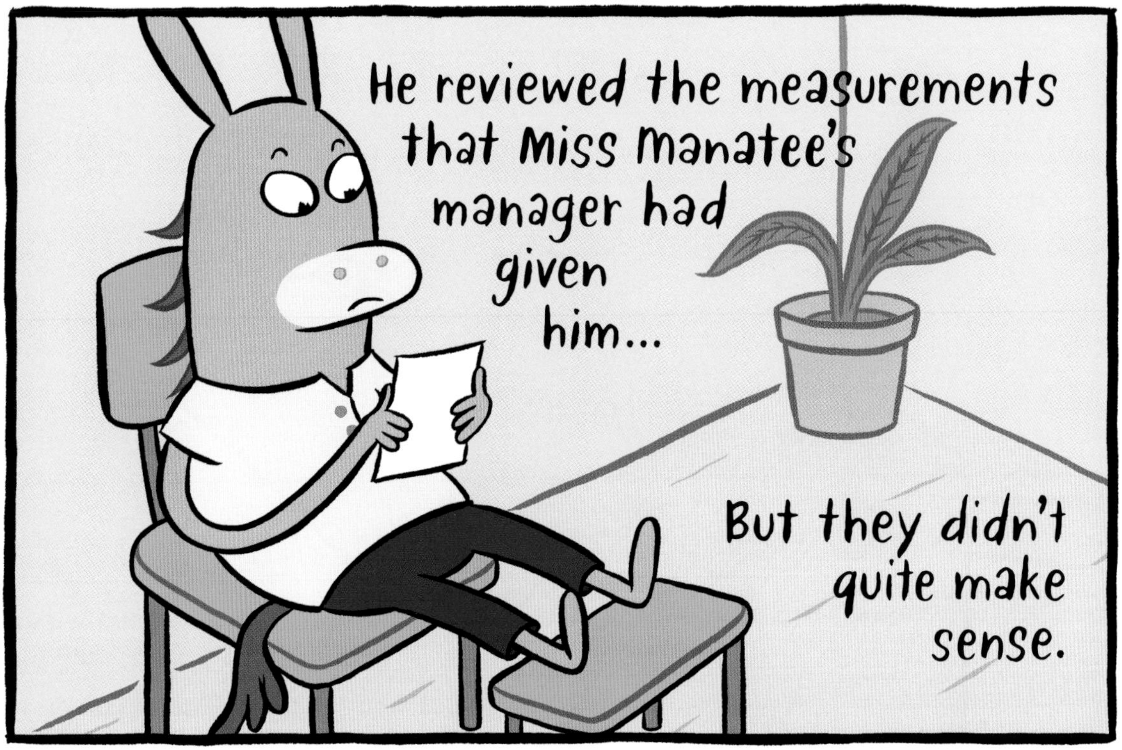
He reviewed the measurements that Miss Manatee's manager had given him...
But they didn't quite make sense.

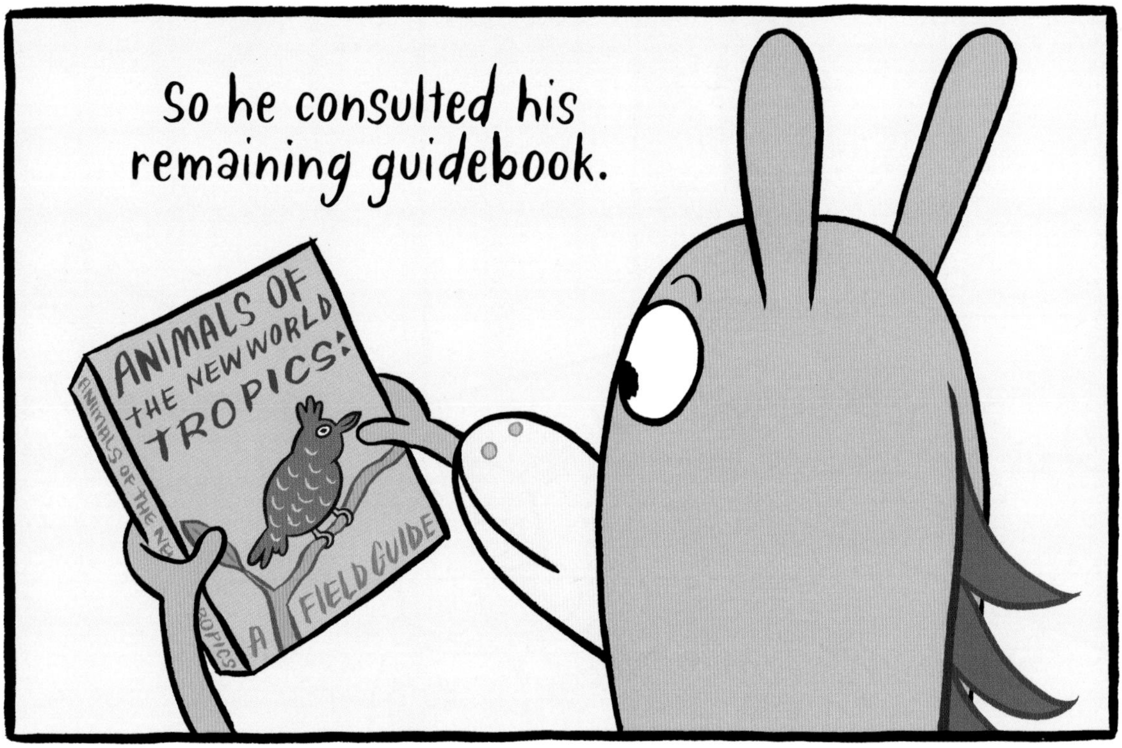
So he consulted his remaining guidebook.
ANIMALS OF THE NEW WORLD TROPICS:
A FIELD GUIDE

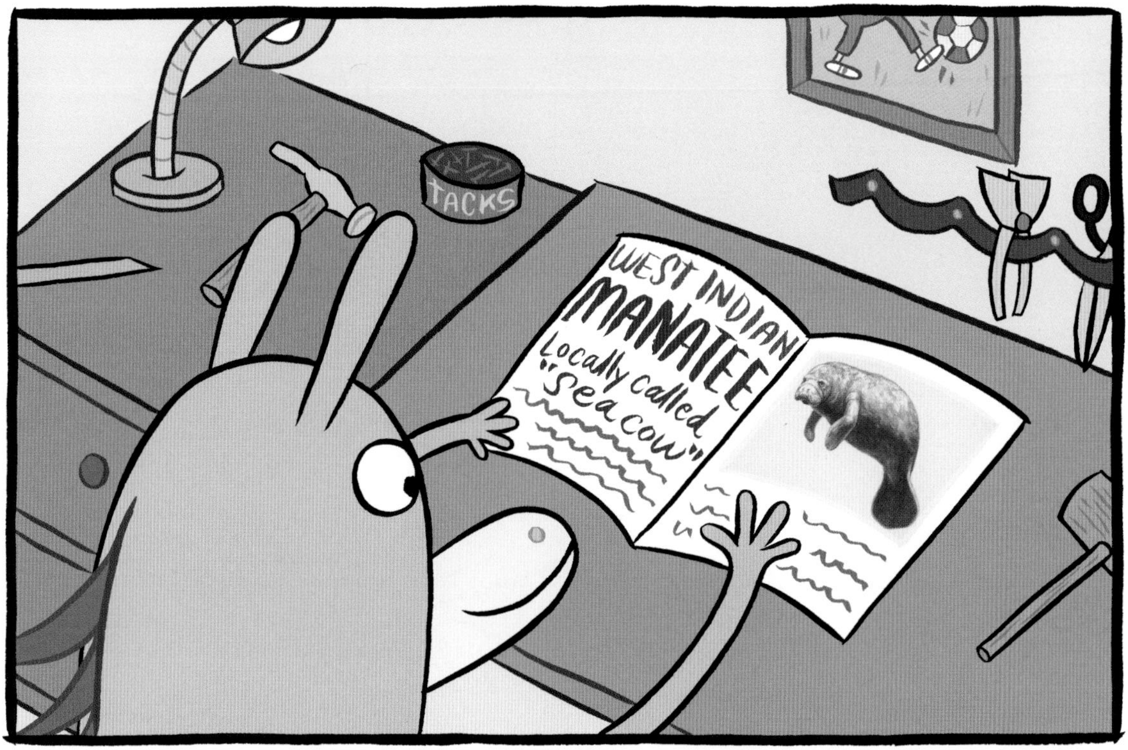
WEST INDIAN
MANATEE
Locally called
"sea cow"
TACKS

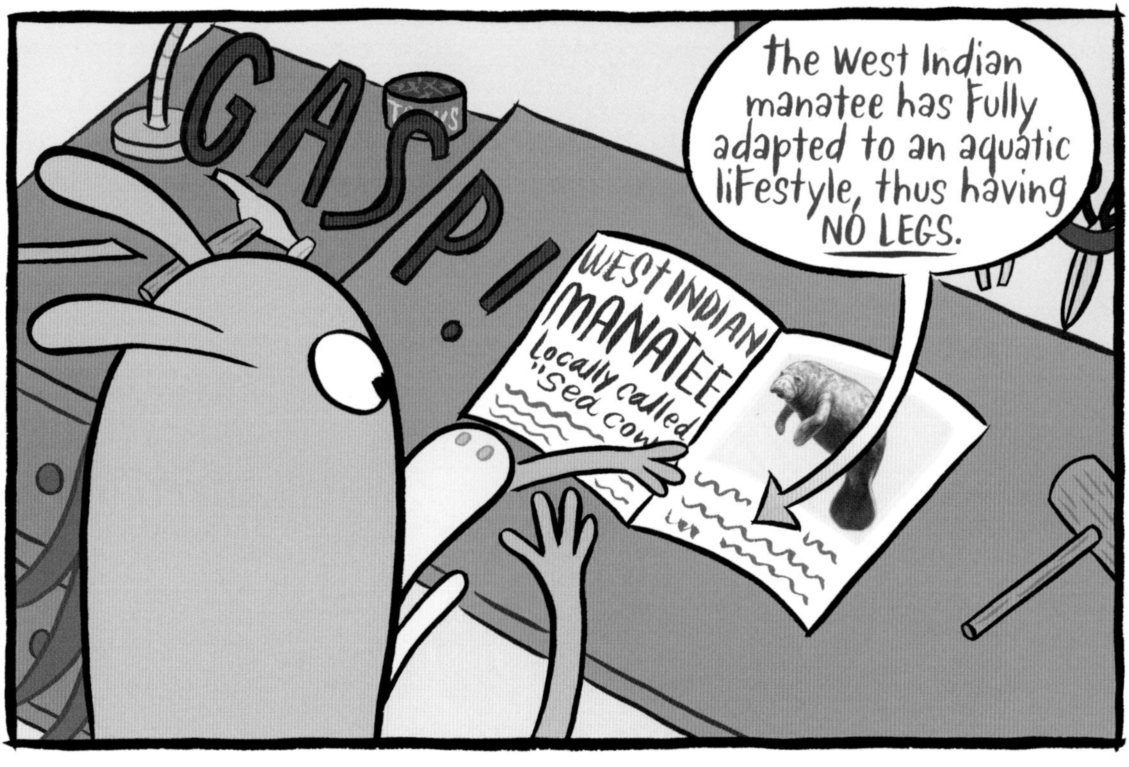
GASP!
the West Indian manatee has fully adapted to an aquatic lifestyle, thus having NO LEGS.
WEST INDIAN
MANATEE
Locally called
"sea cow

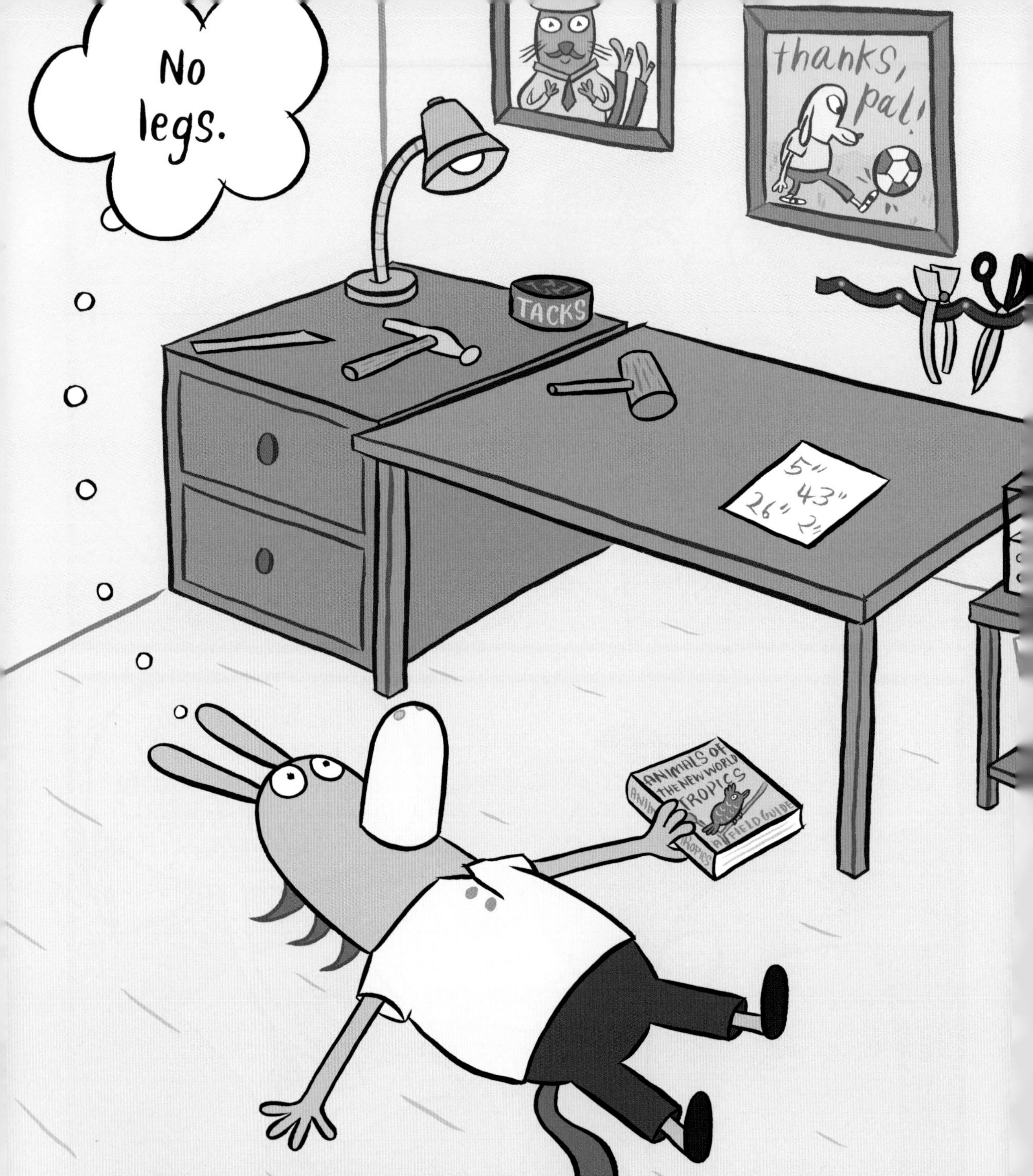
No legs.
TACKS
thanks, pal!
5" 43" 26" 2"
ANIMALS OF THE NEW WORLD TROPICS
A FIELD GUIDE

Before his journey,
Francis would have been stumped. He might even have had to turn down the job.

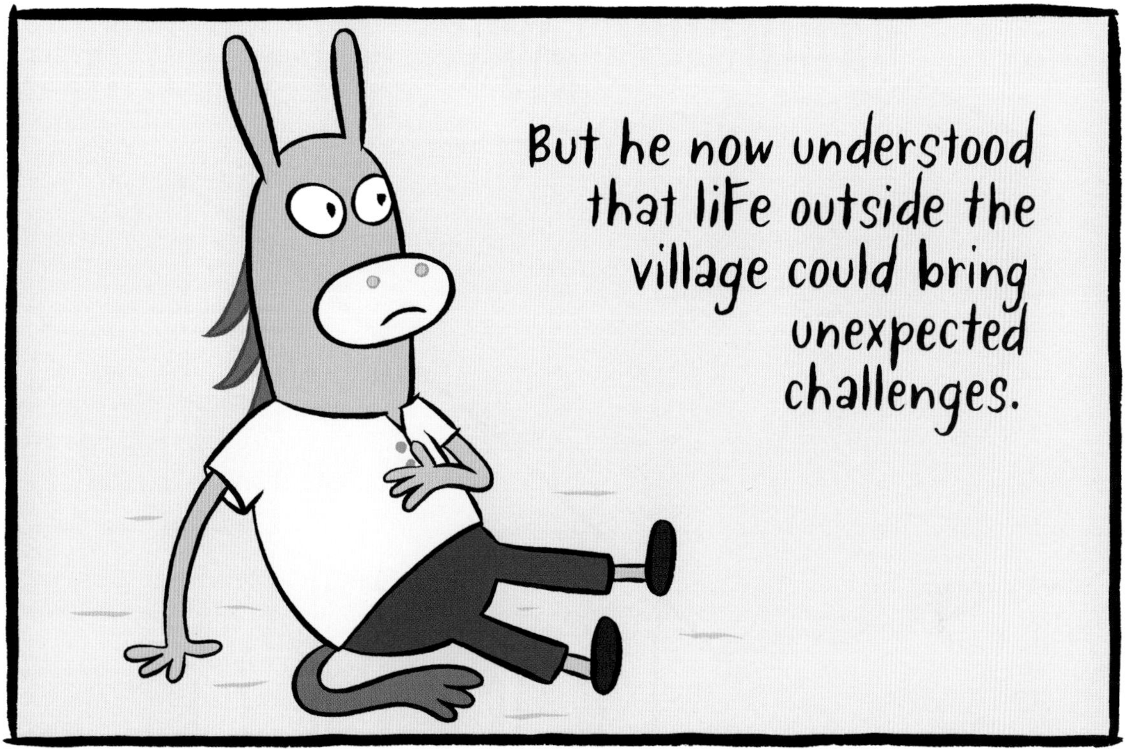
But he now understood that life outside the village could bring unexpected challenges.

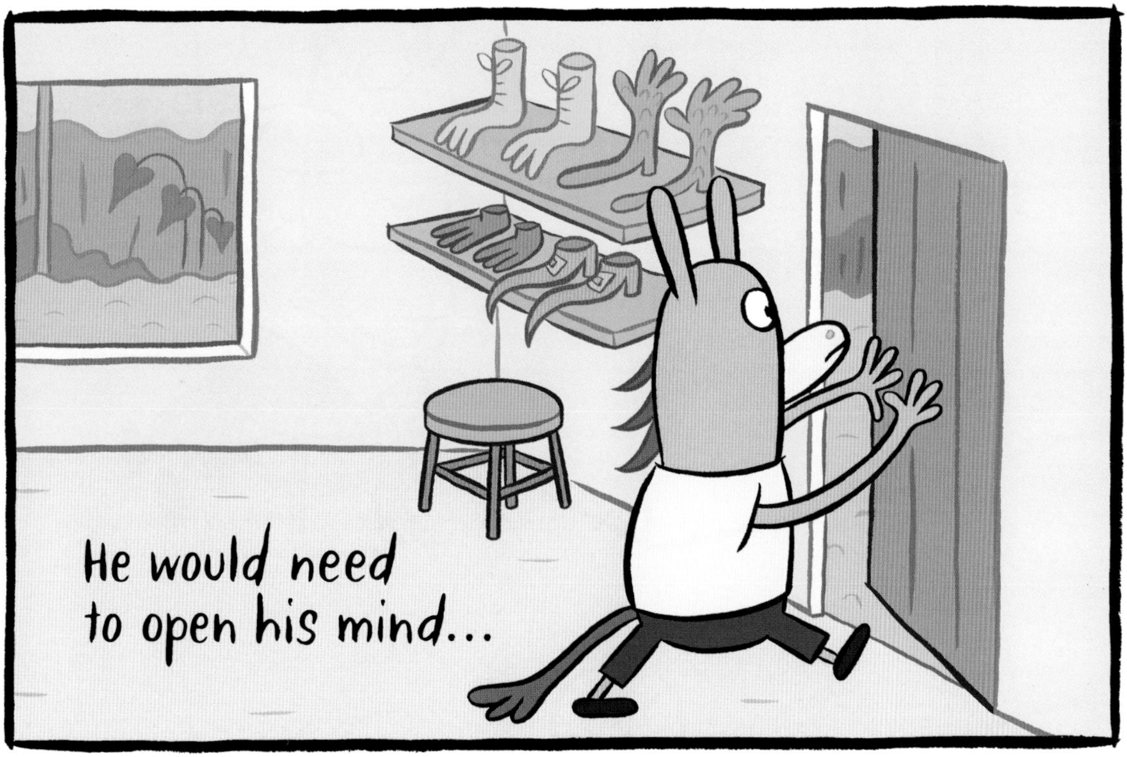
He would need to open his mind...

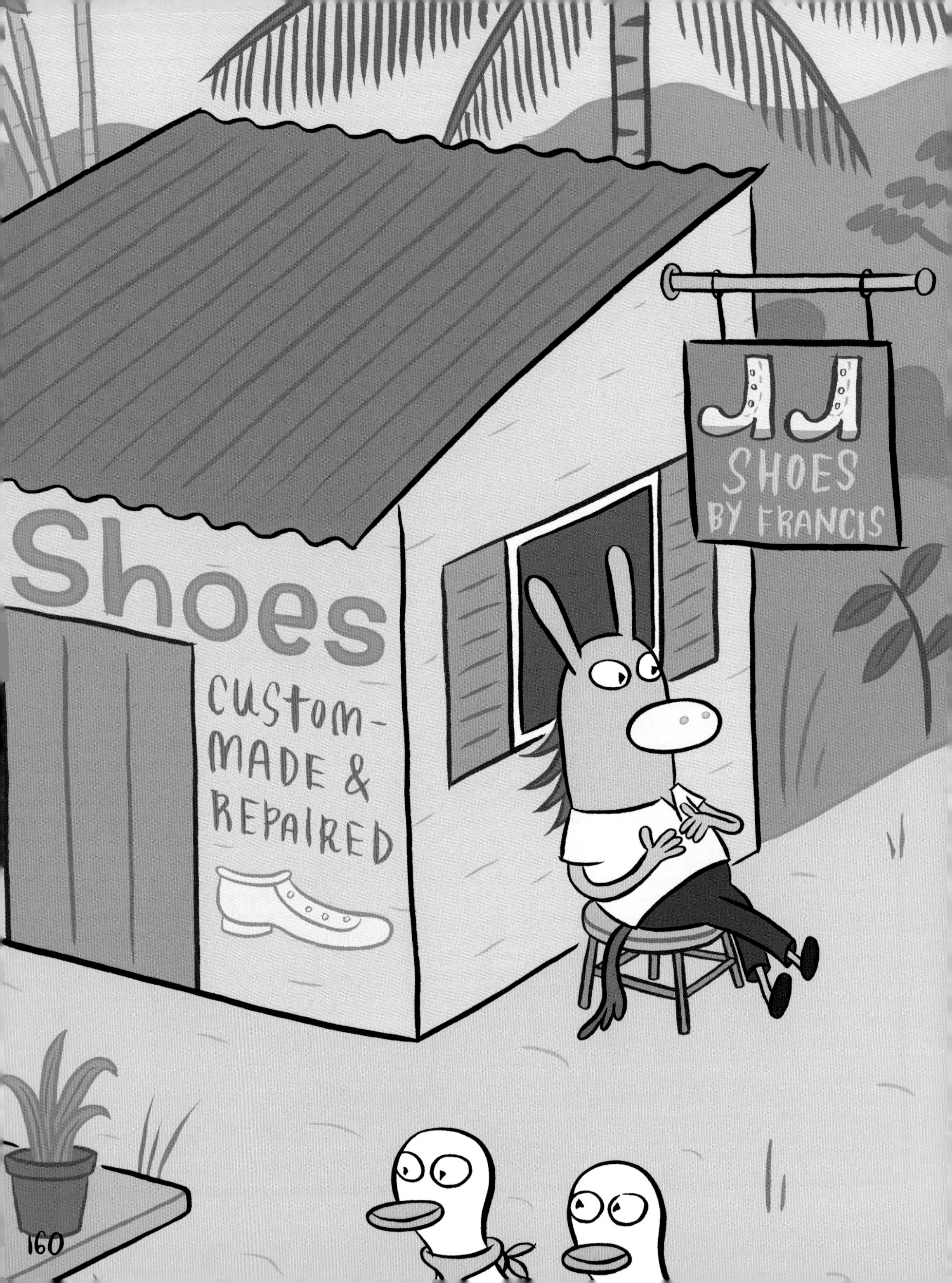
Shoes
CUSTOM-MADE & REPAIRED
SHOES
SHOES BY FRANCIS

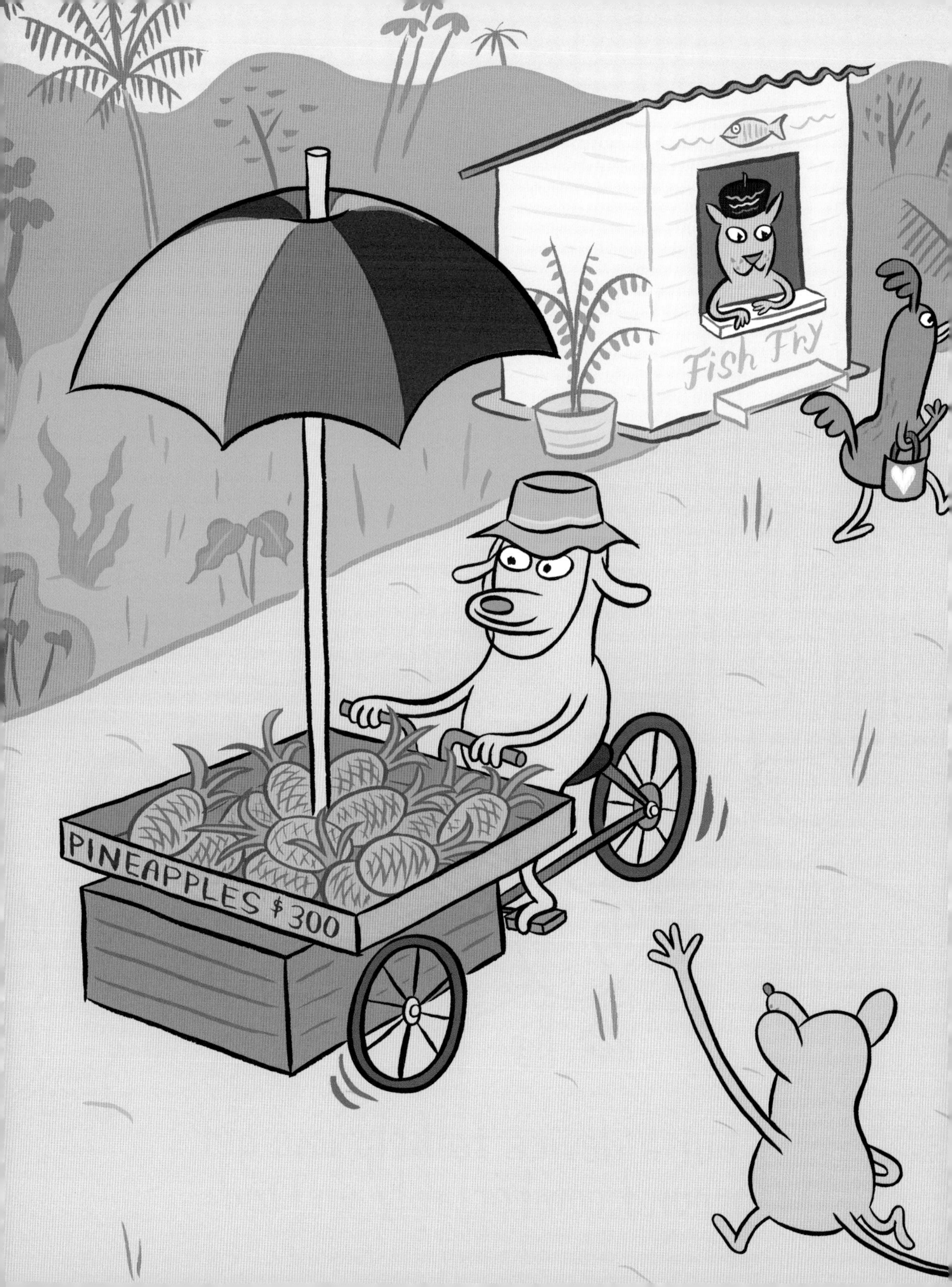
Fish Fry
PINEAPPLES $300

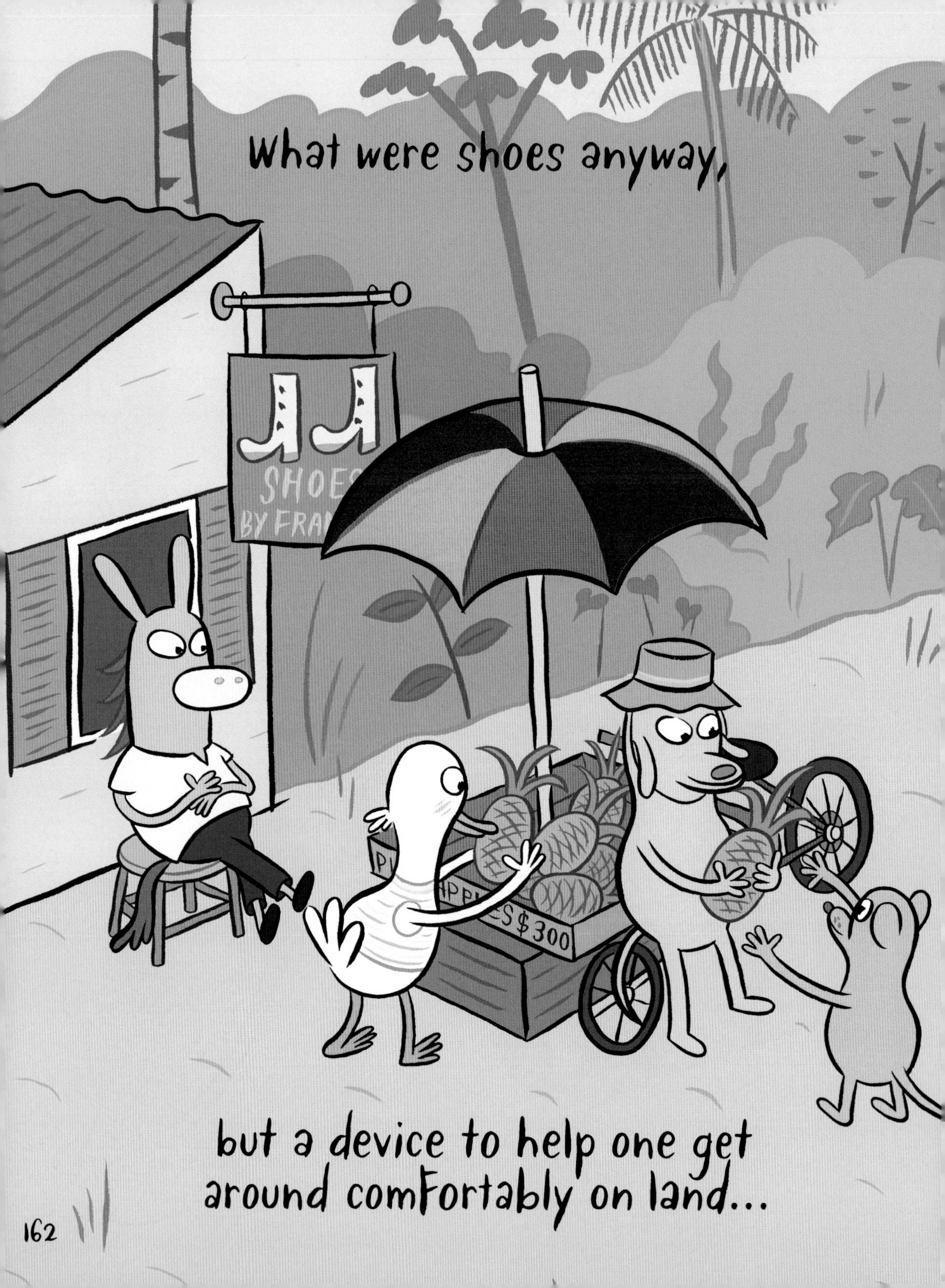
What were shoes anyway,
but a device to help one get around comfortably on land...
SHOES

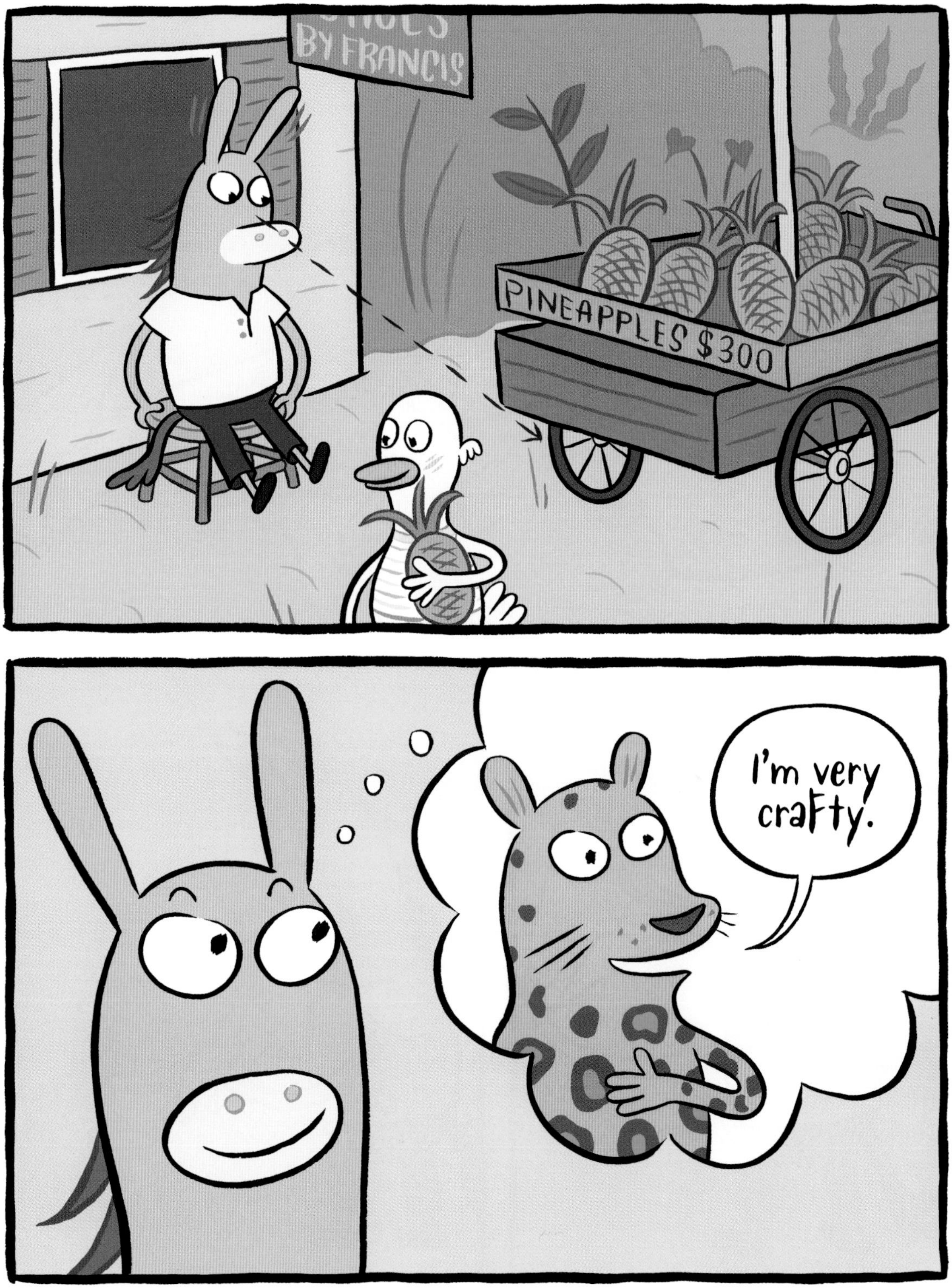
BY FRANCIS
PINEAPPLES $300
I'm very crafty.

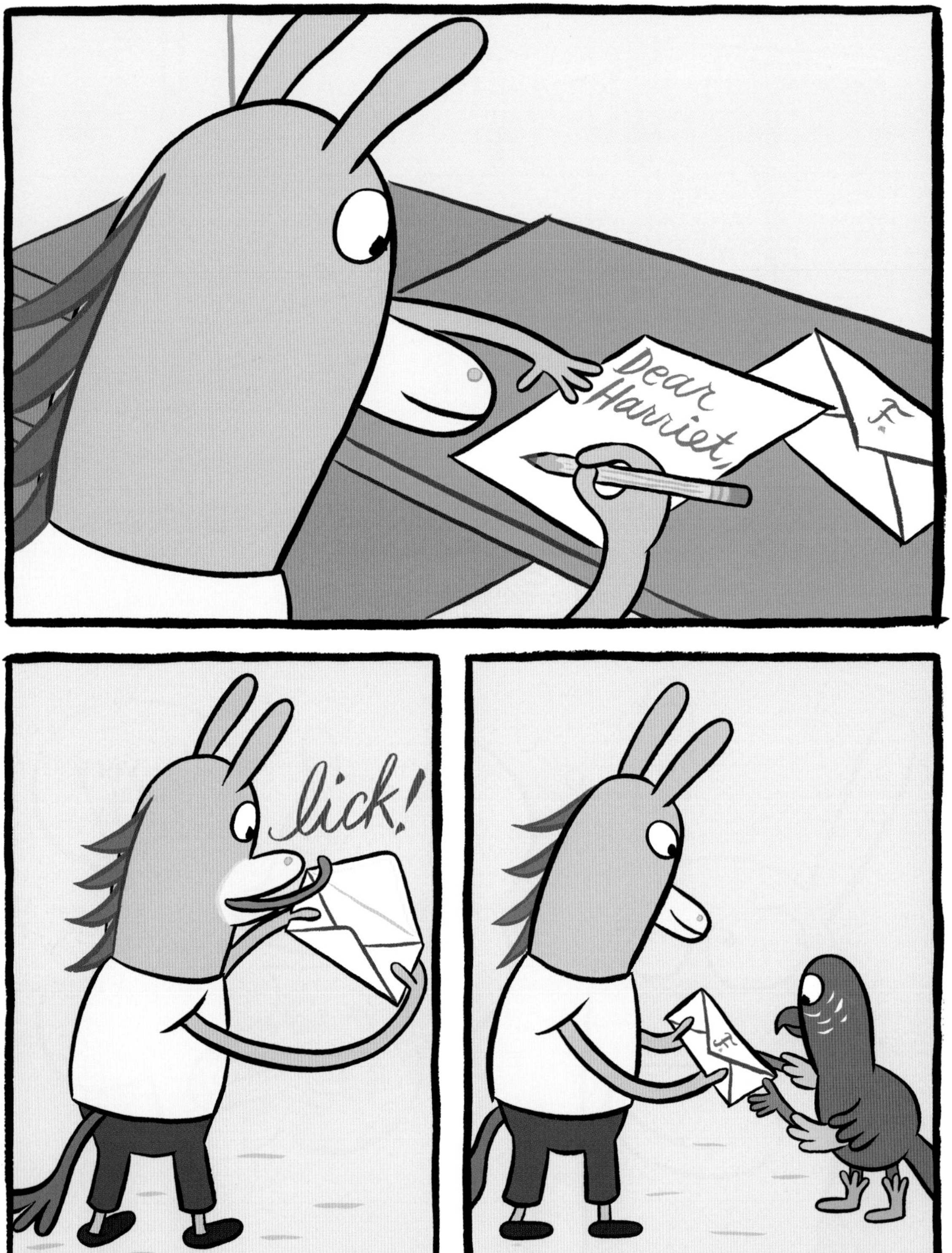
Dear Harriet,
F.
lick!
F.

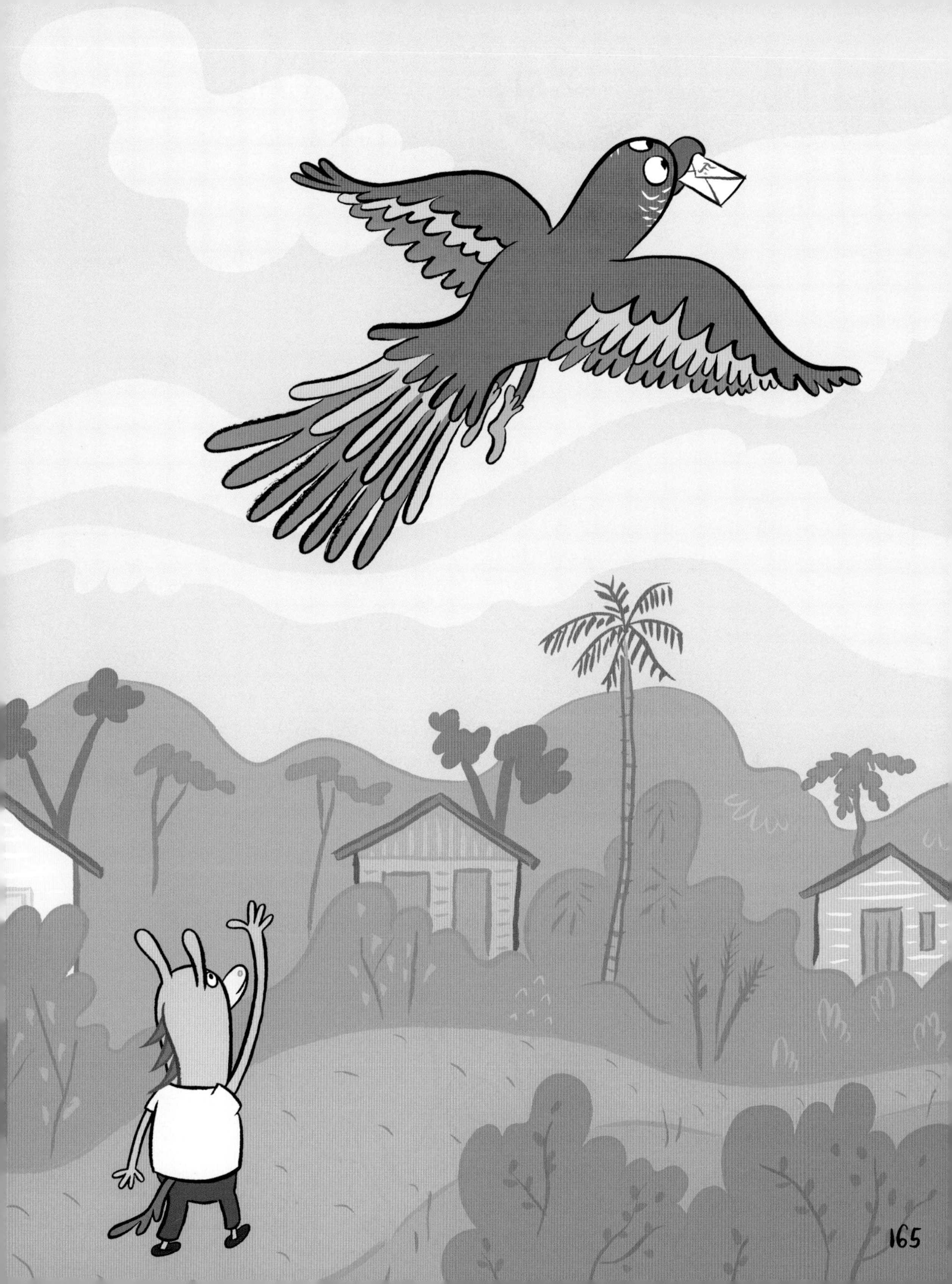

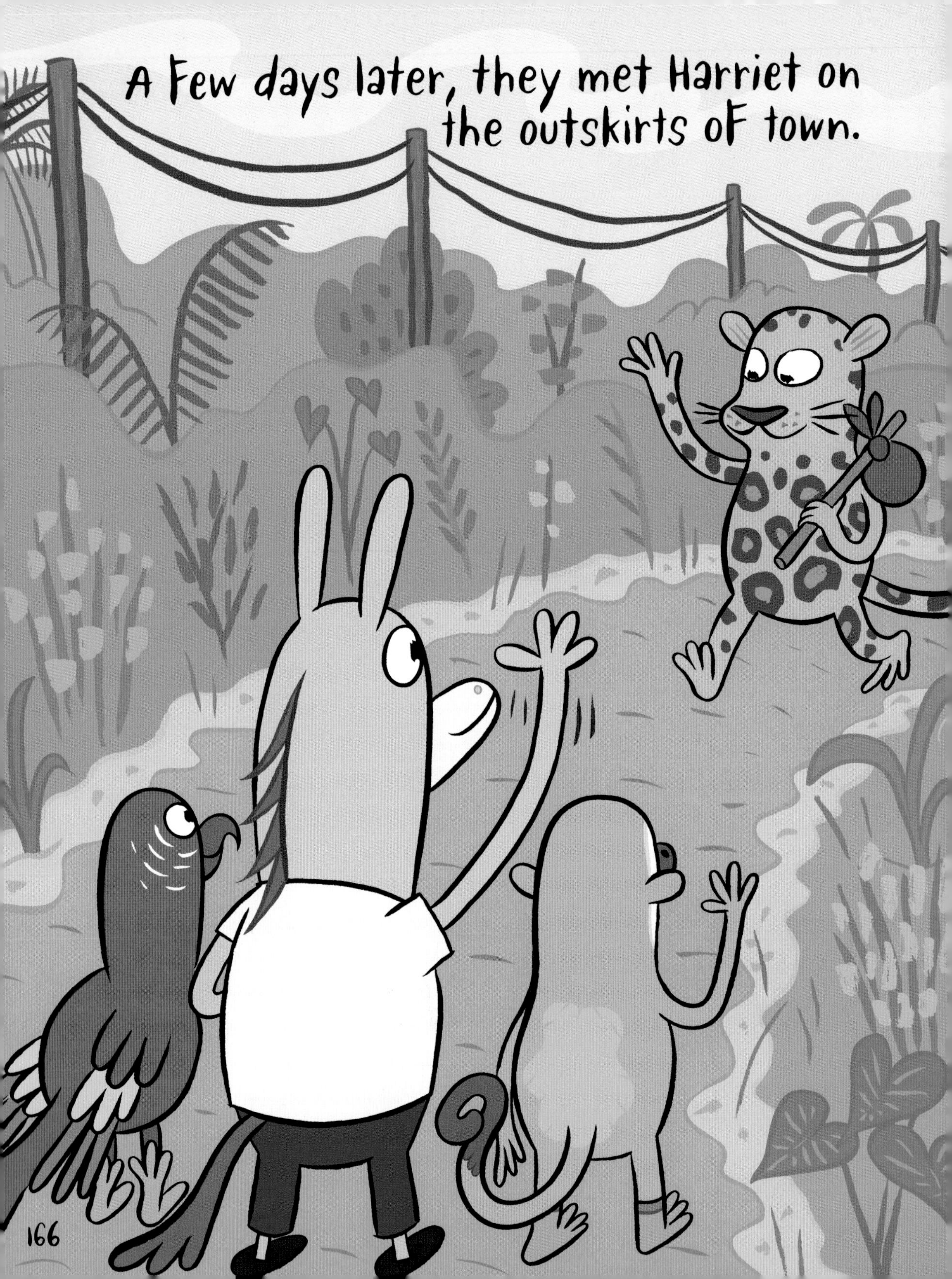
A Few days later, they met Harriet on the outskirts of town.

Nigel was still wary of Harriet after their most recent encounter, but they both apologized for their past actions and agreed to put everything behind them.

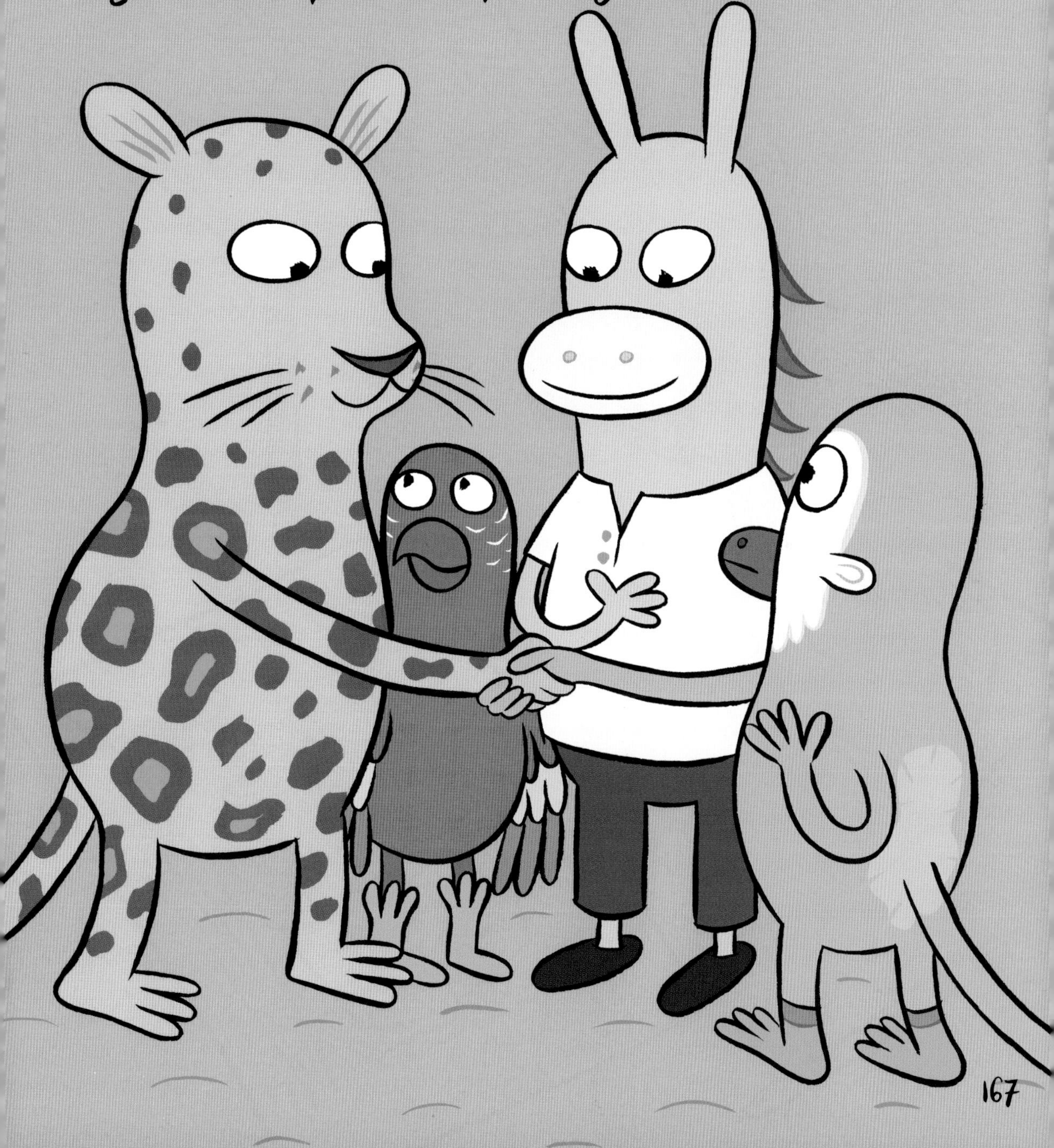

Back in his shop, Francis drew out some ideas.

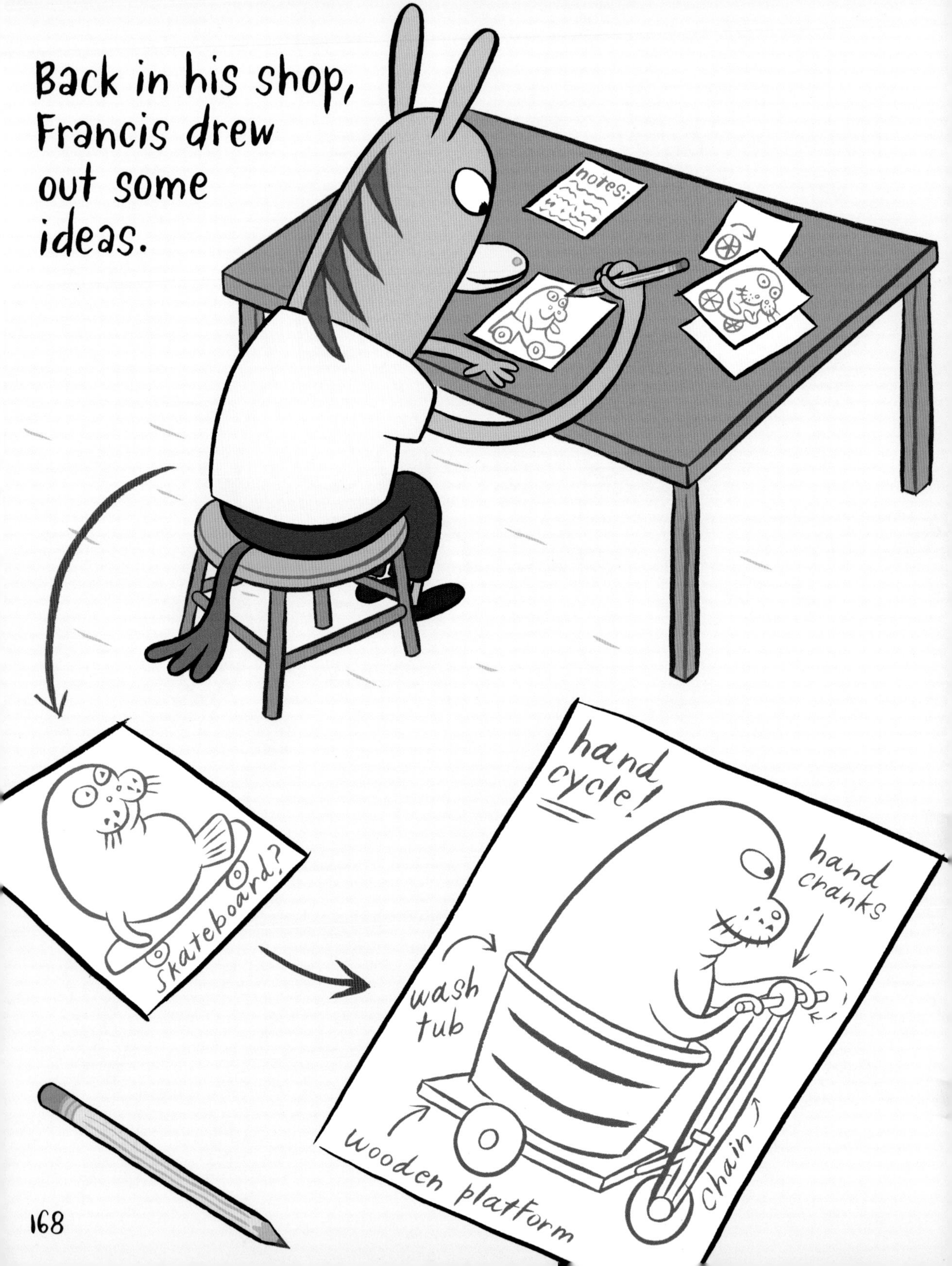
notes:
skateboard?
hand cycle!
hand cranks
wash tub
wooden platform
chain

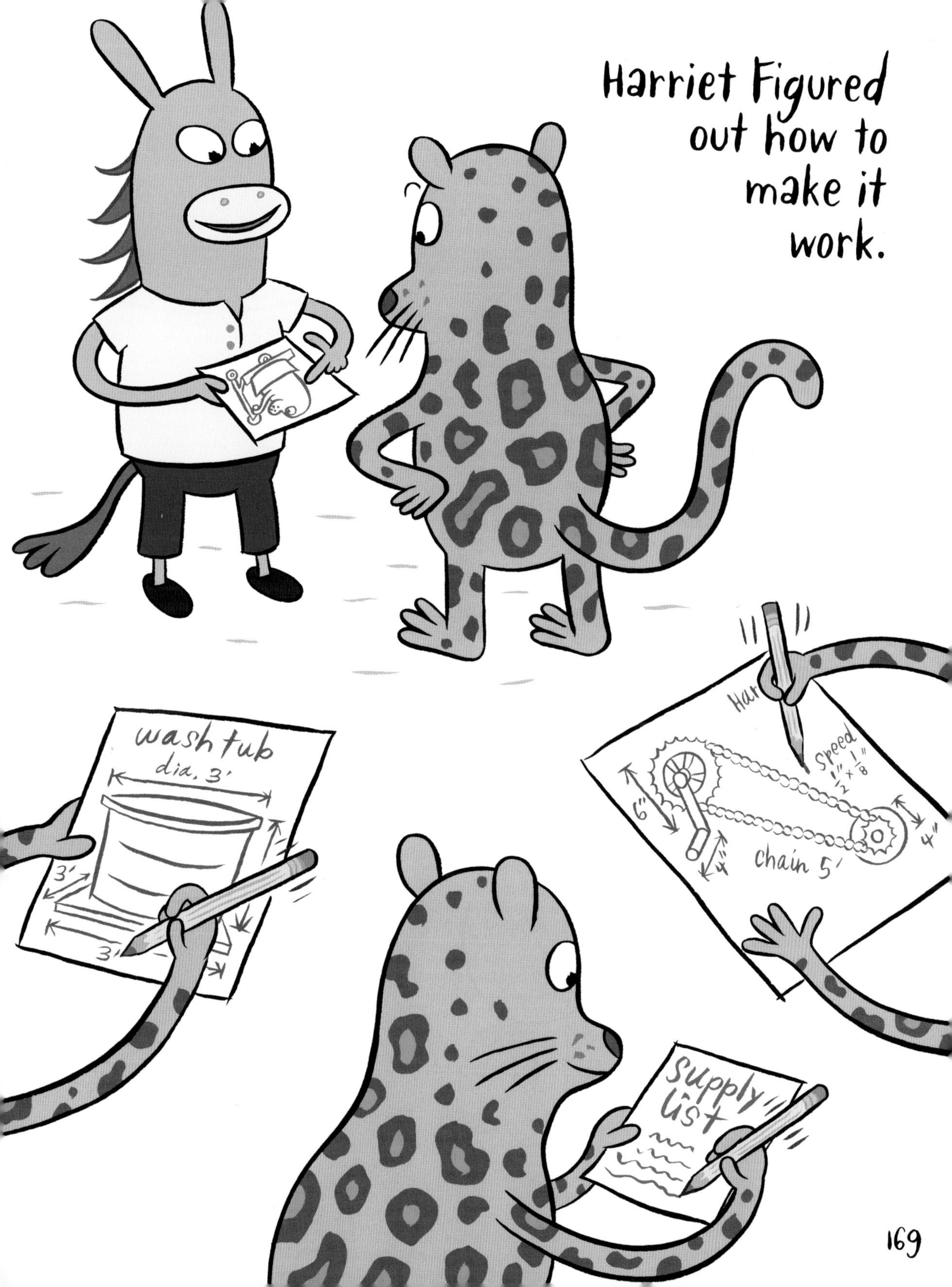
Harriet Figured out how to make it work.
wash tub
dia. 3'
3'
3'
Har
Speed
chain 5'
6"
4"
Supply List

Nigel brought the materials they needed.

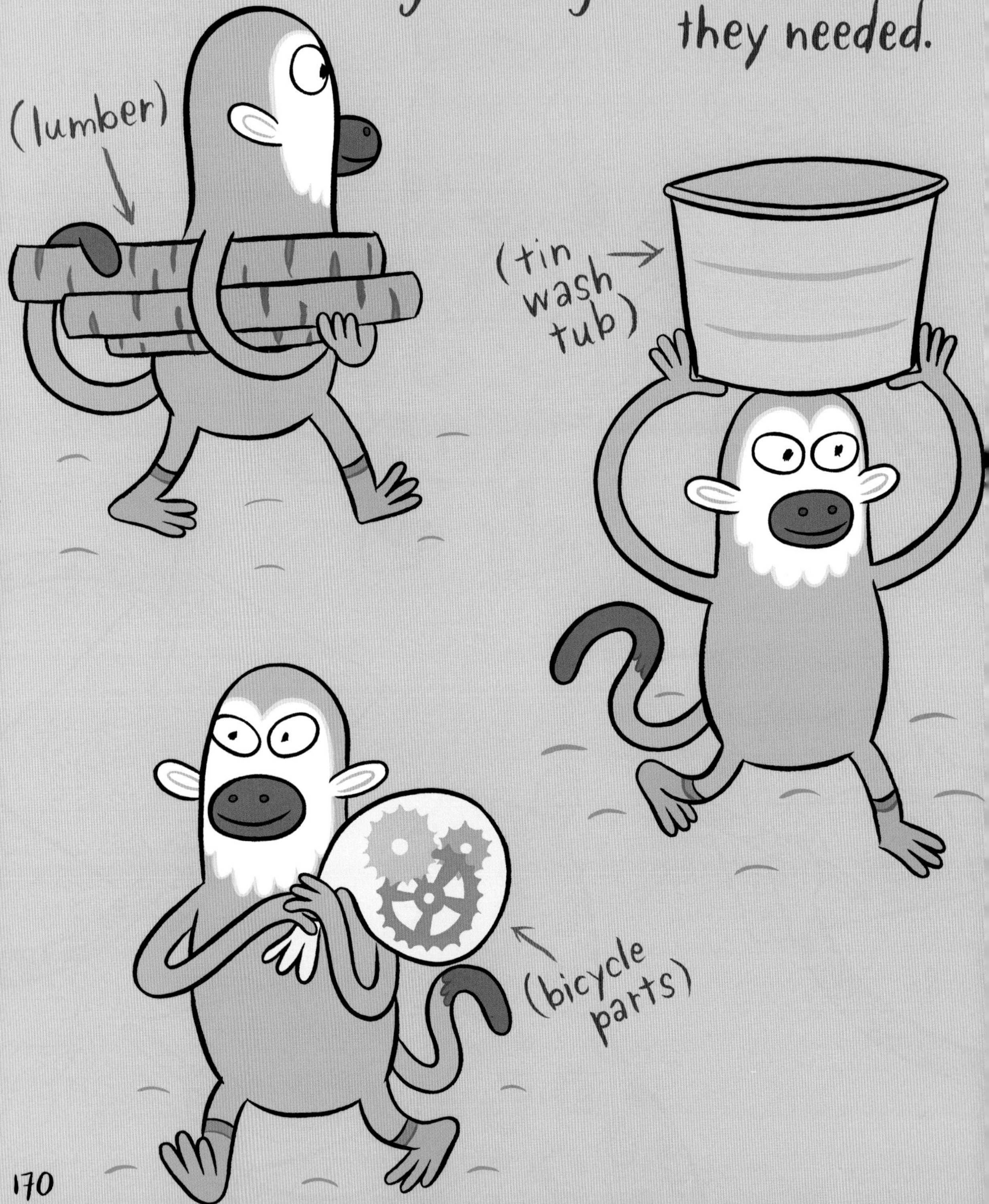
(lumber)
(tin wash tub)
(bicycle parts)

And Rhoda played DJ while they worked.

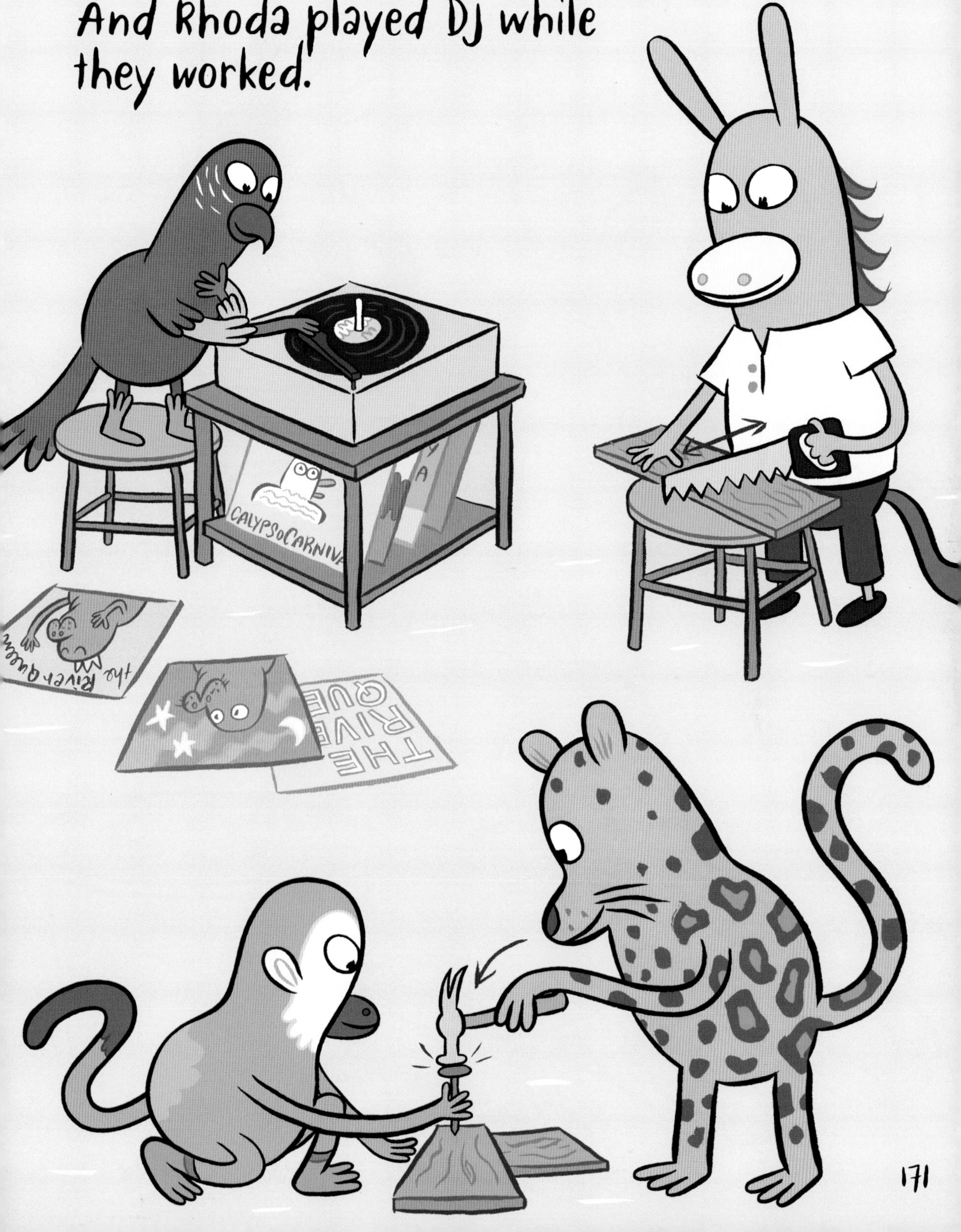
CALYPSO CARNIVA
the River Queen
THE RIVE QUE

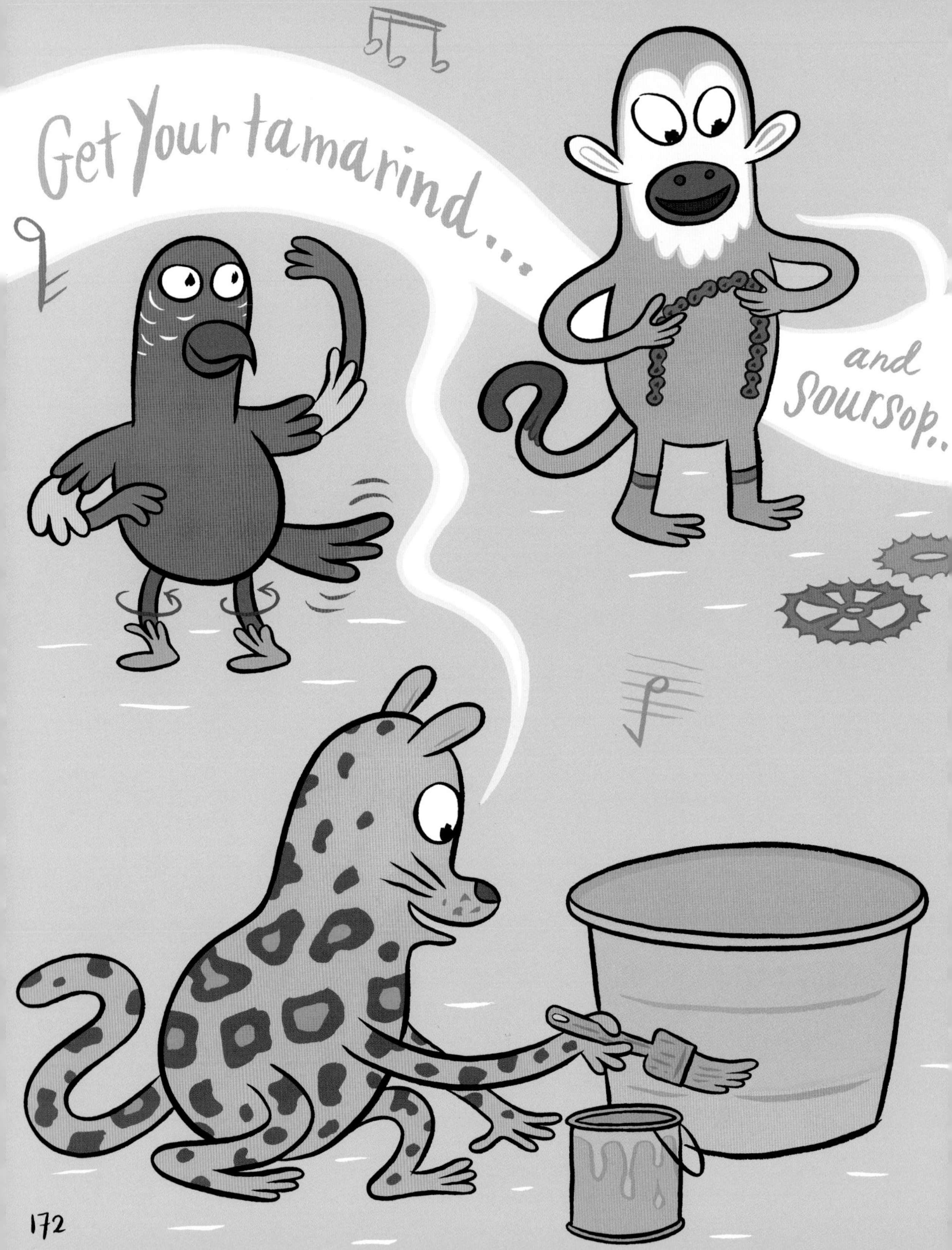
Get Your tamarind...
and Soursop..

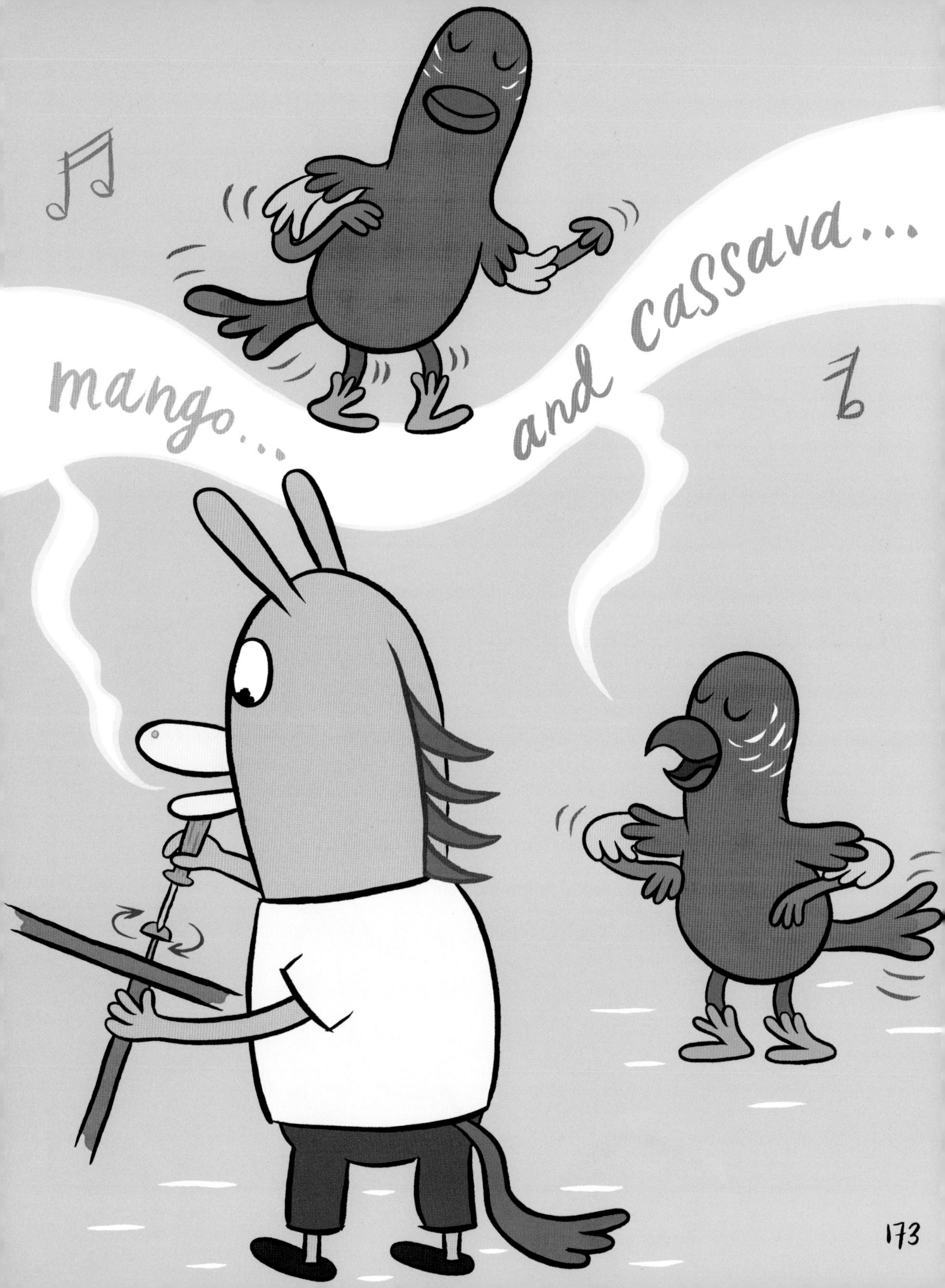
mango...
and cassava...

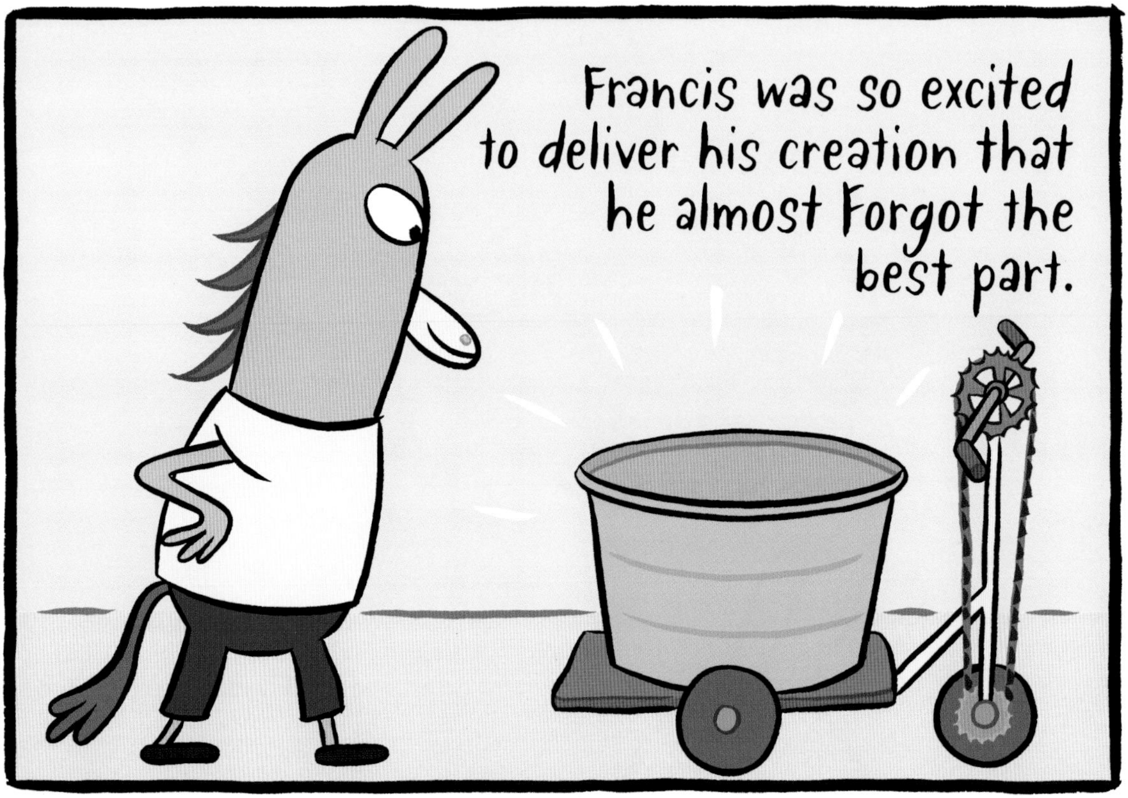
Francis was so excited to deliver his creation that he almost forgot the best part.

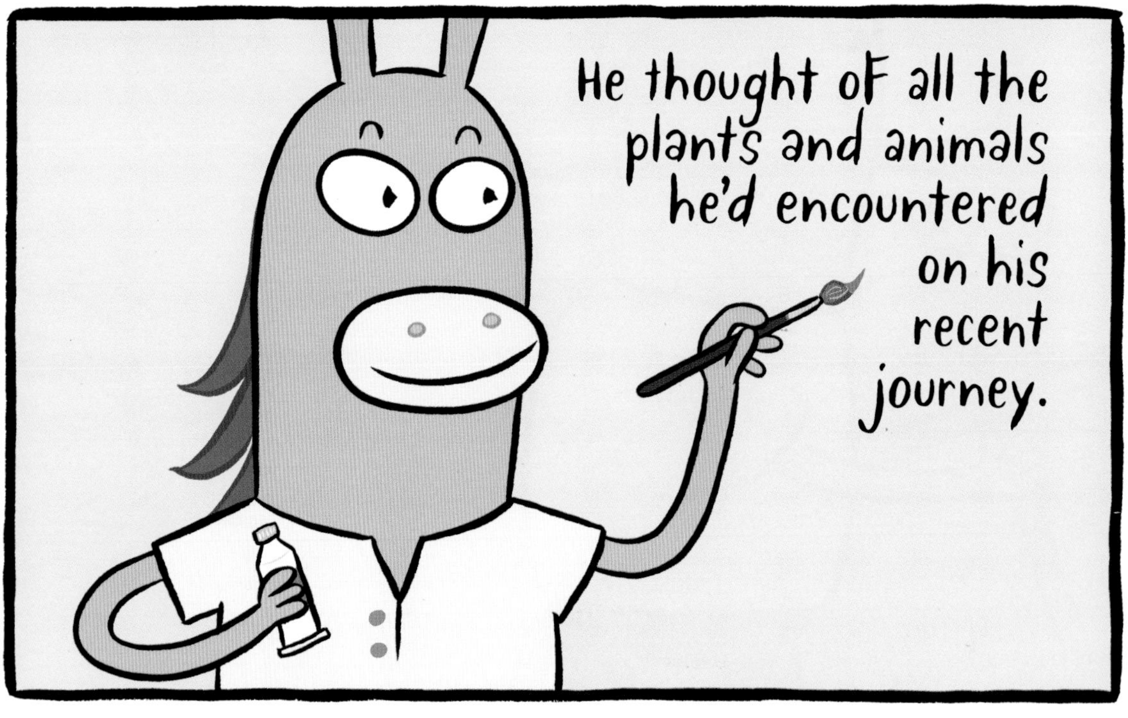
He thought of all the plants and animals he'd encountered on his recent journey.

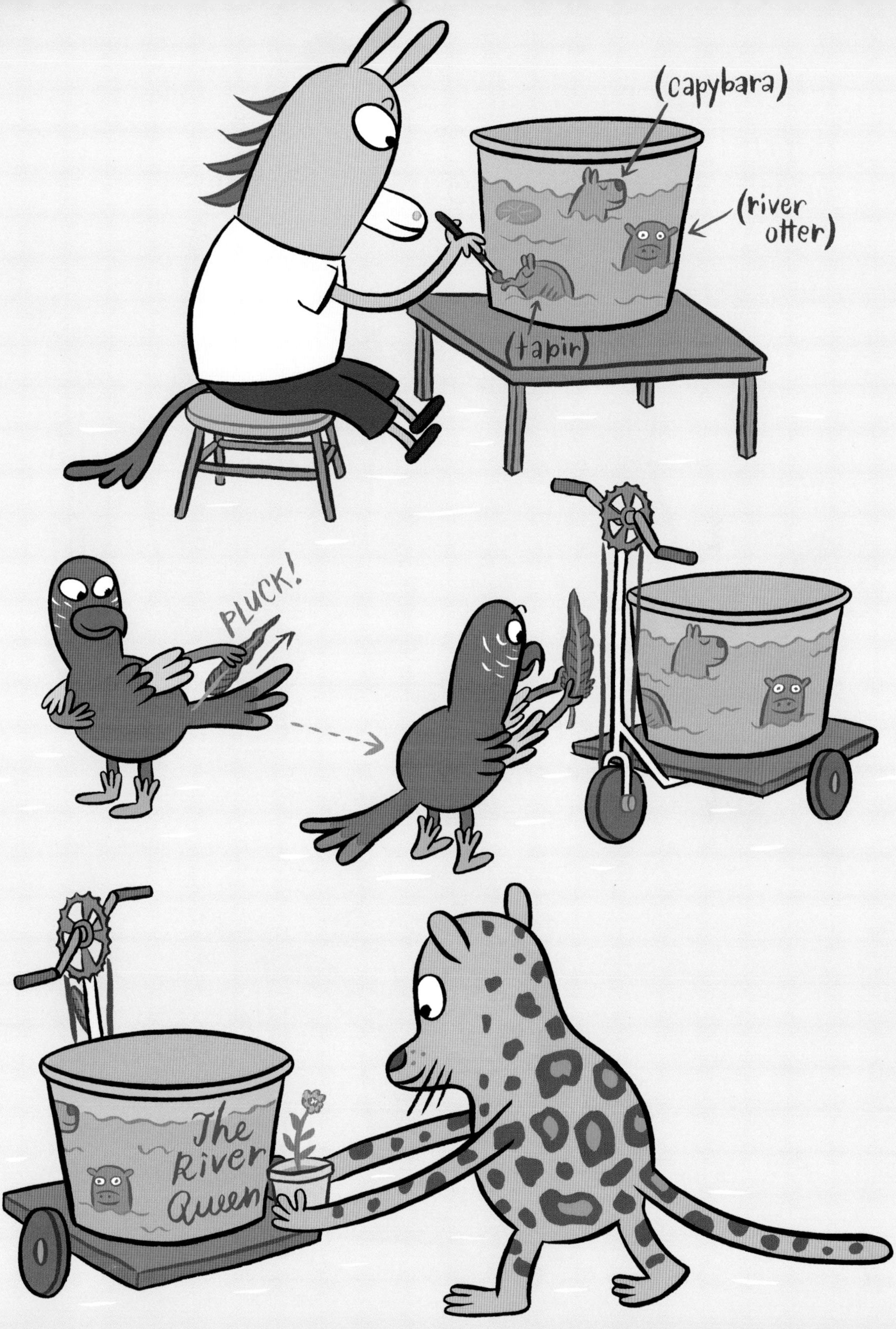
(capybara)
(river otter)
(tapir)
PLUCK!
The River Queen

When they Finished Miss Manatee's vehicle, Harriet tested it. The tub would be Filled with water so Miss Manatee could travel comFortably.

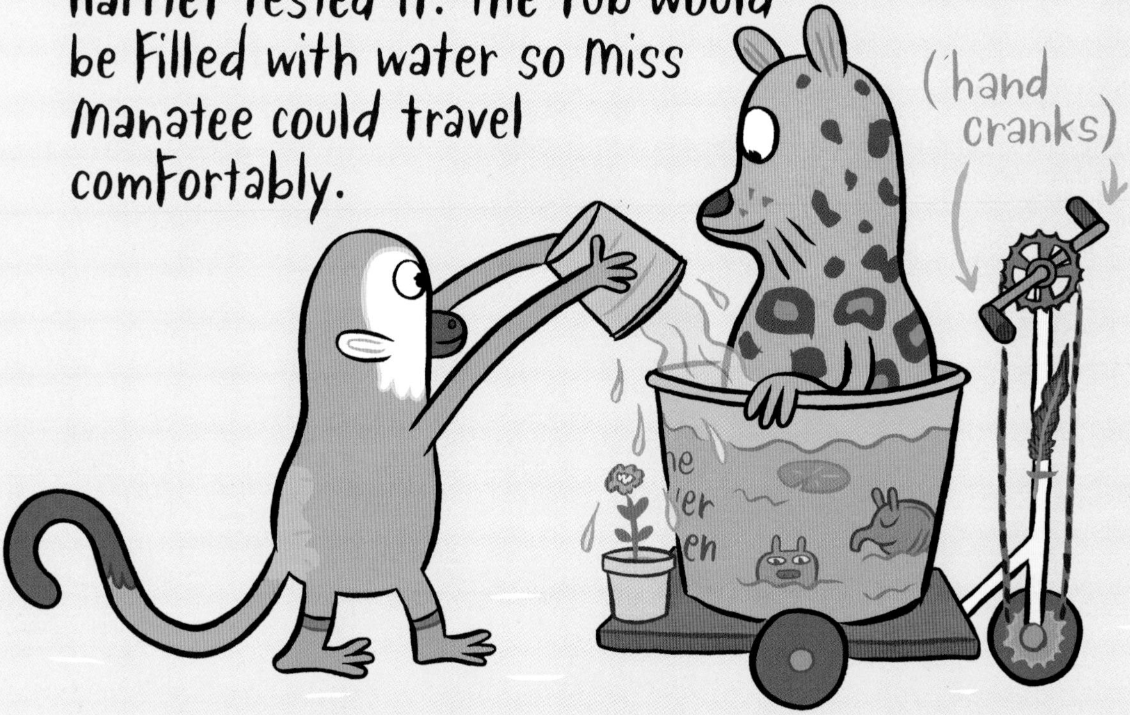
(hand cranks)

By turning the hand cranks, she could move the vehicle Forward.

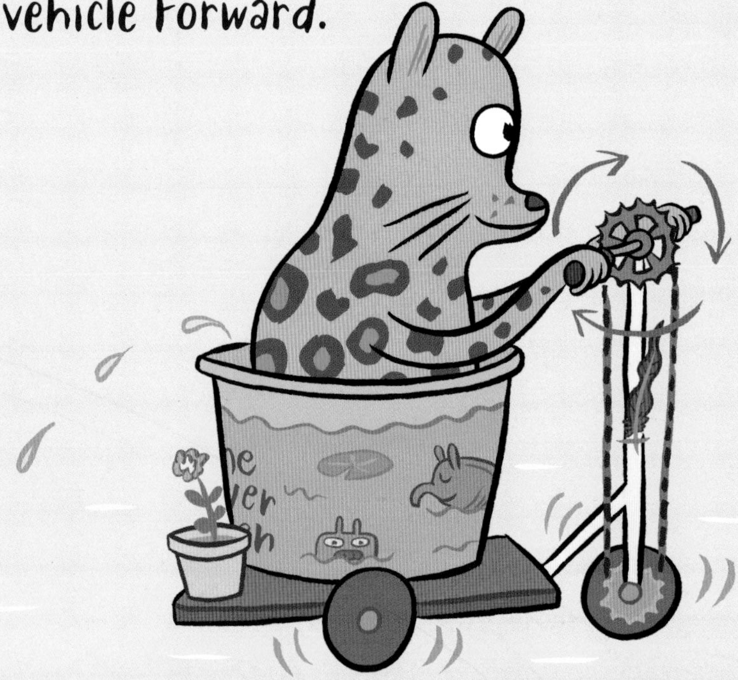

When Miss Manatee was going to perform, she could rotate in the tub so that the hand cranks, which were a bit unwieldy, would be behind her...

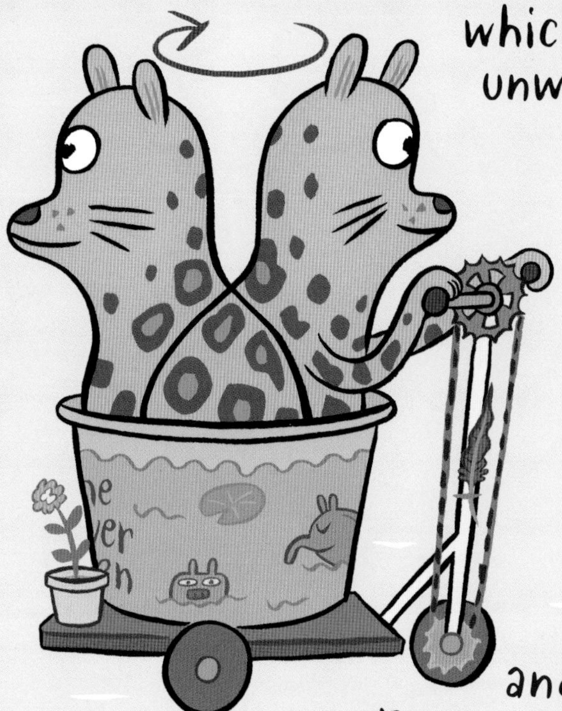

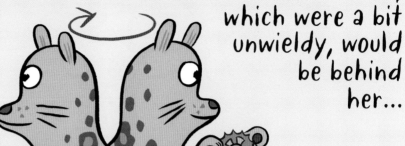

and she could perform unobstructed.

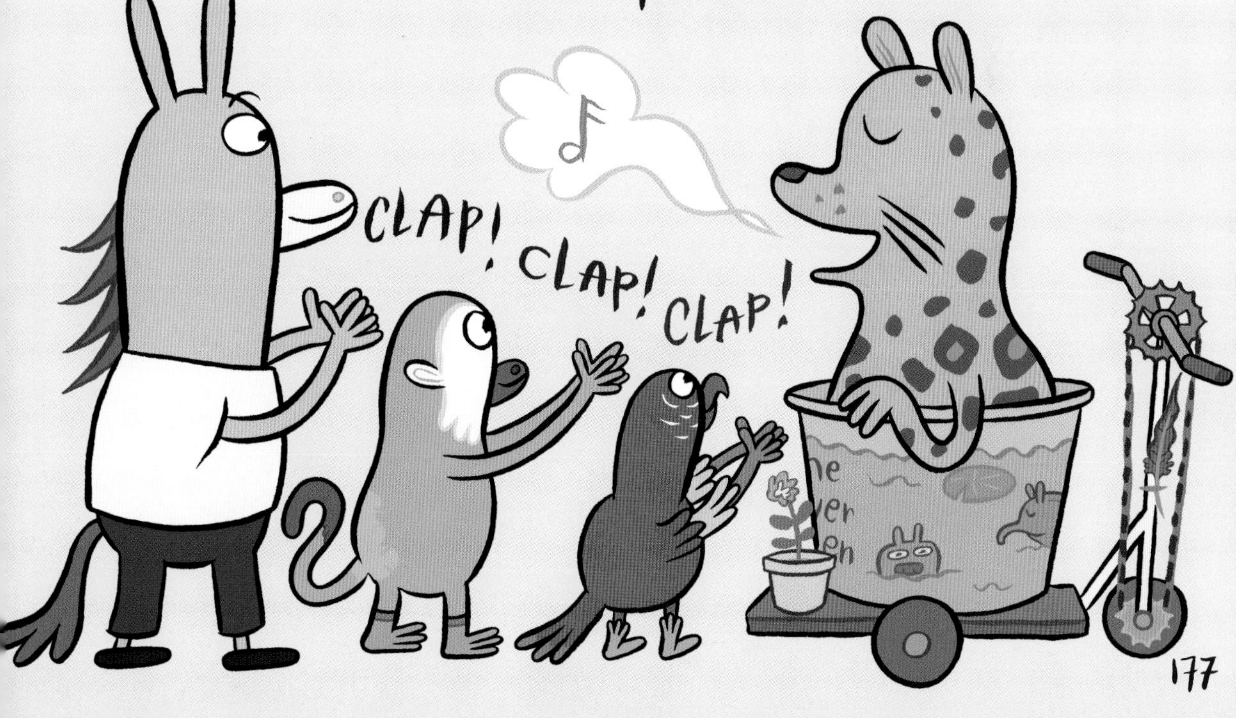
CLAP! CLAP! CLAP!

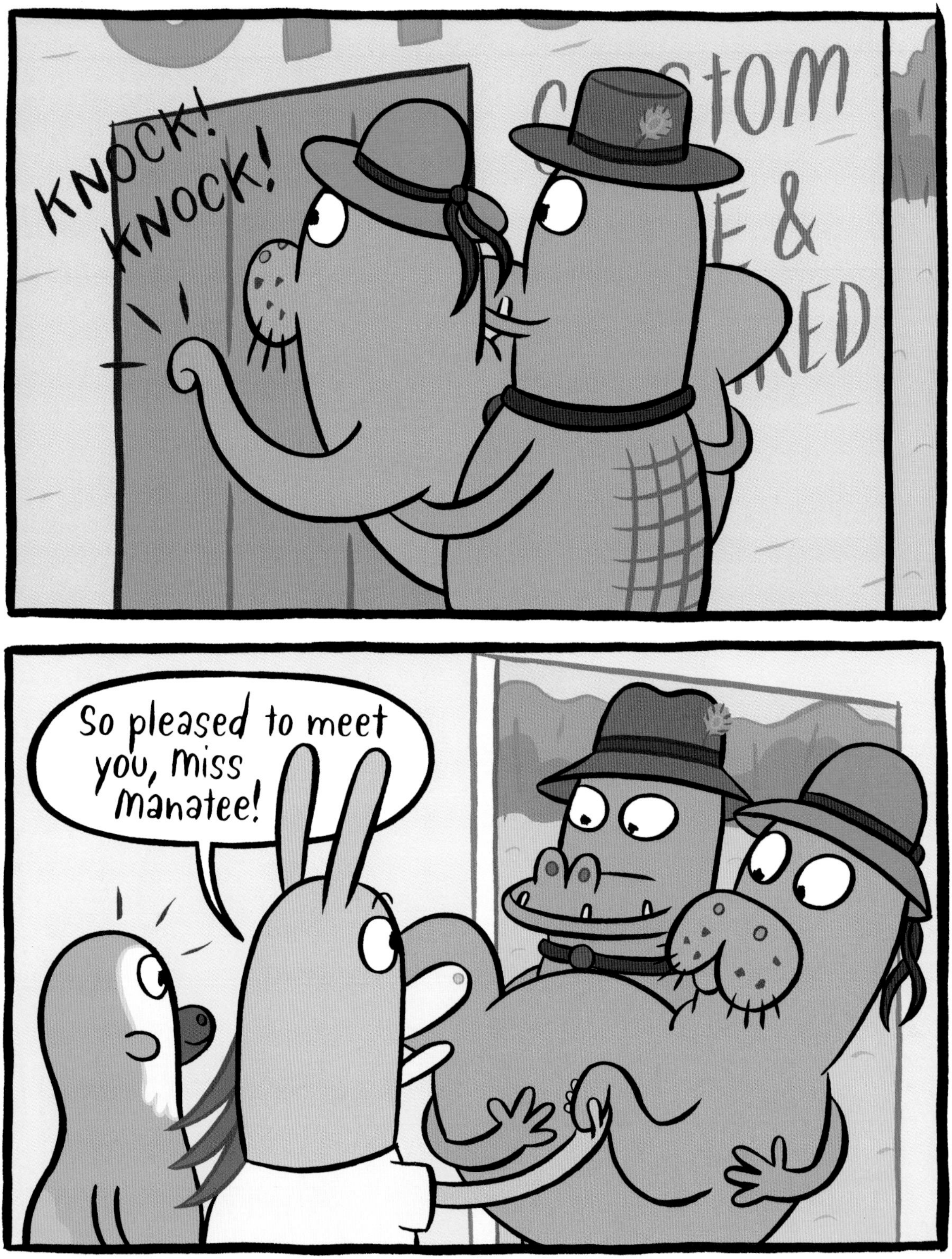
KNOCK! KNOCK!
So pleased to meet you, miss manatee!

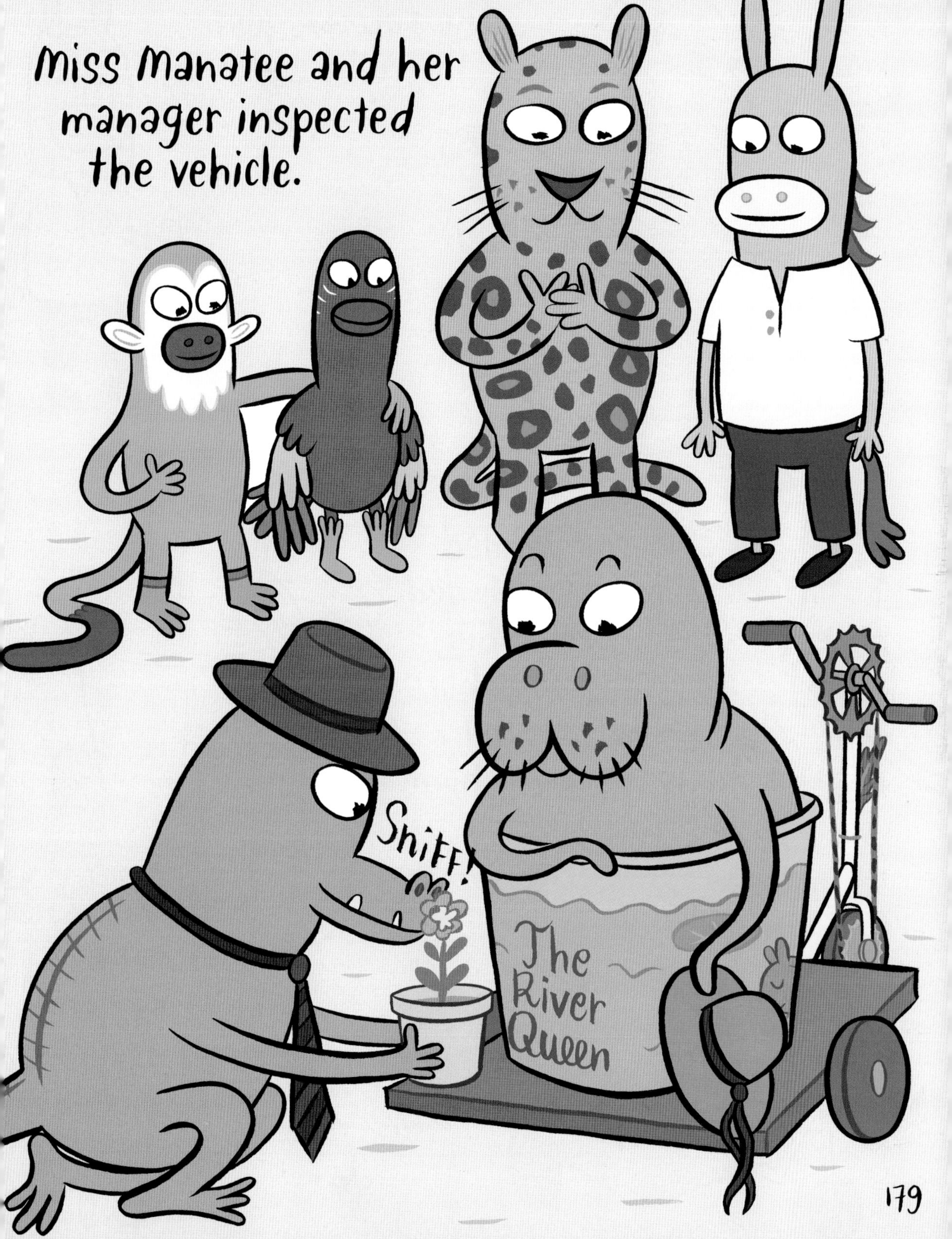
Miss Manatee and her manager inspected the vehicle.
SNIFF!
The River Queen

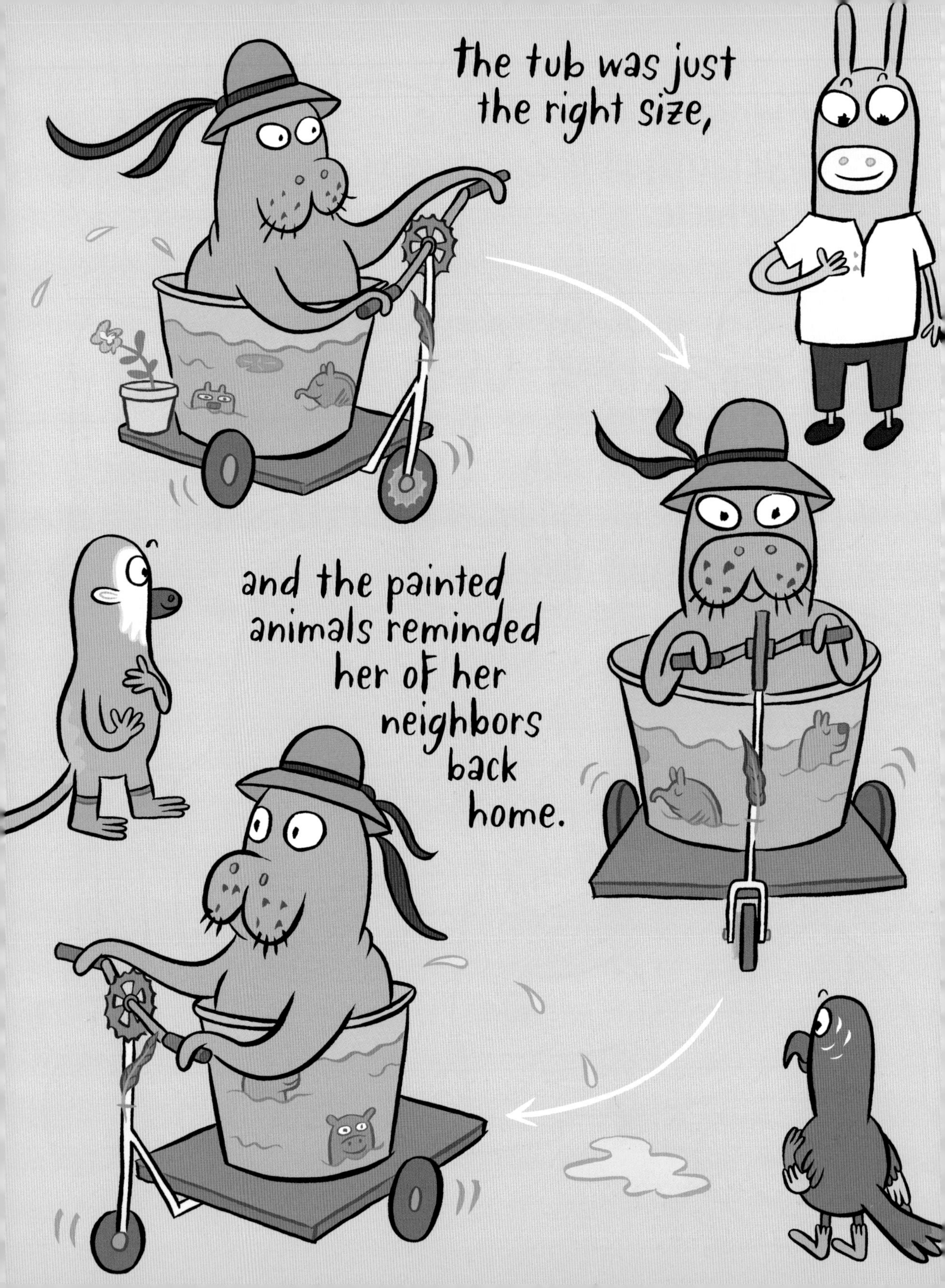

the tub was just
the right size,

and the painted
animals reminded
her of her
neighbors
back
home.

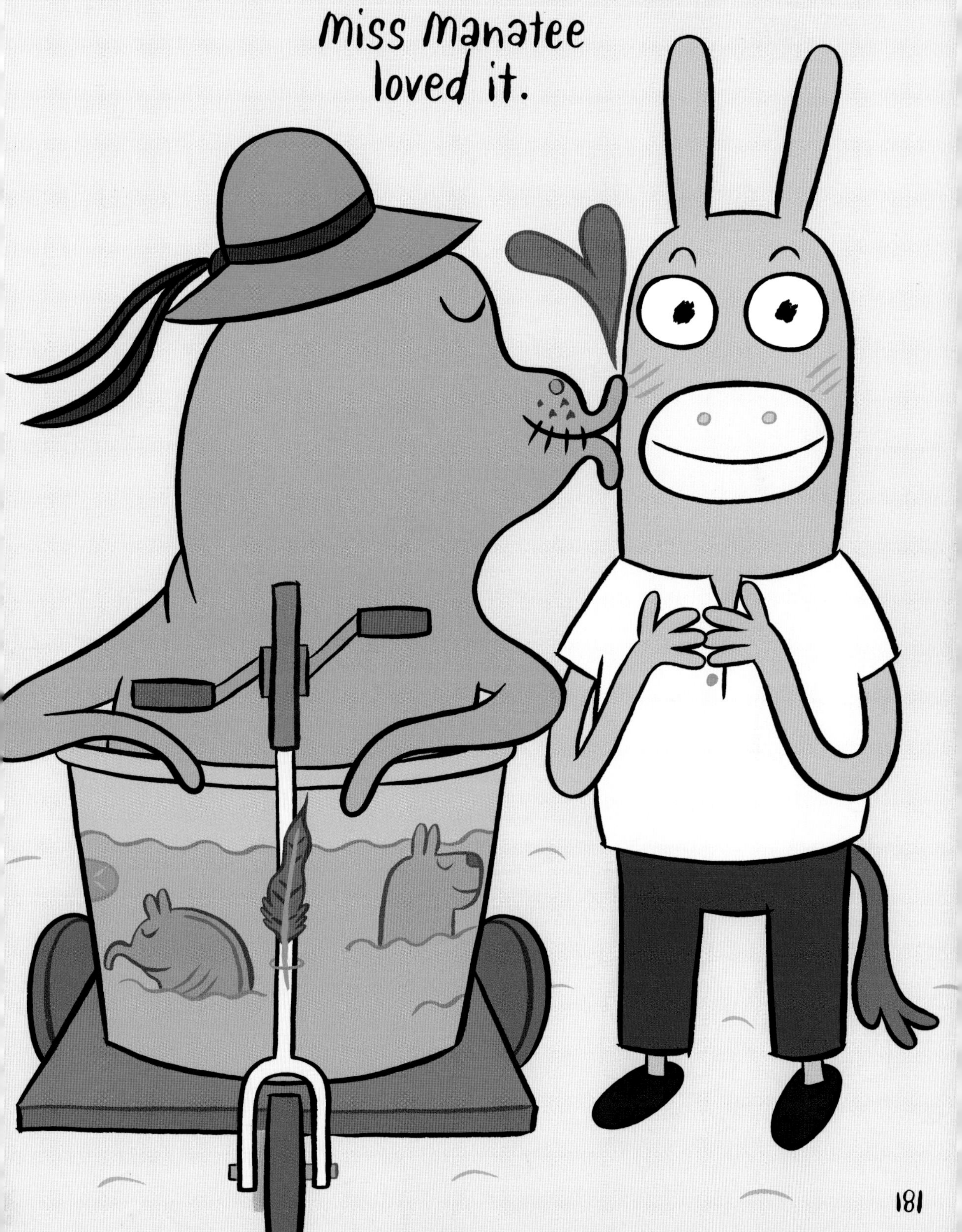
miss manatee
loved it.

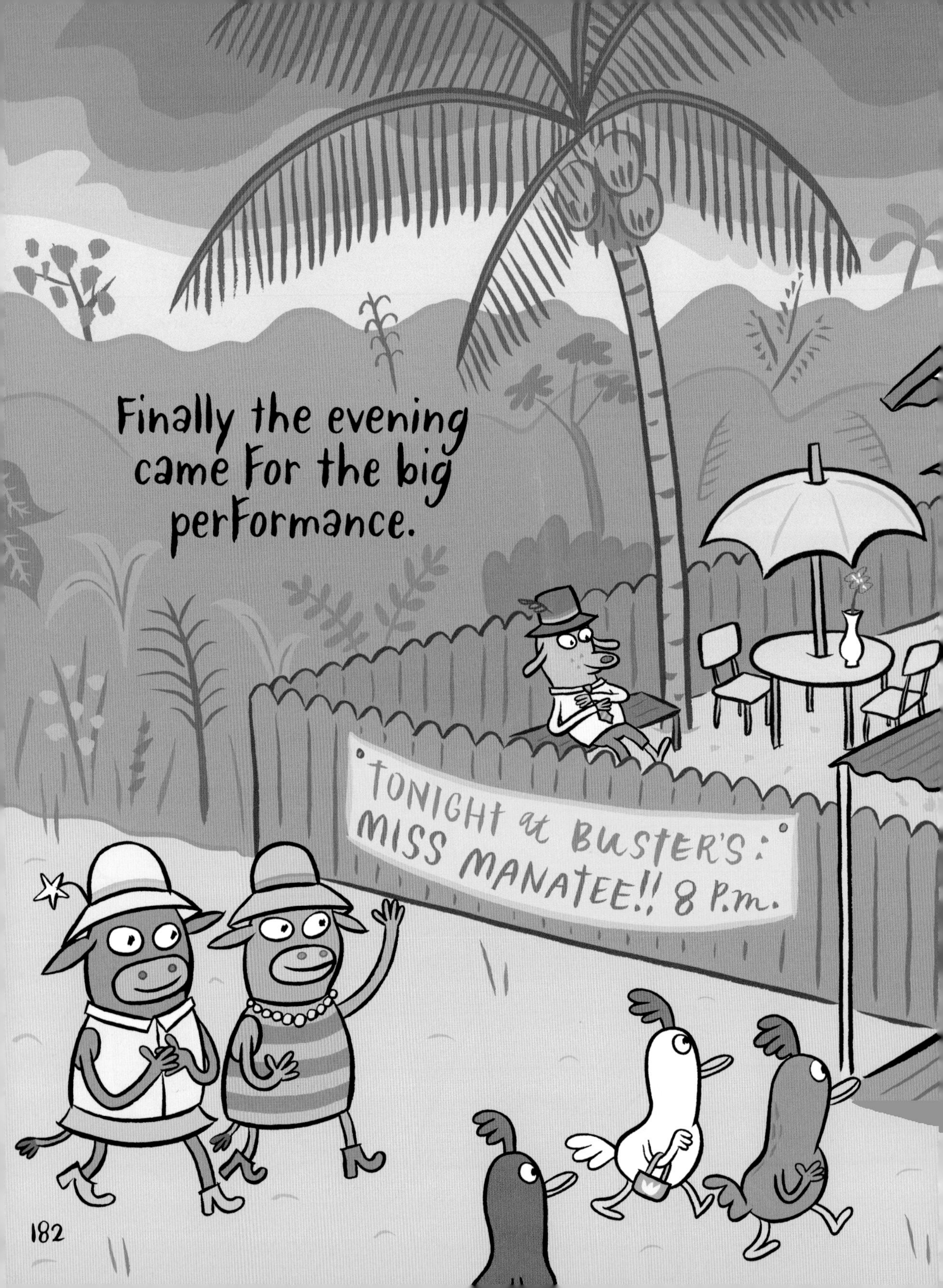
Finally the evening came for the big performance.
TONIGHT at BUSTER'S: MISS MANATEE!! 8 P.m.

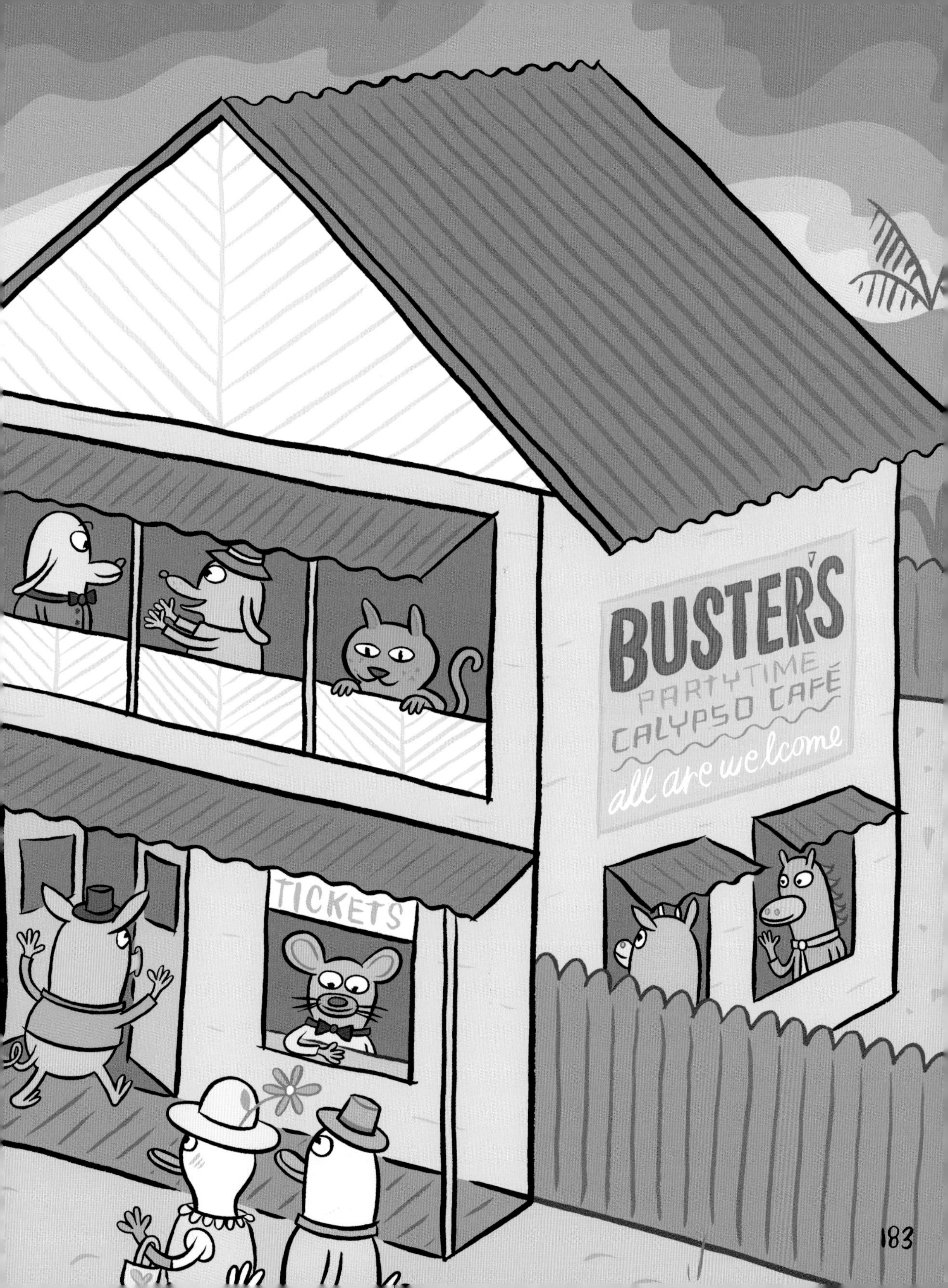
BUSTER'S
PARTYTIME
CALYPSO CAFÉ
all are welcome
TICKETS

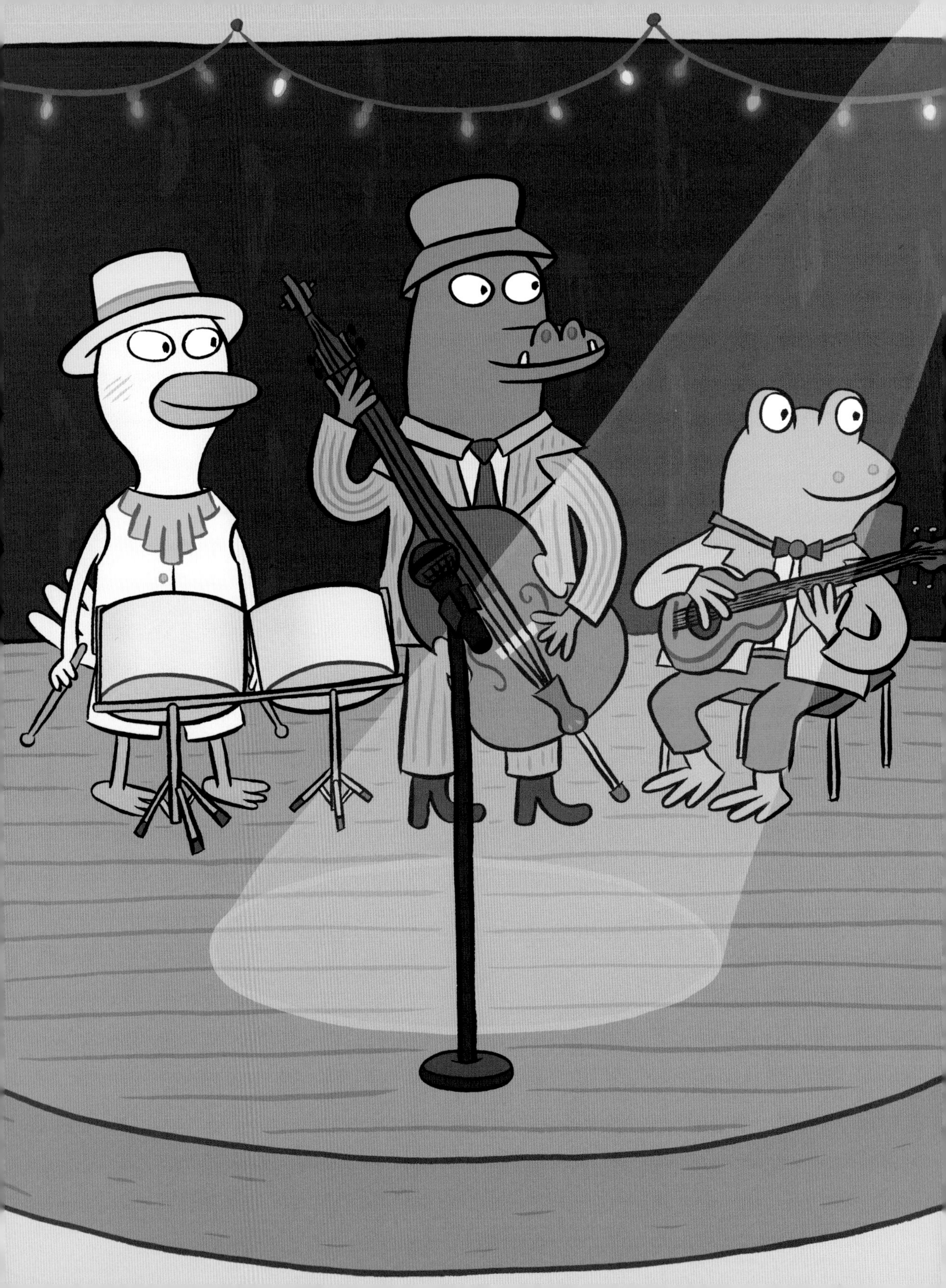

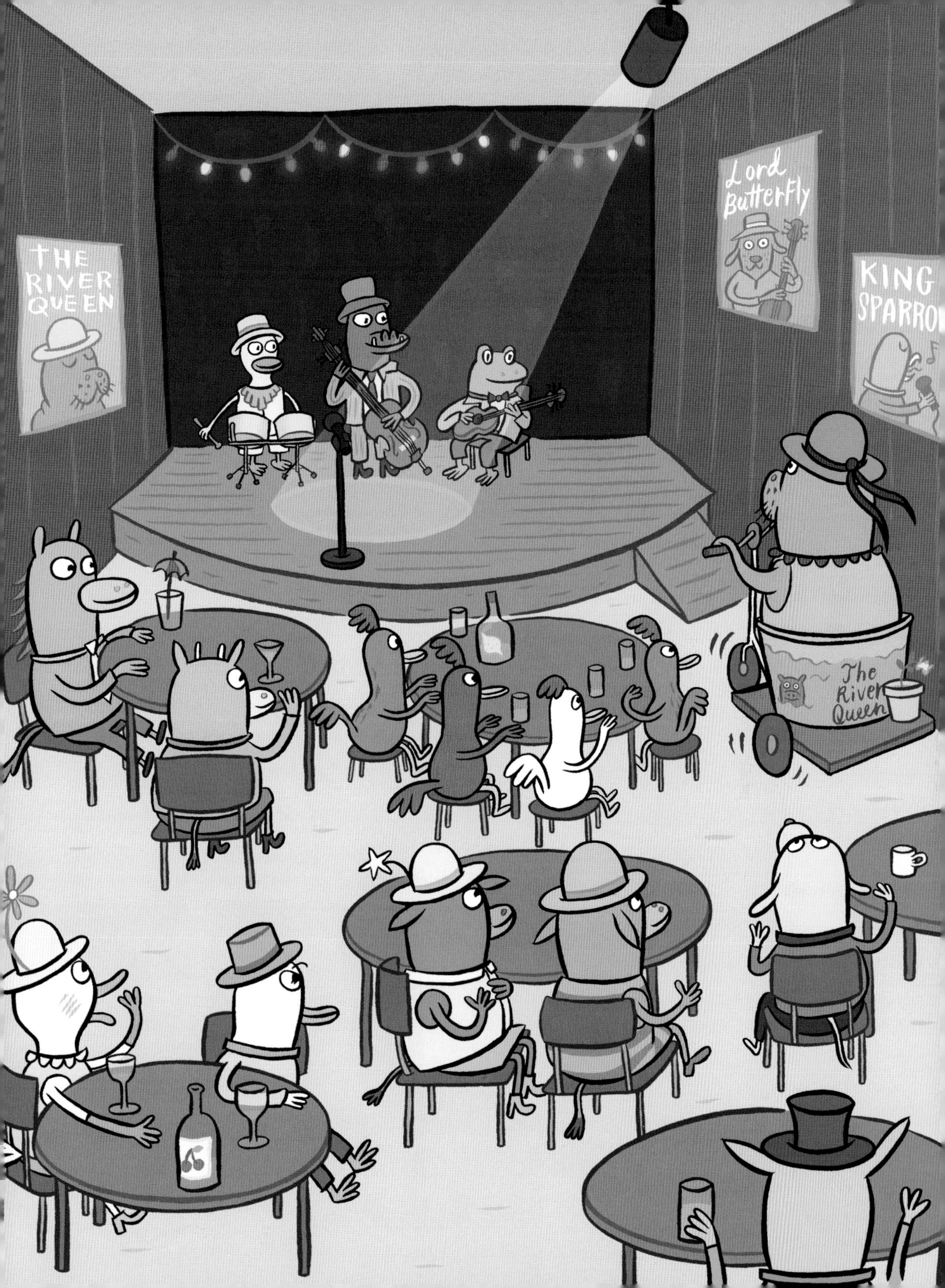
THE RIVER QUEEN
Lord Butterfly
KING SPARRO
The River Queen

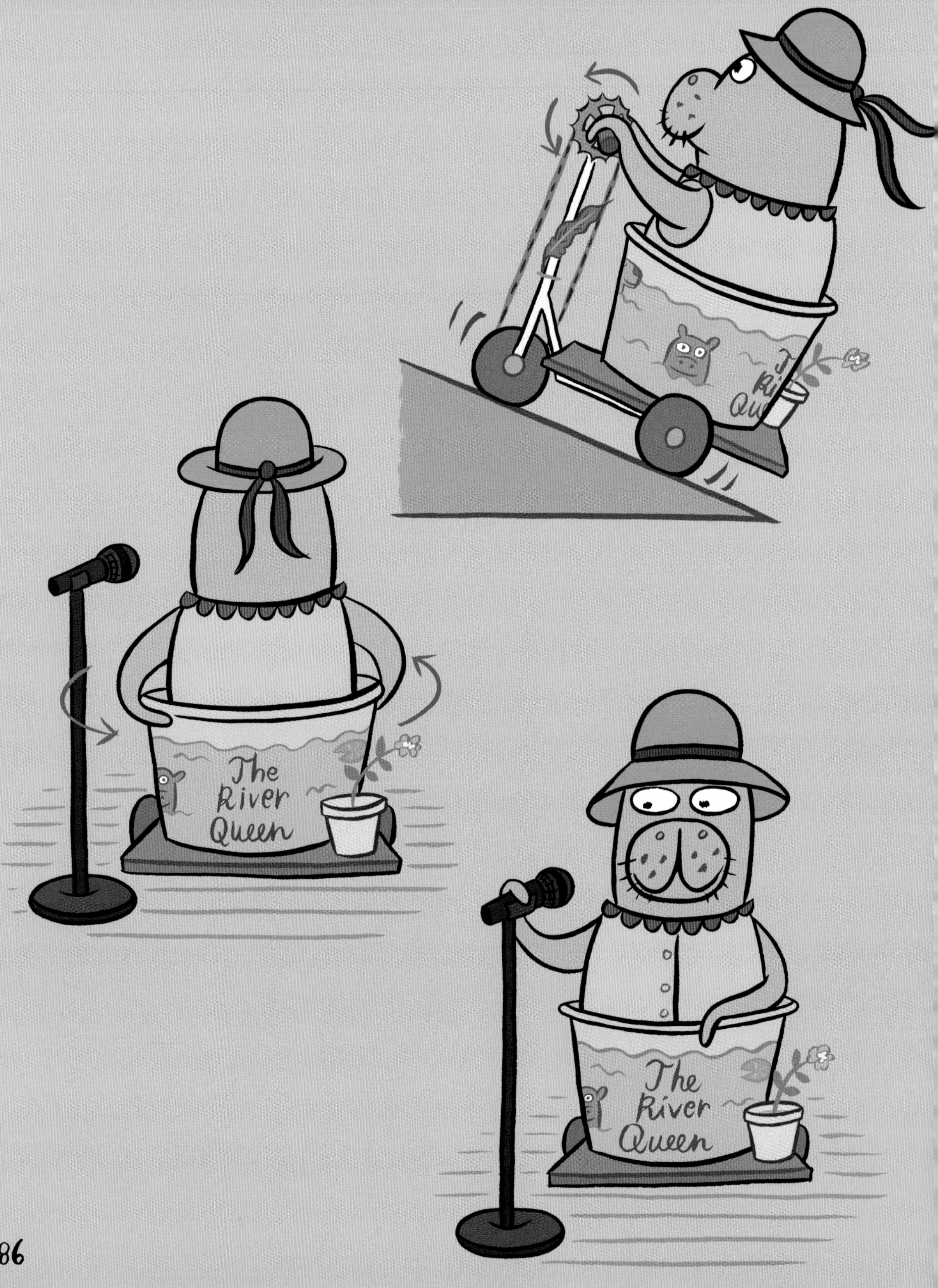
The River Queen
The River Queen
The River Queen

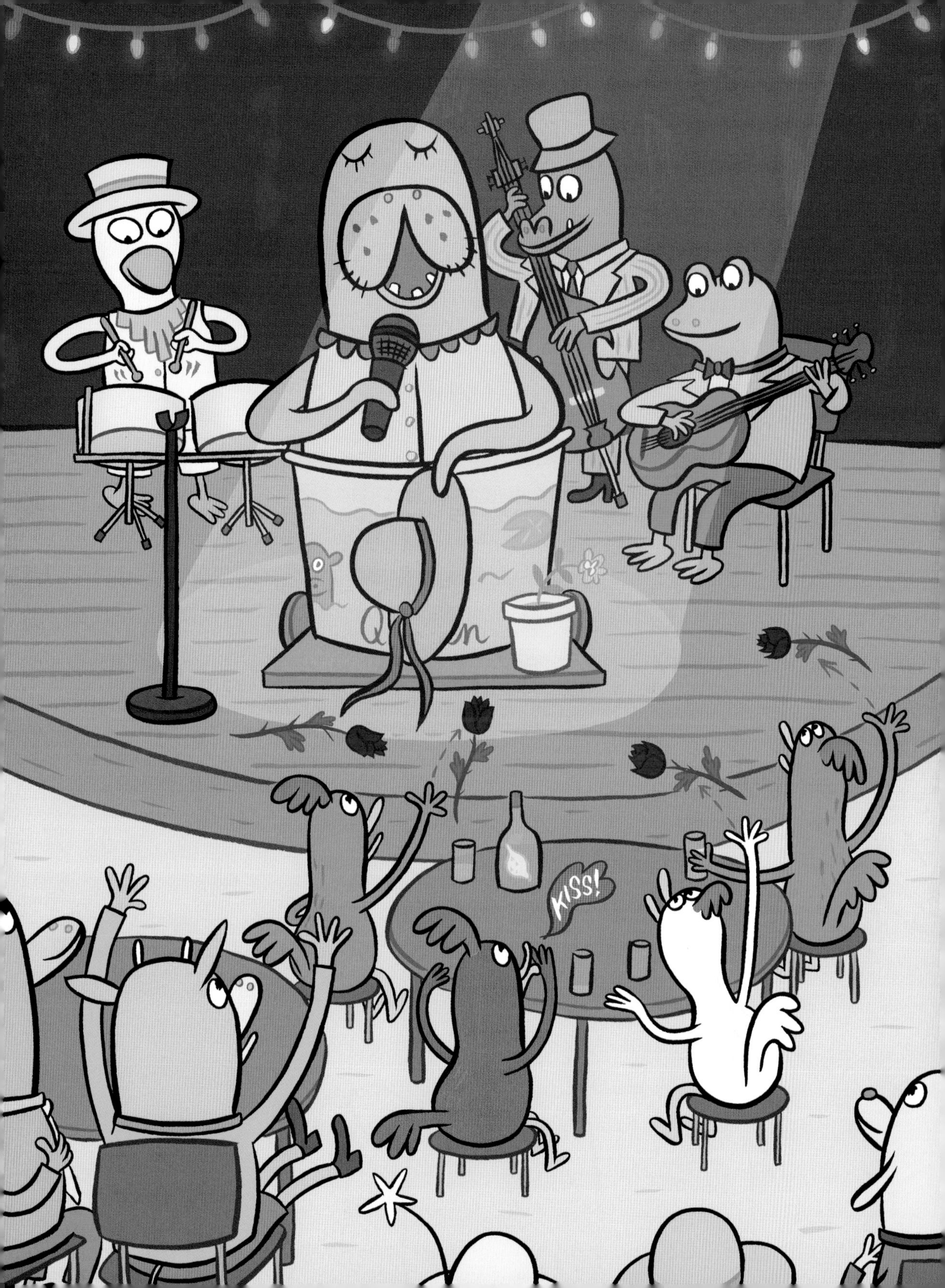
KISS!

As Miss Manatee sang, Francis looked at his friends—Nigel, Rhoda, the downstairs chickens...

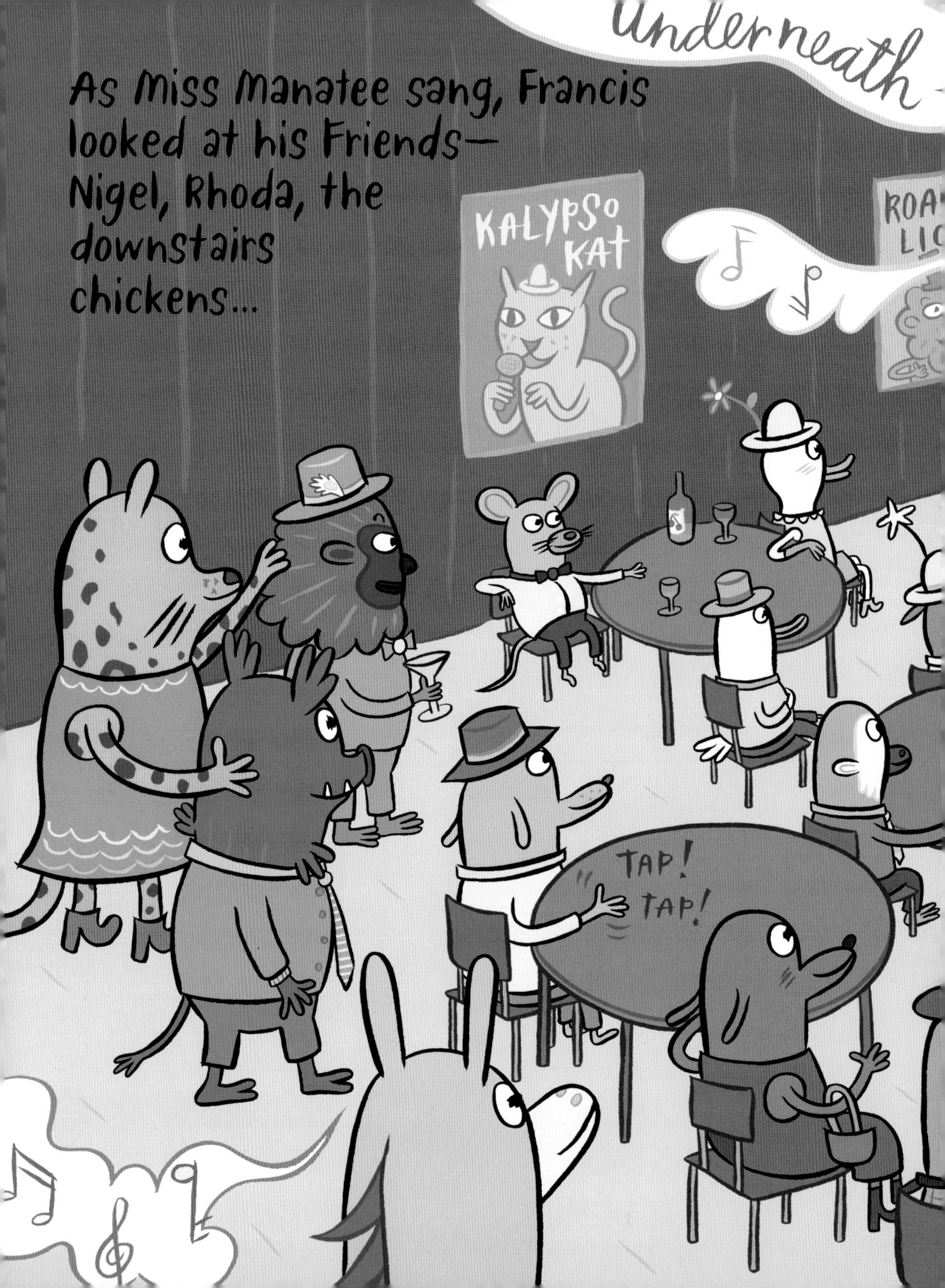

underneath
KALYPSO KAT
TAP! TAP!

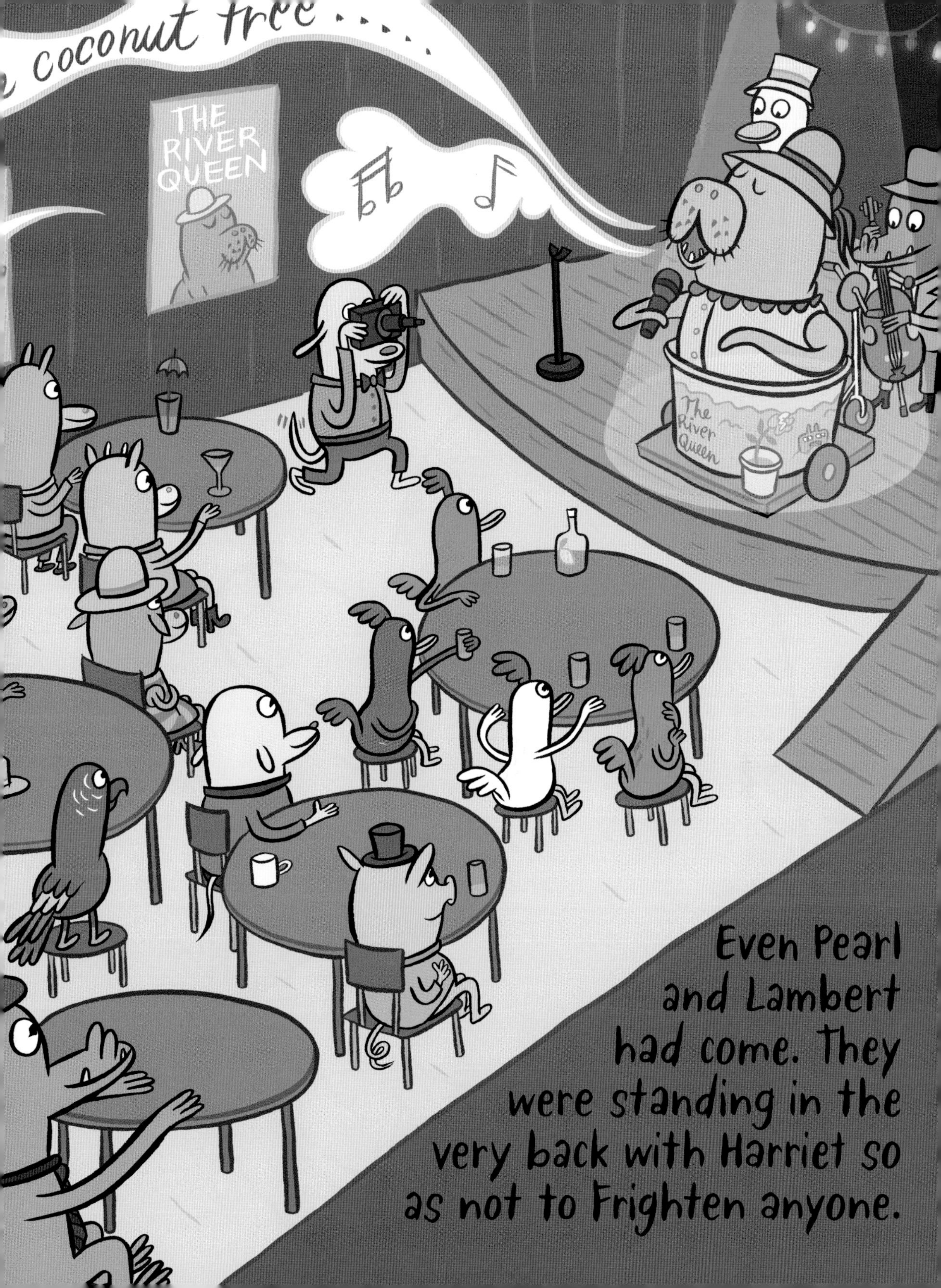
coconut tree . . . .
THE RIVER QUEEN
The River Queen

Even Pearl and Lambert had come. They were standing in the very back with Harriet so as not to frighten anyone.

Francis was sure it was the sweetest music he'd ever heard.

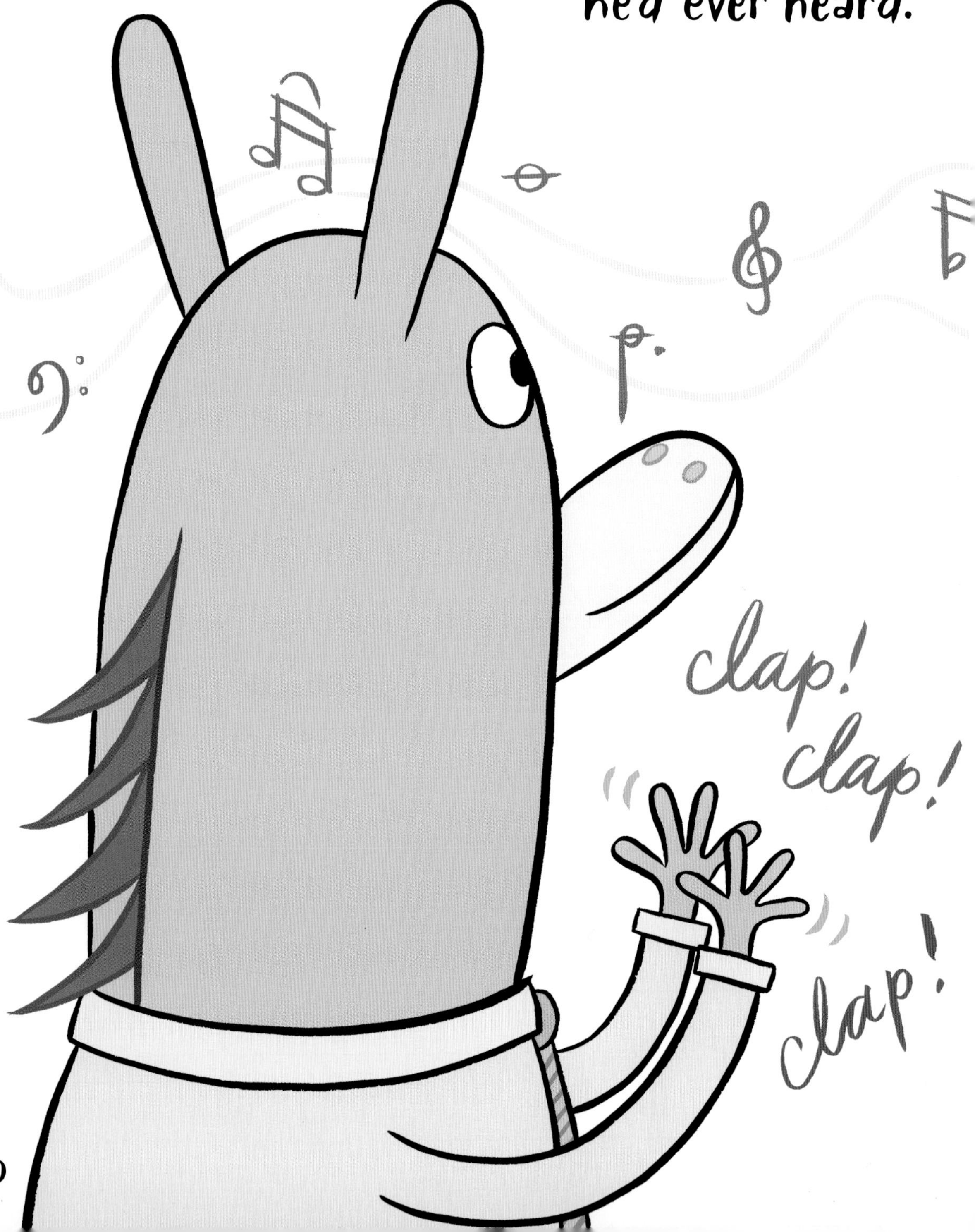
clap!
clap!
clap!

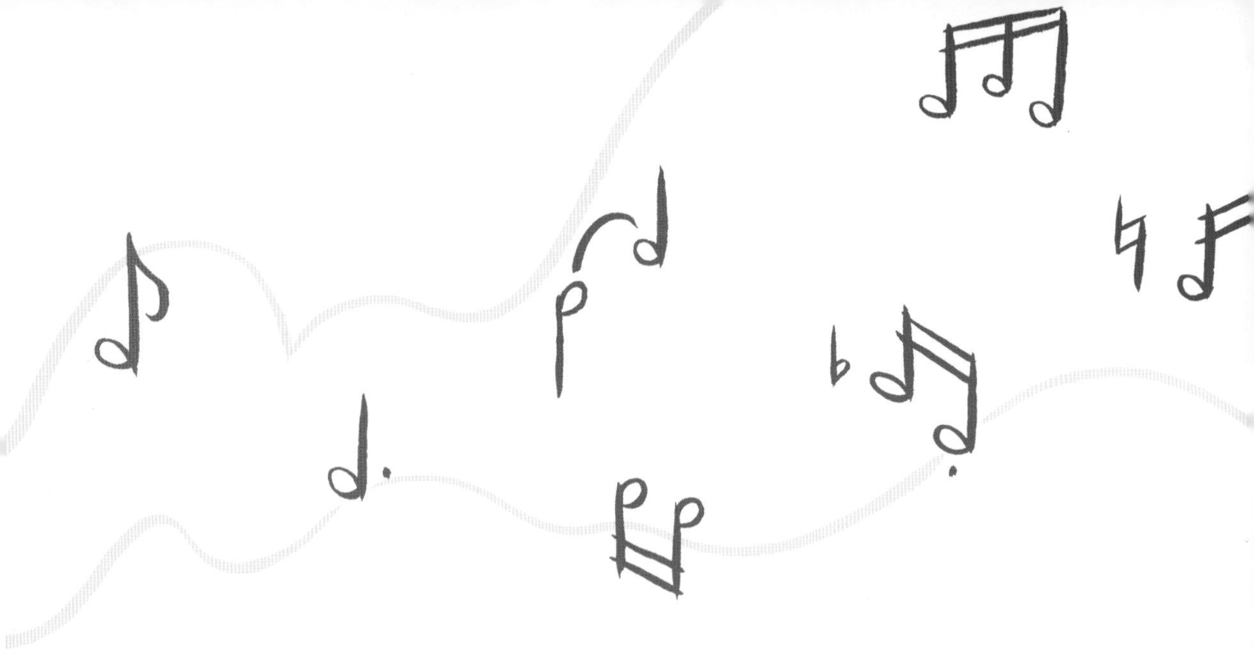

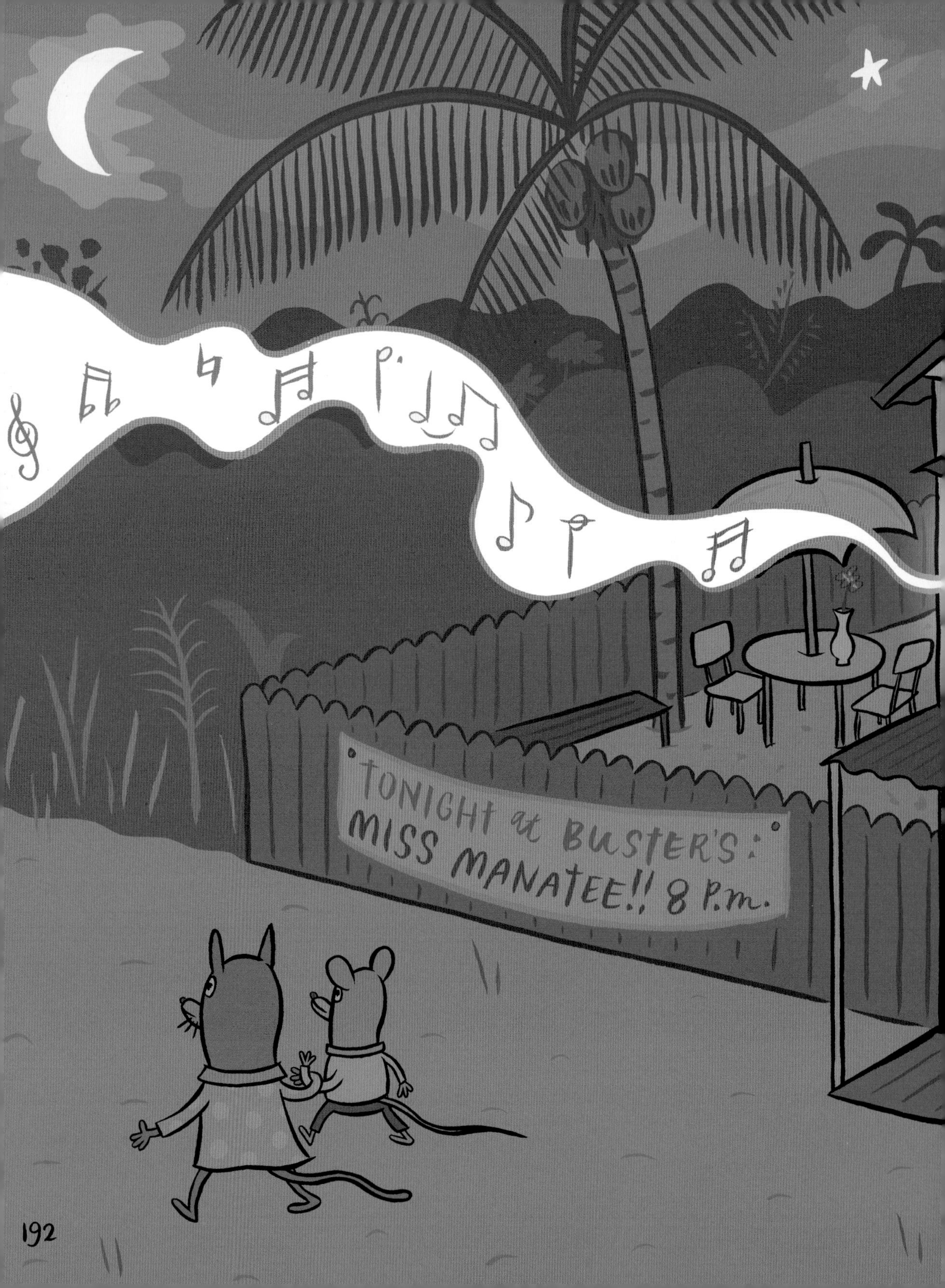
TONIGHT at BUSTER'S:
MISS MANATEE!! 8 P.m.

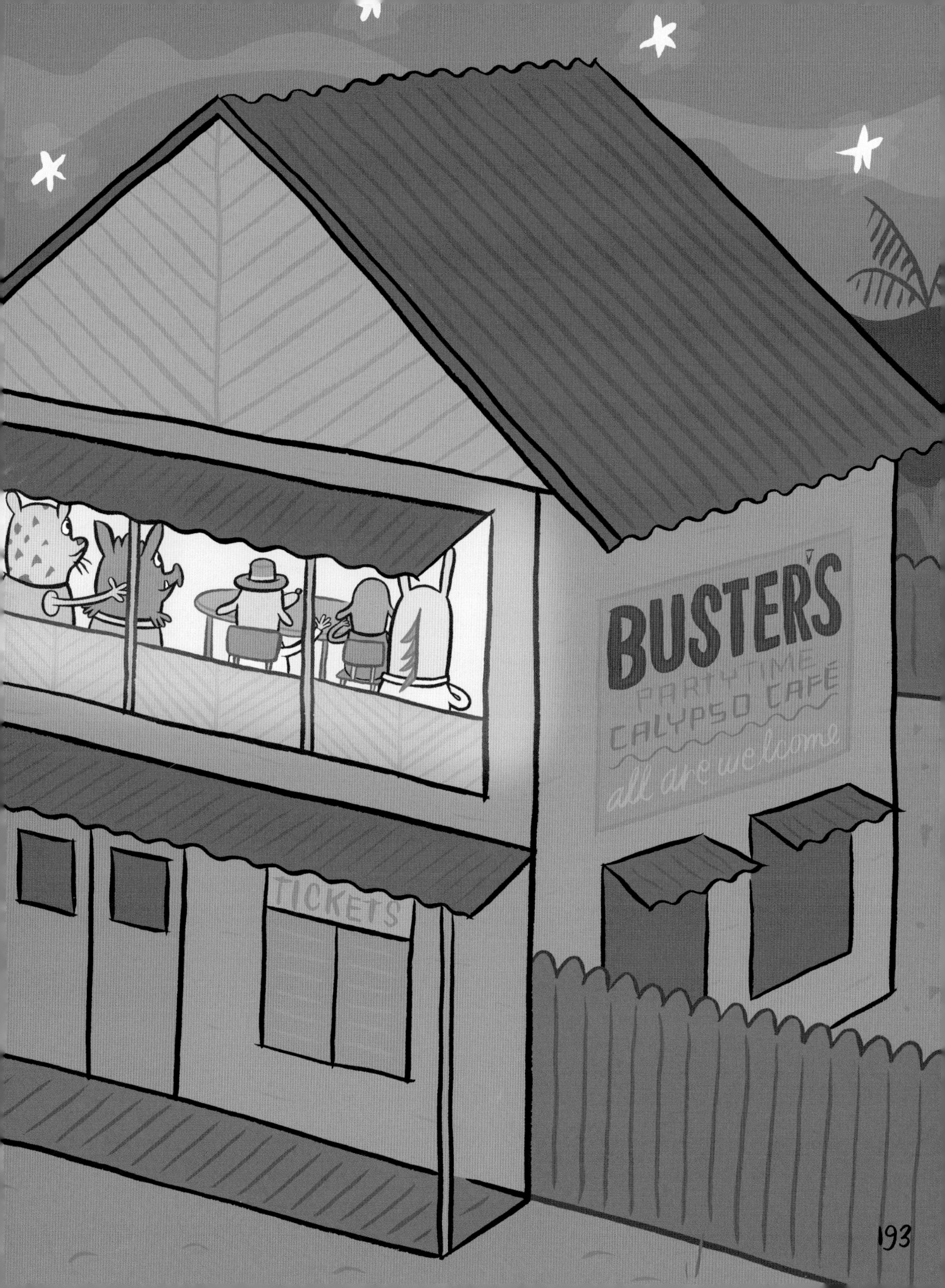
BUSTER'S
PARTYTIME
CALYPSO CAFÉ
all are welcome
TICKETS

thanks, Sheila O'Donnell, For giving me the seed For this project.

thanks to John's Family in Linden (especially JenniFer) For always hosting us on our visits to Guyana.

thanks to Elvis at Iwokrama Centre, who will probably never see this, For double-checking my birds and Fruits (even iF the Fruits mentioned wouldn't all be ripe at the same time) and For his amazing knowledge oF local plants.

All the thanks in the world to Dona, Lynn, and the Sendak Fellowship, and to Maura For her walks in the woods.

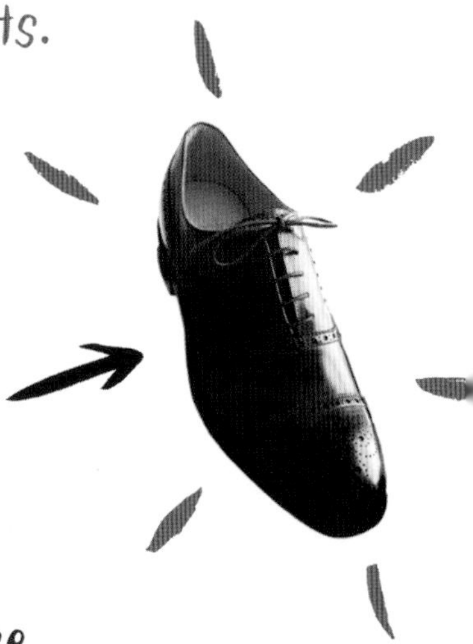

thanks to Perry Ercolino, in Doylestown, PA, For explaining how to make shoes by hand (even iF I didn't include much oF the inFo).

thanks, Ada Price, For having the good sense to tell me to trace my thumbnails.

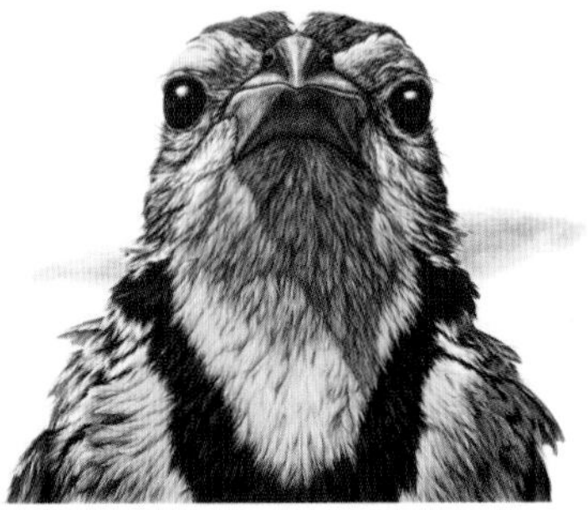

Thanks to the talented George Boorujy For illustrating the animals in the guidebook! www.georgeboorujy.com

thanks to Mark Siegel and Tanya McKinnon For their excellent editing, and to Danielle Ceccolini For her great design.

Huge thanks to John and, as always, my mom.

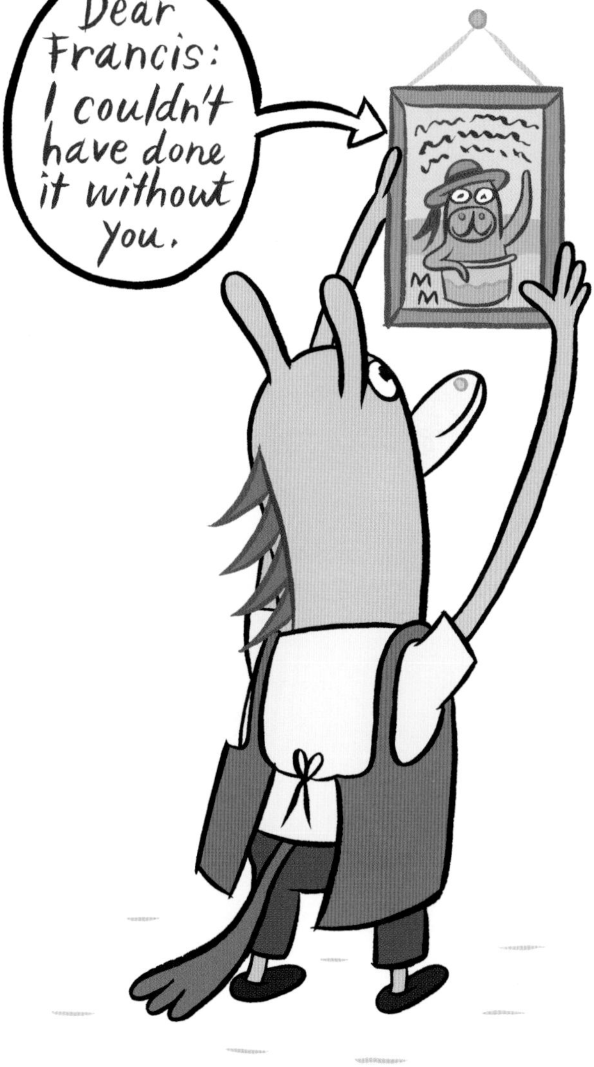
Dear Francis: I couldn't have done it without you.

to make this book, I took a few thousand reference photos. I photographed things that gave me ideas or that would help me draw things I wanted to include in the story. All of the photos were taken in Guyana; most were taken in the town of Linden.

the houses are such great colors. I love the skyline of coconut trees and power lines.

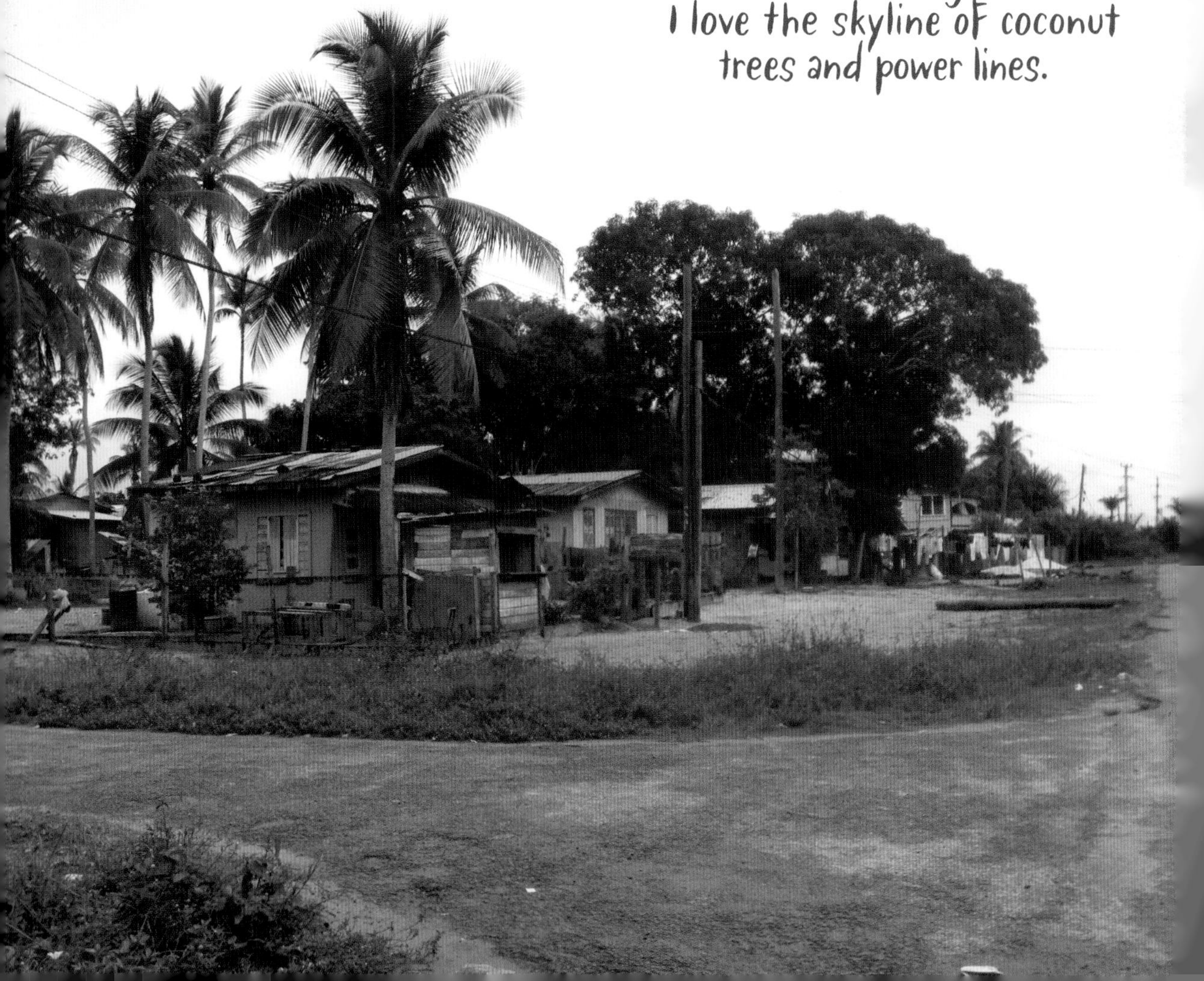

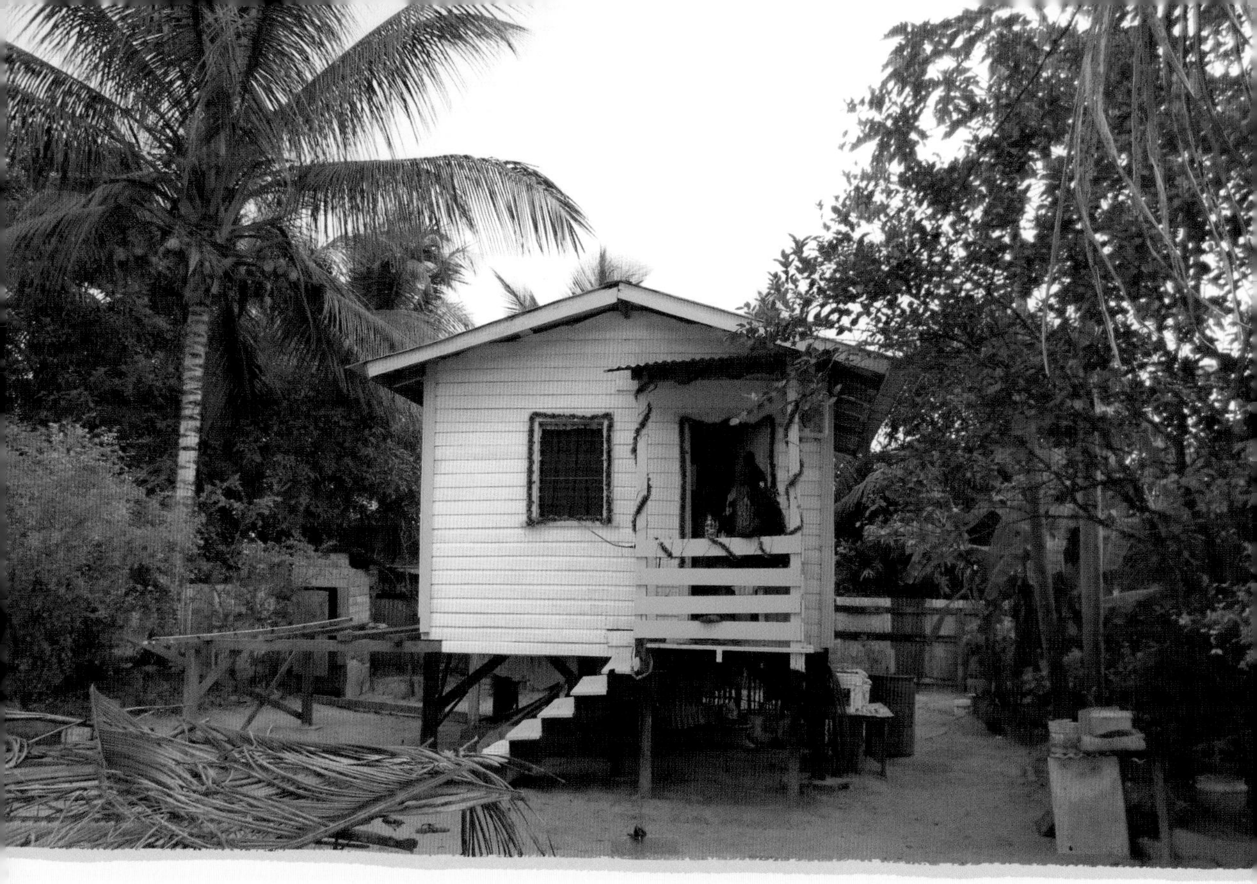

reference for Francis's house

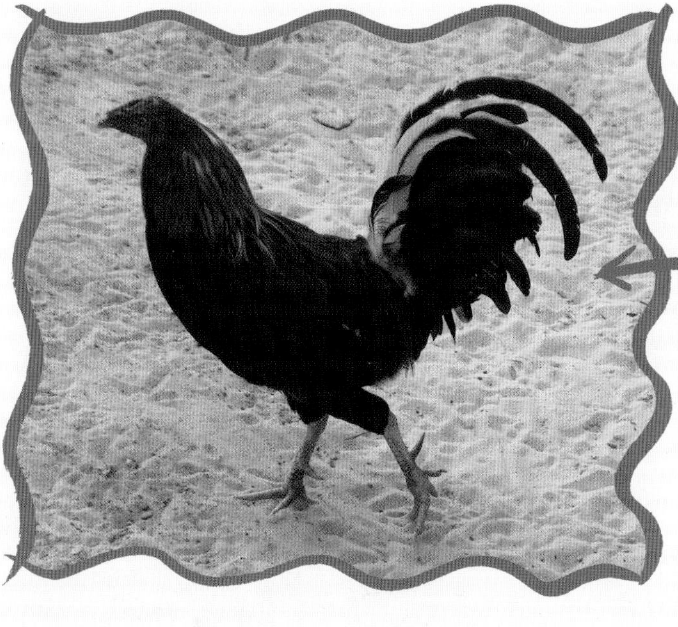

Animals are all over the place.

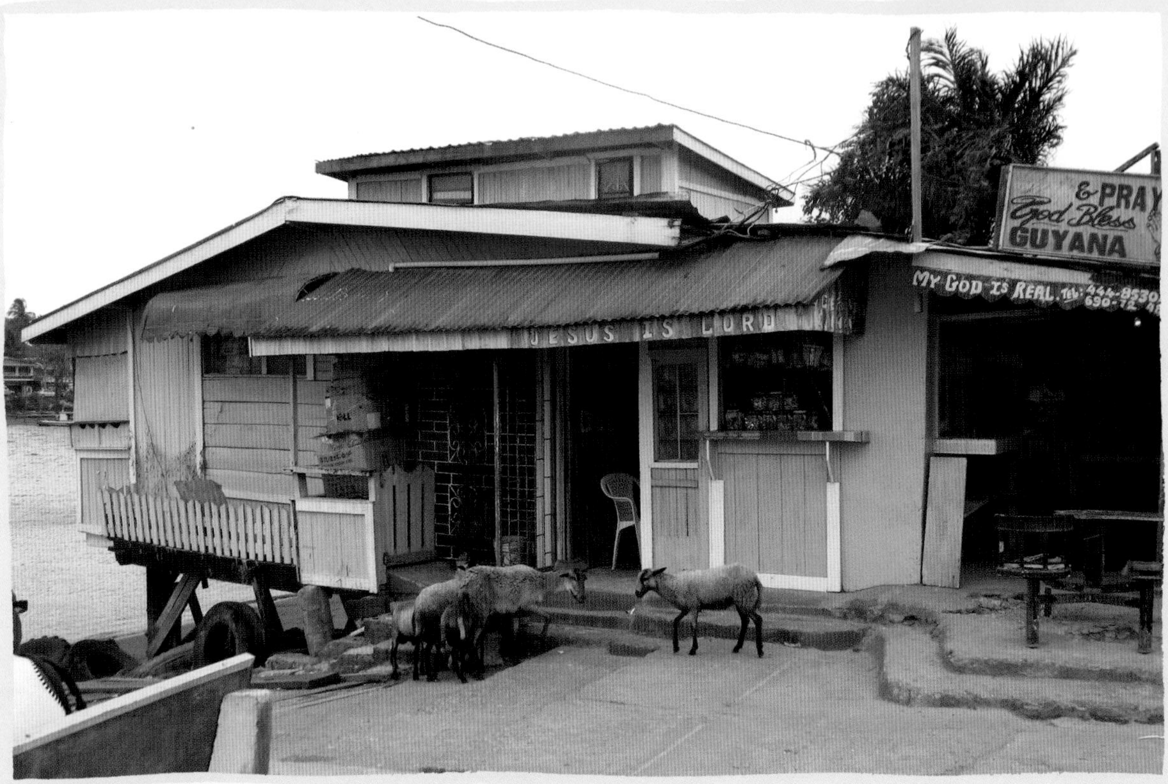
& PRAY
God Bless
GUYANA
MY GOD IS REAL
JESUS IS LORD

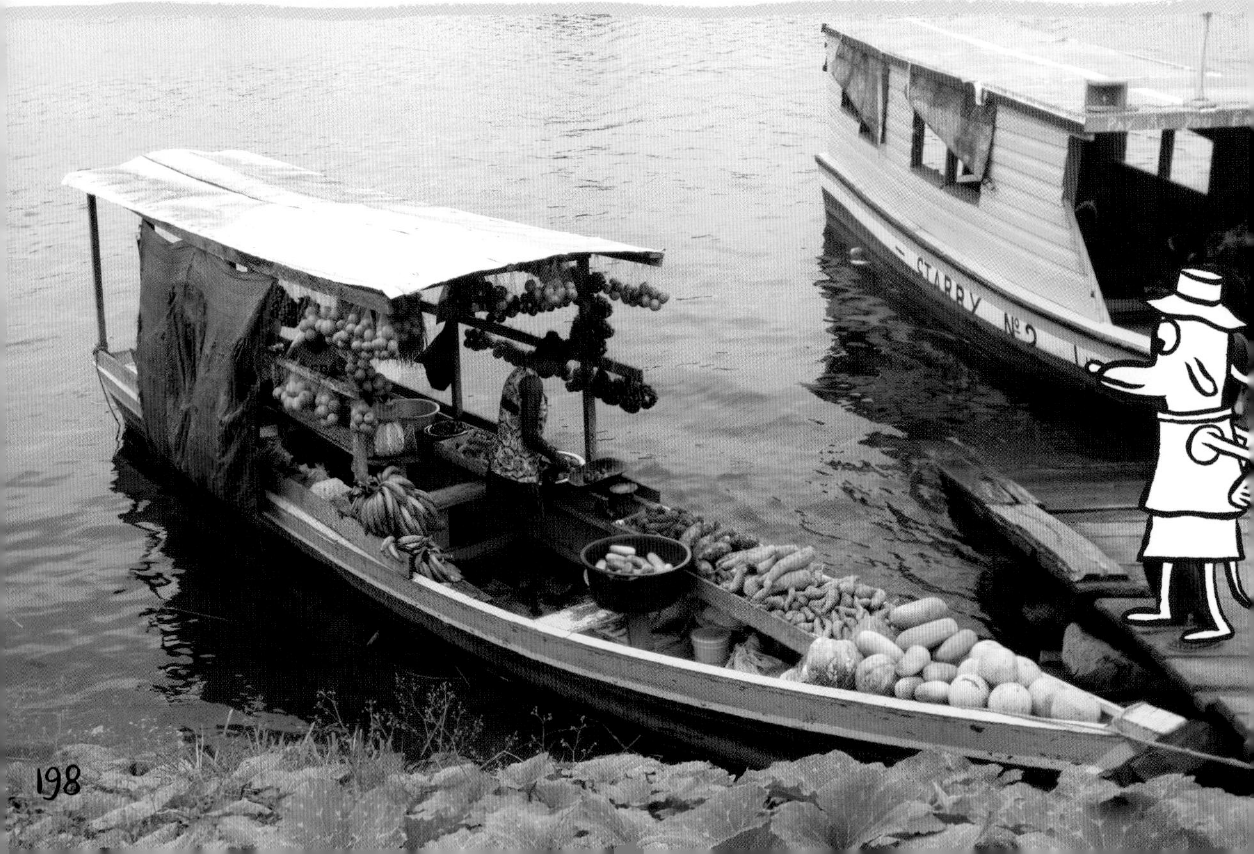
STARRY No 2

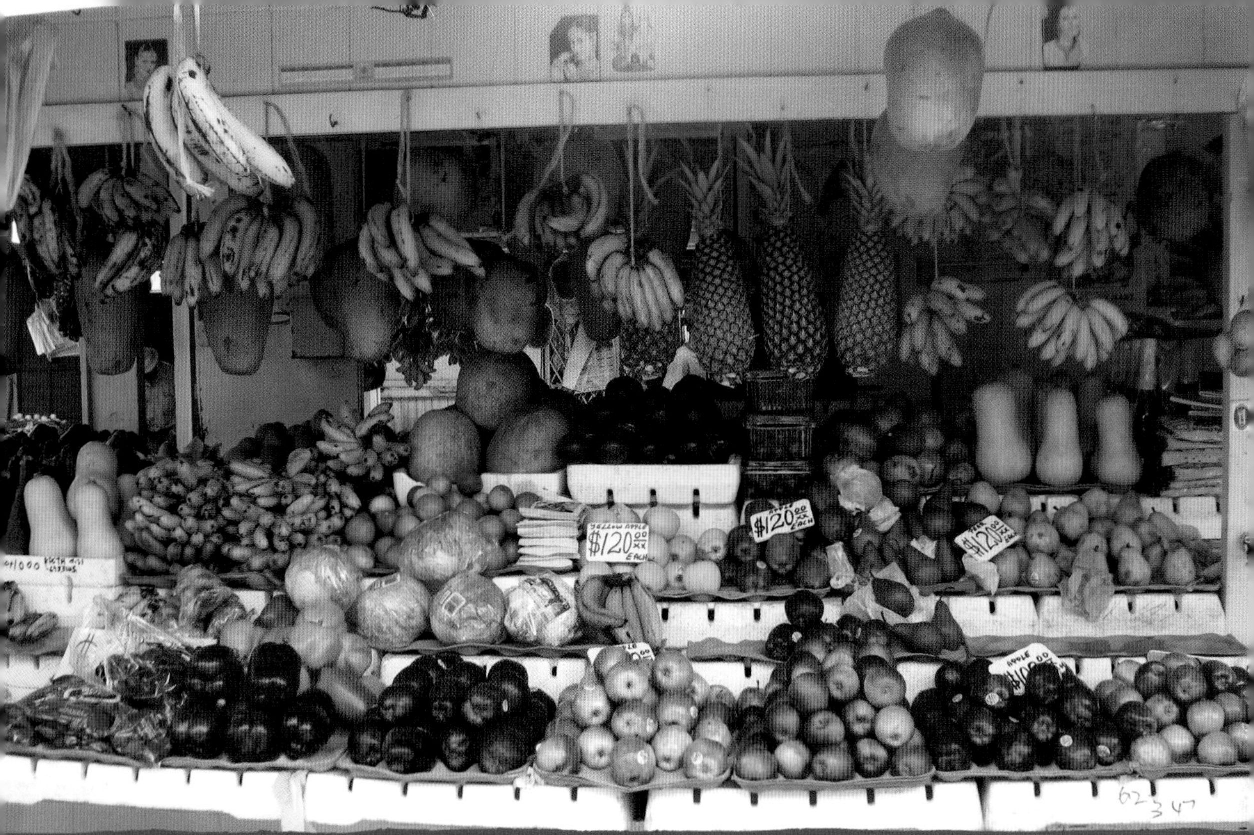
YELLOW APPLE
$120.00
EACH

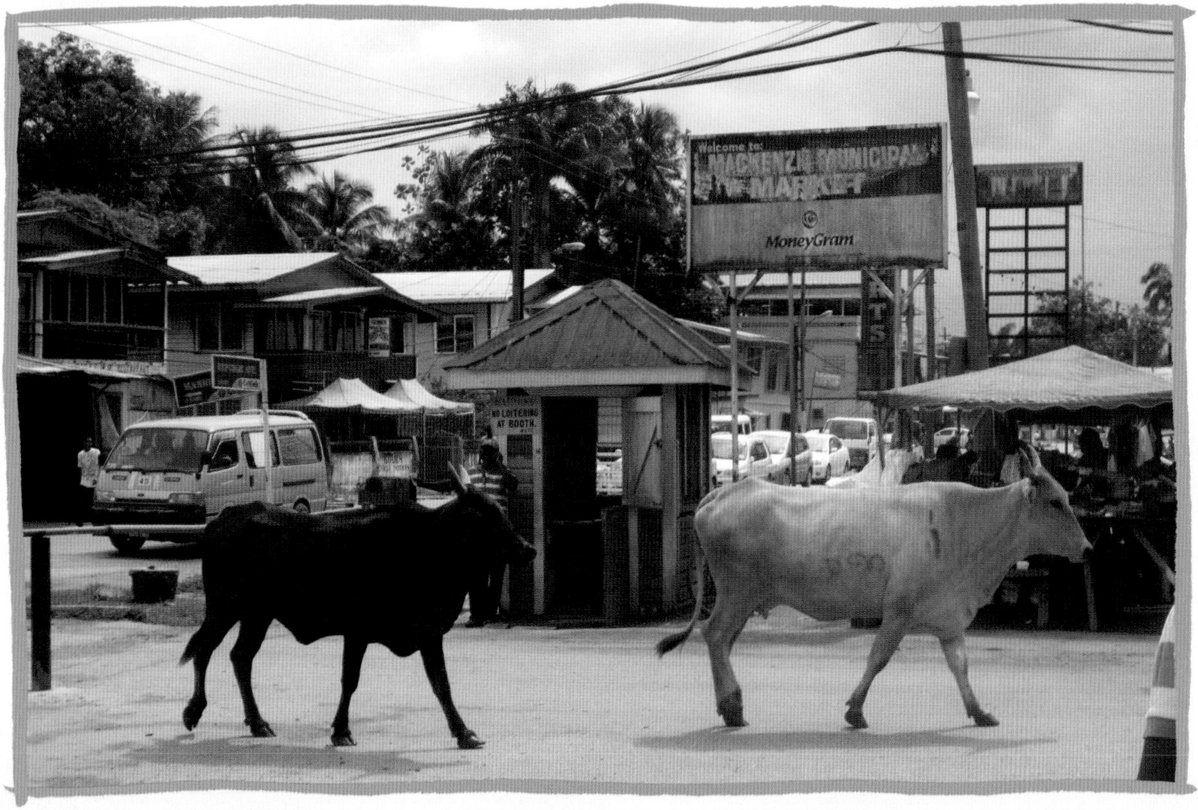
Welcome to:
MACKENZIE MUNICIPAL
MARKET
MoneyGram
NO LOITERING
AT BOOTH.

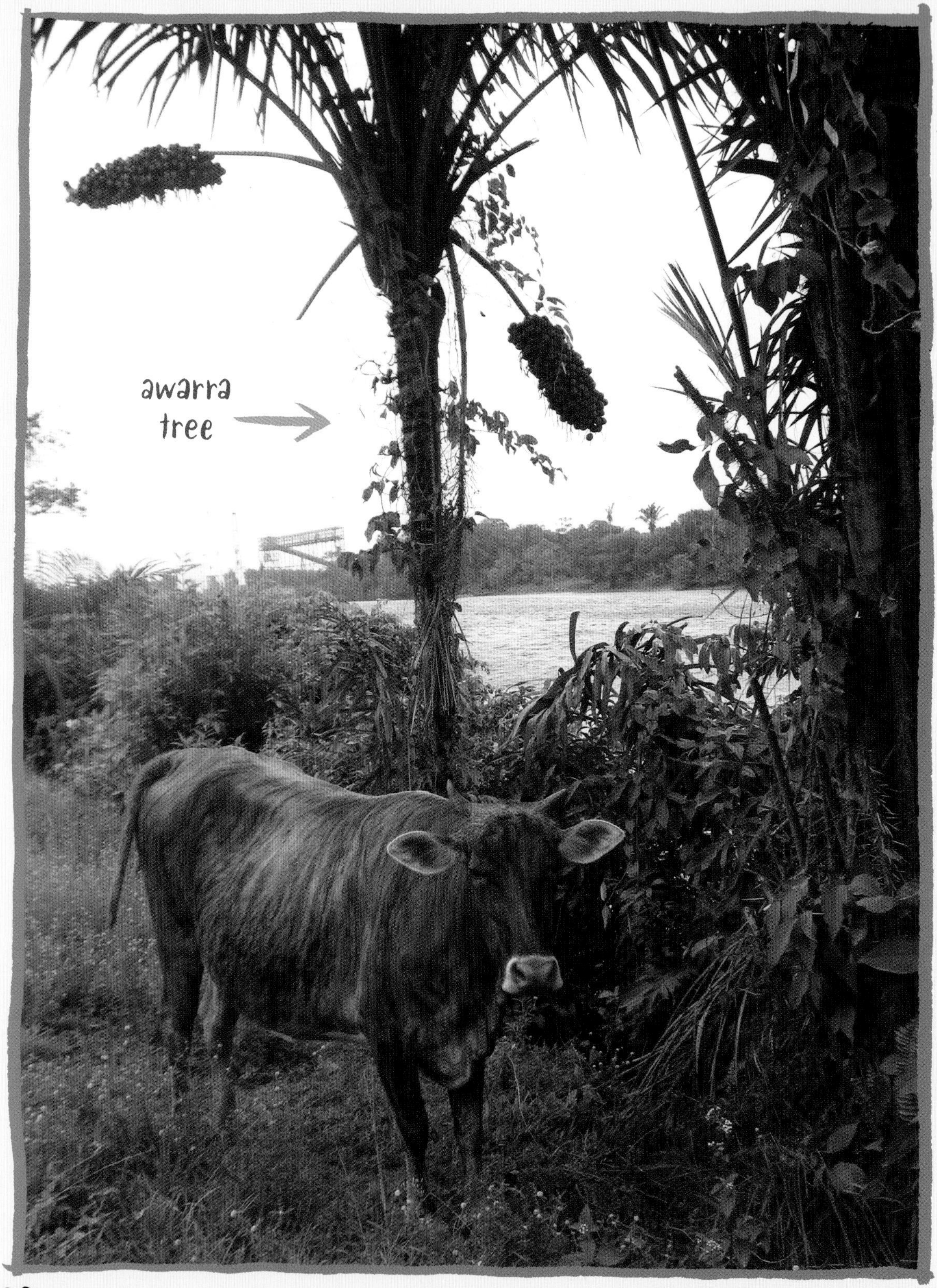
awarra
tree

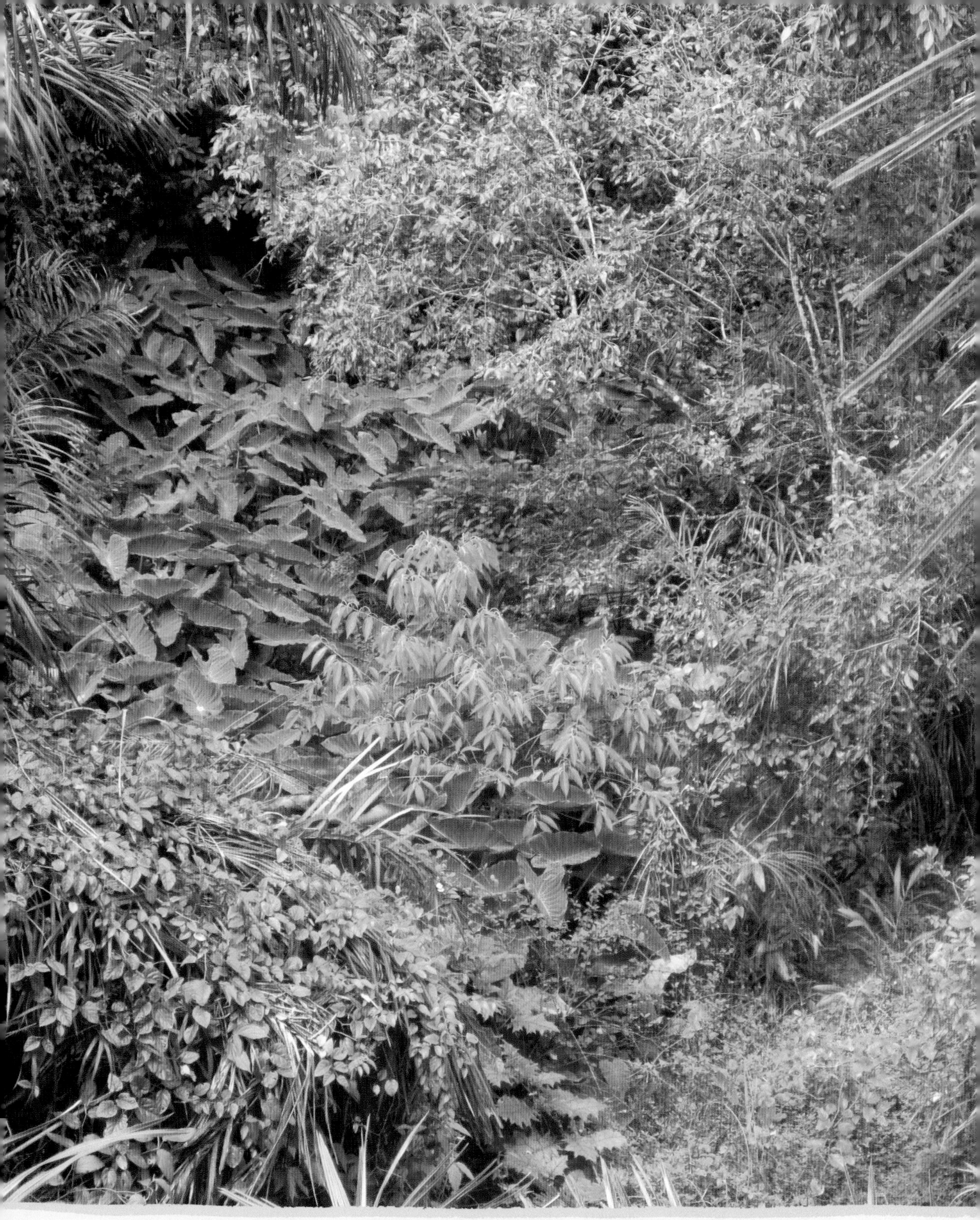

the plants come in so many diFFerent shapes, patterns, textures, sizes, and shades oF green.

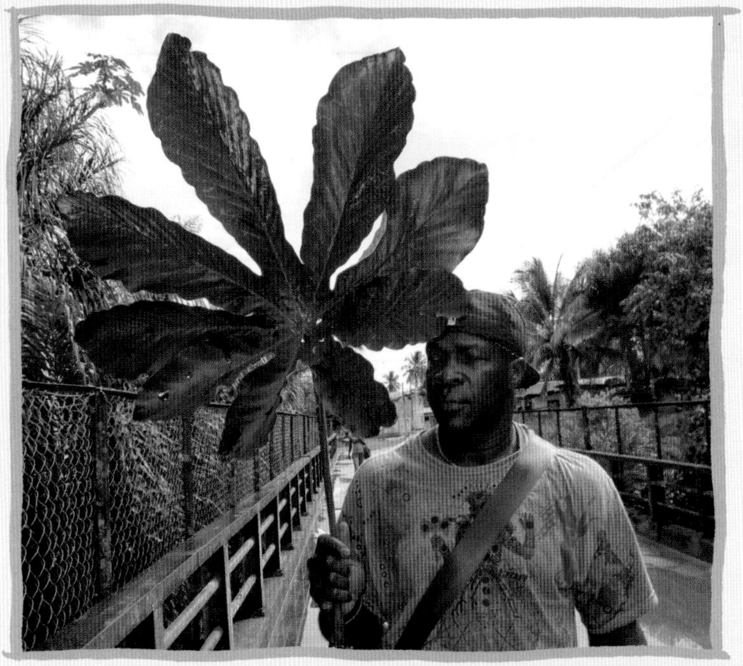

dried out
cecropia leaf found
on the ground

cashew fruit on tree

Here is
John
holding
a cashew
fruit
upside down.

the red
part is the
fruit and
this is the
cashew
nut.

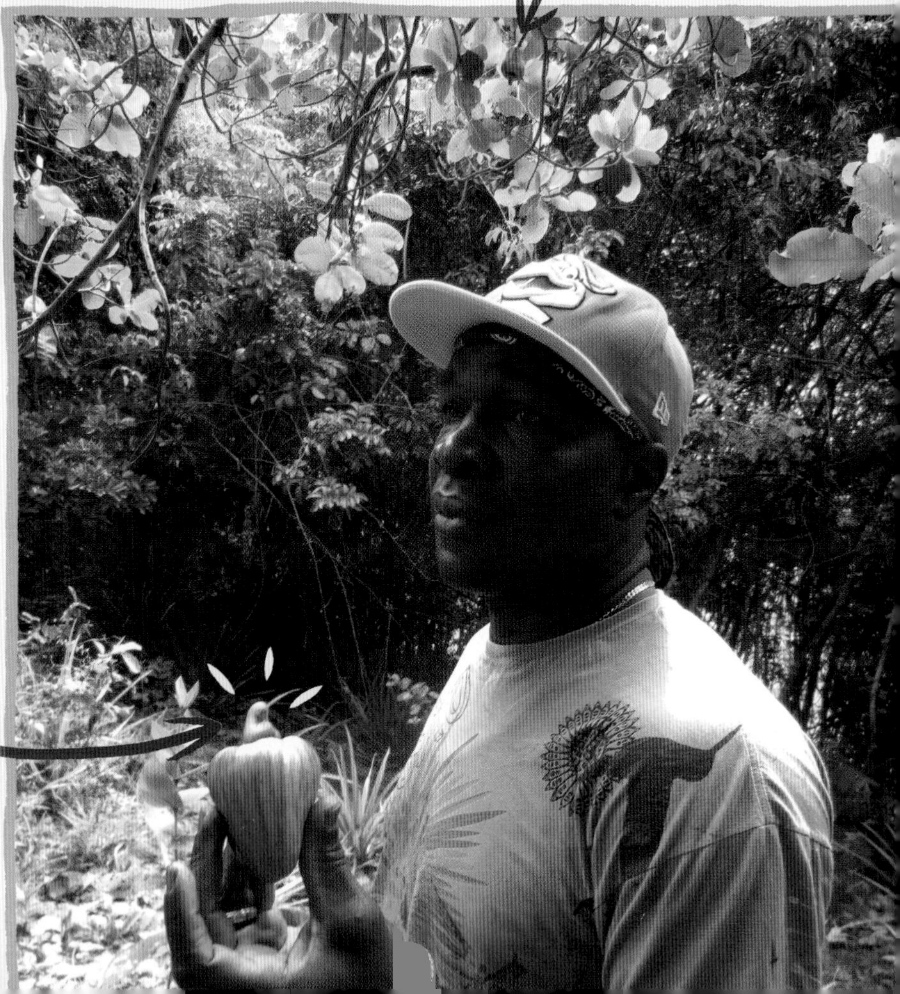

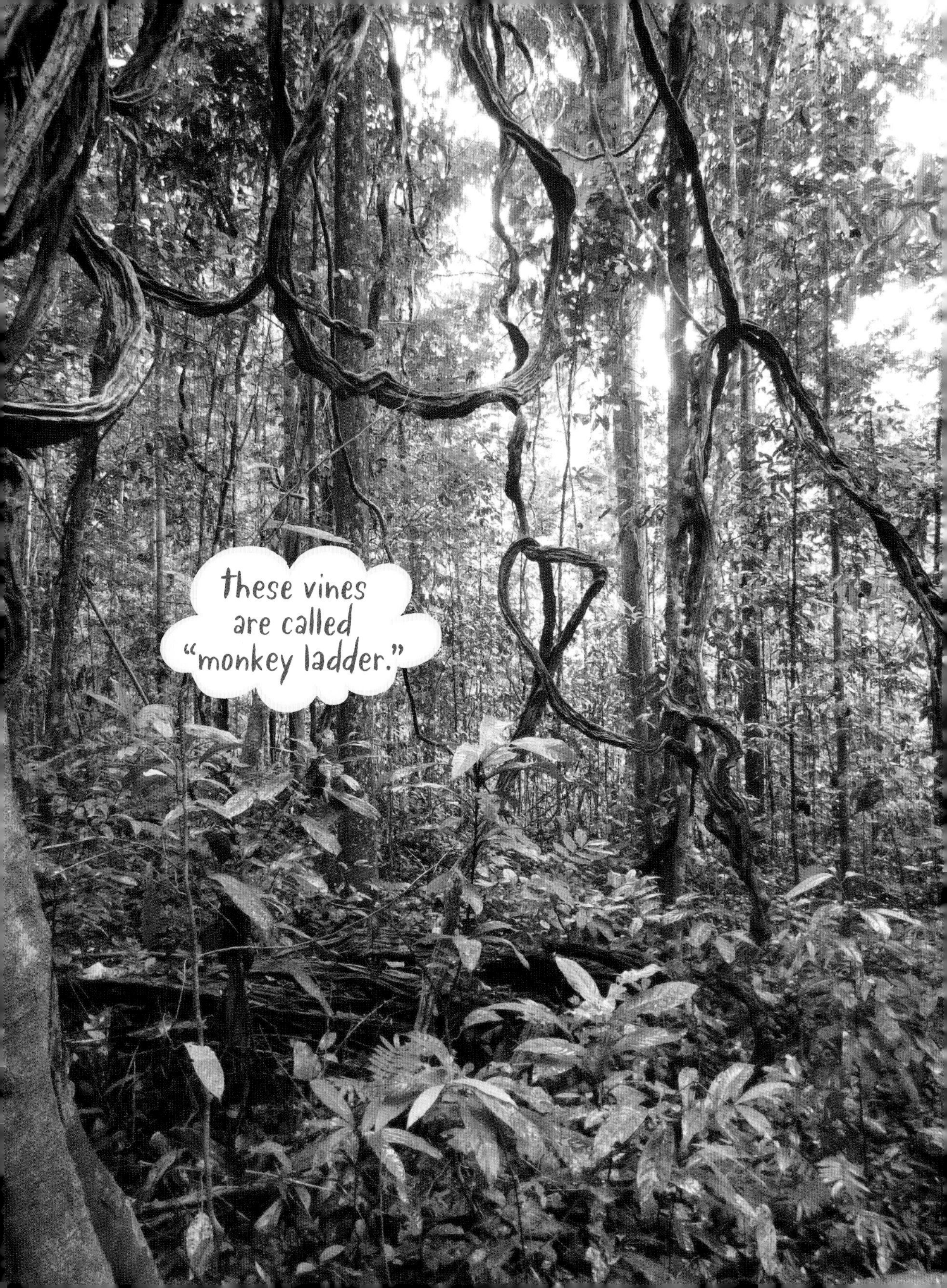
these vines are called "monkey ladder."

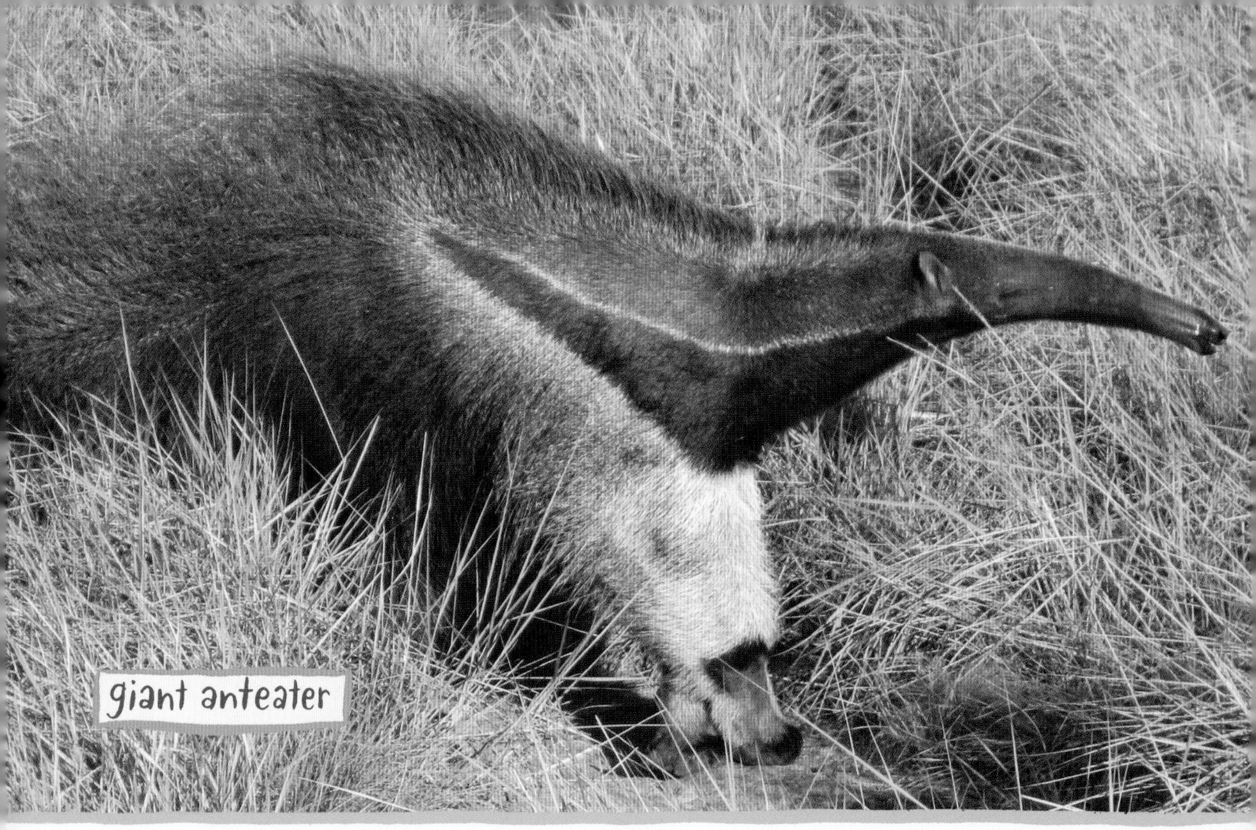

giant anteater

so many really great hand-painted signs

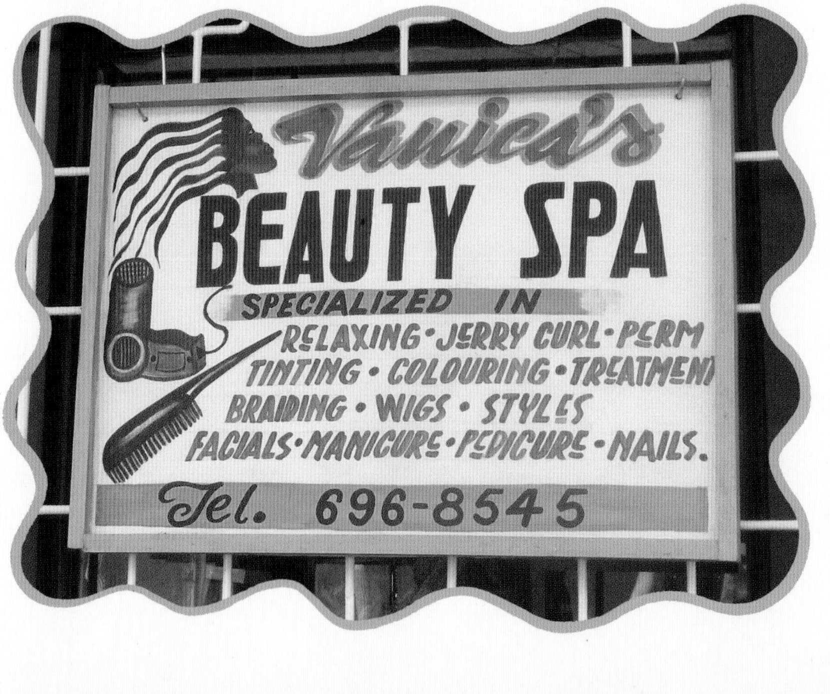
Vanica's
BEAUTY SPA
SPECIALIZED IN
RELAXING · JERRY CURL · PERM
TINTING · COLOURING · TREATMENT
BRAIDING · WIGS · STYLES
FACIALS · MANICURE · PEDICURE · NAILS.
Tel. 696-8545

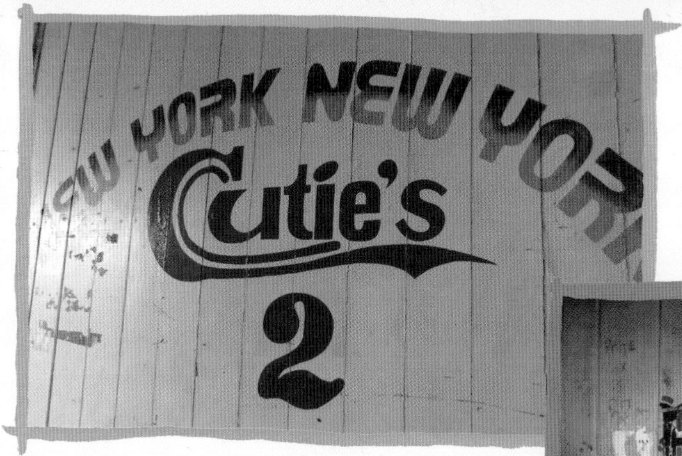
YORK NEW YORK NEW YOR
Cutie's
2

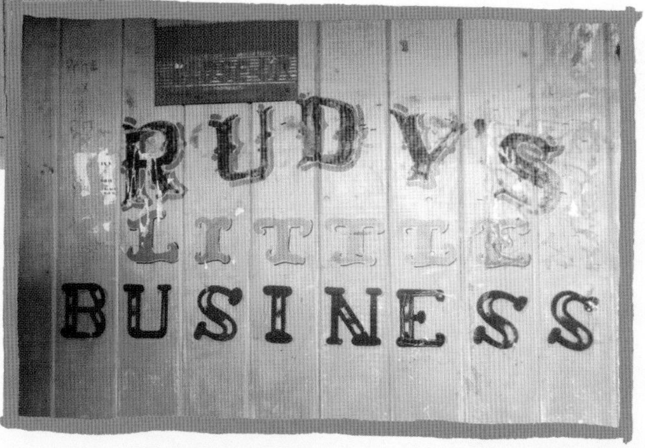
RUDY'S
LITTLE
BUSINESS

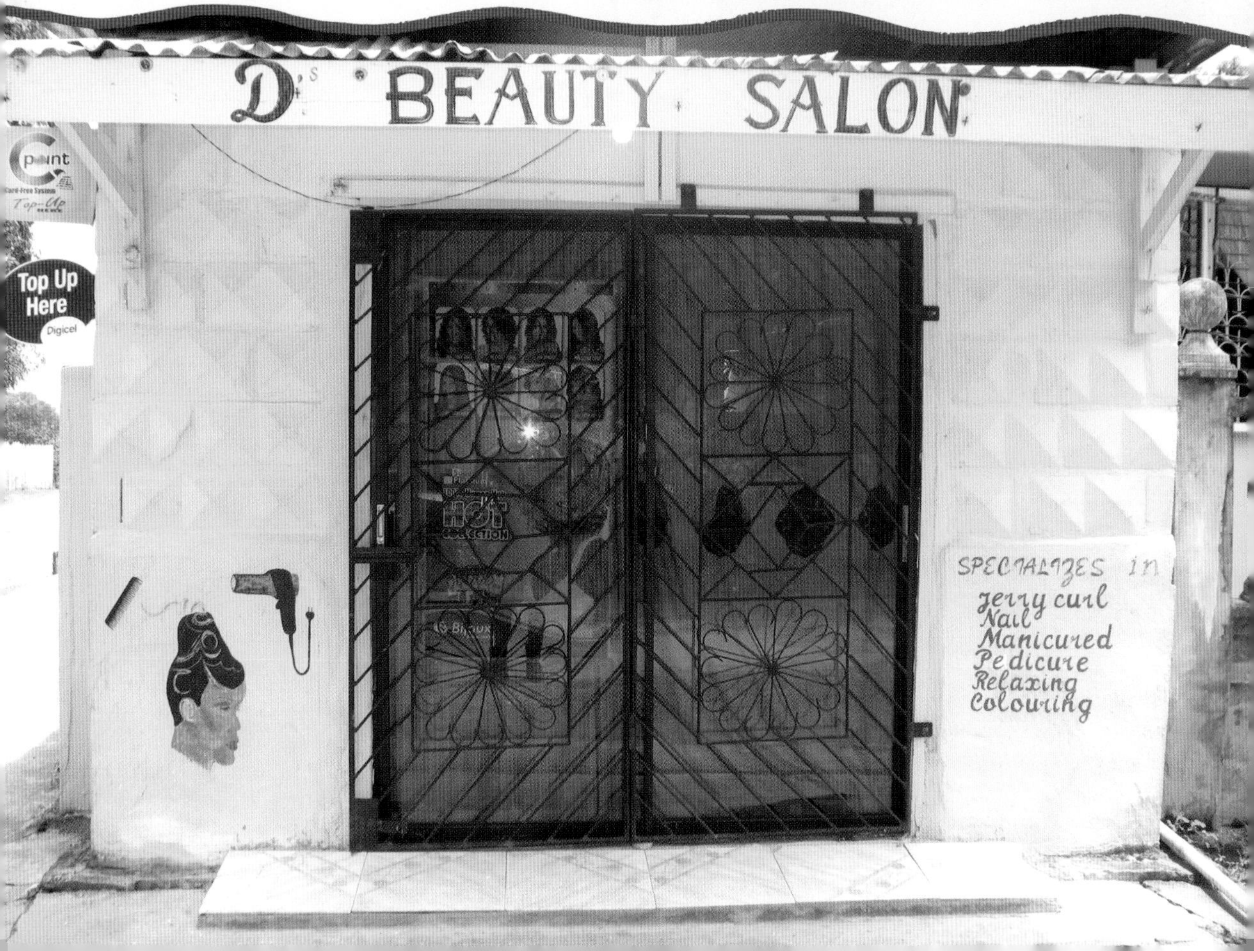
D'S BEAUTY SALON
Top Up Here
Digicel
SPECIALIZES in
Jerry curl
Nail
Manicured
Pedicure
Relaxing
Colouring

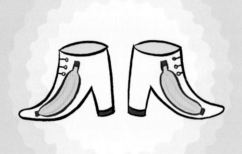

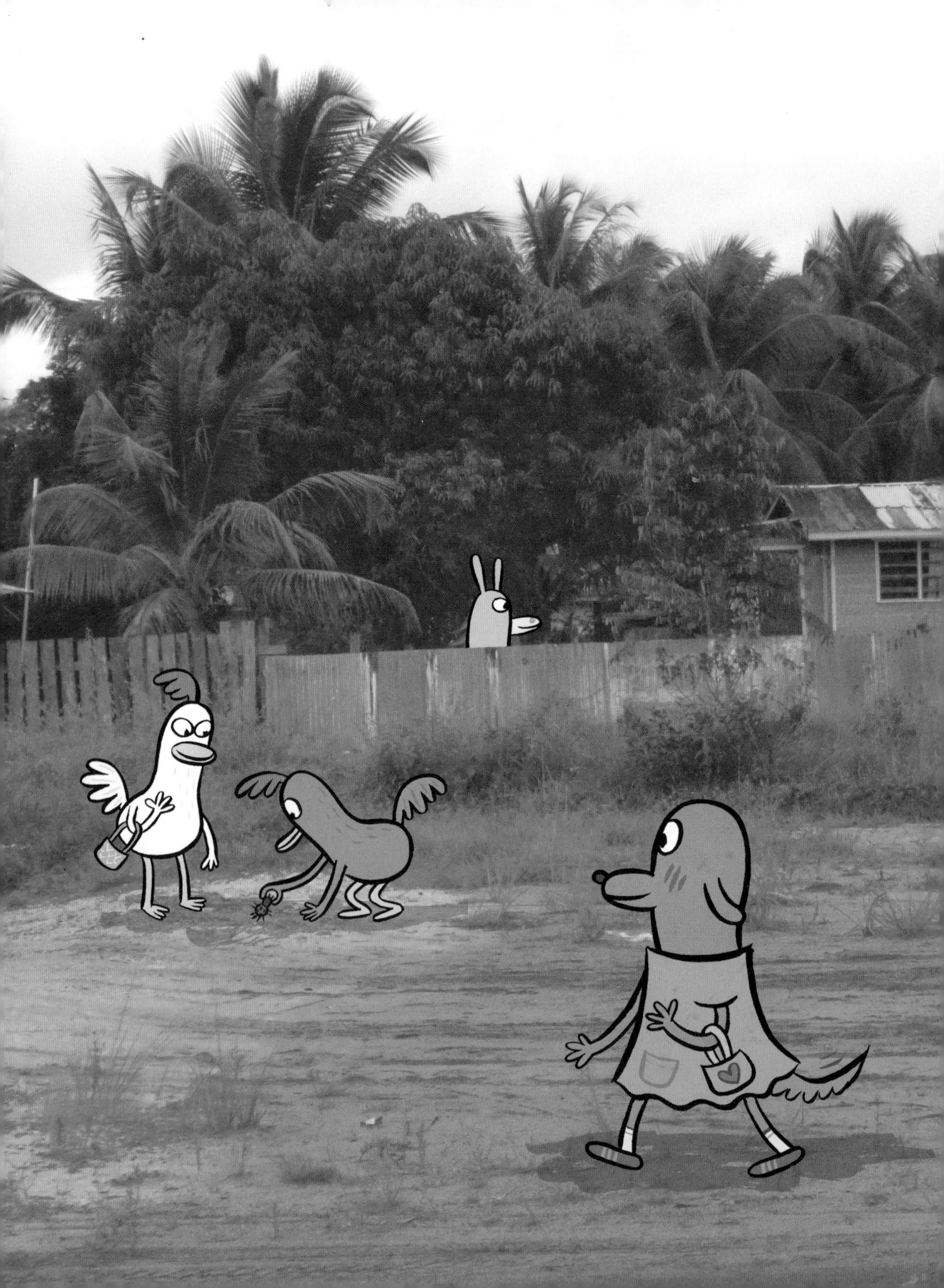